ESCAPED THE NIGHT

I hope you enjoy my story!
Jenn
xo

ESCAPED THE NIGHT

JENNIFER BLYTH

ESCAPED THE NIGHT

Copyright © 2011, 2015 Jennifer Blyth Starlight Creative Expressions Ltd.
www.escapedthenight.com

All rights reserved. No part of this book may be used or reproduced by any means, graphic, electronic, or mechanical, including photocopying, recording, taping or by any information storage retrieval system without the written permission of the author except in the case of brief quotations embodied in critical articles and reviews.

This is a work of fiction. All of the characters, names, incidents, organizations, and dialogue in this novel are either the products of the author's imagination or are used fictitiously.

iUniverse books may be ordered through booksellers or by contacting:

iUniverse
1663 Liberty Drive
Bloomington, IN 47403
www.iuniverse.com
1-800-Authors (1-800-288-4677)

Because of the dynamic nature of the Internet, any web addresses or links contained in this book may have changed since publication and may no longer be valid. The views expressed in this work are solely those of the author and do not necessarily reflect the views of the publisher, and the publisher hereby disclaims any responsibility for them.

Any people depicted in stock imagery provided by Thinkstock are models, and such images are being used for illustrative purposes only.
Certain stock imagery © Thinkstock.

ISBN: 978-1-4917-8632-1 (sc)
ISBN: 978-1-4917-8631-4 (hc)
ISBN: 978-1-4917-8630-7 (e)

Library of Congress Control Number: 2015921130

Previous ISBN (978-0-9878238-0-9) has been discontinued.

Print information available on the last page.

iUniverse rev. date: 12/30/2015

Contents

Acknowledgements vii
Ouija 1
The Day 12
Blackness 21
Blackwood 28
Elements 39
Connected 44
Second Date 53
Opened Eyes 63
Stars 71
Visions 78
The Stranger 87
First Encounter 96
Another Chance 104
Prisoners 114
Trapped 123
Plan in Motion 132
Tingles 141
Forever 152
The Forest 159
A Glimpse 169
Decisions 175
Union 186
Changes 194
United 205

Rekindled	216
Named	231
Reasons	238
Truce	244
Sauda	254
Destiny	262
Healing	273
Contact	280
Fangs	286
Lights	300
Sunlight	309
Author Note	321
Sammie Street Adventures	322
Reader Reviews	323
About the Author	327
Author Photo	328

Acknowledgements

Shanntal Elizabeth Blyth, when you were little, stories were part of our daily life. The stories we made up will always stay close to my heart, but this one needed to be shared with others. You're truly my source of inspiration. I love you more than anything. Always. XO

Betty Blyth, thank you for telling me I should write books. I'm glad I decided to take your advice to heart. Mom, you helped me find my passion, my calling. I hope you enjoyed watching the seeds you planted finally blossom. I love you. XO

Dave Wright, a very special thank you goes out to you for being such a great friend and reading my first draft chapter by chapter as I wrote it. Your continued encouragement kept me on track. This one's for you!

Michael De Jong, a special thanks goes out to you for introducing me to the people who helped make my dream come true. I hope you enjoy the magic.

Carol Hoenig, you are my mentor. You've taught me so much about writing as well as the industry. I appreciate the time you spent helping me and for your encouraging words that kept my drive alive. Thank you for believing in my dream.

Greg Percy, thank you for putting a picture to my words. I hope everyone enjoys the book cover as much as I do. Art is a way of life. I hope you keep dreaming and never quit creating. Cheers!

Tiffany Cole, Lori Whitwam, and **Rachel Whitwam,** a special thanks goes out to you all for helping shape my story.

Sabrina Ford and **Kristina Haecker,** you're my first and favorite 5-star reviewers. I'm grateful to have established the relationships we have. Cheers to sharing the love of books, always!

Valerie Farrell and **Jade Pepper,** you are a couple of my biggest fans. The two of you ladies have believed in me so much that I couldn't help but believe in myself too. Thank you. XO

Morgan Giles, thank you for supporting me while I chased after my dreams, and especially during crunch time. I'm thankful you weren't too upset with me on the day I smashed into you with all my heavy books. Instead, it gave us something to talk about and brought you into my life. XO

This wouldn't have been possible without all the help and support I've received. To anyone who used their time to read one of my books, told a friend about my books, pushed me when I was ready to give up, or believed in me when I didn't … This special thanks goes out just for you. You've helped make my dreams come true!

☾ **************************** ☾

Never stop chasing dreams

****

Ouija

~ Chapter One ~

*D*istraught and alone, I rushed through the forest. I heard the sound of my feet stomping while gasps leaked out between labored breaths. My heart pounded wildly, yet I stopped abruptly. I couldn't believe this was happening ... I was being hunted.

I attempted to remain hidden, but the smell of blood took control and lured me into the open. I licked my lips involuntarily as I took a few steps closer. I wanted a taste, even craved it. But why did I want it so badly?

The dark figure with vicious red eyes knew the answer, and he reached out for me. I screamed, but no sound escaped my lips. He smirked right before he brushed against me. We touched, and suddenly I felt different—a chill in my bones, hunger in my stomach, and a lust that could not be tamed. He was the remedy for it all. He moved closer, only this time, I didn't pull away. Instead, I accepted the offering and embraced his bloody hands.

I woke up in the midst of a panic attack, desperately wiping my hands off on my pants. Thankfully, no blood. I found myself safe and sound in the car, surrounded by my family. Just another one of my horrible dreams; I wondered if they would ever stop.

I wasn't sure if anyone had caught wind of the fact I'd momentarily dozed off. My parents continued chatting casually in the front seat while both of my sisters kept busy looking out the backseat windows. There I sat, screaming on the inside, haunted by twisted dreams whenever my eyes closed, and to them it was another typical day. A frustrated sigh slipped out.

My sisters used this as an open invitation to squish me in the middle.

I jostled both, trying to get them back to their own sides of the car. "Hey, move over!" I snapped, sounding crankier than I'd meant. My sisters were eight and ten, but for some reason they decided to cling to me like toddlers afraid of being lost.

"Really?" My sisters repeated, one right after the other.

From their tone, I knew what I had done, but it was too late.

"You want us to move over?" Sweet giggles filled the car as they simultaneously squeezed even closer, looping their arms around mine. Two against one. I wasn't any match for their innocent faces, blonde hair, and crystal blue eyes.

"Brats! You guys are lucky I love you so much." There was no way to win the battle for more space, so I sat defeated and squished.

"You're the lucky one." My sisters remained snuggled up. "You get to love us."

Despite their cuteness, I couldn't wait to get to Ginata's house for the night. Life had become so hectic with her new job that we hadn't seen each other for nearly a month. I missed her and knew we had some serious catching up to do.

I consider Ginata the coolest girl ever, and I'm lucky enough to call her my best friend. She's two years older, and we met a few years ago when she babysat for my younger sisters. The cute guy who lived down the road had asked me out on a date. I begged and pleaded with my parents to let me out of watching my sisters for the evening. They agreed and called Ginata—the neighborhood babysitter—who thankfully was available.

My so-called date hadn't gone anything like expected. We ran into some of his friends, and he decided to devote his attention to them. Actually, more to the flirty blonde persistently flashing her bright smile and abundance of cleavage his way. I sat alone, feeling ditched and ignored by both my date and the group, so I decided it would be best just to go home. When I got up to leave, I never received a word or even so much as a look from him, because he'd been far too busy to notice with his eyes locked on her chest. She smiled and intently watched as I left, all the while knowing my departure meant her evening would go exactly how she'd planned.

I beat my mom and dad home, so Ginata and I hung out. She listened as I threw a pity party, divulging the terrible details of my date, while ranting about Little Miss Blondie. Ginata comforted and reassured my crushed ego, saying there wasn't anything wrong with me, and reminded me this was, in fact, his loss. That was the very moment our friendship began. I'd found my missing piece, my kindred spirit, and Ginata felt the same. Best friends till death, we vowed.

I started to overheat with my sisters pressed so close, which brought my mind back to the matters at hand. I was hot, tired, and cranky. Thankfully, we were almost at Ginata's house.

My father turned down the music in the car. I noticed but paid little attention due to everything racing through my mind.

"So ... what are you girls doing tonight, Shanntal? Will her parents be home? No one else is coming over, *right?*"

He was always protective of us girls and liked keeping me on a tight leash by knowing what I was doing at all times. He meant well, but I still found it utterly annoying.

"Girl stuff, don't know, and no," I shot back shortly, hoping to end the conversation.

My father grunted at my response, then tightened his grip on the wheel, turning his knuckles white.

Ginata and I had been friends for a couple years, so why did he have to act like this now? And seriously, why couldn't he just leave me alone when he knew I was so edgy? He'd picked the wrong point in time to ask me anything.

"Here we go," I muttered under my breath. I rolled my eyes and flipped a piece of long brown hair off my face. I wasn't in the mood to deal with his constant hovering.

"No need to get defensive, honey." My mother spoke softly, trying her best to ease the rising tension. "We just want to make sure you stay safe; that's all." She looked back, and I saw the warning in her eyes ... Don't push it.

But, the words slipped out of my mouth anyway. "Safe? Are you kidding me?" Sometimes I forgot how to keep my big mouth shut. Unfortunately, it was the fuel to make the fire rage.

"Shann–tal!" His voice grew sharper with each syllable.

I watched my mother stroke my father's arm in an effort to calm him down.

This drama made me even more eager for my sleepover. I loved my family dearly, but tonight they'd clearly be better off without me around, especially when I was in this kind of mood. I didn't want to fight but saw where the situation was heading, so I caved and disclosed the details before it turned into an all out argument. "We're staying in, doing girl stuff. Probably watching movies, talking, nothing out of the ordinary, I promise. I'm sorry. Guess I'm cranky from not sleeping well. My dreams sometimes ... sometimes they seem too real."

My apology lowered the tension, and my father loosened his grip on the wheel. The color quickly flooded back into his hands.

My mother turned around and mouthed 'thank you.'

"Remember, dreams are simply that, nothing more. They can't harm you. You've got to think of them as your mind's way of entertaining. They're not real, so there's no reason to be afraid." My father pulled onto the road adjacent to Ginata's cul-de-sac.

I decided to keep my mouth shut this time, even though I totally disagreed. My dreams were intense. They felt as though they'd happened before, like memories rising to the surface. Not to mention all the blood. That alone was more than enough to keep anyone fearful.

I spotted the red brick home with fancy French doors and white window trim, and felt an instant sense of relief. A night away from home meant no more arguing with my family or talk of nightmares. Just the break I needed!

Upon our arrival, Ginata swung the front door open and came toward the car with her Saint Bernard, Berkley right on her heels. Her welcoming smile was lit up by the sparkle in her big brown eyes. Ginata's long dark locks were pulled into a tight ponytail, and she wore a violet backless top I'd never seen before. It fit perfectly, allowing her to show off the flower garden tattoo that covered her back and climbed up her neck. It was full of various shades of pinks, purples, yellows, greens, and reds. The flowers and vines intertwined, forming a stunning blend from one color to the next.

"Hiya!" she greeted us cheerfully.

Ginata leaned inside the passenger window and kissed my mother on the cheek, then a quick thumbs up to my sisters in the backseat. She pulled her head out of the window and proceeded around to my father's side, leaned in his window, and gave him a hug.

"It's good to see you guys," she said, opening the rear door for me.

I climbed over my youngest sister in order to get out.

"Pleasure to see you too, dear. Are your parents home?" my father asked, giving Berkley a pat on his head after he jumped up to say hello.

"Nope. They're out on date night," she wiggled her eyebrows playfully.

"Really?" My father gave me the eye.

"They won't be out too late, though," Ginata interjected, taking notice of the look I'd just received.

"We'll be good. Here all night," I promised.

Ginata and I said farewells to my family. I inhaled deeply as we passed by the large, flowery bushes outside the doors. The bushes were at least seven feet tall and filled with beautiful sweet smelling blossoms. Their scent was so welcoming it could put anyone at ease.

"What was that all about?" she asked once inside.

I shrugged. "Everyone just seems off today, or maybe it's me and the lack of sleep is finally catching up."

"You're still not sleeping? More dreams?"

"Not at all, and there's way more now, like every time I close my eyes. I don't know what's going on with everyone else. Sure feels like something's up, but I don't know what, and they haven't said."

"Well, remember they love and worry about you. That's actually a good thing. It's what family's all about." She gave a caring smile. "Chin up, girly. You're here now, so no more stress. Let's get the fun times started!"

Her words were right. They loved me, so of course they worried. I was lucky to have such a caring family. Instantly the heavy burden I'd been lugging around lifted. I felt better and excited for our night.

Ginata was a great friend who could always make me smile, even when I felt down. I loved how she wore brightly colored clothes, making her the happiest looking person around. The night we first met, she'd told me her name meant 'flower,' and she truly resembled one.

We headed upstairs to her room to gossip about random things, but it wasn't long before the guy subject came up. Neither of us had been on a date within the past six months, so talk in this department didn't usually amount to much.

"Have you met anyone?" Ginata asked.

I shook my head. "No, I haven't. What about you?"

"Well, there is this one guy at work who's really cute." She sighed heavily. "But we aren't allowed to date coworkers."

"That sucks. Maybe he'll fall so madly in love with you that he'll quit his job and you two can live happily ever after."

"Ha! I wish! Anyway, this talk, or should I say *reminder* of our non-existent love lives is starting to bring me down. I've got an idea of what we can do instead." Ginata got up and went into her closet and pulled out her Ouija board.

She smiled brightly, and I cringed. The thing freaked me right out. I'd used one of these boards with some friends at a birthday party, and the Ouija told us I would die in the near future. It had been the longest year of my life, waiting to die. I didn't know how or when, but since the board said so, it must've meant it was true. Well, there I was, still alive, and I'd never trusted the board since. I didn't want to mess with it, in case I received any other dire predictions.

"Why don't we watch a movie, do our nails, or something else?" I suggested, trying to avoid using the board.

"Don't be such a baby. Using the Ouija won't hurt you. We're just going to have a bit of fun. We'll watch some movies later, okay?"

I sighed, knowing I couldn't change her mind.

I helped her clear off the desk and pull it into the middle of her room. Next, we placed chairs on either side and a black velvet dress on top. Finally, she set the board down carefully, as if it were made of glass and would break if not handled gently.

Ginata was totally into witchcraft, and in far more ways than I ever dared to attempt. She had runes, tarot cards, smudge sticks, books, pendants, and the list went on and on. I'd never put much faith in any of it. After my run-in with the board, well, that led me to the end of my believing days.

We burned a few candles and incense for effect. I shut off the light, and we assumed our positions. We placed our hands on the triangle sitting in the middle of the board.

I peered around. Her room had gone from girlish to intimidating in a matter of minutes. The candles cast strange shadows across the walls while the incense left a faint fog. The darkness crept over everything, leaving nothing untouched. I'd never seen shadows behave this way. They seemed alive. The darker parts shifted forms and closed in around us, giving tonight a whole new eerie sensation.

Ginata spoke in a low, spooky voice. "Ouija, we would like to ask you some questions. We mean no harm. We only want to know more about you. Give us a sign if someone wishes to share with us."

We paused for a moment. Nothing happened, no movement.

She spoke again, this time in a normal voice. "Ouija, give us a sign you're here and wish to speak with us."

Just when I thought nothing would happen, the triangle scratched slowly along the board. It slid up to the left corner and pointed directly at 'yes.'

The sound of the triangle moving made me tremble. I squirmed in my seat. I didn't like using these things. They were creepy and never said anything good. Who really wanted to talk to dead people, anyway?

Ginata looked at me, excitement in her eyes. "Who are you? Will you tell us your name?"

The triangle moved. It landed on the letter "D" and slid to the "A."

I panicked. "Ginata, are you pushing it?"

Her scowl told me she wasn't.

I looked down at the triangle now resting on the "R."

"D-A-R," Ginata said, but the triangle rushed to the "A" again, and then the "Y" before stopping.

"Daray?" we said in unison.

"Is your name?" Ginata guessed.

The triangle moved to 'yes.'

Something about this name made me feel uneasy.

"How did you die?" Ginata pried.

She was always the bold one, getting right to the point, no goofing around or wasting time with idle chitchat. If she wanted to know something, she'd come straight out and ask.

The triangle spelled out V-A-M-P-I-R-E.

A shiver shot down my spine. "Vamp—" My voice squeaked. I cleared my throat and continued. "Vampire? Uh, do you think this is a horror movie or something?"

I felt spooked, but at the same time this was beyond ridiculous. Vampire. Like vampires, creatures of the night with the ability to seduce and make you powerless so they could drink your blood were real. Come on! I'd had about enough and contemplated taking my hands off when the triangle moved. This time spelling I-AM-HERE.

A light breeze filled Ginata's room. The candles flickered similar to someone breathing on them or blowing gently. We both looked around mystified. Was someone else here? What felt like a hand gently brushed across my shoulder.

"Oh no! Did you do that?" I snapped at Ginata, squirming in my seat. "This isn't funny. I'm totally freaking out!"

"Do what? I never did anything." Ginata looked over at me, and I saw the fear in her eyes.

The triangle moved again. MY-SWEETS-I-WILL-FIND-YOU.

I looked at Ginata, completely horrified, but the triangle kept moving. I lowered my eyes to focus on what was being spelled. I-HAVE-NEVER-STOPPED-SEARCHING.

Suddenly, I felt like crying. This conversation brought up all kinds of emotions. I felt afraid and sad; only I didn't understand why. Maybe I was getting too wrapped up in this, but Daray seemed to be talking to me.

WE-WILL-BE-TOGETHER-AGAIN-SOON. Then, in an abrupt movement, the triangle shot to the bottom of the board and landed on goodbye. When the triangle stopped moving, the candles no longer flickered strangely.

Ginata asked the board, "Daray, are you still here? Please, talk to us!"

Nothing happened. There was no more movement.

I lifted my hands off the triangle and shook them, hoping to remove any lingering bad vibes. I was done with that creepy thing. Right then, I swore to myself that I would never, *ever* touch one of those boards again.

We sat silently in the dark room for what felt like a very long and awkward time. I assumed she was thinking about the contact we'd made and trying to find some way to make sense of it. I know I sure was.

How could we justify what happened? Had a vampire just communicated with us? I never could've seen that twist coming, not even in my wildest dreams. What about the breeze blowing the candles? There was no plausible explanation because the window had been closed. So what made the flames flicker like that? Worst of all was feeling someone touch my shoulder. It was messed up!

The nagging voice in the back of my head spoke up. *If you find the thoughts so absurd, why let them bother you so much? Maybe not everything is as it seems.*

I turned the lights back on and blew out the candles. I left the incense burning, because, in truth, I found the musky smell somewhat comforting. I sat down beside Ginata on her bed, still pondering things.

Ginata shifted her body slightly and turned to face me. "Are you sure you weren't pushing?"

"No!" I snapped, harsher than necessary. "I'd never do something like that. I thought you were being a jerk because you know I don't like using them. I thought you … I thought you were trying to freak me out."

"I would never do that to you," she said, sounding hurt.

We both shivered. It was clear neither of us would admit to pushing the triangular planchette. Perhaps it was because neither of us did. What if we were contacted? Who exactly was Daray searching for?

The Day

~ Chapter Two ~

I couldn't shake the feeling Daray had been referring to me. There was something familiar about that name …

"Enough witchcraft for one evening? How about a movie?" I said, trying to turn our night around. "A change of pace is needed in order to get this out of my head."

"Enough witchcraft!" Ginata agreed.

We made our way downstairs, pillows and all. First stop, a beeline to the kitchen. We grabbed some cans of soda, chips, and two candy bars out of the pantry.

"Chips, pop, and chocolate … yum. Doesn't get much better than this. We're set!" she dropped her can of pop, but I caught it before it landed on the floor. "Good save."

We proceeded into the living room, plopped the treats down on the coffee table, tossed pillows to our designated ends of the couch, and went over to search through the overstocked DVD rack.

"Maybe a comedy or romance?" I suggested. "I think I've had enough frights for one night."

"A comedy sounds good to me." Ginata stood up on her tiptoes and grabbed a movie off the top shelf. She took it out of the case and placed it in the DVD player while I headed over to the couch.

Ginata was about a footstep away from joining me on the couch when Berkley charged through the living room, his protective barks echoing throughout the house.

We both screamed. Ginata grabbed my hand, yanked me up, and held my hand tightly as she pulled me uneasily toward the window. Berkley continued to growl and bare his teeth until Ginata placed her hand gently upon him. Then, nothing but silence remained. The house became too quiet. I swore I heard my own heart beating in my chest.

We simultaneously pulled back the curtains and looked out into the darkness, our eyes scanning high and low.

I thought I saw a flash of red streak by. Suddenly, I felt strange chills run through my body.

"Did you see that?" I asked.

"See what?"

"A red streak," I said, backing away. "Something's out there."

"Where?" Ginata pulled me back over to the window. "Show me."

I hesitantly looked out, afraid of what I might find. My eyes scanned everywhere, but this time saw nothing out of the ordinary.

"I must've imagined it. But seriously, Berkley, come on, talk about perfect timing. Dog, your barking totally just scared me." I patted his head and stepped away from the window. "Okay, I'm honestly about to admit something pretty silly. So here it goes. Somehow, I just convinced myself that a vampire was out there."

"A vampire?" She chuckled. "That's pretty ridiculous."

"I know. My imagination is on complete overload." I forced a laugh, even though I probably could've cried at that moment.

"No kidding. To be honest, though, he scared the crap out of me, and I kind of half expected to see one too." Ginata shook her head, trying to get herself back in order. "Wow ... movie ... right! That's what we were doing."

"Yep, movie," I said.

"Okay, let's do this. I need some serious laughs. My nerves are shot."

Ginata looked shook up to me. I could only imagine what I must've looked like to her.

We arranged ourselves on the puffy sectional with our heads near each other. The Ouija board incident and Berkley's strange behavior had clearly affected us more than we thought. After a few seconds of shuffling around blankets, we snuggled ourselves in for the next couple hours.

The movie played on the screen, but I couldn't pay attention because I kept thinking about the board's warnings in spite of myself. Vampires weren't real, were they? Could Daray actually be looking for one of us? Every once in a while I caught myself glancing over at the window. Had something really been out there?

My mind finally started to slow down. I felt tired from lazing around on the couch and looked at the clock. Just after one o'clock a.m. No wonder I was starting to fade.

Before long, Ginata woke me up to say she was heading upstairs to call it a night.

I checked the clock again, close to two-thirty a.m. I let out a big yawn, grabbed my pillow, and followed Ginata upstairs. On the way to her room, we stopped for some extra blankets and pillows from the hall closet. With loaded arms, we made our way to her room where I created my makeshift bed on the floor. A few moments passed, and I easily entered dreamland.

I woke to brilliant sunshine filling Ginata's room. The dark shadows of the night before were nothing more than a distant memory. I checked my cell phone—just after eleven. I had slept soundly, so completely comfortable wrapped up in all the blankets and pillows. No dreams intervened or conquered my mind as I'd expected.

Ginata still slept peacefully in her bed. I stood up, reaching my hand out to try and gently wake her, when suddenly her eyes shot open. She wore a strange look on her face, but before I could ask, she promptly sat upright. She hopped out of bed without so much as a stretch and said, "I'm starved. Let's eat!"

I decided to let it go and simply followed her downstairs. We walked into the kitchen, also bright from the beaming sunshine.

"Good morning, girls!" Ginata's mom smiled warmly.

"Good morning," we said, and each took a seat.

"Sleepyheads, since its pretty much lunchtime, what're your thoughts on that fancy midday meal some people like to call brunch?" she teased.

"Brunch sounds great." I smiled, but right at that moment, my stomach growled loudly. "Oops, exactly what it said."

We all had a good giggle. While Ginata's mom prepped our meal, she casually asked, "So … what'd you two get up to last night?"

Ginata spoke up first. "Oh Mom, you know, the same thing we usually do. Played around with some makeup and gossiped. Later on, we pigged out and ended up watching a movie."

When her mom focused back on the food, Ginata gave me a look, warning me not to let her in on our scary encounter.

I completely understood.

"Sounds like a fun time. Any big plans for today?" Her mom continued.

We both shrugged. I didn't really care what we did. I always enjoyed myself around their family. They were truly happy people, and the happy rays, as I liked to call them, always rubbed off.

"No plans yet," Ginata answered.

"Well, your father and I were thinking of taking Berkley for a good long walk. Perhaps you girls could join us?"

Ginata and I nodded in agreement. A walk was always a good thing. Especially after all this food we were about to eat.

"Great! It's settled." Her mom smiled as she flipped a pancake onto a plate. "Dad should be home around two, so try to be ready by then."

After brunch, we went upstairs to get ready. Per my usual, I put on a black sweater and a pair of old, beat-up blue jeans. Ginata, on the other hand, looked like a summer flower in her pink sequin top and white skirt. The sunlight hit her shirt, making it glitter like a thousand sparkling diamonds.

The front door opened, and a male voice called out. "Hello, family, I'm home. Who's happy to see me?" There was a pause, followed by a short session of barks, and, "I know Berkley is always happy to see me. Good boy!"

I gathered up my stuff before going downstairs to meet up with her parents. Berkley waited for everyone in the front foyer, his tail wagging nonstop. He knew we were going for a walk, and his patience or bladder would not hold out much longer.

As Ginata's dad drove us out of the city limits, I watched the buildings eventually give way to big maple, lush birch, and thick evergreen trees. The further we drove, the further I went from my worries. About thirty minutes later, I felt calmer than I'd been in months. I felt rested, happy, but even better, I felt normal.

We pulled over on the outskirts of a thick forest. Berkley panted with excitement. He raced off once Ginata's dad undid his leash. Ginata's dad simply chuckled and said, "Look at him go! You'd think he knew his way around this place like the back of his paw or something."

Berkley tromped ahead through the lush forest. He'd speed ahead, come back around to check on us, and all the while his tail never stopped wagging once. He was our scout, letting us know we were safe to proceed.

We came to the top of a small hill, and to my surprise, just on the other side ran a beautiful creek. I never knew such beauty lay hidden within the vast forest. The water sparkled as the sun hit its little rushing rapids. It was a secret paradise.

Berkley tore off into the water at full speed. He swam back and forth a number of times. Afterward, he'd run up, stand beside us, and shake, sending a spray of water sailing through the air. We tried to dodge him, but Berkley liked his game. He'd shake off the water and go directly back into the creek, only to chase us down again.

It was getting close to dusk, so we decided to head back before ending up caught in the forest at dark. This long but exhilarating day managed to push the previous night's events and other worries to the back of my mind. I was completely relaxed, ready to go home to my family, and hoped for another peaceful sleep.

"Ginata, we'll drop you and Berkley off first," her mom said on our way back to the city. "You need to bathe him because he smells kind of funky. We can take Shanntal home and pick up something quick for dinner on our way back since it's getting pretty late."

"Okay," Ginata agreed. "Sounds good."

A short while later we pulled into their driveway.

"Come on, boy." Ginata opened the back door to let Berkley out. "I'll call you later," she said to me. I waved, and not even a moment later we were on our way to drop me off at home.

We pulled on to my road, and I said, "Thank you for having me over last night, and for everything today. I really enjoyed myself."

"It's always a pleasure to have you. You already know the door is open for you, anytime." Ginata's mom smiled warmly.

I was about to return the smile, but as we pulled into my driveway, an uneasy sensation came over me. Something wasn't right. We had a family custom to leave the outdoor light on until everyone was home, safe and sound. Why hadn't they left the light on for me? My dad's car sat parked in the driveway right where it belonged.

The lights from the vehicle lit up the front of my house. Just as Ginata's dad gasped, I noticed deep claw marks starting from the garage and leading all the way up to my front door. My mind raced. Why weren't any lights on inside? Where was my family? What was going on? Panic set in, my hands trembled, and I felt nauseated. Holy … what happened here?

I wasn't the only one upset by the sight of my house. Ginata's father ordered us to call the police, lock the doors, and stay inside the car no matter what. He climbed out of the driver's seat, and then hesitantly walked toward my front door. I grabbed my phone to call, but Ginata's mom reached back and grabbed my hand, causing me to drop my phone. Squeezing each other's hands tightly, we watched him disappear inside.

I fumbled around, trying to find my phone with my free hand, but I couldn't take my eyes off the front door. A few minutes passed by, and then a few more. There was still no sign of Ginata's dad or my family.

Ginata's mom grew antsy and unbuckled herself. "I'm going to go check and see what's taking him so long." She took a deep breath and unlocked the door. Hesitating for only a second, she got up from her seat.

I begged her not to go, but she wouldn't listen.

"I need you to call the police. Shanntal, do it right now," she ordered, before relocking her door and closing it. I sank helplessly back into my seat, watching her walk away.

As soon as she was out of sight, I felt along the floor until I found my phone. I called 9-1-1, sobbing uncontrollably. "Someone's broken into my house. My friend's parents went in to check on my family, but they haven't come out. No one has. I'm scared, something's not right. Send the police now!"

Ginata's parents had been gone for what seemed like an eternity. Minutes felt more like hours. Why hadn't anyone come out? I saw no sign of movement. None of the lights went on—nothing but sheer darkness.

I heard the sirens' blare coming down my street. Three police cars pulled up in front of my house. One after the other, the officers piled out of their cars and carefully approached, guns drawn. An officer noticed me sitting alone in the SUV. He lowered his gun and came over to knock on the window.

I stared intensely at my house, hoping everyone would walk out now that the police had arrived. Instead, my eyes met the same red ones I thought I'd seen outside Ginata's house. Only this time, they watched me through my bedroom window. I pointed frantically up to the window, trying to show the policeman, but by the time I looked again, nothing was there.

The officer spoke loudly through the window. "Are you the one who called us?"

I nodded. I'd been crying so badly; he looked like a blur holding a flashlight. I wiped away my tears and saw his hat and uniform clearly. At that moment, I knew I was safe ... but what about everyone else?

"I need you to come with me. You'll be safer in my cruiser. Unlock the door so I can help you," he said sternly.

I wiped away more tears in time to catch the movement behind him. At least ten other officers were now closing in on my house with their weapons drawn.

That really freaked me out. I unlocked my door and flung it open wildly. I got out of my seat and nearly tumbled to the ground. My knees were weak, and my head spun. The officer placed his arm around my waist for support and rushed me over to his cruiser, placing me safely in the backseat. He shut the door and stood in front of his car.

We remained across the street, watching the chaos unfold. Police were everywhere. Neighbors poured out of their comfortable homes to see what was taking place on our normally quiet street.

Lights went on in my house shortly after the armed officers entered. Room by room, my entire house lit up, but no one I cared about came out. I felt super dizzy and thought perhaps I'd blacked out, yet oddly I still saw what was going on. Everything just appeared blurry—dream-like.

The officer climbed all the way into his car when a voice came on the police radio. "Car six-five-nine, you've got to get her out of here. Media's gonna have a field day with this. Man ... this is bad ... it's ... uh ... nothing like we've ever seen before."

The officer slammed closed the car door and we sped off. I sobbed hysterically while the officer drove us away from the life I'd known.

Blackness

~ Chapter Three ~

Between the bouts of hysteria, all I could ask was, "What about my family?"

The officer pulled his cruiser over to the shoulder of the road once we'd gotten far enough away from my house. I saw regret in his eyes when he turned around to face me.

"Honey, I know you heard what they said on the radio, about the … incident. I mean the ummm … you know, the ummm, deaths." His voice cracked as he stumbled around looking for the right words. "Do you know who was inside the house?"

"My mom, dad, two sisters, then Ginata's mom and dad went in, but no one came back out." My voice quivered.

"That matches the descriptions I was given. I'm sorry to be the one who has to tell you, dear …"

"Did they catch him?"

"Him?" He pried carefully. "How do you know it was a him?"

"I saw his red eyes looking at me from my bedroom window when you arrived."

"Red eyes?" His asked, his voice somewhat comforting. "My dear, I understand it's been an extremely difficult night for you."

I nodded.

"I hate to have to tell you this, but they weren't able to find anyone alive inside the house."

"They're all gone?" I sat in the backseat, unable to comprehend anything going on. I felt safe in the presence of the officer, but when I realized I was alone in this life, the feeling quickly disappeared.

"I'm afraid so," he replied sympathetically. "There were no survivors."

"Everyone is dead? I'll never get to see my ..." I slumped down in the seat, allowing the sadness to leak from my eyes and spill down my cheeks.

The officer watched me carefully while I struggled in my moment of despair. A few minutes had passed when he jolted upright, filled with a new sense of spunk. "Actually, I was wrong. There was a survivor. *You!* You are safe and alive. You're the lucky one, honey."

I nodded, still overwhelmed. I didn't feel lucky; I felt quite the opposite. "I am only alive because I was too scared and stayed in the car. I hardly consider that a survivor."

The officer continued talking, just ignoring my comments. He was on a roll spouting optimism. "You have been given another chance. You were too strong to be defeated. My dear, you are meant to be here."

I rolled my eyes. I knew he meant well, but it sounded like utter nonsense. It was a fluke. Nothing more. The police arrived at the right time, and that's why I was alive. If they hadn't, well maybe, just maybe, those red eyes would have ended me too.

"I've seen cases like this before, and I must warn you, please, please, please, you mustn't listen to what the tabloids are going to say. Speculation, it's all they've got to go on. They'll point fingers everywhere—maybe even at you."

"Me?" I was shocked by his comment.

"Just do your best to ignore what they say, and stay strong. I personally promise, we will catch whoever did this. They'll never get away with it."

I was the only survivor. I tried my best to process the fact, but nothing about this made any sense. Several minutes passed before a clear thought came into my mind. "Ginata. Please, I need to go to her. She's my best friend and has lost just as much as me tonight." I gave the officer her address.

"Okay," he agreed. "But it has to be between us. I could get in a ton of trouble for doing this."

I agreed to keep the secret, and he turned the cruiser around. We headed to Ginata's house and he pulled up the driveway. Before he could let me out of the car, Ginata had burst through the front door and was racing down the front path to us, Berkley following her every step.

"What's going on?" she demanded. "Why is my friend in your car? Where are my parents?"

The officer lifted the handle, and my door clicked open. I overheard him gently trying to explain what had happened. The strength in my legs returned, so I climbed out of the cruiser just in time to see Ginata collapse into a heaping pile on the front lawn. Berkley stood guard beside her, growling at the officer whenever he reached out to comfort her.

I stood in silence as my best friend fell to pieces. I watched all her brightness turn completely dark. Her body shook as though she was crying, but no sound came out. I no longer heard Berkley growling, only silence. Suddenly, I couldn't breathe and felt super dizzy. The crazed world around me spun faster and faster—I hit the ground. Then, blackness.

I awoke in a very different place. Everything was bright, white, and sanitized. I jerked upright in bed, but noticed a pounding ache in my head like I'd never experienced before. I felt along the left side of my head and felt a large goose egg protruding through my hairline. It was about the same time I realized that this place was a hospital. What else had happened?

I tried to get out of the bed but moaned loudly from the pain shooting through my head. I fumbled around, feeling weak and nauseated. A nurse passing by saw me and hurried into the room. She assisted me, somewhat forcefully, back into the bed while speaking calmly, as if this occurrence seemed perfectly normal. "You were brought in earlier tonight because you've taken a spill and hit your head pretty good. We're keeping you here for observation. There is an officer stationed outside the room for your protection. No one is coming in, nor will you be going out. You've been through so much tonight, poor girl. Now just lie back and try to relax. You're safe here. Please, try to rest and let us take care of you."

Everything came flooding back. I remembered the events of the night, but worse was the fact I had no family left. I was eighteen—not exactly a child anymore, but not quite ready to be considered an adult. What was I supposed to do?

Hysterics took over, but before I could react to what I was doing, the nurse pinned my arm down and injected me. I felt the slight burn of the sedative make its way through my system. I couldn't keep my eyes open any longer.

While under sedation, my dreams decided to take on a new path. Darkness became more of a comfort to me. I didn't have any pain or sadness in the dark, and I wasn't afraid of being alone. The presence of shadows kept me company by wrapping me in their arms and keeping me there, safe and calm. Most of all, they kept me hidden. It wasn't long before I realized I was no longer alone. The silhouette of a man appeared repeatedly. He never revealed himself completely, his face always stayed partially hidden, but wherever this figure went, the trail of blood followed. It didn't take long for me to understand that the faceless man in the darkness was death. He was searching for me because I had escaped him.

I awoke feeling quite numb. My dream left me under a false illusion that I'd somehow managed to come to terms with the fact my family and best friend's parents were gone. I still felt lost and hurt, but never shed a tear.

The same nurse came into my room and gave a candid smile. However, her expression exposed how she was mentally preparing for our daily meeting. What would today bring?

I returned a smile.

She seemed stunned by my gesture.

"Hello. How are you today?" I asked politely.

She looked at me curiously and replied, "I am fine. Thank you for asking. How are you feeling today?"

"I'm all right, considering." I shrugged and then continued, "What's the date today?" I spoke using my typical voice, not the hysterical one she'd recently become accustomed to. I needed to gather my bearings. I had no idea how long I'd been in and out of consciousness.

"Today is Saturday, June the eleventh."

She studied my every move, looking ready to pounce with another sedative injection at any given moment.

"Oh …" was all I managed to say. I didn't cry or turn into a raging lunatic as I had on previous occasions. I simply sat there quietly processing how long I'd been in a daze. Feeling this kind of numb, I couldn't have managed more tears even if I'd wanted to.

My reaction took her off guard. She spoke in a much softer, sweeter voice. "You've been in here for a few days now, Shanntal."

"I've been sedated for days?" I felt confused. I tried piecing everything together. That dreadful night, my dreams, they all played in my memory again. None of this felt like it had happened days ago; everything still seemed so fresh.

"You had a horrific thing happen, but you are strong. You've already gone through the worst of this. There are doctors here who can help you. I mean, whenever you're ready to talk to someone about things."

I could literally feel myself slipping back into a depressed state, but a vision of a happier memory took control over my mind. I saw the face of someone—Ginata. I needed to speak with her; she'd understand everything. I reached over the bed and picked up my purse from a nearby chair. I rifled through it and pulled out my phone, only to find out that it was dead too.

I was frustrated and furious, but before I fell apart I got an idea and asked the nurse, "Please, may I use the hospital phone? I would like to call my friend."

The nurse agreed and handed me the phone in my room, but there was no dial tone.

"It doesn't work either." I hung up the phone.

The nurse picked it up and wiggled the cord a few times. "Strange, it must be broken. You'll have to use the one over at the nurses' station."

She helped me over to the long desk a few feet down from my doorway. I called, the phone rang once, but an operator's voice came over the line stating the number was no longer in service. That couldn't be right. Why was Ginata's number disconnected? I dialed again, only to get the same response. I decided to call 4-1-1 to see if they could track down another number. No luck. I was left wondering what happened to my friend. Soon the questions started to build. Where did she go? Did she leave town? Was she okay? Or was she dead now too?

The nurse saw how pale I turned and asked the nearby officer for some assistance. They escorted me back to my room and into bed.

Now I really was all by myself. When the thought of isolation hit me, I didn't breakdown; instead, I'd force myself to stand strong and tall. I'd survived that horrific night, and I owed it to all of them to live my life to the fullest and make them proud.

Over the next few long weeks, I had lots of therapy, especially after the funeral for my family. It had to be kept small and discreet, so the media never caught wind of it. The whole ordeal caused me to sink into a deep depression, but a helpful doctor taught me how to overcome my fears and battle the sadness. He demonstrated various coping methods, giving me the skills required to process the loss of everyone I loved.

I had been improving every day, and even found myself looking forward to my daily therapy session. I went to my regularly scheduled appointment, but today was different. Today the doctor decided I was finally in control of my thoughts and emotions. He told me I was free to go, but only if I stayed under constant supervision.

Free to go? Was this some kind of joke? Supervision? Ha! Where … in the graveyard? Did he forget I had no one left to keep an eye on me?

I was about to blurt my irritated thoughts aloud, but stopped when two people caught my attention as they came through the double doors of the hospital. I recognized them at once.

"Auntie Stephanie, Uncle Danier!" Happy tears filled my eyes. I ran over, opened my arms up wide, and gave them a joint bear hug.

I felt so incredibly relieved to see them. I wasn't alone anymore. I still had a family. Maybe not the family I wanted, but they were, without any doubt, the family I needed.

Blackwood

~ Chapter Four ~

After leaving the hospital, Uncle Danier and Auntie Stephanie took me to the police station where I spoke with the officer who had helped me on that terrible night. I wanted to find out for myself if he had any leads, versus what people were saying. He confirmed their means of death remained a mystery, but then he told me something I hadn't heard. He said the bodies had been drained of all liquids and every victim sustained various bites, including our pet cat, which also perished. Before we left, he suggested it might be best to leave Greyton and move to Blackwood where Uncle Danier and Auntie Stephanie lived.

This situation was extremely weird. My family died from bites? So did our cat? We never even owned a cat. They must've been confused, or a stray wandered in while the door was ajar. Poor thing. So now we were left with no suspects, drained bodies, and a dead cat.

We discussed my moving as we walked to the car. I wasn't sure I really wanted to move. Auntie Stephanie and Uncle Danier were debating a move closer to me, but when we passed by a newsstand, I stopped walking and covered my mouth as I gasped. The policeman had warned me about what might come, but what I saw was unbelievably horrible. The headlines said everything he'd prepared me for, but worse. My picture was plastered across every front page with a different headline. Guilty! Who Really Did It? Coincidence—A Lone Survivor. How Did She Pull It Off? Killer Teen Walks!

A reporter popped out from behind the rack. "How did you kill them? What kind of weapon did you use?"

"I didn't do anything." I pushed the microphone away from my face.

"What was your motive? Abused? Ignored?" He shoved the microphone back in front of my face.

Uncle Danier stepped in and shouted at the reporter to leave us alone and go away. I turned just in time to see more reporters gathering. Uncle Danier also saw them and hurried us to the car. Auntie Stephanie hopped in first and fired up the engine while Uncle Danier sheltered me in the backseat.

"Why are they doing this?" I tried my best to hold back the tears. No use, they streamed down my face. "How can they be so cruel?"

"They're grasping." Uncle Danier placed a protective arm around my shoulders as we drove away. "These ridiculous theories are all they've got in order to make themselves feel better, feel safer. A monster is loose out there. They've got to place blame somewhere, and doing this is easier than not holding anyone accountable."

I knew what he meant; their deaths remained a mystery with no real suspects or clues. They still had no idea of how my family died, so the tabloids did what they do best and created their own story.

However, I was particularly bothered by the headlines pointing to me as a "person of interest" simply because I was a teenager who wore black clothes and ripped jeans. Sure, the piercings, highlights, and tattoos probably didn't help in my defense, but these were a sign of the times. Everyone my age had them or thought about getting some. What a joke! How could they get away with insinuating things like this? I'd just lost everyone I cared about. Didn't they have any sympathy or pity? Why couldn't they just leave me alone and allow me the chance to heal?

While we drove, the suggestion of moving away came up again, and this time I couldn't object. It was clear there wasn't much left for me in Greyton other than a few friends I never really saw, and a ton of memories I needed to put some distance between. It was evident my life would never be the same.

We proceeded to my house so I could collect some of my belongings for the move. We sat in the driveway, but I couldn't bring myself to go in. The thought of what happened inside was far too painful. The memories of that night flashed fresh in my mind.

Uncle Danier went inside while Auntie Stephanie sat in the rental car with me. She reached back, held my hand, and assured me again and again that everything would be okay. No one else would be hurt. We were safe.

My heart beat erratically while waiting for my uncle to return. I found it hard to breathe; my body trembled with fear. He had to come out ... I needed him to come out. I was about to start screaming my face off when he emerged, carrying two overstuffed suitcases.

The sheer sight of him made me cry. I felt so relieved he'd come back safely from my house. He walked quickly to the car, put my bags in the trunk, and got into the passenger seat. He turned to Auntie Stephanie, gave a smile, and then put on his seatbelt. I saw right through his façade. His eyes insinuated he'd never go back in my house, ever again.

Then he spoke softly to me. "I didn't grab too much, just some clothes, and a few other basics. You can check out your things when we get home. We will pick up whatever else you need."

Silently, we made our way to the airport. I thought about all the good memories being left behind. Sadly, those were now outnumbered by the bad memories residing in their place. I found myself somewhat relieved to be leaving. It would've been far too difficult trying to put myself back together in Greyton with all this uncertainty. Uncle Danier remained extremely quiet, which wasn't like him, so I assumed it was because of what he'd witnessed inside my house. I was actually thankful no one spoke. I wanted to leave all the bad stuff behind, and not get caught up in the stress of the unknown life waiting for me.

We arrived at the airport, dropped off the rental car, and proceeded to the airline counter to check in. The airline took our bags as we made our way through security. When we boarded the plane, I began to feel more apprehensive. What about Ginata? I should have stopped by her house to say goodbye, but I couldn't bring myself to say those words to her. Maybe it was because I was afraid to face her again. After all, it was my fault her parents were gone. I should have been the one who went inside my house, and then none of this would have ever happened. It should've been me who died so she and her family could be living out the rest of their lives together. Then another chilling thought crept in. Was leaving everything I'd ever known the right thing to do? I took a deep breath, trying to correct my state of mind. I reminded myself change was a good thing and sat down in my seat and fastened my seatbelt. A fresh start was exactly what I needed.

Once this plane takes off, I'm never coming back here.

I stared out the window, waiting impatiently. A moment later the plane took off. I took another deep breath, this time inviting the change.

"Well, this is it," Auntie Stephanie said.

In that moment, I realized the small island where my aunt and uncle lived was now considered home.

Uncle Danier hauled our suitcases up the front walkway. I was about to offer him some assistance, but he stopped. That's when I noticed him wipe his eyes. He'd been crying. It dawned on me that he'd lost his sister, just as I'd lost my mom. I went up to him, only before I got a chance to say anything, he said, "Aww, kiddo. I'm glad you're here." He hesitated a moment and added, "I really wish it were under different circumstances, though." He attempted a smile, but it didn't hide his pain.

"Me too." It would be a hard adjustment, but at least we didn't have to go through it alone.

Auntie Stephanie gave us both a warm smile and to my surprise, her small gesture made me feel a bit better. She wrapped her loving arms around Uncle Danier and myself. Together, as a new family unit, we entered our brightly colored home.

The walls were painted in shades of deep cranberry reds, rustic oranges, and welcoming yellows. The furniture was made up of prominent dark woods and leathers while the house was decorated with various vases, pictures, statues, and masks. They had so many interesting artifacts. I'd forgotten how stylish their house was. As I looked around, past visits with my family resurfaced, placing a lump in my throat.

Uncle Danier led me down the hall. We entered the bedroom on the right, and he put my suitcases on the bed.

"I'm sorry this isn't quite like your old room, but we can fix it up however you wish." He patted me on the shoulder then left the room, allowing me to get myself situated.

I took in the surroundings of my new bedroom. Unique sculptures of couples were positioned on the driftwood shelves, while scented candles sat on both corners of the dresser with an oversized mirror. The tall bedposts were composed of rustic dark wood, while deep red and black linens covered the mattress and pillows.

The room was lovely, but quite different from what I was accustomed to. Mind you, everything had changed for me. I'd

Escaped the Night

never have my old life back again, or the people in it. I sighed and began unpacking my clothes, all the while trying to decide if I should keep the room as it was. Amidst the piles of clothes, I pulled out a picture of my family that Uncle Danier had stowed away for me. I stared at their photo resting in the pewter frame and wondered who could have done such an awful thing to them. Especially my sisters, they were both so young and innocent. I ached to be back home and close to my family. I cried as I placed their photo in the middle of my dresser to ensure I got to see their faces every day.

I continued to unpack and was about to put my empty bags in the closet when I heard a dull jingle. I scrounged around, looking inside the suitcase. Something on the inside pocket tangled around my fingers. I pulled my hand out, now holding my amethyst sphere and silver moon. They hung together on a black strap of leather. More tears stung my eyes as I remembered back to when my family gave it to me. I'd been having a stressful day; my parents and sisters wanted to cheer me up and they did, with this necklace. My mother told me how the sphere held special powers of luck and protection. My sisters each kissed the amethyst so I could always feel the power of love. My father was the one who put the necklace on me. I had added the moon later on, which was a gift Ginata gave to me. I placed the necklace securely around my neck. I would treasure it forever, keeping their memories close to my heart.

Days, weeks, then months passed by, and I had settled in nicely. I felt like I belonged somewhere again. Auntie Steph and Uncle Dane were all too easy going, and even welcomed the new nicknames I'd given them.

I had an occasional roller coaster mood swing every now and then, but tried to overcome them so I wasn't a burden. My dreams still haunted me; however, they became fewer as each night passed.

Either Uncle Dane or Auntie Steph constantly stayed near me to ensure I never got lonely and that I was okay, but even with their company I found I missed my sisters and Ginata. Their bonds were hard to replace.

I'd been in Blackwood for close to three months before feeling settled enough to brave the would-be shopping center alone. I needed to have a life again. Besides, there really wasn't too much to their shopping center, unlike the giant malls back home.

Uncle Dane pulled up to the front entrance. "Shanntal, call me whenever you're ready to come home. Here's a bit of cash." He stuffed a wad of crumpled bills in my hand. "Now, go buy yourself some lunch or clothes or both. Just have some fun!"

"Thank you." I climbed out of the car and started toward the entrance.

He sat in the car, watching my approach to the main doors. I felt his eyes on me, so I waved, hoping to put us both at ease. I turned back around and entered the mall.

It was a lot busier than I expected. I braved my way through the crowds, moving back and forth so others could pass by. I couldn't believe this many people lived here, yet I knew no one. A few sets of eyes looked in my direction, but none of the faces smiled.

The tiny shopping center suddenly felt larger than the malls back home. I felt small and alone, which brought up thoughts I didn't want to think about. But my thoughts were too loud, and I found myself wondering why I hadn't died too. Why did I have to be the only one left? I shook the dark thoughts from my mind. I'd done enough pondering over the past few months; it was starting to get on my own nerves.

Friends. You're here to make friends. Being so incredibly lonely, I decided to accept friendship from anyone who offered. I'd become somewhat desperate for some kind, actually any kind, of companionship from people my own age.

I ambled over to a rack of clothes. The colors were too bright for my liking, but the group of girls standing nearby was what had drawn me over to this particular stand. I began sorting through the shirts. I smiled at one of the girls, but she turned away, paying zero attention to me. This wasn't going to be easy.

I took a blue tank top off the rack and held it up. I asked the girls, "Could I have your opinion on this?"

A girl with brown hair and thick makeup gave me a once over from head to toe before she laughed and said, "I wouldn't be caught dead wearing that ugly shirt."

"Me neither," laughed the blonde with a large nose.

The group snickered at me as they walked away.

Flustered, I threw the shirt on top of the rack, left the store, and made sure to walk in the opposite direction the girls went. I debated calling Uncle Dane to come pick me up. I even pulled out my cell to check the time, but only twenty minutes had passed since he dropped me off. I sighed and shoved the phone back in my purse.

What now? Then my nose caught the smell of food, really yummy smelling food. I walked up to the counter, waited in the line at the burger place, but changed my mind at the last minute. Now wasn't the time to try and eat my feelings away. Instead, I went over to the counter with no line and ordered a veggie sandwich and a bottle of water. Upon paying, I decided to sit at a table on the far side of the food court. I glanced up every once in a while with a smile, but the strangers looked at me like I had six heads or they just didn't take any notice.

"Grrrrrr. I hate this," I said under my breath. "Never knew I was invisible."

I looked up in time to witness an extremely good-looking, brown-haired guy wearing a baseball cap come straight toward me and sit down at my table. He wore a black t-shirt and blue jeans, and had a patch of hair just under his lip. My heart raced as I looked at the tattoo covering his muscular arm, some kind of Celtic knot going down to his elbow. He was downright irresistible.

I went to speak, but my voice only squeaked out a quiet, "Hello."

He raised an eyebrow then said, "Hello, I'm Jayce."

I couldn't believe such an attractive guy was talking to me.

He smiled. "And you are?"

"Shanntal, my name is Shanntal," I mumbled, so embarrassed I must've been crimson red.

"Shanntal, that's a nice name." He leaned back in the chair. "You don't look like you're from around here."

"Wow, glad to know I stand out so much." I felt my face redden. "Actually, I just moved to Blackwood a few months back." I leaned forward in my chair, and Jayce did too.

"Does everyone pass by without acknowledging others? I feel like I've come to a forbidden island, no newcomers allowed." I noticed a weird look on his face and leaned back into my seat.

He smirked and eyed me carefully. "Are we that obvious?"

I panicked. His reaction wasn't what I'd expected. *Are we that obvious?* What was that supposed to mean?

"What brings you here?"

"Here? You mean the mall or …"

He kept his eyes firmly on me. "Here, as in this forbidden island."

"Forbidden? Really?"

"I'm only joking around." He laughed. "You're just meeting the local mall snobs."

"Oh." I relaxed. "I'm here because I'm staying with my aunt and uncle."

He didn't say anything, just nodded, expecting me to continue. However, I wasn't sure I should share all the details of my life, at least not yet. So I took a bite of my sandwich.

"Well now …" He leaned in closer, flashing a fantastic smile. "A girl full of mystery, hmmm … I like that. Guess there's something you might want to know about me. When you act like this, I only want to know more." He winked, and I melted.

"My family was killed and I'm the sole survivor," I blurted.

I expected him to run away and never look back, but he didn't budge.

"Your entire family? Wow, that's tough. I'm sorry. What happened?"

I tried not to tear up as I told my story. I wrapped my arms around my stomach, as if giving myself a hug. "I don't really know. I was at a friend's house the night it happened." I paused, trying to stay strong. I didn't want to become a bawling lunatic. "My parents and two sisters were home, when someone or *something* got into the house."

Jayce gave a puzzled look.

This was really hard to talk about, but Jayce had a way about him. Something seemed familiar in his deep brown eyes, so I held myself together and went on. "We could tell something wasn't right when I got dropped off. My best friend's parents went into my house to check things out." My voice quavered. "Whoever killed my family remained inside and finished them off too."

"How did you escape?"

"I never got out of the car."

Jayce stared, his brown eyes wide and jaw dropped. Guess it wasn't the type of thing he expected to hear upon a first introduction.

I tried to read his expression.

"You said someone or *something*? What do you mean by *something*?"

I took my napkin and dabbed at the tears coming to my eyes.

"Sorry, I didn't mean to upset you. I … I like you. You look nice. I only wanted to get to know you better. But wow …" Jayce's voice trailed off.

I felt myself blush again. I managed to stop crying and smiled. He liked me.

"Are you okay?" he asked.

"I'm good."

"Yes, yes you are."

Elements

~ Chapter Five ~

I realized I hadn't actually told anyone what happened before this moment. Uncle Dane and Auntie Steph avoided the topic, at least whenever they were around me. I still needed to make sense of what happened, or at least have someone else hear how crazy everything was.

"The police never caught the person or people responsible, but they said everyone had been repeatedly bitten. There were different sets of bite marks, but not one was an exact duplicate. I'm not even sure what that means."

Jayce stared intensely into my eyes. "That's one interesting story you've got there, Shanntal. Sounds like you've been through an awful lot."

I nodded. "Please, can we keep this between us? I don't want any rumors going about me. I'm trying to start fresh."

"Sure," he agreed. "I don't blame you."

We sat quietly for a couple minutes. It felt nice having a friend my own age again. Jayce was easy to open up and talk to. I couldn't believe we hadn't known each other for a longer period of time.

Jayce leaned closer and asked, "Do you consider yourself open-minded?"

I thought about his question and wondered what he meant. I blurted out, "I suppose I do."

"I'd like to show you some, umm, things. Then all, or at least some of this, might become easier for you to understand. We'll need to leave here, though." He got up.

"What? You want me to leave here with you?" He must've thought I was nuts. I stood up, but not to go with him—to get far, far away.

"I didn't mean to freak you out. Come on ... you've gotta be able to tell I'm not a weirdo. I just thought I could help you take your mind off the horrible events taking place for you lately. If you don't want to come, I won't make you. I'm not going to make you do anything you aren't comfortable doing, Shanntal."

"Where do you plan on taking me?"

"The beach."

"I need to call my aunt and uncle first." I thought this would make him run, but instead, he nodded and agreed it was a good idea.

Auntie Steph answered the phone.

"Hi, Auntie Steph."

"How's things?" she asked.

"Great. I've made a new friend. He wants me to go to the beach with him for a while."

"What beach, and who's the guy?"

"His name is Jayce," I said. "And the beach is—"

"Mystic," Jayce responded.

"Mystic," I repeated. "Don't worry, I will be careful. Any funny biz, trust me, I'll be calling for backup while kicking butts and taking names."

"Keep the phone near you at all times, but sweetheart, we both know it's time for you to have some sort of social life again. I've heard his name around town before, and from what I've heard, he's a really nice guy."

"I promise I will. Thanks, Auntie Steph. I love you."

"Love you too."

I shoved my phone into my pocket. "All right, I'll come."

"Glad to see you don't think I'm a creeper after all." Jayce's dark brown eyes sparkled when he smiled.

"A girl can never be too careful." I gave a reserved grin.

"Very true."

We headed out the main entrance of the mall and into the parking lot. I followed Jayce to a car parked in the very last row. There wasn't another anywhere around.

"Why'd you park so far away?"

"Didn't want anyone to scratch my beauty," he said, approaching the shiny black car with tinted windows and fancy rims. Jayce pressed the car alarm disarm button on his key ring, and both doors instantly unlocked.

We drove for a few miles with the radio blasting. I'd never been a really good judge of distances, but knew we'd been traveling for some time now. I remembered we were on an island, so at least he couldn't drive me to another country or something. I focused on the smudges of greens and browns blending together, hoping for the same sense of ease I had on my final night with Ginata and her family. But, it didn't come, and I remained on guard. I stared out the window at the moss layered trees and jagged rock faces that covered every rolling hill we passed.

I glanced at Jayce inconspicuously every once in a while. Sometimes, when he realized I was looking, he would turn and share the warmest smile. I'd have to look away when the butterflies took over.

The car slowed as I spotted a glimpse of the water. We made our way around the sharp corner of a steep hill. Midway down, he lowered the music. We passed by a sign and I read it aloud. "Mystic Beach."

Not long past the sign, the terrain changed. Rock faces were now covered in lush green trees blending perfectly with the grassy hillside. He slowly took another sharp corner, and that's when I caught a full view of the magnificent ocean and sandy beach.

"Wow!" I saw waves rolling in along the shoreline and felt like I'd found paradise. "Simply beautiful!"

We drove along the coastline until Jayce pulled into a makeshift parking spot. We maneuvered our way across the driftwood and rocks. After a few more feet of debris, the beach turned into beautiful seamless sand swallowing my shoes, so I bent down and took them off. There weren't any pebbles or stones, just soft sand on my feet.

I noticed some people farther down the beach. Behind them rested a mountainside hollowed out with caves. Jayce grabbed my hand, and we started in their direction. My knees weakened as his big hand cradled mine. There was something special about Jayce. I felt connected, like I truly knew him.

"I'm really glad you decided to come."

"Me too."

"I want you to meet some of my friends. You don't mind, do you?"

"Nope. It's cool." Surprisingly, I found myself looking forward to meeting more people and hoped they were also friendly.

The closer we got, the more apprehensive I became. Suddenly, I felt guilty for going out and having fun after everything that happened. I didn't know what to do with myself once the panic set in. All the training the doctor provided was momentarily forgotten in the midst of an adrenaline rush.

Jayce squeezed my hand. "Please don't feel guilty. This is your life, and it's meant to be lived. You're healing, that's all. You'll be okay. I promise."

Had I just said it all out loud? I felt myself blush. *Brain, shut off now.* Thinking only seemed to get me in trouble.

We closed in on four people.

"Shanntal, I'd like to introduce you to some of my closest friends—Terran, Aiden, Makan, Meriel." He pointed in the direction of the strangers standing before us. "And Layla," he added, gesturing toward the black cat at their feet.

I was shocked I'd just been introduced to a cat. *People here are a wee bit different.*

Jayce let out a muffled snicker, leaving me to wonder how he always managed to do things on cue.

"Hello." I waved to the group. "Oh … wow!" I noticed the cat's eyes were a brilliant purple. "Beautiful cat."

Terran stood closest to the cat and replied, "She's a rare breed. We were lucky to find one that's remained so loyal after all this time."

Meriel leaned down and patted the cat on the head.

"Shanntal, have you ever heard of the elements before?" Jayce asked.

"Elements?" I shrugged.

I felt unsure, which made me miss being home in the comfort of my room. I was safe there, hidden, protected.

"Let me show you something." Jayce reached into the left pocket of his jacket and pulled out a small velvet bag. He loosened the drawstrings and gestured for me to hold out my hand, which I did. He poured four tiny containers from the bag into my palm.

"What are these?" I said, studying the glass containers. One held a water-like substance, and another appeared empty. There was a small burning flame in the third, but the last one stole my breath. A tiny earth spun around in the glass. It was the strangest thing I'd ever seen. I almost couldn't bring myself to stop staring at the tube, until I realized everyone was watching me. When I looked up, I found them all smiling.

"Those are the four elements," Jayce said. "Earth, fire, wind, and water." He gestured back to the four people standing before us. "Allow me to re-introduce my friends."

Connected

~ Chapter Six ~

Jayce re-introduced the closest girl. "Terran represents the earth element, which is the provider of life."

Terran wore beige and brown clothing, accompanied by a decorative scarf full of blue and green splashes. She had big green eyes and a wild mess of curly, sandy-brown hair. The resemblance made sense, but I didn't say so, at least not out loud, yet Jayce laughed like he somehow knew what I was thinking.

Jayce moved on to the tall fellow standing beside Terran. "Aiden represents the fire element. Fire gives people warmth, light, among many other things."

Aiden had the brightest shade of red hair, not carrot top, but more of a deep burgundy. His eyes were a light but piercing brown. He wore simple clothes that accented his body by showing off his rippling muscles.

I realized I really could identify them. They each resembled the element they were attached to. Normally anything supernatural freaked me out, but I found these people completely fascinating.

"I know this. I know this one!" I blurted before Jayce could tell me more. "Makan represents the wind element." I smiled, pleased with myself. I knew I had his element right.

Jayce nodded. "The wind element supplies us with the air we all need to survive."

Makan's prominent gray eyes had various blue specks spun throughout. His silver-toned hair was relatively long. His muscular frame didn't appear old, although his hair stated otherwise.

"And there's also our sweet Meriel." Jayce smiled. "The water element gives us our much-needed hydration."

Her spiked blonde hair popped out in every direction. Meriel was a blue-eyed stunner. Her clothes swayed around her, not clinging in any way. She had a way about her that just seemed so refreshing.

"Well ... I'm pleased to ... and umm ... thankful?" I stumbled to find my words. "I'm happy to meet you all."

They laughed, putting me at ease.

Even though everything they'd shown me was far beyond reasonable comprehension, I found myself believing them. They were the most unique people I'd ever seen.

"Let me guess, now you're going to tell me there's something special about the cat?" I was kidding, but after I said that, I heard a 'whoosh' noise.

A beautiful, dark-skinned girl stood before me with the same unforgettable purple eyes. In another blink of the eye, the 'whoosh' happened, and the girl was gone, but a large black panther stood in her place. I gasped and stumbled backward as the large cat growled.

I started to worry, while everyone else laughed. I began to feel unsure about these people. I considered this stunt pretty far from funny.

"Enough showing off, Layla," Jayce warned.

Right before my eyes, the panther changed into the beautiful girl again. Layla spoke in an enchanting voice. "I'm sorry if I scared you. I never meant to, I was only having some fun and wanted to show off my skills." She held out her hand to shake mine. "I'm Layla, the shapeshifter. As you can see, I'm able to take any form I choose."

"It's good to meet you, Layla." I returned the shake.

"I have to protect my secret, so I generally keep the form of a house cat. It keeps suspicions down because cats are pretty common around here. There are only a handful of shifters left, so I'm pretty choosy about who gets to know about me. I've got a good feeling about you, though." She placed her hand on my shoulder. "I can already tell we're going to be great friends."

If I hadn't seen this first-hand, I never would've been able to comprehend any of it. This was truly unbelievable! I'd just made the most amazing friends, but another thought popped into my mind. If Jayce hung around such mythical beings … what did that make him?

Before I could ask my question aloud, Jayce began to answer. "I'm what some call … connected. I'm also the keeper of the elements."

"Connected?"

"To the elements and certain other minds. I mean, so long as they're open. When connected, I'm able to share their thoughts, experiences, secrets, fears, dreams, you get the drift." He looked relieved to share this.

"You said certain minds?"

"I'm able to connect … umm … normally … What I mean to say is, I'm usually only able to connect to immortal minds," he said, his voice low.

"Immortal minds, that's cool," I said, not fully convinced of what he was implying.

"What I mean is, you're the first human I've been able to do this with."

"Oh, I see." That explained why he always laughed at the arguments in my head. I hadn't been saying them out loud; he was in my head hearing the whole conversation.

I felt the embarrassment starting to build, and blood rushed to my face. Wow, I had to learn to watch my thoughts from now on, considering I wasn't the only one aware of them. I'd already had about a zillion thoughts about him. *Shut up Shanntal, he can hear you!* Then I felt anger. He should've told me about this little gift sooner, like when he first started to read my mind. Hadn't he ever heard of privacy? I was about to erupt when he looked deep into my eyes. His stare was penetrating.

'I'm truly sorry, Shanntal. I should've told you sooner.' He apologized without saying any words aloud.

Totally bizarre—I heard his voice perfectly in my head. "Whoa! How'd you do that?"

He winked.

Just then, my cell rang. I pulled my phone out of my pocket, recognizing the number. "My uncle must be getting worried. I have to take this call." I moved away from the group and answered.

"Shanntal, where are you? Why haven't you called? Is everything okay?" His voice sounded panicked.

"I'm fine." I walked further away from the group. "I'm sorry. I should've called sooner, but I met some nice people and wanted to hang out more. We're down at Mystic Beach. I told Auntie Steph what I was doing, and she said it was okay. I didn't mean to make you worry. I'm all right, I promise."

He let out a big sigh of relief. "Well, time to start heading back. Should I come get you?"

I looked at Jayce, who mouthed, "I can take you home."

"I can get a ride home. My new friends are really nice. Can I *please* stay longer? Maybe a few more hours?"

I heard mumbling in the background as Uncle Dane tried to cover up the phone. I overheard him say, "Come on, Steph, of course, I want her to have friends … yeah, I know … fine, all right." Then he came back onto the phone. "Okay, Shanntal, you can have a few more hours, but don't stay out too late."

"Thank you! Thank you! Thank you!"

"Okay, see you in a while."

"See you."

Just when I thought we were done saying goodbye, Uncle Dane piped up. "Hey, who are you with? Do I know them?"

"Jayce, Layla ..." I stopped. Were their identities a secret? I felt unsure how to answer, but if I didn't say something, I knew Uncle Dane would flip out.

Jayce's voice entered my mind. *'Jayce Fallon. Tell him you're with a few of my friends and me, but you don't remember all their names.'*

I never mentioned Layla again, hoping Uncle Dane hadn't heard me say it the first time around. "I'm with Jayce Fallon. We came down here to meet some of his friends. I just met them a few minutes ago. You know how bad I am with names. I already can't remember them." I paused. Then in a lower voice, I said, "Their names are funky and pretty strange." That was the truth; I'd just omitted a few facts about them.

"Jayce Fallon. Could you spell that?" I heard paper shuffling.

"J-A-Y-C-E and F-A-L-L-O-N." My response took me off guard. Jayce was a relatively unique name. How had I known the proper spelling?

'You're connected to my thoughts, as I am yours. When we're connected, if either one of us knows the answer to a question, it will naturally come.'

Jayce stood yards away, facing the opposite direction, but it felt like he was next to me having this conversation.

"Shanntal?" Uncle Dane said. "Still there? Hello?"

"Yeah, sorry." I half expected a lecture like my father used to give and was preparing to turn on my attitude.

"Get back to your friends, kiddo. Call me if you need anything, but don't be too late." His voice lowered, and he added, "I love you, sweetie. I don't want anything to ever happen to you."

How could I be upset at him for caring? Tears stung my eyes. "I won't be late," I said. "I love you too. Have a good night, Uncle Dane."

"You too! Please say hello to Layla for me."

"Lay—How do ...?" He hung up before I could finish.

Jayce interrupted. *'It's a small town. Everyone knows everyone, that's all. Come back over here. You're safe with us. Nothing's going to harm you.'*

'But ...'

'Get over here. It's time to relax and have some fun.'

'Right.' That's when I realized I was standing halfway down the beach all by myself. I went back and took place beside Jayce. Everyone smiled upon my return, which made me feel like I fit in with these people quite nicely. Even though I didn't look anything like them or have any powers, I felt like I belonged. I'd never had such chemistry with my other friends, minus one exception—Ginata. My heart sunk heavily as I wondered where she was now.

Jayce picked up on how much I missed my dear friend and felt the emptiness left in her place. In an attempt to comfort, he wrapped his arms around tightly and pulled me in close. His gesture worked. The simple hug felt so good; I found myself never wanting him to let go. I was safe and secure locked in his embrace.

'I can feel how much you miss her. Just know that you aren't alone anymore. You have us now. We aren't going anywhere.'

'Thank you, it's sweet of you to say.'

'I speak the truth.' He squeezed tighter.

All I could do was smile. I was honestly happy again.

It started getting chilly, so we decided to copy a few of the other groups along the beach that had made small fires. Terran and Makan gathered some driftwood and arranged it, then Aiden snapped his fingers, and just like that our fire was going.

I chatted back and forth with my new friends, getting to know each other better. I enjoyed finding out more about their special gifts, but decided to leave out the horrific details of my past, and instead gave only the basics. Jayce knew what had really happened, so I figured that was enough. Our bond seemed to grow stronger by the minute. I felt incredibly close to Jayce and everyone else. They were all very accepting, making them extremely easy for me to get along with.

A short while before the sun set, Jayce decided it was time to say goodbye to our friends and take me home. Meriel, Terran, and Layla hugged me before parting ways while the guys waved and invited me back soon. Everyone felt like old friends.

Jayce and I walked hand in hand back to his car. I breathed deeply, taking in the magnificent smells of the water. With the small waterfall, seamless sand, and various caves, this place could have been called perfect beach.

On the trip home, Jayce held my hand the entire way, leaving me in a state of giddy schoolgirl.

"So, what did you think of my friends?"

"They're totally amazing. I actually can't believe how well I got along with them."

"I can tell they really liked you." He flashed his perfect smile.

"I'm glad." My heart fluttered from the way he glanced over.

I didn't need to tell Jayce where to go. He passed by the small grocer and gas station, then turned left onto my road and stopped his car directly in front of the black and white bungalow.

I got possession of my hand back, but before I got out of the car, I said, "Thank you for everything today, Jayce. I had a really great time." I wondered when I'd see him next.

"Tomorrow." He grinned. "Just send me a thought when you're ready for me to come pick you up." He leaned in and gently kissed my cheek. "Sweet dreams, Shanntal."

"Sweet dreams, Jayce." My cheek felt extra warm where he kissed me. His kiss lingered, like I'd always be able to feel it.

Jayce chuckled, and I was beyond embarrassed. I needed to try much harder to control my thoughts or risk becoming bright red for all time. I hurried out of the car, waved at Jayce, and quickly headed up to my house.

I reached for the door knob, but lost my balance when the front door flung wide open. Uncle Dane stood in the doorway, looking directly past me in order to get a peek at Jayce.

Jayce noticed what was happening and rolled down his passenger window. He called out, "Hello, I'm Jayce. I'm in a bit of a hurry now, but I'll meet you properly tomorrow. Enjoy the rest of your night." He waved goodbye and drove away.

My uncle gave me a look, and I saw the question in his eyes. *Tomorrow?* Surprisingly, he never said the words I expected; instead, he moved out of the way, letting me by.

Auntie Steph and Uncle Dane must've had a really good talk, I thought to myself. I went into the living room and glanced at the clock on the mantel. Wow, almost ten-thirty already. I sat down on the couch to spend a few minutes with my uncle before heading to sleep. Auntie Steph had already gone to bed. She was a ten o'clock kind of woman. Ten o'clock every night, she went behind closed doors and entered dreamland.

"I tried talking to some girls at the mall," I started, "but they weren't very kind to me. Come to think of it, they were downright rude. I debated calling you, except I got some food, and then Jayce sat down. We talked and instantly clicked, and before long, hours passed and we were down at the beach meeting some of his friends."

"You went alone with him?"

"Yes, but Auntie Steph knew what I was doing and where we were going. Trust me, I asked her first, and she said okay." I tried getting his mind off worry mode. "It feels good having friends again. I really missed it. The girls I met are super nice ... speaking of girls, how exactly do you know Layla?"

"Small town," he answered.

I was looking forward to seeing Jayce again tomorrow, so I got up from the couch before it ended up any later. I didn't want to accidently sleep all day. Before getting too far, I turned and gave Uncle Dane a quick kiss on the cheek. "Good night and thank you for today. I really had an awesome time."

"Good night, Shanntal. I'm glad you made some new friends."

"Thanks. Me too." I went into my room, ready for the greatly needed sleep that waited.

Second Date

~ Chapter Seven ~

My dream flashed from one scene to the next. I tried to remain focused so I could examine the details more thoroughly.

In one part, I appeared very young, only about five or six. I was playing on swings in the neighborhood park on a warm, sunny day. Whenever I swung up real high, I saw something. I peered harder at the spot every time I went up in the air, then finally I saw an older boy standing just outside the playground. He was watching me. However, he didn't scare me because I felt like I knew him. I felt safer knowing that he kept a watchful eye over me.

My dream spiraled, taking me into another time. Here I appeared to be about thirteen and standing in a shopping center with some friends. There were crowds of people all around us. We were giggling and having fun. I looked around and spotted the same boy. He didn't appear any older, yet he was still there watching me, protecting me.

I associated the boy in my dream with Jayce, all grown up. They must've been the same person, because I got a similar connected feeling with Jayce as I did with the boy in my dream. Knowing he was there made me feel safe.

My dream went on yet another path. Things appeared entirely different, but the boy remained beside me. This time, we were older, about the same age. He stood close, not far out in the distance as he had before. I took a few moments to savor every small detail of his being and just as I'd suspected, he turned into Jayce. The same Jayce I knew now. He grabbed onto my arms, shook me hard, and yelled at me to run.

We weren't in friendly places like the park or shopping center anymore. We were in a dark alley with doors everywhere, but they were all locked. A thunderous snarl sounded behind us. Jayce and I ran away from the sound, but I wasn't scared, even though I knew it was a vampire. Jayce pulled me along, trying his hardest to find a safe place for me to hide.

Terrifying screams rang out from close behind. Wood broke apart with loud crunches, and the cries grew louder. Then silence followed until the next sets of screams began. We needed to run faster. It was getting closer, and we had to get away.

I finally became aware of how scared I was. Fear rose up from my feet and continued throughout my entire body. My heart pounded, but I swallowed the overwhelming urge to scream. I clenched my hands into fists and prepared myself for the upcoming fight.

The vampire was so close I could smell the stench of blood all around me. More screams rang out from people nearby. I was so frightened, yet I couldn't bring myself to turn around to see what it looked like. I just knew I needed to get away. I couldn't die like this.

We yanked and pulled, but no success. Every door we reached was locked. I turned a dark corner and crashed into something hard. The collision almost knocked me down, but I managed to regain my balance in time to notice slimy drool run down my shoulder. A werewolf let out a loud rumbling growl, its breath reeking of death.

I looked around for Jayce; I needed help but couldn't find him. My life was about to end, but suddenly, the beast transformed. A lone man stood before me. I grabbed ahold of the man by his shoulder and told him we needed to get away, this place was too dangerous. The man gave me a strange look, and with a quick thrust from his other arm, he jabbed a wooden stake through my heart.

Jolting awake, I gasped and clutched my chest, feeling the sting as if he'd actually stabbed me. I blinked my eyes in a total frenzy until they refocused. The sun gleamed vibrantly through my window, lighting up my room like the Fourth of July, nearly blinding me in the process.

I decided to stay in bed for a few minutes longer, recalling the dream that had turned into a nightmare. My heartbeat slowly returned to its normal rhythm, as did my breathing. I told myself over and over again, it was just another dream.

I remembered most of the details, yet something still seemed strange. I knew I'd only just met Jayce, but he felt like a distant memory coming back. He'd been in every part of my dream, watching and protecting me. Did I know him? Had he been on the sidelines of my life all along? How come I couldn't remember my childhood? Only small tidbits had ever revealed themselves, but they always seemed surreal, like they didn't belong to me.

Certain areas of the dream stuck in my mind—especially the parts about the vampire and werewolf. There was that word again. *Vampire.* Only this time it had a partner. Jayce had been there too. He tried keeping me away from the monsters, but where had he gone? Did they get him too? More importantly, why did the man stab *me* with the stake?

Why were vampires arising in my thoughts so frequently? They'd been mentioned the night Ginata and I used the Ouija board. That whole encounter seemed so strange because those boards were supposed to contact the dead, not the walking dead. Now vampires were intruding my dreams. After everything I found out yesterday, could it be possible they were real too?

I was going to have a million questions for Jayce when I saw him. Then I realized he probably already knew my questions; it would be just a matter of him passing along the answers.

'*Good morning, beautiful.*' His voice entered my head.

I loved the sound of his voice, a perfect deep pitch. His voice sounded how every man's voice should—profound and strong, yet somehow sweet and sensitive.

It wasn't fair, knowing he knew everything I thought. Why couldn't I do the same with him? Could he see me too? I lifted the blankets and looked down. Perfect! I rolled my eyes. I'd worn mismatched pajamas to bed.

"Argh," I said aloud, pulling the blanket over my head. I felt ugly and embarrassed. To top everything off, I knew Jayce was listening and possibly saw exactly what I'd just done. This could potentially become a really bad thing, and pretty quick. We needed to set some boundaries. Fast!

'Has anyone ever told you, you look really cute when you're frustrated?'

'Geez, Jayce.' Yet again, I felt myself blush. *'Can you see me?'*

'Only if I focus all of my attention, I can get glimpses, you know, small scenes. I can't watch every move you make, so there's no need to worry.'

This had already spun into a full time relationship between us. We were linked together in so many ways, and it felt more intimate than what I was used to. I'd never really had any serious boyfriends. My longest so-called relationship lasted a total of three months, and we were already far more serious than that had ever been. I took a moment to think about everything. Then, one major question popped into my head and it couldn't be ignored. Was I ready for all this?

'All we can do is take this one day at a time. I promise I'll behave myself and give space whenever needed. Right now though, you should get yourself ready because I can't wait to see you.'

'Okay, okay I'm up!' In truth, I really wanted to see him too.

I got up, let out a big stretch, went over to my dresser, grabbed my hairbrush, and tried to brush through the tangled mess of bedhead. Wasn't happening, I needed a shower. I left my room, but heard Uncle Dane and Auntie Steph already up, so I decided to go say good morning.

They sat together at the breakfast bar, sipping on morning coffee while eating fruit and toast. They smiled happily back and forth, exchanging conversation while enjoying their breakfast.

I admired the cute couple before announcing myself. It amused me how they shared the same traditional style, yet managed to keep their look modern. They had the same shade of brown hair; his short and hers shoulder length. Both had bright blue eyes. He stood a few inches taller, but overall, they were very similar. I knew the saying, 'the longer you were with someone; the more you would start to resemble them.' This rang completely true in their case. I sneezed, giving away my location.

Uncle Dane raised his cup of coffee to me, and Auntie Steph said good morning.

"Good morning." I gave them each a kiss on the cheek. I went directly to the coffee pot and filled up the cup waiting for me on the counter. I fixed myself a piece of toast and grabbed some fruit out of the refrigerator.

Breaking off a piece of her toast, Auntie Steph said, "I'm meeting a friend for a fun-filled day of shopping. Then we will be heading out for lunch, and if time permits, may possibly go watch a movie before we head home. Shanntal, you're more than welcome to tag along."

"Oh sure," Uncle Dane said, "just leave me home alone to watch the game!"

Auntie Steph and I both laughed since we knew that's exactly what he wanted to do.

I blew on my coffee then said, "Thanks for the offer, but Jayce and I are meeting up today. He said he'd pick me up in a little while."

"Oh, so you're hanging with that Jayce guy again." Uncle Dane pried.

I waited to hear his objection, but he never got the chance.

"Ohhhh, do tell, do tell!" Auntie Steph absolutely beamed as she started questioning me. She placed her elbows up on the counter, leaned forward with her head in her hands, waiting for me to spill the details.

"Jayce, you know, the guy I met at the mall yesterday. We hung out, and well he introduced me to some of his friends. He's pretty cool. They all are." I tried leaving things at that.

"Is he cute?" Her head tilted sideways as she prodded for more details.

I tried to act casual, but my face grew warm. I merely nodded and took a bite of my toast, hoping she'd just let this go.

"You like him!" She squealed, throwing her arms in the air. "You like him, a lot!"

'I like your aunt!' Jayce intruded. *'I'm looking forward to meeting her. She'll be easy to win over. Your uncle on the other hand ... he might be a bit more challenging.'*

I saw the concerned expression my uncle wore. He apparently didn't share the same enthusiasm as his wife.

"Jayce is really nice and polite. He's a real gentleman." I hoped this would help put his mind to rest.

"Well, keep your cell handy at all times," he said, the worry lines noticeable on his forehead. "Remember, we're only a phone call away."

I stood up and gave him a big hug. "Well, I guess I better start getting ready. I told Jayce to pick me up at eleven." I'd never actually picked a time for Jayce and wasn't sure if he'd caught the clue I just dropped for him. I couldn't tell if we were still connected. I'd verify with him when I had a little more privacy.

I loaded my dishes into the dishwasher and started down the hallway toward the bathroom. I was in desperate need of a shower. I stopped by the hall closet and pulled out a towel. I closed the bathroom door and began stripping down when I realized I wasn't sure if I was alone. A shower with Jayce in my head, oh my ...

"Jayce, are you there?" I asked aloud.

'Well now, hello, hello!' he answered playfully.

I was about to vent, but he interrupted.

'I know. Trust me. You don't even need to ask. I'll try to think of lots of other things. Even though I'd really rather be thinking about you.'

'If you prefer me to show up smelly, continue to think about me, Jayce. I dare you.' There was no way I could shower with him in my head.

'All right! You win. You've got my word, okay? No thoughts,' he promised. *'How about you send me a thought when you're done. Or better yet, I'll just see you at eleven.'*

Thankfully, he'd picked up on my not so subtle hint. He was a tricky one, and I had to lay down some ground rules, plus make sure I stuck to my guns. *'Thank you ... now out you go.'*

The feeling surprised me; I actually felt him leave. At least I'd learned something with all this. I now knew what it felt like while he was connected and when he wasn't.

I took a quick shower, just in case this whole ordeal was too tempting for him. After all, he was a guy, and this clearly asked a lot of him. I swiftly toweled off and put clean clothes on. I brushed my hair and teeth, and applied a tiny bit of makeup.

'I'm ready for you,' I thought to Jayce, hoping he'd hear me.

'Give me twenty minutes, and I'll be there.'

'Jayce, were you connected this entire time?'

'No, I swear. It's eleven so I knew you'd be ready.'

'Really?'

'Yup, promise. See you soon.'

Not even fifteen minutes passed by before I heard a knock at the front door. Uncle Dane opened it.

"Hello, I'm Jayce Fallon. I'm here to pick up Shanntal. I'd like to apologize for not introducing myself yesterday. I was running short on time." I watched Jayce reach his hand out, awaiting a return shake from my uncle.

"No worries, Jayce. It's nice to meet you. I've already heard lots about you. The name's Danier, but you can call me Dane." He reached his hand out and shook Jayce's.

Auntie Steph had already left to meet her friend for the day. At least there wouldn't be any embarrassing drama. A handshake, I could handle. The squealing, well, that would've been something else entirely.

I grabbed my jacket and purse and slipped my feet easily into my running shoes. I kissed Uncle Dane on his cheek. "See you later."

"See you," Uncle Dane replied. He stood in the doorway watching us make our way to the shiny black car.

Jayce opened the door for me, then ran around to the driver's side and climbed in. The butterflies in my stomach were unbearable. I was happy to see him, but extremely nervous at the same time.

"Me too, I know what you mean." Jayce started the car, then shot me a wink followed by a flash of his perfect grin.

Uncle Dane remained positioned in a protective stance in the front doorway. I waved to him when Jayce pulled the car away. Uncle Dane waved back, and I watched him hesitantly close the door.

I felt terrible that he worried so much about me. I felt safe around Jayce and wanted more than anything for Uncle Dane to accept him.

Jayce and I spent the entire day driving around. I'd expected to go meet the others, but Jayce said he wanted me all to himself for the day. He showed me around the island, taking me to the top of various hills so we could admire their views. He proceeded to show me a couple of other beaches too. None of them compared to Mystic Beach, which I considered to be the most beautiful one by far.

We decided to stop at the seafood restaurant and grab a late lunch. Jayce and I took a seat in a booth by the window. A lone candle burned in the center of our table, it was accompanied by two white roses and a single red. We admired the spectacular view overlooking the water. A dark-haired, slender waiter came over to take down our drink order. We both ordered lemon water with the fish and chip meal off the menu board.

While Jayce and I conversed, the candle burning in the middle of our table kept grabbing my attention. This would've been so much more romantic if it were dark outside.

Jayce leaned over, and with a smooth motion, took the red rose out of the vase and tucked it safely behind my ear. "Perfect!"

I smiled.

He held my hand and told me more stories about the island and some of his favorite places to go. I was completely mesmerized, hanging on his every word.

The food was served promptly to us in our booth.

I squirted an obscene amount of ketchup on the plate beside my fries. When I realized what I'd done, I fought back the tears. I'd always shared with my sisters, so I made sure to put enough for all three of us, an old habit. I expected Jayce to make a comment, but instead he gave a quirky grin then dipped a fry. I couldn't help but laugh.

We ate the delicious fish and chips while sharing the big ketchup blob on my plate. After we had finished our meal, Jayce went over to the front counter to pay the bill. I used the opportunity to sneak in another look out the window with the magnificent view. Picture perfect.

We got back into his car to continue on with our touring adventure. We spent a delightful day together seeing sites and just hanging out. Then, came the trip back. We'd driven quite a way up-island. Our trip home to Blackwood took close to four hours. Another day had raced by. Jayce and I pulled in front of my house as the clock in his car read ten-thirty p.m. It wasn't fair how fast time flew whenever I was near Jayce and stood still in situations where I wanted nothing more than to have it pass faster. Time sure was a funny thing.

Before I got out of the car, Jayce leaned over and planted a warm, lingering kiss on each cheek. Then he grazed my lips, and I pulled him in closer. Butterflies filled my stomach as we shared an impassioned kiss. Afterward, the biggest smile spread across my face. I felt so incredibly happy; it was absolutely impossible for me to hide the fact. I didn't want him to leave, but I fought against every urge pushing me to stay and climbed out of his car. I headed up to my house, but before reaching the door, I turned and waved good night.

Opened Eyes

~ Chapter Eight ~

Over the next few months, Jayce and I became pretty much inseparable. We saw each other every day and spent every waking minute together. He always held my hand while we were out, and each night we said good night with a passionate kiss. During this time, I also became very close friends with the elements.

Layla usually stayed in human form around me, trusting me completely to keep her secret. Every now and then she'd shift into a house cat, but mostly when we were down at the beach or around others that she didn't know very well. Layla and I had a strong bond; she was quickly becoming my best friend.

Terran, Meriel, and Layla weren't like any of my other girlfriends. We got along extremely well, but on a totally different level. We never gossiped about cute boys we had crushes on, or complained about how we spent too much on shopping sprees. We talked more about the environment and simply being alive. Around them, I felt like I was experiencing life for the first time. Nothing seemed the same, and I had a new-found appreciation for everything around me.

Aiden and Makan clearly enjoyed Jayce's company, and it was easy to tell they'd been friends for some time. I was amused watching them attempt to roughhouse like ordinary guys. They danced around with anticipation, trying to get a handle on each other's moves before lunging forward. Most times, they'd go sailing past each other and land on the ground. They'd shake off their misses, laugh, and get up to try again. However, Jayce always seemed to have the upper hand. Aiden and Makan would charge, but Jayce would predict their moves, and with one quick move to the side, down they'd go again.

Even though these were superior beings, they were first and foremost my friends. I didn't feel odd hanging out alongside immortals, because they made me feel like I finally belonged somewhere. They'd openly accepted me into their circle.

One Friday afternoon Jayce picked me up to go for a drive. After driving a while, he turned the car around, and we headed in the direction of Mystic Beach.

"Back to the beach?"

"My favorite place!" He squeezed my hand tightly.

Once in a while, I was still caught off guard with how natural this felt. Almost as if my hand belonged there, the two of us specifically made for one another. We fit perfectly.

Jayce nodded in agreement.

I looked out the window, slightly embarrassed. I'd done it again. There I sat, fantasizing about the beautiful man beside me, and was most likely freaking him right out. This would've been the same as walking up to someone and blurting out something along the lines of, 'take me, I'm yours.'

Jayce laughed. "You aren't the only one feeling this way, Shanntal. We are feeling twice the emotion of any normal person right now. Trust me, you aren't alone. I feel it too, maybe even more than you do."

His reaction put me at ease. He thought the same way about me. Now, I felt utterly ecstatic! I needed to keep my cool, so I turned to hide my big smile, watching the trees and rocks flash by as we traveled along the curving road. We pulled into our usual parking spot and walked the same path just as we always did. Out of habit, I looked down the beach to see if our friends were around.

No one else was around. Being alone scared yet excited me all at the same time. My chance had finally arrived. We were always hanging out with the others, but now that we were alone, I hoped to figure out a few more intimate details about Jayce. In the few months we'd known each other, we had really only discussed my past, the island, and his friends and their importance. Today, I wanted to learn more about him.

Mystery surrounded Jayce. He'd totally captivated me with those deep brown eyes and impeccable smile. Despite the romantic tension evident between us, he'd somehow managed to remain partially distant. I knew nothing about him other than the basics. I wanted to get through all the small talk, because our relationship kept heading toward a more serious level. I needed to know more about him.

We walked a ways down the beach, my hand cradled in his. I found it nice, just the two of us. I was thoroughly enjoying our alone time so much that for a few moments I'd forgotten about wanting to interrogate him. Jayce led the way to a flat rock. It was kind of shaped like a bench sitting along the shore, so we sat down on it.

"I'm the keeper of the elements." He looked at me cautiously. "Do you know what that really means?"

I thought for a minute then shook my head. "No, I'm not exactly sure."

Letting go of my hand, he got up off the rock. I sat and watched him pace back and forth, looking somewhat nervous. "Where do I even start?"

"From the beginning," I said, unsure if I was ready to hear what he was about to say.

"All right." He squared his body off in front of me. "There's no simple way to say this, so here it goes. I'm immortal. You're looking at the keeper of the elements, and you've already realized I am able to connect to certain minds. What you don't know is …" He fidgeted around for a moment before steadying himself. "I'm the reason the elements function together as a whole and not against each other. I came to them a very long time ago. I was three years old the night my parents were killed by werewolves. Being so tiny, I managed to escape unnoticed. Meriel was the one who found me wandering alone by the water. She took pity on me and brought me home to the others. They've taught me everything I know. Once I learned how to use my gifts, I was able to keep peace between them. Back then, they were having some real power struggles, and I figured it was the least I could do after they'd treated me so well. And that's how I became their keeper."

"Jayce," I said. "It's kind of a wonderful thing. You're a survivor too. As for being immortal, well, that just means you get to live forever. Most people only wish they could do such a thing."

He kept his stance firm and spoke more hesitantly than before. "There's more … something I must tell you. There's a fight brewing among the immortal world, and I've got a feeling you're right in the middle of this mess. I don't know which side's going to prevail. Immortals are talking, and some of them say the outcome will basically be up to you. They believe you'll be our savior and think you're the key to keeping peace in the immortal world." He paused and looked at me, waiting.

I sat quietly for a minute. I'd been introduced to some odd things throughout my life. Especially within the past few months, the strange things just seemed to multiply and get even more unimaginable.

I'd met people who resembled the four elements because apparently they were, in fact, the elements. I'd seen house cats shift into large wild cats and then into people right before my eyes. So sure, this could be believable. Why not? After all, I'd seen so many things that made "normal" jump right out of my head. What was normal anyway? Surely, I no longer knew.

"I believe you, and we'll figure this out." I moved closer to Jayce. "I'm just not quite sure about the savior part. It really doesn't make much sense." A million questions raced through my mind, but were quickly dismissed when I saw Jayce's dark eyes penetrating me.

I longed for him. I couldn't deny him or bear to be away from him for even a second. I'd never experienced anything like this. I needed him in every way possible.

Jayce suddenly grabbed me, using such a force, that in a split instant, my body was pressed up against his. His breath on my neck, and the smell of his cologne sent tingles racing through me. He kissed me slowly and gently at first, but then his kisses grew intense and fierce. We shared the most passionate kiss I'd ever had, and for a few moments we remained lost in our desire.

The kiss was so powerful, I couldn't imagine there would ever be another one able to top it. All our thoughts, dreams, and fantasies were shared. He was in my mind, and I was in his. We experienced all of our burning desire together.

I felt lightheaded, and my lips burned hot. They stung in such a good way. My lips and tongue felt as though I'd eaten a bunch of cinnamon hearts. This sensation was absolutely irresistible.

Together, we sat back down on the rock. I felt so comfortable around Jayce. I never had to hide or act like someone I wasn't. The best part? I was positive he felt the same way about me.

He took this opportunity to explain more about the existence of the different immortals. He shared stories about the elements and shapeshifters. Soon he was describing beautiful fairies, glorious mermaids, fierce werewolves, and the dreadful doomahorns.

"Doomahorns?"

"You've probably never heard of them."

"Never. What exactly is a doomahorn?"

"A rare breed of nightwalker. I'm honestly not sure what or who created them. I just know to steer clear. Promise you'll do the same."

"How will I know if I see one?"

"Take my word, they're pretty unmistakable."

I hoped to never cross paths with one. 'Nightwalker' was one word that made me want to stay away. I listened while Jayce continued to fill me in on the details of various immortals.

"Nightwalkers use scouts, which are the doomahorns. I'm guessing you might want to know what they look like so you know what to stay away from." He shot me his quirky smile.

"Sure, might help."

"They're dark horse-like creatures with two devilish horns on their head. They have a large deformed bulge on their back, and big, jagged fangs. Their unmistakable trait is ferocious blood-red eyes. Trust me, you can't miss them. Doomahorns are used to track prey. Then, the werewolves get the dirty work out of the way, and the vampires come in for the final kill. They've mastered the ultimate ambush."

Wow! This was so much to process, and everything sounded direct from a movie script. Overwhelmed, I sat down and shook my head multiple times. For a few minutes, I didn't move or speak as I tried to comprehend everything. Whenever I went to speak, I couldn't find my words, so I stayed quiet. I never could've imagined anything like this. Not even in my wildest dreams, and my imagination was pretty vivid. Then I remembered back to the night my family died and how the police said no one had seen anything like it before. A flood of emotion came over me. I began crying hysterically, tears streaming down my face.

Jayce had been giving me some space while I took this all in. However, he couldn't help but take notice of my meltdown. "Shanntal, please talk to me."

"You ... s ... s ... said," I choked out the words in between my hysterical sobs. "You said vampires are real?"

Jayce focused on trying to comfort me. He rubbed my back and hugged me tightly. Unfortunately, his reaction made me sob even harder. I sensed his growing frustration on top of this pain. I had to get my tears out of the way in order to speak again. I just didn't know how long it would take. I'd held myself together for so long. Eight months had passed since my family was killed, and a couple months since I'd shed any tears. Only now it felt like this horror was happening all over again.

Eventually, I calmed down. I took a couple of deep breaths and looked at Jayce, while wiping away tears from my swollen eyes. "So, there's a vampire named Daray, do you know him?" I asked in a shaky voice. "Is he real?"

Jayce took a long, cautious pause before speaking. He eyed me up and down and carefully started. "Yes, I know him. Daray is one of the most powerful vampires of all time. I believe it's because of him the vampires and werewolves have joined alliances. I personally consider him a real danger to everyone, mortal or immortal."

Again, the hysterics took control. I couldn't make myself stop, even when I tried. The tears kept on flowing, but in order to explain more to Jayce, I thought long and hard about the night at Ginata's house when we had used the Ouija board. I revisited the night before our families were killed to show how Daray contacted us.

"I'm very sorry, Shanntal." He squeezed me harder, and I knew he'd seen what I needed him to. I knew it would help him figure out who or what killed my family, if he didn't already know.

Well, at least I had a real idea of how my family died. I'd never received a straight answer from the police on what really happened. Only that they'd never seen anything like it before. Now I finally understood what was meant. They'd never seen this type of scene because vampires, werewolves, and doomahorns had killed them. These creatures weren't supposed to be real; they were supposed to be make-believe.

This was a lot to absorb. I'd just found out the significance of my new boyfriend, who also happened to be immortal. No big deal! Not to mention, there was a war about to break out in the immortal world, which somehow involved me. For some unknown reason, I felt I could handle those parts. The part I was having the hardest time with was realizing vampires and werewolves were what killed my family. Finally knowing how they died made it feel as though I'd gotten the air knocked right out of my chest.

Once I pulled myself back together, enough to make the tears stop, I began asking Jayce questions. "What do bad nightwalkers eat besides humans? How do immortals die, or can they be destroyed? How do I defend myself should one attack? More importantly, what do I have to do with any of this?"

Jayce began honestly answering my questions. "It's very difficult to destroy an immortal. You basically need to be one in order to do so. Please, don't get me wrong. Humans have managed to overcome immortals for centuries, but with far more difficulty simply because they don't have the same strength."

I shot him a helpless look. I was human, after all.

Stars

~ Chapter Nine ~

Jayce ignored my discouragement and continued answering my questions for the most part. There were a few he overlooked, but he did provide me with tons of information about the immortal world.

"Some immortals are born, while others are made. The ones born begin as babies and grow until they hit their destined maturity. They stay that age forever. The ones made from the bites of vampires and werewolves remain the age they were when they were bitten. Vampires and werewolves are the only immortals capable of changing a person's mortality."

I shivered, but had to ask. "Why didn't my family change into nightwalkers? Why did they just die?"

"I'm not sure," Jayce said.

"Oh," I replied solemnly.

I saw sympathy in his eyes.

Jayce continued. "The greatest honor for any immortal is to go to the heavens. This doesn't mean we die; instead, we shoot up into the stars to be joined together with our true love or soul mate for all time."

"That's beautiful," I said.

"You know when you see a shooting star? Pay particular attention next time to see if it's rising or falling. Falling stars mean an immortal has just been born or created. You can tell by the night sky, this happens all the time." Jayce pointed up at the sky. "Rising stars, well, let's just say you'll witness quite a spectacular sight."

I followed his gaze, wondering what he was looking for.. I saw the sky beginning to change the same as it did every night when the sun went down.

"Created immortals only turn because of a nightwalker bite, and afterward they must assume their role within the pack or coven where their master resides. It's a dark life they must live out, a cursed life. Born immortals have a cycle somewhat similar to a human. In the beginning, they age the same, but the difference is they can only mature to the age they're destined to be. Some stop aging when they are sixteen, while others don't stop until they are in their forties. It's all kinda pre-planned. I guess you could say it's part of the deal they have to make for this creation. They won't get sick or suffer any other negative aspects of human life. The best part of being immortal is what I mentioned to you before. Once an immortal finds their soul mate, they get sent up to the heavens together. This rings true for both daywalkers and nightwalkers. When the timing and circumstances are right, they become one entity for all time."

He sounded excited, sharing secrets of the immortal world, and I couldn't help but change my mood. I was thoroughly intrigued by Jayce.

Again, he pointed up at the sky. "Have you ever wondered why the stars are different colors?"

I had to think about his question. I'd never really paid much attention. I shrugged, unable to answer. I'd never even realized there were different colors.

"Some stars shine yellow, while others sparkle light purple, baby blue, and even orange. There's only one that burns white, and it's also the largest. A special privilege was bestowed upon them to be the first and last star in the sky each night."

I looked up, searching for stars. None were out yet because the sky was still too light. I looked back at Jayce, hoping he would tell me more.

"The oldest immortal is named Sitara," he said, initiating her story. "She's the first known immortal, and she lived on earth for five thousand years before finding her soul mate. Sitara crossed the world numerous times in hopes of finding what she longed for—her other half. The search became an obsession, which took a piece of her heart. For many, many years she couldn't love entirely because of it. However, she did end up meeting another immortal who managed to hold all the pieces of her heart. That's how she's up there with him today."

As the sun disappeared below the horizon, the sky quickly darkened. We looked up in time to see Sitara and her true love making their nightly appearance.

"Wow, that's kind of heartbreaking. I can't believe she had to wait so long to find her true love."

They twinkled brightly at me. Almost like they'd heard what I said.

"Don't feel sad," Jayce assured me. "They're happier than humanly possible. That's why they all shine so bright. Going up to the stars is the greatest gift an immortal can receive."

Jayce placed his arms around me. We snuggled up watching more of the different colored stars emerge. The happy couples twinkled brightly when they made their appearances one by one. In no time at all, the sky was full.

Jayce explained what the different colors meant. "Sitara is the only white star. She received this honor because she was the first immortal to live among the humans for so long. The immortals that get sent up to the stars typically find their soul mates much faster. Do you see those blue stars bunched together over there?"

I nodded.

"Their color means those immortals remained on earth for around four centuries. Yellow, orange, and purple also stand for the number of years they were here. The colors are a kind of ranking system. Does this make sense?"

"Yes, I understand."

I felt so comforted by Jayce's presence and realized why he seemed somewhat familiar to me. With every passing minute, I believed more and more that I'd found my true love.

Then, my purpose became clear. Jayce had told me about the immortal fight because I was a survivor. They thought I would be their savior, and although I wasn't quite sure why, I decided I wouldn't let any of them down. I'd choose the good side over evil any day. Evil had killed my family, so there was no way on earth I would ever help them win a fight.

We walked along the beach heading toward the car when something caught my eye. I saw it flicker. I looked, but the light had gone out. Suddenly, the flash appeared again, this time glowing in the tall grass. "Jayce, look." I pointed.

"That's a fairy house. Their mushroom houses glow blue whenever the moon is high."

We went over to the light, and I knelt down to examine it a bit closer. Sure enough, a patch of glowing mushrooms sat hidden in the tall grass. A beautiful blue glow glistened off their tops and along their stems. I stood up to find myself surrounded by colors I hadn't seen moments ago. A peach-colored flash caught my eye, flying quickly at us. I flinched when musical wings buzzed by my head. The glow stopped moving, and I saw the figure of a tiny female. She was absolutely beautiful. Her long curled hair flowed freely with her fancy white dress. Her shiny wings opened and closed, keeping a perfect rhythm. She left a trail of sparks behind as she whipped away, her laughter caught on the wind.

"That was a fairy, right?" I asked. "Who is she?"

"Yes, her name is Shea."

"I never knew someone so tiny could be so beautiful."

In a quick wisp, she was in my face again. "I'm Shea, Queen of the Fairies. You're welcome on our land whenever you wish."

"Thank you," I said, bowing.

She winked at Jayce before saying, "We've heard all about you from the elements, and well, actually more from Jayce. Seems someone can't stop talking about this wonderful girl who came into his life."

Jayce blushed, and I felt my own cheeks heat.

"Friends of theirs are automatically considered friends of ours. We're glad to have you as our friend, Shanntal."

"Thank you, your majesty." I bowed another time to the tiny queen.

She let out a sweet giggle. "I said we were friends, friends call me Shea. Please, there's no need to bow. I'm simply a girl, just like you."

"Shea," I repeated, slightly embarrassed.

Apparently, I happened to be the court jester of the immortal world. Every one of them had laughed at me during our introduction. In any event, I was delighted to be such a success with them and felt honored they'd accepted my presence.

A flood of new glows filled the air around us. Hundreds of fairies flew everywhere, leaving trails of sparks. They were so beautiful, each one different. Some of the females had long straight locks, or short spiky hair, while others had masses of curls. Males flew past in all different shapes and sizes. I even noticed some cute children laughing as they played.

The sound of their wings fluttering was breathtaking, and it combined perfectly with the waves splashing gently behind us. The sounds reminded me of an orchestra playing music. Jayce must have felt it too because he grabbed my hand and pulled me in close. There were so many sparks between us—our fireworks, combined with the fairies' tender music, made tonight perfect.

Jayce kissed my lips, and I melted from the sensation of the sweet sting taking place. I found myself wondering if this would happen every time our lips met. Was it because of the electricity flowing through us that our kisses lingered, or because this still felt so new to us?

We hung out on the beach for a bit longer, enjoying the company of my new miniature friends. I stood off to the side as a group of girls surrounded me. At first I felt intimidated by the number of small beings gathered around. However, I was quickly put at ease as I found myself wrapped up in tales of their history and things they'd foreseen in the future. They explained everything to me, right down to how they lived, their rules and laws, and even the foods they ate. We were virtually the same, only they were miniature with wings. And yes, chocolate was a weakness for them too.

Jayce interacted with some of the male fairies. I smiled, thinking about how much he resembled a giant. He smiled back at me, thinking the same thing.

Shea fluttered close by, but the others spread out to join Jayce's group. Shea asked me to stay behind so she could explain to me in greater detail about their hidden homes.

"I want to tell you more about the glowing houses we live in. I'm sure they resemble the ones humans live in ... well, on the inside, anyway. I'm going to let you in on something very few know about, with the exception of us fairies, of course." Shea winked. "The number of caps tells you the size of the family residing there. Each cap represents a bedroom. All houses have a master room which humans call a basement. The master room is underground so you aren't able to see it, but this room is used for the entire family to gather. Families always eat together because it gives them an opportunity to check in and see how everyone's doing."

"That's amazing, Shea. I'm so grateful you shared this with me. It's all beyond my wildest dreams." I smiled at my tiny friend.

"Let's go join the others now." She flew away, leaving a trail of sparks.

I followed her over to Jayce and slipped my arms around his waist.

As the night went on, the fairies told us more stories from their various adventures. The scene reminded me of sitting around a campfire, only the fairies' glow was our flame.

Jayce whispered in my ear, "Once you believe in fairies, you can always see them and their homes. If you don't believe, they will remain invisible. Invisibility is good protection from those who aren't accustomed to the land of the fairies."

I nodded, and he leaned in and planted another kiss directly on my lips. This felt like a fairy tale to me. I was accompanied by amazing companionship and surrounded by the most beautiful scenery. Nothing could ruin this wonderful evening. Absolutely nothing!

Visions

~ Chapter Ten ~

A sliver of the moon peeked out from behind thinly scattered clouds. It was as if someone had hand-painted the clouds just so the moon could make this brilliant appearance.

We stood side by side, basking under its beauty, but a gust of wind carried a howl in our direction. The mere sound sent a shiver through me. "What was that?"

Fear marked Jayce's expression. I'd never seen him like this, so my anxiety level increased. He grabbed my hands and locked them in a secure grip. Flashes from different visions raced through my mind. I closed my eyes, trying to focus on what he was about to show me.

Wolves entered the vision. Only these wolves didn't look like any normal ones I'd ever seen. They were much larger and their coats far more ragged. The harder I concentrated, the clearer the vision became. Their evil gray eyes were piercing, with no sign of a soul in sight. Razor sharp, jagged teeth lined their blood-stained mouths.

My dream started coming back, but Jayce squeezed my hands tighter and pushed more of the vision on me, commanding all my attention.

Dark figures strolled in a V-formation just behind the pack of bloodthirsty werewolves. The shadowy figures all wore similar long, dark attire, and shared the same distinct movement, practically floating. Their clothing and garments flew out behind their bodies, resembling wings.

Knowing these were real vampires absolutely terrified me. I couldn't believe what I was witnessing. It seemed surreal. I had my own personal spy-cam into the immortal world. I carefully pieced together the visions, but one part remained unclear. Why was Jayce showing me this?

Then one specific face emerged from the crowd. I knew instantly that he was Daray, even before Jayce pointed him out. My heart began to beat in the same strange rhythm from my dreams, while the blood pumping throughout my veins felt ice cold. This sensation felt like the fear I'd experienced in my dreams. I needed to run, but at the same time, I felt drawn to him.

I never filled Jayce in on the fact that I'd recognized Daray, or my reaction when I first saw him. I tried my best to ignore the situation, but Jayce picked up on everything despite my attempts. He just carried on through the vision.

Daray stood out from the others. He radiated strength and stamina. His deep, commanding eyes and pulled back dark hair made his dangerous façade both seductive and appealing. His skin was pale but absolutely flawless. His clothes were fashionably put together, even though the style appeared to be from a much earlier era.

Daray led the group. This was clear by the way the werewolves walked in front, like nothing more than dogs on a leash. It was also obvious because of the way the others followed his lead. Four other vampires were equally spaced apart, making up the rear of the group. They all had the same dangerous, yet luring features. Then I saw a lone female who stood out in the crowd. I focused all my attention on her. Jayce tried to redirect me, but I needed to know more about her. Who was she?

She looked different. Her wild features weren't nearly as alluring, nor did she glide gracefully along with the others. She came across unstable, even somewhat awkward compared to the rest of the group. She didn't walk up front near the werewolves nor walk beside the vampires. She was just there, mixed among them. After a moment of pondering the reason she acted so differently, Jayce filled me in on the fact that she was a half-breed. She was both vampire and werewolf. *'Lakylee.'* Her name came easily.

I felt pity toward her because I'd known a similar feeling once before. She was alone, one of a kind, and I could completely relate. I was the only reminder my family ever existed, left to carry on alone. Sometimes life could be so cruel.

Jayce ignored my empathy spiel and pushed through to the conclusion of his vision. He showed me the group approaching ... then, the vision was gone. I couldn't see anything except blackness. I opened my eyes only to find the beach surrounding us. I watched Jayce crinkle up his face in frustration as he tried to concentrate. Suddenly, his eyes shot open. "I'm pretty sure they're coming here."

Panic rushed because I automatically assumed this meant they were coming for me. The immortal fight was going to start tonight. Which one would kill me to win this battle? I appeared to be the biggest obstacle standing in their way, so it made perfect sense for them to eliminate me.

"They will be here in a matter of minutes. I'm sorry. I never sensed them until now."

I grabbed onto Jayce's sleeve. "Are you kidding? We're out in the middle of nowhere! No place to hide, no shelter." I spotted his car but automatically thought about how easy it would be to break through the glass if they wanted to. Maybe if we drove really fast, we could outrun them? Not likely. "What are we going to do?

This is bad, oh Jayce … this is really bad!" My voice trembled. I scanned everything high and low, but there wasn't anything big enough. There was no place to hide. Fairies scattered in different directions, sparks flew everywhere as they frantically searched, trying to help us find some form of shelter. They were doing their best to keep us safe from what was coming our way.

During all the chaos, another vision flashed into my mind. I tried blinking a bunch of times to make the vision go away. Clearly now wasn't an ideal time to watch. I needed to find somewhere safe. However, the harder I resisted, the more forceful it became, and I had no choice but to be still and watch the message unfold.

I saw a man drop to the ground. I had to concentrate harder in order to see him clearer. His body lay motionless, blood pouring from a wound just out of sight. I knew he didn't have long because of how rapidly the pool of blood grew. I gasped in horror when I finally saw his face. The sight took me by surprise when I realized the man was Jayce, but even worse was when I saw myself on the ground beside him. I didn't appear to be hurt as badly, but I knew I was dying too.

Jayce shook me out of the vision. "You weren't supposed to see that, Shanntal. It's not our destiny. The future can always change. Just takes a single moment or altered action. Please understand, just one different choice is all it takes."

"Is that what's going to happen to us?"

"No, you've got to believe me. What you saw will never happen, *ever*!"

I didn't have time to argue. Jayce grabbed my arm and dragged me down the beach in the direction of the waterfalls and caves. When we reached the far end of the beach, Jayce ducked into the first cave we approached. He immediately popped back out shaking his head, and I knew that meant we both wouldn't fit. We tried another one. Jayce went in first, and I quickly disappeared inside after him. It smelled musky, and I couldn't really see because of the darkness. I waited, blinked a couple of times hoping my eyes would adjust, but it wasn't any use. I fumbled my way around in the darkness. Everything I touched felt cold, wet, or slimy.

Fairies began flying in, and their glows lit up everything allowing us to take in our surroundings. Two tiny waterfalls streamed down the back side of the cave, while markings covered the walls. Some of the markings looked like they were from ancient times, but others were noticeably more recent.

Suddenly, a wave of terror riveted my body. I darted around, unable to ignore the claustrophobic feeling taking over. "We're stuck in a stupid cave! What were we thinking? Why did we come in here? A cave doesn't have a door to close, so now what? We're trapped, sitting in a dead-end while the hunters stalk nearby."

Jayce put his arms around me. "It'll be okay," he whispered.

Large, thunderous booms and thudding crashes sounded near the entrance. My body shook from the rumbling, but I felt frozen to the spot. My legs wouldn't move.

Jayce pulled me back a few feet and yelled, "Terran, now!"

The ground rippled as the earth shook. The powerful earthquake loosened boulders, beginning to seal us in.

"No!" I cried out.

We would be trapped. There was no way to get out. Were we going to die in here?

Jayce was listening to my thoughts. *'They'll get through the boulders. They know we're in here. Terran is trying to buy us a little more time. The fairies need all the strength they can get.'*

I gave him a confused look. Now wasn't the time for riddles.

"You'll see soon enough." This time, Jayce said the words aloud.

I watched fairies swarm the entrance of the cave. Using amazing grace and speed, they maneuvered around the fallen obstacles like none existed. There were so many pouring in, there was barely enough room left for us. I expected their glow to be brighter, but the fairies seemed to have put on their dimmers. Guess they didn't want to blind us.

I didn't think I could feel any more claustrophobic, but that was before there were more of us in the cave. In an attempt to calm myself, I imagined I was sleeping. Safe and sound, at home in my bed, and this was nothing more than another bad dream. I backed my way into a corner and Jayce followed. We'd let the fairies stay toward the front. After all, the vampires weren't going to be sucking their blood.

The thunder of colliding rocks continued outside, and I thought back to my earlier vision. Is this how the end happened? No, it couldn't be. Something didn't feel right. In the vision, we were both wearing different clothes, and the atmosphere hadn't been this cold and wet.

Shadows crept along, covering everything as the fairies began shutting off their glows. We'd soon be left in complete darkness. The earth rumbled a final time, and Terran's earthquake sealed us in.

The fairies gathered tightly along the front of the cave. Minutes passed while we sat motionless in the dark, expecting the hunters to come. Silently and anxiously waiting. It was too much to handle, so I remembered back to a time when the darkness had actually brought me comfort. After a few seconds of deep breathing, the same peacefulness returned, and I found I didn't mind the dark so much. Even though I knew danger lurked close by, it felt more like an escape.

A voice interrupted my zone. I tried releasing myself from the mighty grip of my mind, but had a hard time letting go. Something about this entire situation seemed somewhat familiar, yet at the same time, unexplainably foreign. Before things became too incoherent or I got sucked further into my mind, I made myself pay attention to what Jayce was saying.

'I need you to believe everything's going to turn out okay. Help will come in time. I see it now. Things will be fine, and the fairies will help play a crucial part in keeping us safe until the others arrive.'

I knew it was a bad time to come across as pessimistic, but asked anyway. 'How exactly do you suppose cute, tiny, flying people are going to help defend us against bloodthirsty, life-sized monsters?'

'Have some faith. I promise you, we'll be all right. This is only a precaution because I don't entirely know what they want. All I know is I won't let them have you. I need you too much.'

'Oh … I've got an idea of what they want to do to me.' I imagined every horror scene I'd ever watched that had vampires; not once did it end well.

'Silly girl, they won't be like that. I love you and refuse to ever live without you.'

I sensed his urgency, and even though the situation around us grew more dangerous, I found myself wrapped up in the comfort of his words.

Jayce sat with one arm wrapped around me. Using his free hand, he ran his fingers up and down my leg, then positioned his hand perfectly back in mine. Whenever he touched me, I felt like nothing else in the world mattered, only us being together. I wasn't afraid when I was near him, and knew my life would never be the same without him in it.

Howls echoed off the rocks outside. They sounded closer, probably only moments away. We sat hand in hand, anticipating the upcoming meeting.

Memories of my father, mother, and sisters came to me. I remembered some of the good times we shared. Strangely, these memories acted more like glimpses or predictions. I couldn't recall having any of these conversations before. I listened carefully, surprised to find my family speaking to me in a present tense.

The voices of my younger sisters spoke lovingly, just as they always had. "Shanntal, you've always been the strongest, and that's why you remain. They won't overthrow you. You're simply too special. You'll never be alone, because we are always with you. Standing on either side, through time and distance. We'll always love you."

My parents took turns speaking. My mother went first. "We're so incredibly proud of you," she said sweetly.

My father spoke in an authoritative, yet calming manner. "We've always been impressed at the paths you've chosen in your life. We're proud to call you our daughter. You're very special and will be until the end of time. You're truly one of a kind."

My mother spoke again. "You'll succeed at anything you do, and the world's full of opportunities. You choose your destiny. No one else can do this for you. You're unique, and that can be both very helpful, and at other times, rather distracting. You'll need to find light whenever the darkness invades. Dark may seem appealing, but please be careful. It's deceiving. The light will always be true and show you a better way."

I nodded, acknowledging that I understood everything she said.

My father's wise voice spoke again. "When trouble comes, do not despair. You will prevail. Your protectors will come, but be very aware, as they are appealing to both the light and the dark. They possess great strength. However, they remain loyal to only you. They'll stand beside you no matter what in order to keep you safe. Consider them your family now."

My family left my thoughts, but I felt reassured by the encouragement they'd given. Even in death, our bond still remained strong. It felt like they were sitting alongside me. I thought back to the words my father said about the protectors, and I assumed he was referring to Jayce or the others. Terran had clearly tried to help, as did the fairies, but no matter how hard I tried, I couldn't picture any of them as protectors. Jayce tried his best to help keep me safe; I understood that much.

Thoughts from the conversation with my mother came back into my mind. She'd spoken about light and dark. Light must have meant good and dark referred to the evil coming. I couldn't really dwell on the details of our conversation for too long, considering where I was. Although I'd never forget the feeling of getting a second chance to communicate with my family. I wondered why Jayce didn't have any input. He'd have usually interrupted me by then.

He asked aloud, "What do you mean by that?"

"I was just remembering my family, that's all. Though some of our conversation, well … it seemed to have more of a present tense."

"Present tense?"

There wasn't enough time to explain. A loud, hideous snarl echoed throughout the cave, letting us know they'd arrived.

Daray's group lurked just on the other side of the rocks. Jayce sensed their group had grown since the vision, and confirmed three doomahorns had joined them. We were really outnumbered.

I wished with all my might that help would hurry up and get to us before it was too late.

The Stranger

~ Chapter Eleven ~

Daray's sensuous voice spoke through the rocks. "Shanntal, I've been waiting a long time to see you. Why don't you come out here to greet me properly?"

Jayce stood up, moved his body in front of mine, and pushed me back into the wall. He barked out, "Back off, parasite. You'll never get her."

A captivating laugh rang back. "Keeper, don't you know you can't keep everything?"

I felt invisible while the war of words shot back and forth bitterly between them. They bickered over which one of them would get to keep me, like I was nothing more than a pawn.

"Daray, Jayce, enough already!" They went silent, and I took a deep breath before speaking. "Daray, I refuse to meet you face to face. It's that simple. Leave me alone."

"Oh? I think otherwise."

"Well, you are wrong. First off, I'm fighting mad with you over the deaths of my family. How dare you speak to me and come here to trap me like this?" I shouted.

"I was extremely upset to hear of their passing," Daray replied solemnly.

Suddenly, I felt strange, and for a brief moment found myself intrigued, actually wanting to know him better. Why would he be upset if he killed them? Was I missing something here? I realized my thoughts and shook them away quickly. This time, I made sure my tone came out sharp. "It's best we never meet. Now go away!"

"Alas, you'll meet me soon enough, my sweets. This courtship is your destiny."

His words sent chills. My destiny?

"It hurts me deeply to hear of your loss. Your family always meant a lot to me. I respected them, even though we shared our differences of opinion, especially when the matters involved you." He sounded quite sincere. "Come out here. You will understand."

Why did he say my family always meant a lot to him? How could he have possibly known them? I opened my mouth to retort, but the noise from hooves and howls overpowered me. The rock wall Terran built shook as hooves and claws landed one powerful strike after another. Large boulders shifted at the top, allowing a dim beam of moonlight to creep into the cave.

I couldn't feel Jayce pressing on me, but found him on the opposite side of the cave. I could just barely see him through all the dust.

"Jayce," I called out.

He didn't acknowledge me. Instead, he remained facing forward, watching the rock wall shift and crumble. I looked around, hoping that by some form of miracle, another way out miraculously appeared. The nightwalkers were coming into the cave, and there wasn't any way to stop them.

The doomahorns' hooves bore such strength that with every kick the boulders turned into sheer dust. The cave soon filled with dusty smoke, burning my lungs and eyes. I tried to clear the dust from my eyes, but it wasn't working. Jayce and I started coughing at the same time, finding it hard to breathe. Soon the tiny fairies were coughing too.

"Makan ... help!" Jayce gasped for fresh air.

A dominant wind howled fiercely outside. Makan's airstream powerfully sucked out the dust. I gasped, taking in deep breaths of clean air. My lungs still burned, but I was quite thankful for the fresh air.

When the last bit of dust settled, I saw they'd pretty much cleared the entrance. Only a small wall remained between them and us. I watched shadows of the doomahorns pace back and forth, guarding the entrance, hindering any chance for escape. Another giant kick stirred up more dust, but before the residual cloud settled, they started to make their way in. However, the moment the werewolves and vampires began to advance, Jayce shouted, "Aiden. You're up."

In sync, the fairies, with help from Aiden, beamed a light so incredibly brilliant it nearly blinded us. I covered my eyes and felt the warmth on my skin like pure sunshine. Their performance worked ... instant sunlight.

The nightwalkers hissed and snarled in agony, retreating into the darkness. The tiny fairies had managed to come to our rescue for the time being. They continued to hold their brightness for another ten minutes. Then their glows began to diminish, granting the nightwalkers access to the entrance again.

"Meriel ... your turn," Jayce said, before they got too far inside.

An enormous wave rolled past the entrance, sweeping away the doomahorns and even a few vampires. The werewolves used their giant claws to grip onto the rocks, but a couple of them were swept away by the water. Meriel had helped clear away some of the enemies, only another problem arose. We were knee deep in water, which was rising rapidly. Within a few seconds, the water reached our waists, then our chests. I looked to Jayce for help, but he also splashed around, trying to keep his head above water.

"Meriel, enough," Jayce pleaded.

Instantly, the water levels lowered. Some of the nightwalkers made their way back into the cave, quite angry and sopping wet. A pair of werewolves used the opportunity to push through the mass of fairies, swatting and snarling at the tiny beings.

The werewolves headed in my direction. I was pinned up against the wall with nowhere to go; I glanced around for Jayce, but couldn't see past the wolves' mammoth bodies. They let out rumbling snarls, baring their jagged teeth as drool spilled out of their mouths. The larger of the two reached a paw out to me. I shut my eyes. In the same instant, what resembled a shock of electricity zapped my arm. I screamed at the excruciating pain radiating along my forearm. I looked down, and my head spun from the sight of blood.

Out of nowhere, a pair of hands pulled the beast's enormous head back. The wolf made a loud yelping sound, and I heard a snap come from its powerful jaws. The injured beast retreated out of the cave. A split second later, the other wolf howled in pain and also withdrew.

Two massive figures emerged. I closed my eyes, waiting for them to finish me off. Minutes passed, but I didn't feel any worse, and the pain in my arm started to subside. I carefully opened one eye and saw a large chest beside me. I shut my eyes tightly. A few more minutes went by, and still nothing happened to me. Confused, I opened both eyes and looked first to my left, and then my right side. Two muscular males stood in the same protective pose on either side of me. Things began making a bit more sense. I clued in on the fact these were the guys who'd just fought off the werewolves.

Outside the entrance, dark shadows still lurked. However, the vampires, doomahorns, and remaining werewolves weren't as close. I was quite thankful for the arrival of these massive figures. Because of them, we now had some space between the nightwalkers and us. I wanted to celebrate our small victory, only

Jayce was nowhere to be seen. My eyes searched frantically for him. Where did he go? Was he okay?

A female voice spoke using such a hostile sharpness that it made my hopes disappear. "Shanntal, if you ever want to see your precious Jayce again, call off your protectors and get out here."

Protectors? Was this what my father had been referring to? He'd told me protectors would come soon, and having them by my side would keep me safe. Now I understood the true meaning of his words. Thanks to these two guys arriving at the right moment, I was safe from the werewolves who could've easily polished me off.

I stepped forward, taking an opportunity to fully view both of my protectors. Looking at their faces, I realized they were virtually identical. A few years apart in age perhaps, but still incredibly similar. They must have been brothers.

The older looking one spoke in a strong, enchanting voice. "I am Kaleb, your protector. I'll guard you with my very life. So long as I'm around, you will always be safe." He swiftly returned his focus back toward the entrance.

The younger one took his turn speaking. He had a bit deeper voice, but still sounded quite charming. "I'm Garrison. I too am your protector. You'll be safe with me at your side. Until death, I promise to stand by you." He winked and returned his focus to the front of the cave.

Even though we'd just met, they already seemed like part of the family. I felt a sense of closeness I couldn't quite explain.

The three of us moved carefully through the remaining fairies. Most of them had fled the cave during the invasion in hopes of chasing the vampires away with their glow. The remaining ones stayed their position, flying right beside us as a sweet gesture to let me know they were still trying to help. Towering over me, Garrison and Kaleb walked cautiously on either side until we came to the entrance. I stopped dead in my tracks as I took my first look at the dreaded doomahorn.

Doomahorns were such ugly creatures. They had large, horse-like bodies with a mutated bulge on their back. Two curled, devilish horns sat on top of their beastly heads. Long, ragged fur coats of dark grays and black patches covered their protruding muscles. Gobs of drool poured out between their rows of jagged fangs. But their most frightening feature was their beaming red eyes—blood-burning eyes.

I turned my head away, unable to look any longer. Garrison and Kaleb moved in front of me, assuming a fighting stance with their massive bodies. They positioned themselves as shields so I was no longer in harm's way.

"Call off your beasts, parasite," Garrison ordered.

"Beasts?" Daray taunted. "Careful what you say."

Garrison remained firm, not bothering with another response. He stood his ground, showing no sign of backing down.

"Look, they are just my dark beauties." Daray stroked one of the ugly creatures. "Don't be afraid, Shanntal. They will never harm you."

However, the beast closest to me rubbed and pounded its hooves on the ground, ready to charge. Instinctively, I moved backward trying to get out of the way. In the same moment, the doomahorn took off, approaching us rapidly, but Kaleb intervened. He swiftly jumped up on its back, grabbed ahold of the horns, and steered the bucking beast away from the crowd. A moment later, he returned alone and promptly took his place by my side.

Daray let out a violent hiss.

That's when I spotted Jayce. The half-breed Lakylee held his arms behind his back. She didn't appear to be using too much force, but enough that he couldn't break free. He looked roughed up, but seemed okay despite some minor scratches on his face. A bit of blood from one of his wounds left a stain on his jacket, but

Escaped the Night

it seemed quite strange to me. Jayce stood completely surrounded by vampires and werewolves, but they weren't obsessing over his blood. I immediately jumped to the conclusion it must've been because he was also an immortal.

My conclusion made me less anxious because it seemed Jayce would be all right. Clearly they wanted me, not him. I suppose that was part of the reason I'd been granted the protectors. I glanced around the crowd. The nightwalkers looked like they were starting to get antsy.

I got nervous and blurted, "Daray, why did you come here? What do you want?"

Daray stepped forward from his group of followers. I did too. I gestured to my protectors to stay behind, and they obeyed. Daray and I stood less than a foot apart, and I couldn't help but take notice of him. He was devilishly handsome, and I didn't fear him like I thought I would; instead, found myself somewhat curious. Why did he seem so familiar? Why had he contacted me through the Ouija board? What did he want with me now?

Daray took a noticeable sniff of my arm and let out a low, rumbling growl.

That's when I remembered my arm was bleeding, and I cringed at the thought. He was a vampire, and the aroma of my blood must've been tempting him. I took a step back, but there were blood hungry beasts were all around me.

The look upon my face obviously said it all. Daray let out an enchanting chuckle. Then he said, "Shanntal, you're not like anyone else. You are so special." He held his hand out. "We do not wish for your blood. We wish for you to join us."

An intoxicating sensation took over. Unable to stop myself, I stretched out my hand to meet his. He took complete control and pulled me into him, and there wasn't a thing I could do to stop it. He ran his icy fingers down my shoulder, while holding me tightly in his cold embrace. "My sweet Shanntal, remember who you are. You are still my queen." His voice flooded my mind with images.

I saw myself standing beside Daray, but in a different place, in a different time. The vision started off foggy at first, then it began to explain a story. We were in a castle, and together as a couple. I wore a beautiful pink gown, while Daray looked handsomely dressed in black tails. The grand ballroom was full of sweet sounding music and lots of laughter. People in beautiful dresses and handsome tails danced throughout the magnificent room. Daray pulled me off to the side. We stood alone on the balcony, and he took me by the hand. I smiled lovingly at him. Then he got down on one knee.

"My sweet Shanntal. I promise to love you, forever and always. Will you please marry me?"

I pulled him up off his knees, threw my arms around him, and showered him with kisses. "Yes, my love, yes!"

Daray and I left the ballroom to go somewhere a little more private to celebrate our engagement. We took a stroll through the glorious gardens, but a stranger appeared from out of nowhere. At first, he stood somewhat hidden by the rose bushes. We paid him no attention, until he spoke our names. Daray told me to run. I tried to pull him, make him run with me, but the stranger moved so quickly he flew over to us in no time. He ripped Daray from my arms, and I stood helpless, watching in horror as the blood began to spray. The stranger gave me a smile, exposing his mouth full of fangs. Then he went back to what he'd come for and continued sucking the life out of my sweet Daray.

Gathering up my gown, I raced back to the castle. I pushed open the doors and shouted. "Help! Daray is being killed. There's a stranger. He … he … he's sucking out all his blood. Please, he needs us to help him. Please, someone … help him!"

No one came to his rescue. They already knew what had happened to Daray, the outcome evident from the blood splatter all over my dress.

"She's one of those nightwalkers." Someone shouted, "We need to kill her!"

"No, no, I'm not. Please, you must believe me."

The angry crowd forcefully removed me from the castle, dragging me back out to the gardens. I kicked and screamed, trying to break free, but they were too strong. Six men held on tightly as they carried me to the area covered in the blood of my beloved. A man with a long salt and pepper colored beard leaned over me, holding a stake in his hand. He looked me in the eye while I begged and pleaded for my life. I thought if I explained again and he saw what had happened here, it would all make sense. He'd believe me when I said I wasn't a vampire. However, the look on his face was enough for me to know he did not believe a word out of my mouth. He reached his arms up high into the air and came back down with an excruciating force. He stabbed the wooden stake directly through my heart.

My blood began spilling out. I gasped and choked, then took my last living breath.

First Encounter

~ Chapter Twelve ~

My next breaths came a while later, long after the crowds dissipated. I awoke remembering I had died. Yet there I was, still breathing. It was completely remarkable. However, questions stuck in my mind. Why hadn't my corpse been disposed of like they would have with any other vampire? Everyone knew the body of a vampire should always be burned to ensure the undead stayed dead. Someone must have saved me. Was it my sweet Daray? Was he a vampire now? Was I?

Nights passed, and my memories started to fade. Soon I could no longer recall who I was, let alone where I'd been. I wandered alone day after day and night after night until a family took me in, my family. They weren't my birth parents, but treated me like one of their own children. They were an immortal family who felt badly for me because of how I'd been turned. I was alone and with no memory. There wasn't any immortal throughout history ever created like me, and they wanted to help ensure I survived.

I did die that night along with my love, only neither one of us had really died after all. We had just taken different paths. He walked the night, and I walked during the day. He'd searched for me every night for a hundred years, but I didn't remember a thing about him. It wasn't until that night at Ginata's that Daray found me again. I felt overwhelmed by his loyalty, but more so by the fact that I was actually an immortal.

Daray whispered more missing information to me. "Due to the fact you weren't a normally made immortal, born or bitten, you weren't able to retain memories like other immortals. That's the price you had to pay for the ability to live forever, but I can help you remember."

What kind of immortals was my family? Were Uncle Dane and Auntie Steph immortal too? How had they kept this hidden from me for so long? Now I understood why I had trouble remembering pieces of my past. I couldn't remember going to school, family vacations, or even birthday parties. All I could ever put together were more like mere flashes. I only knew the teen life I had lived with my family, and they'd done their best to make sure I lived a normal lifestyle. I was shocked to find out I had a case of immortal amnesia, but my memories were back now, and there wasn't any way I would forget again.

Daray spoke softly, his cool breath upon my skin. "You are different because you're more human than anything else. You stayed alive because of the blood of the newborn vampire, not the bite. When my tainted blood twined with yours, I gave you just enough immortality for everlasting life. My blood ensured your survival. It helped you live throughout time, and has now brought you back where you belong."

I opened my eyes, nearly forgetting we were down on the beach in light of all that had just happened. I felt startled for a brief second, seeing everyone's eyes focused on me. I broke out of the embrace and looked directly at Jayce. He looked betrayed, but my gaze was quickly drawn back to Daray, who remained in front of me. Daray looked at me now just as he had in my memory.

Another realization came to me. They'd never attacked when I stood before them bleeding because of the immortal blood running through my veins. Daray was no enemy of mine. He was my savior, and once upon a long time ago, the love of my life. I moved a step forward, placing my hands on his cold face, taking in every single detail. He looked slightly different than I remembered from his human life. The tiny scar along his lip from when he'd fallen as a child was no longer there. The one along his eyebrow had also vanished. Ironically, he sported two beauty marks in the exact spot where the stranger bit him.

Our reunion had cooled off the confrontation. I felt relieved for that much anyway. Everyone around us was immortal, either good or evil, and it left me feeling torn. A few hours ago, Jayce was my world. Now, everything had changed because of Daray.

I looked back at Jayce, but this time he did not meet my gaze. Instead, he kept his eyes focused on the ground. I tried speaking without words, but our connection no longer linked us together.

I managed to pull myself away from Daray and went back over to stand between Garrison and Kaleb. I felt safe between my protectors.

Layla and the elements were coming down the beach. Lakylee let go of her grip on Jayce and he passed by me without even a look. He headed toward the others and I wanted to go after him. I wanted to follow my friends, but felt uncertain. My body felt heavy, like it had been turned into stone. With my memory back, I wasn't sure where to go, so I stayed still.

Layla shot me a glance, clearly asking why I wasn't coming. Jayce lifted his head and looked her in the eyes. Her face told me she understood. Jayce reconnected us for a brief minute so I could get a hint of what he told her. *'The parasite's right. I'm not the keeper of everything. I couldn't even keep the one who meant the most to me.'*

My heart shattered as he spoke these words to Layla. I felt him leave and feared this would be the last time I'd ever feel connected. I didn't want to hurt Jayce. I honestly loved him, but part of me couldn't hurt Daray either. We were supposed to have been married, a hundred years ago of course, but there was definitely some kind of loyalty and love remaining. He'd never given up searching for me; that was true commitment.

Jayce and my dear friends disappeared down the beach. I called out to Jayce before he was out of sight, but he didn't bother to even turn around. I'd waited too long to stop him. I felt a lump rise in my throat, and wondered if or when I'd ever see any of them again. I knew what I had to do. For now, I needed to stay neutral, just until I figured out exactly where I belonged. I felt safe around Daray, but not the company he kept. I felt secure near Jayce and my friends. However, I couldn't fight the feeling that I owed Daray some form of recognition. After all, it was because of him I was still alive.

I approached Daray and embraced his cold hands. I paused for a minute; his icy hands didn't fit quite right with mine. I really enjoyed Jayce's warmth and how perfectly our hands fit together. It was a minor detail, but seemed important in my eyes. Jayce fit.

"Daray, it's almost dawn. You should head back to your dwellings before daylight arrives. I want to let you know that I won't be coming with you right now either."

"Pardon?" he said, clearly agitated.

"Please don't be upset. I'm feeling torn, and honestly, I'm not sure what I should do. I need some time to think things through."

"I understand, my sweets. Please know I've never, ever stopped loving you. I've searched for you every night for a hundred years. I'll never lose track of you again. You are my love." He kissed me fervently.

As his cool lips breezed swiftly on mine and moved downward on my neck, I fell back under his undeniable trance. It wasn't long before Garrison intervened, grabbed my arm, and placed me safely beside Kaleb.

Daray hissed at my protectors in protest. Nevertheless, he knew daybreak was coming soon, and I wasn't joining them, so he and his followers headed down the beach away from us.

I remained along the shoreline, stuck between Garrison and Kaleb, watching as the sun made its way over the horizon. The sky and clouds turned marvelous shades of pinks, purples, and oranges as the new day began.

A brand new day, and I was stuck down at the beach. How would I get back home? I'd come with Jayce, and no one else drove cars. I was immortal, but being mostly human, it would take me hours to walk home. I let out a disappointed sigh.

Just then, a voice I knew very well asked, "May I offer you a ride?"

I turned around, and my heart fluttered when I saw Jayce alone on the beach.

"I knew you wouldn't be able to get home easily if you stayed among us daywalkers. I mean ... I have to admit, I'm very happy you didn't go with Daray and the others." He mustered up a smile.

I felt so ashamed about how I'd changed right in front of Jayce. It wasn't fair to him, and I felt incredibly guilty. We walked silently toward his car. I waited for Garrison or Kaleb to get in first, hoping one of them would claim shotgun so I could hide out in the back until I got home.

Garrison spoke to me reassuringly. "You're no longer in any danger, so we won't be coming now. If you need us, we will be there. We're always around for you, Shanntal. Whenever danger's close, we will stay by your side. You can count on that."

I gave my protectors each a hug. "Thank you, for everything," I said, getting into the car. I took a long, deep breath while Jayce got in and started up the engine. This had started out as a perfect day, but ended up the complete opposite. I never meant to hurt him, but seeing how I had tore me up inside.

We shared an awkward ride home. Jayce didn't hold my hand like usual, nor did he read my thoughts. He just happened to be there, driving me home, like there was nothing ever between us. I leaned my head against the window, and tears filled my eyes. I didn't want him to know I was crying because I had no right to. It was my fault he felt hurt now. A tiny sob slipped out, but he took me by surprise and grabbed my hand.

He pulled over. "This isn't your fault, Shanntal. At least we're aware of what Daray wants. But it leaves you with a big decision to make. I promise you won't receive any pressure from me. You know my heart belongs to you, and it's yours whenever you want. On one condition though, you have to take the whole thing, in exchange for yours."

I wiped my teary eyes. "I'm so sorry, Jayce. I never wanted any of this. I never knew I was immortal, let alone the fact Daray and I were once engaged." I squeezed his hand tightly. "I didn't think anything could come between us."

"Me neither."

We drove the rest of the way home in silence. He continued to hold my hand, but it wasn't the same as before. We pulled up in front of my house, and I looked over at Jayce. "I'm truly sorry … I'm not sure what I am supposed to do." I went to get out, but had to say one more thing before I lost the chance. "Please know I care for you deeply, and this is hurting me too."

He enticed me back over and left a warm kiss upon my cheek. I wrapped my arms tightly around his neck and hugged him as hard as I could. When I pulled away, he moved forward, taking me by surprise by placing a sizzling hot kiss directly on my lips. I couldn't help but react, and kissed him back. Something about kissing him felt so right.

"I'll be here when you want me, Shanntal. Just let me know whenever you're ready."

I nodded and got out of the car. I closed the door but stood on the curb as I watched him drive away, taking a piece of my heart along for the ride. I felt a void, an unbearable pain that made me stumble. After he was completely out of sight, I slowly walked up to the house. I stood outside the front door for a moment, trying to fix whatever makeup was left around my eyes. If any remained, it would've been smeared halfway down my face, and I didn't want Auntie Steph and Uncle Dane to worry.

I went through the front door and found them sitting in the kitchen having their morning coffee and breakfast. Today seemed to be just another typical day for them, and I found myself envious. Why weren't my days ever typical?

"Is it good morning or good night?" Uncle Dane said, anger present in his voice. "We have been worried sick. You never answered your phone, never called. Why would you do that knowing how much we worry about you?"

"It's been a really long night." I shrugged, unsure of what else to say.

When he realized how filthy I was, his harshness vanished. "Shanntal, is everything okay? Where have you been?"

Auntie Steph gave me the once over. "Shanntal, did something happen?"

"I'm all right. We were at the beach all day, hiding in caves. Guess that's why I'm dirty. I also ran into an old boyfriend, which caused some friction with Jayce, that's all." I tried downplaying the ordeal.

"Old boyfriend?" Uncle Dane gave me a doubtful look. "Here?"

Auntie Steph placed her hands on her hips, sharing a disapproving look.

"Yeah, I haven't seen him in years," I said.

"How did he find you at the beach?" she interrogated.

"We simply ran into each other."

"Do I know him?" asked Uncle Dane.

"I doubt it."

"Try me." He wouldn't let it go.

"Everything happened a long time ago. There's nothing to tell. His name's Daray, and honestly, I'd forgotten all about him."

Auntie Steph made a weird face, and Uncle Dane began fidgeting strangely. "Go get some sleep, kiddo, we'll talk later." He turned to Auntie Steph, making a face I shouldn't have seen.

I was too tired and stressed to argue or pry. I knew he wasn't behaving in his normal manner, and I wanted to know why, and if they were immortal too, but instead I gave them each a kiss on the cheek. "Good night, good day … whatever. I'll see you guys in a while."

I walked into my room and closed the door behind me. I flopped down on the bed. I didn't bother pulling back the covers or even changing my clothes. I was too exhausted and passed out right where I lay down.

Another Chance

~ Chapter Thirteen ~

I awoke from my slumber to realize I hadn't taken the short nap originally planned. My room was quite dark. I pulled back the curtains and saw the sun had already begun to set; I'd slept the entire day away. My long hair felt like a giant mess of tangles. I tugged on a strand of hair supposed to be highlighted blonde, only to find it more of a gray tinge. Even my clothes were covered in lingering dust and dirt, a constant reminder of the previous day's adventures/disaster. Of all the things I'd ever forgotten, why couldn't yesterday be one of them? I had just found happiness and was finally coming to terms with my new life. I'd accepted everything that had happened, no matter how unfair. Why did this new inner peace come with such a hefty price to pay?

Jayce had opened up and willingly shared everything about his world. Is this the reason why he told me? Had he known the entire time that I was an immortal?

Bits and pieces from my history with Daray resurfaced. I paid attention for a brief while, but everything I saw happened so long ago. Nothing was like that anymore. I didn't have my family alive, nor did I really know Daray. Soon, the memories wore on my patience; I wanted to live in the moment, not the past.

I cleared the thoughts from my head, got out of bed, and headed straight for the shower. Stripping out of my filthy clothes, I kicked them in the corner. A small dust cloud rose up and settled back down on the pile of fabric. I shook my head in disgust as I stood in front of the mirror, taking a good long look at my face. Smears of dirt covered my cheeks, and eye makeup ran halfway down my face. Now I fully understood why Uncle Dane seemed so worried. I was a sad sight that matched an equally horrible day.

I'd chat with him later to let him know everything was okay, and try to explain what had happened. Then I thought about how I could tell him. What could I do? Blurt out, 'Hey, guess what Uncle Dane. I'm an immortal.' He probably wouldn't believe me, even though I was telling the truth. He'd figure I was having some sort of breakdown and would undoubtedly try to lock me up in the loony bin. Perhaps this would be better left unmentioned.

I turned on the shower. Warm water flowed while steam leaked out from behind the curtain. I climbed in, but the water stung my arm. I looked at the wound; it wasn't nearly as bad as I'd thought. The wolf had basically scratched me, and my arm seemed to be healing quickly. A perk of being immortal, I assumed. While enjoying the rejuvenating warmth, I found myself wishing I could wash away my sorrows with all the filthy dirt. I got so wrapped up in my thoughts that I didn't bother washing my hair until the hot water ran out.

Jayce and I were never going to be the same. I felt ashamed and couldn't get over how badly I'd treated him. It wasn't right. I cared so deeply about him. I'd fallen head over heels, and he meant everything to me, so how could I do this? I pushed the thoughts from my head because imagining his pain hurt too much. Why did Daray have such control over me? How could he make me turn away from the people I loved and cared about? Why couldn't I resist his magnetism? I let out a sigh, forcing myself to face the facts. Daray was in the picture now, and like it or not, he wasn't going anywhere.

Frustrated, I sunk into a ball on the bathroom floor and wondered how to choose between the two of them. Why had Daray come back into my life after all this time? What did he really want from me? Was it possible he loved me that much? Could this be some kind of trick to start the immortal war? No, no, he wouldn't do that to me ... or would he?

My thoughts drifted over to Jayce, who'd just entered my life. Why couldn't we have met sooner? Did he love me as much as I loved him? Would he love me for the long haul?

I fought with myself over both of them. But, for some unexplainable reason, something inside made me feel obligated to give Daray another chance. I supposed it all boiled down to the history we'd once shared, or maybe because he had been the one who saved me from dying. He would get another chance because of this. I just had to get past all the differences in how he behaved back then versus now. His entire being had changed, and not just the subtle differences on his face. He'd become almost sinister. I also didn't really care for the intoxicating feeling that happened every time he came around; it felt like a spell. I'd have to find a way of keeping better control over myself. I imagined the possibilities of what life together could be like. I remembered a gentle, caring, thoughtful, and considerate man. In reality, he didn't show any of those qualities on the surface. Instead, Daray seemed dangerous, perhaps even wicked. Still, I hoped to be strong enough to bring back the gentle man I once knew.

To be fair to everyone, I knew what had to be done. Leading them both on wouldn't be fair, so I needed to make a choice, and soon. Jayce was all the things I wanted, but Daray held the key to my past, which made me feel a sense of closeness to him. However, people change, especially when a hundred years had gone by. If we were to have any sort of a future and move beyond this current mess, I needed to know the person Daray was now. My mind was settled. I'd give Daray another chance and somehow make all this up to Jayce. There wasn't any reason why we couldn't remain friends, right? Clearly my selfish motives were in charge, but I needed Jayce in my life. He understood me like nobody else, and I wouldn't give that up.

I picked myself up off the floor and shook off the remaining insecurity and self-pity. I got dressed in a black tank top and black jeans. I ran a brush through my hair and applied some eyeliner and mascara. I didn't bother wearing too much makeup, because this time the boys were going to have to impress me, not the other way around.

A knock sounded at the front door. I hadn't been expecting anyone. Actually, the only one who'd come to get me lately was Jayce, and I knew all too well that wouldn't be happening today. I waited for someone to answer, but there was another knock. I walked into the common room to find myself home alone, so I opened the door.

"Hey, you guys," I said, happily surprised. I moved out of the way, letting my giant protectors and gorgeous purple-eyed friend in. Garrison and Kaleb did a walk-through around the entire house, checking top to bottom, making sure everything was safe. Layla and I ignored them while we said our hellos.

"Layla, I can't believe you're actually here," I said, hugging her. "It feels like we haven't seen each other in forever." We'd grown close, spending every day of the last few months together. When I hadn't seen her in forty-eight hours, time felt more like weeks rather than days. "Where's Terran and Meriel?"

"They couldn't come ... you know how it is." She sounded distant.

"Is everything okay?"

"Jayce explained everything. He wanted me to let you know he'll be staying away for a while in order to make things easier.

Jayce loves you, but he wants you to be true to yourself. He also mentioned that you and Daray were once engaged?" She shook her head in disbelief.

The message came across direct and to the point. Jayce wouldn't be coming around any time soon. I'd figured that much out long before she'd finished her statement. Layla was the messenger. It was also the reason she'd come, not for me, but for him.

"Yeah, weird or what? Who would've thought?" I snorted. "I don't think even Jayce saw that twist coming."

I tried making light of the situation, but this whole thing was extremely difficult for me too. I already missed Jayce. I'd never meant to do this to him and wanted to take his pain back more than anything. If I had some kind of superpower that could've changed the outcome of all this, I would've used it a long time ago.

"Super weird," Layla said, sounding friendlier. "So, what else has been going on?"

We went into the living room and sat side by side on the couch so we could catch up. She was my friend, after all, and I couldn't be mad at her for being the messenger. I found it easier to hear the news from her because I knew she cared about us both.

Garrison came out of the kitchen with a big smile, but suddenly his eyes shifted toward the front door, and the smile faded. "Lover boy's pretty much here."

I was confused. Last night, or this morning, my protectors had left me alone with Jayce. They didn't sense any danger when we were together, meaning I was truly safe around Jayce. I'd always felt that way, so this must've meant Daray was coming. Everything progressively became more complicated by the minute. I wanted, no, *needed* a simpler time, one that didn't make me feel at odds with myself.

I looked at Layla, who now sported a serious expression. "I'll be staying with you through the duration of this. I'll assist any way I can, even if it's just to talk or listen. I'm here for you ... I can't imagine how difficult this must be."

"Thanks, Layla. I'm glad to know you're a true friend to us both. I appreciate—" I stopped talking when Garrison and Kaleb assumed their fighting stance in the front hallway. I couldn't remember what I'd been saying; my heart pounded so hard I thought it might beat right out of my chest. I didn't want a repeat of our last run-in. A wave of fear consumed me.

The doorknob rotated slowly, letting out a small squeaking sound. All eyes remained focused on the door. The door began to open, and two familiar voices spoke—Auntie Steph and Uncle Dane were home.

I let out a sigh of relief. Kaleb and Garrison raced back to join Layla and me on the couch. My friends created a diversion by chatting about random things and giggling. I smiled, even though it brought up more questions. Why didn't they want to alarm anyone that danger lurked nearby? Wouldn't it better to know so we could have a chance to defend ourselves? Who was going to attack? Doomahorns? Werewolves? Other vampires? No, that stuff wouldn't happen again. Daray had told me they didn't want to hurt me. This was all too confusing. I took a deep breath, let it out slowly, and felt my anxiety ease. I looked down and saw my trembling hands had steadied.

Uncle Dane came over to greet our group nestled in the living room. Auntie Steph gave a warm smile before going into the kitchen, her arms loaded full of groceries.

"Layla, always a pleasure, my dear," Uncle Dane gave her a wink.

"Danier," she acknowledged.

"Garrison and Kaleb. Been a long time. Good to see you boys," Uncle Dane patted them on their bulky shoulders. "Shanntal, I'm glad to see you're keeping such good company these days." He looked me square in the eyes.

I was dumbfounded, completely confused. How did he know everyone?

"A word?" He gestured toward my room.

With no hesitation, I got up off the couch and followed him. We stood alone in my bedroom. Uncle Dane closed the door slightly, not all the way, but enough to allow some privacy.

"Am I missing something?" I asked.

"Everything's starting to come back, isn't it? I see you remember who you are now."

"Who I am? Don't you mean what I am?" I shot back. "You knew about this? Why didn't you tell me?" I said, my voice growing louder. "After everything that's happened to me in the last twenty-four hours, let alone the past year, how could you keep this from me?"

"The last twenty-four hours? What happened?" he shouted back.

"Oh, never mind, you wouldn't understand."

"Please, calm down. I understand far more than you think. We were only trying to protect you."

"Protect me? From what?" He sounded just like my father always had.

"From him. We didn't want Daray to finish what he started. He accidently created you. It's a fluke you're still alive. He may fluff the story up and act like he saved you, but that isn't the case. You were dead. Something unexpected happened, and *that's* what saved you. Nothing he did. You must understand he isn't the same man you once knew. He isn't human. He's nothing but dark and evil. No good can or will ever come from him." Uncle Dane walked to my dresser and tugged on a latch, which opened a secret panel. He reached in and pulled out a long scroll of paper. He placed the scroll in my hand. "This lists all the lives Daray's taken this past century. Our family took great care in hiding you from him. Garrison and Kaleb have come and gone from our lives over the years. Whenever Daray was close enough to find you, they'd come. When he lost track and you were safe, they'd leave."

I stood, my world spinning too quickly for me. I wanted nothing more than for everything to slow down. I fought back the urge to break down. I was strong and couldn't afford to fall to pieces like the last time I received bad news.

I threw down the scroll. I didn't want to look at this. I wanted no part. Enough was enough. "All the lives he took? What about the life taken from him, or from me, for that matter? Let's get one thing straight. Daray is the reason I'm still here. You should take a minute to remember that. His death is why I got to live. Accidental or not, in my books, he saved me!" I shouted, waving my arms like a total lunatic. Tears spilled down my face. I could no longer fight them back.

I felt hurt and betrayed. My whole life was nothing like I believed it to be. It was a life full of lies and deceit. Daray was the only one who hadn't hidden the truth from me. He wanted me to remember and helped me do so. I wiped my eyes, yanked the door open, and then stormed out of the room. I heard a thud when the door bounced against the wall. Pretty sure I'd just made a dent, but, too late, I couldn't take back what I had already done.

I headed hastily toward the front door and rushed so no one could talk me out of leaving, but Uncle Dane trailed right behind me. "Shanntal, we did what we thought was best. I'm sorry. Please … stop, don't go."

I ignored him and acted like I was alone because that's how I felt. I ignored everyone's pleas and concentrated on tying my shoes. I left the house without so much as a word and darted down the dark street, slipping on my jacket while I ran. I heard my steps hitting the ground and soon noticed they weren't alone. I glanced back to see who it was and saw Garrison and Kaleb.

I felt too angry to appreciate their loyalty, so I turned and yelled at the top of my lungs, "Just go away. Leave me alone! I don't need you."

I ran full speed, hoping to put some distance between us. The night air felt cold, but it didn't stop me. I was burning hot from the rage consuming me. My past either never existed in the first place or had been totally forgotten. I decided I needed to go find Daray. I knew he had to be close because Kaleb and Garrison had said he was near.

"Daray, come get me, take me away from this. I want to be like we were before." Tears streamed full force down my cheeks. "I want things to be the way they once were. I want to go back."

I needed security and remembered how life felt before that awful night. Up until the moment Daray died, I'd never been so happy. The memory of that life seemed close to perfect. Sure, time changed things, and I had to accept Daray was different from my memories, but he was still the man I used to love. He'd been everything to me. More memories of our time together flowed, making my urge to see him even stronger. I pushed myself and found the strength to run even faster.

Foolishness! My legs burned from running. I needed a break and leaned against a light post to catch my breath. I closed my eyes for a minute, but oddly, all I saw was Jayce's smiling face. Could it be a sign telling me that I should be with him?

I felt the butterflies return and realized the sign sent from my heart to my brain couldn't have come in any clearer. Jayce was the only person able to comfort me. He could feel my feelings, and maybe could be the one to help me see the light in this messed up situation. I tried connecting. Nothing ... I felt nothing. He'd completely cut off our connection.

Frustrated, I opened my eyes. Daray startled me. He stood under the streetlight, looking devious and mysterious in a black overcoat. I'd never heard any footsteps letting me know he'd arrived. He stalked as silent as a shadow. Leaving the safety of the house had been a huge mistake. I panicked and backed away from him. I was supposed to be with Jayce. I loved Jayce and never should have been out here alone.

The familiar intoxication took control when Daray stepped closer. I helplessly wrapped my arms around his neck, allowing him to run his fingers down my cheek. Suddenly, my mindset completely changed, and I was happy he'd found me.

The man who stood before me was so seductive and welcoming. I pressed my warm lips intensely against his icy ones. He kissed back powerfully, sending an erotic charge through me. It was magnificent. I opened my eyes to find we no longer stood on the dark street; instead, we flew through the moonlit night. We weren't up very high, but enough to clear the rooftops. I remembered back to how the stranger had flown at us in the gardens, the night our lives changed. With the memory fresh in my mind, I hugged Daray tightly.

Prisoners

~ Chapter Fourteen ~

It felt marvelous, just the two of us flying through the night sky. The world had completely changed for both of us. We needed to get reacquainted, and from the way things were going, this was a good start. Daray held me securely, soaring even higher. I felt the intense power he held over me, but didn't fight the feeling. Trance or not, in this moment, it was where I wanted to be—fearless and free with the night breeze flowing in my hair and rippling my clothes.

We flew near the outskirts of town and saw the moon's reflection sparkle off the rolling waves at Mystic Beach. Daray flew us lower to get a closer look. The beach didn't feel the same to me. The beauty was now replaced by shadows. I looked for the fairies, but never found them, causing my mood to drop. What exactly was I doing here? Daray sensed the change in me, and he scooped me up snugger in his arms. We flew toward the densely grown forest on the far side of the hillside. Out in the distance, among the thick trees, rested an old, battered stone house.

Daray brought us down gently, but I stumbled when reunited with the ground. He tried to support me, but my jacket slipped down, exposing the tattoo on my bare arm.

He hissed. "What have you done to yourself?"

"This? I actually really like it. The armband's made up of all the zodiac symbols, but notice the tattoo doesn't join?" I twisted my arm around to show him a better view. "Well, that's because I heard your soul could never leave your body if it were connected. The thought of being stuck in one place for all eternity freaked me out at the time, so I left it undone." From the look on his face, I saw he wasn't impressed.

"I do not approve of the fact that you've dishonored your body in such a vile way. You are a lady."

I was taken aback, unsure of how to respond. My tattoos held stories, meaning, and memories. They were an important part of me. "I understand you don't care for my tattoo very much, but I'm quite proud of it. I've got the entire world wrapped around my arm. The best part is, they're all joined in harmony."

He hissed again, not showing any sign of agreement. I decided to keep my ankle tattoo hidden. Seeing I had another one would probably send him on some kind of rampage. I'd let him stumble upon that one at another point in time. Once again, I felt his intoxication creep over me while we strolled through the overgrown garden. Daray lead us through a broken brick archway, which was mostly covered by dead vines and branches. The stepping-stone path twisted and turned, bringing us closer to the neglected house.

Upon reaching the front door, I felt more like myself. Daray had eased up on his power, and I was pleased by that gesture. His intoxication left me unable to think straight. "You don't need to put a spell on me. I'm here now. Okay?"

"Yes, my love. You are here." He slid open the front door. "Welcome home."

At first glance I saw cobwebs hanging from crooked and smashed picture frames, broken railings lining a neglected staircase, and a dangling chandelier looked as if it were about to fall at any moment. Thick dust coated everything, but the entire place had a dark, eerie feel. Too scared to leave, I cringed and followed Daray as he led the way to an adjoining room.

I looked around, taking in my new surroundings. This room wasn't much better. It too was poorly lit. The only exception was candlelight coming from wine bottle candleholders and a few wall sconces. The flames were hard to see through the thick dust and cobwebs surrounding everything in the room. Dark drapes covered the windows where the boards didn't. Dead flowers rotted in old vases while torn books occupied most of the tabletops.

I stumbled, and my heart beat faster when I took notice of the four vampires in the room. They lounged on a few oversized chairs and a worn out couch. I refocused my attention on them because I'd seen more than enough of the house.

They seemed quite comfortable sipping glasses of red wine, and I found myself mesmerized, even envious, of how at ease they appeared. My world was upside down. I would've given anything to enjoy the kind of peacefulness they reflected. I watched in awe until I realized something about this wasn't quite right. Suddenly I was rattled. Most people didn't enjoy drinks by seductively running their tongues up and down the glass. That's when I realized they weren't drinking wine; it was blood.

Tremendously uncomfortable, I grabbed tightly onto Daray's hand, hoping for protection. A male vampire had me locked in his sights. He didn't shift his eyes off me for even a split second. "Daray, is there somewhere else we can go?"

Lakylee, the half-breed, lunged forward, her fangs exposed as she snarled and headed right toward us. I jumped out of her way instinctively and called out for help. The name that came from my mouth was Jayce.

Daray hissed at both of us in protest.

She retaliated by giving me an evil glare.

"Her? All this, for her? You've searched for so many nights, then she calls out for another man, and you're okay with this?"

"Watch your tongue, Lakylee," he warned. "And your eyes."

Irritated, she stormed across the room and sat back down. However, the intimidation process continued. Lakylee proceeded to lick her lips and smear blood across her mouth, then with a wicked chuckle she playfully asked, "Something the matter?"

"Nope, nothing at all," I lied. I wanted Jayce, my protectors, anyone who could come save me from the mess I'd gotten myself in.

"You sure about that?" She wasn't fooled. Her eyes penetrated the depths of my soul.

Unsure of what to do, I turned to Daray, hoping he'd provide me with some assistance.

"Mind yourself," he scolded. Then he led me by the arm out of the uncomfortable room.

Lakylee objected. She lunged from her seat, trying to follow us.

Daray snapped at her. "Enough!"

She groaned and rejoined the others, her head hung low.

Loud rumbling noises came from the basement. I tried ignoring the sounds, attempting to pull myself back together. Lakylee had gotten under my skin, and I couldn't shake the feeling she wasn't about to let this go. I was on her turf, and it was clear that she didn't like me here one bit. I heard another noise, and clearly recognized the sound of a growl.

Obviously, I'd made a giant mistake. I couldn't stay in this house. These beings were more monster than human. I needed to get far away from them and fast. *'Jayce, please, I need your help.'* I couldn't feel him and knew I was on my own. I looked around for an escape route and spotted a loose board in the far window. Knowing I could squeeze through, I started toward it, but Daray grabbed my hand. I tried to pull away, but he shot me a look that made me flinch. I stopped fighting and let him lead me down the darkened hallway.

I really doubted Daray and this whole situation. He didn't speak to me much, and I seriously disliked the trance he kept placing me under. I wanted to be in control of myself and keep my head on straight. His followers, well, they were something else altogether. I didn't care if I ever set eyes on those skin-crawling beasts ever again. Why weren't they like the beautiful vampires in the books I'd read or movies I'd seen? Those vampires were flawless, sensual, and ever so seductive. Irresistible wasn't anywhere close to how I'd describe the monsters in the other room. The ones Daray kept company with were scary. Their dark eyes, pale skin, and sheer wickedness weren't flattering to me whatsoever. Still, they somehow managed to maintain a strange appeal, and even came across somewhat captivating, but it was clear not one hint of goodness remained. Their souls had vanished the day they changed.

Daray picked up on my overwhelming fear and turned to face me in the dark hallway. I felt his power regain control. "My sweet, they shall not cause you harm. Come …" He teased his fingertips along my cheek. "I want to show you something."

It felt like a dream. Was he going to show me how to make the mean vampires treat me better? Were we going to redo that awful introduction and start again? Instead, he opened a secret door behind him and let go of my hand. I heard the same growling noise and held my breath, terrified of what I was about to see. Even though I was free from his grip, I felt I had no choice but to follow.

Daray led our descent. A rotten musky smell, mixed with other scents I couldn't quite recognize, stung my nose, and I fought back the urge to gag. The narrow stairs squeaked under our every step. My mind raced wildly. Where was he taking me? Thick, dirty black pipes lined the ceiling, while a patchy mixture of gray and brown cement covered the walls and floor. Toward the bottom of the staircase, the room became darker, and the growls grew louder. Frightened and unsure, I grabbed onto Daray's cool hand for reassurance, except he pulled away, leaving me scared and alone. I was about to lose it when he turned on the light. The piercing, burning red eyes of the doomahorns stood only a few feet away. I covered my mouth, gasping. I could feel their breath upon me as they huffed and struggled, trying to break free from the thick restraints. My eyes shifted over to the steel cages containing the werewolves, who let out angry growls. A mixture of drool and blood splattered when they smashed violently against the bars.

These beasts were vicious, downright awful, and for some reason appeared angrier now than at our first encounter. They seemed disturbed by my presence, so I tried to back away, but Daray shoved me closer. I stood within arm's reach of a doomahorn. I saw its terrifying eyes, but then I noticed something else. Deep in the middle of that red eye, there was a look of distress.

In that same moment, something else stood out to me. They were being kept as prisoners, not allies like the other immortals had suspected. I turned, ready to face off about this unjust cruelty, when he spun me toward the beasts and back to him. He twirled me around a bunch of times, placing me under another kind of trance. Deciding I'd had enough, Daray grabbed ahold of my hand, shut the light off, and we went back upstairs.

"You wanted to show me something?" I asked once we were back in the hallway.

"I already did, not to worry."

"You did?" However, I almost couldn't remember leaving the hallway. Everything felt like a dream. But I remembered the look I saw in that red eye. It was something I could never forget, no matter what hold he had over me. "Oh right, yes, you did."

He looked deeply into my eyes. I had his full attention, and deep within his eyes rested a sense of kindness I hadn't noticed before. He seemed different, not quite so cold, and he spoke in a much gentler manner. "My sweets, you are always safe. Until the end of time, your heart will beat by my side, where it always belonged." His cool lips breezed along my neck, making me tingle. Finally, I'd found the resemblance of the man living in my memories. He wasn't dead; he was alive, thoughtful, caring, and standing right in front of me.

I followed Daray upstairs into a rather large room, looking quite different from the rest of the house. The room appeared to be clean and the furniture well-kept. Surprisingly, even color was present—darker shades, but it was a start.

"A bed?" I said, puzzled. "Don't vampires sleep in coffins?" I tried to imagine myself sleeping in something so confined, but it was too awful. The thought made me shiver.

"Yes, yes we do." He chuckled. "The bed is for you, my love."

"Thank you for your thoughtfulness. The bed's perfect." I moved further into the room, observing the ancient, beautiful items he had on display. I touched a shiny silver mirror, and my mind surged back to a memory of a girl brushing her long, brown hair. This had once belonged to me. I was the girl, and the mirror had been a gift from Daray. I ran my hands over it, reeling in my past.

My memory flooded back quicker than I could absorb. Every new experience caused more old memories to resurface. I went around the room, eyeing and touching every tiny detail. I found it truly amazing how he'd kept everything in such immaculate condition. If we would've been married, I imagined our room would've resembled this one exactly.

Daray walked toward a small chest located on a table on the far side of the room. He opened the chest, pulled something out, and tried inconspicuously to hide it behind his back.

"Daray, are you hiding something?" I tried peeking. "What do you have?"

"There's something I gave you a very long time ago, and, well ... it will always belong to you." He hugged me tightly. The chill of his skin oozed straight through my clothes.

"Let me see." I reached around, taking his hand.

Daray allowed me to pull it out. I held his clutched fist in my hands. He looked at me deeply, but it wasn't hard to see his eyes no longer held warmth like they once had. They seemed hollow, causing a chill to race through me.

"I asked you a question a hundred years ago." He got down on one knee. "Shanntal, will you be my queen for all eternity?" He opened his hand, and the ring looked just as beautiful as the first time he'd given it to me. Consisting of a one-carat round diamond, accompanied by three smaller diamonds down either side, it sparkled brighter than the stars on a clear night. All of this shine lay embedded in a delicate band of gold.

"Oh, Daray, I can't believe you kept my ring after all these years." I felt blown away, and for a moment was almost caught up in the fairy tale, but I knew deep down inside that I couldn't bring myself to say what he wanted to hear. I paused, unsure of how he would handle my response. "I cannot honestly say I'll be yours forever ... well ... not right now, anyway."

He pulled away.

"Please, let me have the chance to explain myself," I said, grabbing his hand.

"Fine," he said.

"We've lost so much time together, and my memories are just coming back. I'm asking you to be patient, and allow me the time I need so we can get to know one another again. We have eternity and don't need to rush something like this. Please, keep my ring safe until the time comes for you to present it again." I placed the ring carefully in his hand.

He allowed me to hug him briefly, but then shoved me away, causing me to fall onto the floor. I looked at him in disbelief. "Daray, what the ..."

"I won't wait forever!" he snapped.

"What do you expect me to say? I am sorry, but you must understand this is all happening way too fast for me. My memory is just coming back. Please, let me have the chance to remember who I am and where I've been."

He snarled and bared his fangs. My heart sunk as I remained still on the floor. In an instant, the sweet man was gone, and the monster returned. I watched him place my ring back in the chest. He slammed the lid shut and stormed past me, growling. At the bedroom door, he gave me an enraged scowl, followed by a hiss, and an even louder slam of the door. I sat alone on the floor, scared out of my mind.

Trapped

~ Chapter Fifteen ~

What had I done? Self-pity hit me, and the tears and sobs streamed out. A few minutes went by when I finally decided I'd had enough and stopped crying. The best solution I managed to come up with was for me to go home for the remainder of the night. Some space between us would definitely be a good thing. I walked over and twisted the doorknob, only to find the knob wouldn't turn. I tried again, but it didn't budge.

"Daray, are you out there?" I shouted. "I'm stuck. Could you open the door, please?" I shoved my ear up close, trying to hear if he was coming, but I heard nothing, only silence. "Daray? Anyone? Let me out!" I hit the door, this time with some force. Then I placed my ear back against the door. Again, no sound. Nothing but complete silence.

Now even more upset, I went and sat on the bed, sobbing even harder. Unbelievable! I'd become another one of his many prisoners. Whatever made me think he could be the same man I once loved? Clearly, he was more of a monster than I was aware of, and I'd tossed away my one chance of real happiness for this. Why hadn't I listened when everyone warned me?

Minutes passed. I wandered around reminiscing through my old belongings. As more memories returned, the more I resented

Daray. He wasn't anything like I remembered. He was more like a figment of my imagination.

I searched through my pockets; during my hastiness I'd left my phone at home. Perfect. I glanced around, searching for a clock of some kind. There wasn't one to be found, and I had no idea what time it was. Time felt like it stood still in this room, and that caused my patience to wear thin. I wanted out; I wanted to go home.

I ripped open the dark blinds and leaned against the window, hoping for some sign of movement, hoping for a way out. Nothing. There was no way down. They'd have to return before sun-up. So worst case scenario, I'd stay locked up until then. I perched myself up on the window ledge and twisted a blanket around me, waiting for the sunrise or Daray, whichever came first.

With all this time alone and nothing to distract me, all I could do was think. Sure as anything, Jayce was first to cross my mind. Oh, how I missed him. He never would've placed me in a position like this. What would he think if he saw me at this particular point in time? No matter how hard I tried, I couldn't feel any connection to him.

No one had ever known me in such depth. Jayce knew the entirety of my being, both inside and out. The best part was he loved all of it because he truly adored me. Why did I screw that up? I regretted behaving so badly and putting him through all this. It wasn't deliberate, and I should've taken the time to explain that properly. I should've picked him; better yet, I should've stayed with him. He'd always been there for me, and as long as I'd known him, he'd never let me down. Above all else, he tried his best to keep me safe and somehow even swallowed his pride when he lost that quest. I'd live with the regret of my decision for eternity, hoping one day he'd be able to forgive me for the pain and betrayal I caused.

Another thought intruded, pushing Jayce aside. Daray had spent every night of the last hundred years searching for me, and remembered every detail about me, even when I couldn't. He'd known me in both lifetimes, even held onto my belongings until we were reunited, and this was how I repaid him? Doubting him, turning him down when he proposed? What kind of person was I? I wanted to pull my hair out from this overwhelming confusion. I loved Jayce with all my heart and wanted only him, but for some stupid reason felt compelled to be near Daray. "Argh! Why is this happening to me?" I yelled out to the empty room. Then a female voice spoke in my head.

'You're confused. This experience isn't something you're used to, but everything will work out the way it is meant to.'

I wasn't sure to whom the voice belonged. "Do I know you?" I asked aloud. Did other immortals have the same powers as Jayce, or was someone else here? I hopped up out of my blanket cocoon and looked around for a sign of the other person. I swung open the wardrobes and closet doors, checked under the bed and behind the curtains. The room was empty. "Hello, is anyone there?"

'You know me very well, better than most. You don't always listen, but trust me when I say you usually end up doing what I want.' A familiar giggle sounded. *'You need to learn to trust yourself more. Listen to what you think is right and wrong. Feel down in the depths of your soul what you need, then act on those instincts, for those may save you one day.'*

I listened carefully to everything the voice said, and it made total sense. Whenever I didn't take the time to think a situation all the way through, things usually backfired. I did tend to doubt myself a lot and always second-guessed things. Most likely, those were the times I needed to listen to my instincts and use them a bit more frequently. The voice offering advice had a certain familiarity. No way, could it really be her? I said the first name in my mind. *'Ginata?'*

'Yes, Shanntal, it's me!'

It brought me a sense of joy, knowing I could once again communicate with my dearest friend. "I'm not sure why I didn't recognize your voice right away. Guess it's been a while. Oh, how I've missed you. I'm so glad to know you're okay."

I must've been quite the sight, locked in a room alone, talking to myself. If someone were watching, they would've thought I'd definitely lost my mind.

Yes, my dear friend, it's been far too long, but I'm here to warn you. Daray's not the same man you remember. Darkness has dominated his light. There's nothing left of the man you once knew. You must be very careful because the crew he runs with is evil. If you stay now, it'll end badly. You need to get far away from them and quickly.

"Ginata, I'm locked in. There's no way out."

I have to tell you, everything about Jayce felt right, and that's because he's full of light. Darkness hasn't touched nor will it ever influence him.

Memories of Jayce resurfaced. I saw his warm smile and sparkling eyes and remembered our passionate sparks. How could I have been so cruel? Would he ever forgive me? I tried the door again, but the knob still wouldn't turn. How could I escape?

Your protectors will come whenever you request. They won't come on their own because right now you are safe. You're alone in the house. Your friend Layla can take the form of any creature she chooses. Tell them to bring her. Send for them now, there's not much time!

I spoke aloud because I wasn't entirely sure how to send my request. "Garrison, Kaleb, I need you! Please come and bring Layla. I'll need her help too. Hurry, dawn's approaching quickly."

Shanntal, I want you to know that I'm not one of the living anymore. He came back to finish what he started. You're not safe. I don't think he'll ever give up looking for you.

A tear ran down my cheek. I was officially the sole survivor. "Who's he? Who did this?" I asked. "Daray?"

Ginata never responded.

"Are you still here? Don't go. Please, you've got to tell me who did this." Despite my plea, I was once again alone in the house.

My dear friend had warned me the best way she could. I took in a final look at my past, and knew inside that some things were better left behind. I had no place here, not living this lifestyle.

"Wow!" I blurted out when my eyes saw something looking back at me.

A large dragon occupied the space outside the window. The creature startled me until I noticed the purple eyes, assuring me Layla had arrived. I went closer to the window and looked down. My protectors had also come; they'd heard me.

Kaleb waved his arms and hollered, "Get out of the way!"

I moved to the far corner of the room, covered my head, and closed my eyes. A fireball smashed through the window, shattering the glass and sending shards everywhere. I felt the warmth of the flames quickly evaporate. I opened my eyes, and to my surprise, nothing but the window appeared damaged.

Layla pushed her way through, crunching broken glass under her giant reptile feet. Regardless of the fact she'd become a scaly dragon, I'd never been happier to see anyone. I wrapped my arms around her thick neck and climbed onto her back. Once I was secure, she turned around and flew us out the window. Garrison and Kaleb raced across the ground with incredible endurance and speed. I was amazed watching them leap over obstacles both big and small, basically anything that stood in their path.

"I'm sorry. I don't know what I was thinking. I'm so happy to see you guys! Thanks for coming to get me," I called to everyone as we crossed the yard and headed toward the beach.

I looked back briefly at the broken window where I'd been held captive and felt a rush of relief. Once again I was free of Daray, but this time I had a better understanding of what he was really like. The gentle man I'd once loved no longer lived. I was alive because of the monster he'd become. My family had taught me more ways to live life, and his way wasn't meant for me. I faced forward; my head held high. I wouldn't look back at the past anymore. Instead, I'd live in the moment and strive for the future.

The path from the vampire house leading down to the beach was out of the way from civilization. After living on the island for a while, I had learned most of the humans knew what lurked around during the nighttime hours, so they did the smart thing and stayed indoors until full sunrise. Which was quite a wonderful thing for us because they were accustomed to nightwalkers, but what would they have done if they saw someone riding on a dragon's back? I couldn't begin to imagine their surprise. We weren't living in the medieval ages, after all.

The sun broke along the horizon. Another day had dawned, welcoming the early hour in which most people were snug in their beds. I was jealous of them and felt so tired, but I stayed alert, knowing Daray and the others had probably just returned to the house. Soon, he'd realize I was gone, if he hadn't noticed already. I pictured the tantrum he'd throw and shook the thoughts of his rage from my mind. There were bigger issues to deal with. He knew where I was, and I needed a way to keep him far from me. I couldn't imagine he'd be quite so forgiving toward me the next time we met. I had a new set of priorities. Fix things with Jayce and find out who killed my family. Whoever did it had to be stopped. The evidence pointed to Daray, but I couldn't overlook a feeling … could he really have done something so horrible … to me?

We closed in on the beach. My heart beat quicker, and I found myself hoping Jayce would be there to greet us upon our arrival. Disappointment rushed through me when I never saw him. I climbed off Layla's back, and she transformed back into her human form. My protectors caught up to us, and we walked to where Terran, Aiden, Makan, and Meriel stood. Shea fluttered close by Terran, making it obvious they'd been talking.

"Quite the little adventure you've been on." Aiden sneered. "Enjoy yourself?"

Meriel shoved him.

"What were you thinking?" he continued. "Can you even begin to comprehend how much trouble you've caused? Did you at least learn anything so you could get this nonsense out of your system?"

"I did, and I'm terribly sorry."

"Sorry is a start." Makan offered me a grin.

"Daray isn't the same man living in my memories. I understand that. What I saw was nothing but darkness and evil." The guilt I felt was immeasurable, and I quickly realized everything I'd chosen to do had affected more than just myself. "Please understand, I needed to find out on my own because that life was once mine. Could you imagine not being able to remember your life? Trust me, it's brutal. I openly admit, I felt lost and even doubted where I belonged. I owed this to myself, Jayce, and Daray. I needed to find out where I'm meant to be."

Terran and Meriel hugged me. I'd lost the love of my life and met an old love, only to find out he'd turned into my worst nightmare. I'd been through so much and was relieved someone recognized or at least acknowledged the pain I felt. The girls tried their best to comfort me, but I needed Jayce. Only his arms around me, letting me know he'd forgiven me, would make the pain of my mistakes go away.

Garrison, Kaleb, and the element boys gathered together in a circle, conspiring.

"What do you guys think you're doing?" Layla said.

"What needs to be done," Aiden snapped, turning his back to us.

"Enough! What's done is done. We need to get over this. Now's the time for us to stick together." Terran was the voice of reason.

The girls listened in to the guys ramble on about fighting the nightwalkers and which one they thought would be the toughest to beat. There wasn't any point. They had no plan of attack, just an overwhelming batch of testosterone and nothing better to do but mouth off. However, one by one, the girls gave in and joined their circular formation. No one was being left out of the loop, even if they were just talking nonsense. Feeling like an intruder, I joined the group last. This whole mess had started because of me, and I couldn't stand by and watch the outcome from the sidelines. I needed to step up and help make things right.

A few minutes of deep conversation passed. Finally, there were some very productive ideas being tossed around, but suddenly everyone stopped talking. Curious to know what had distracted the group, I followed their stares. Jayce came down the beach toward us. I suddenly felt dizzy; I couldn't breathe. More than anything I wanted to run, wrap my arms around him, and explain how sorry I was and that I'd never leave him ever again. I started to move, but the look on his face made me decide otherwise. His anger and sadness were because of me. I'd done this to him. His eyes wandered in my direction, and he gave a nod of acknowledgment as he passed by.

Terran whispered, "He'll be okay, just give him a little time. Once this is all sorted out with Daray, I'm sure he'll come around." She squeezed my hand.

Her small gesture gave me hope. I couldn't help but think of how I'd managed to ruin my happiness in the blink of an eye. Everything had changed. It had only taken a few minutes for my world to be flipped upside down yet again. If I'd only listened to Uncle Dane and not run out, things might've been so different. It wasn't fair. I'd just found my way and managed to let my new life get ruined by a man I couldn't even remember, destroyed by a memory forgotten for over a century. Yes, Daray had saved me, but by the sound of things, it was purely accidental. I owed him nothing.

I'd make things right with Jayce, even if it ended up being the last thing I ever did. He'd shown me how to live and love without being afraid. He'd taken the time to teach me what love truly meant. Things became clear; I was in this so-called battle as the middleman. It all came down to a battle of good versus evil. I'd seen both sides and knew the leaders each had one major weakness—me.

Seeing the concerned expressions of the friends made me realize I'd inadvertently begun the battle among the immortals. I hadn't meant to, nor had I known until it was too late. We couldn't turn back. It seemed Daray would have to be destroyed; that could be the only way for us to have some kind of resolution. His destruction would set things right, and I felt deep down in my bones this would also be the only way he'd ever leave me alone. So long as Daray stuck around, there'd always be chaos, and I'd always live in fear.

Plan in Motion

~ Chapter Sixteen ~

Another brilliant morning shone vibrantly upon us. We had spent hours pitching ideas on how to beat Daray and the rest of the nightwalkers. After all points were considered, not one person believed Daray would ever simply walk away and let this go.

I looked around the circle, waiting to see which sets of eyes would land on me. A confrontation seemed inevitable at this point because of my stupidity and selfishness. Surprisingly, no one within the group looked to place blame. I felt a smidgen guiltier for assuming they would. Kaleb shifted closer to me. I was thankful for his support. His thoughtful gesture made me feel a bit more at peace with myself.

While we stood there, I couldn't help but look across at Jayce. I felt so badly for how I'd treated him. I tried being inconspicuous while quickly eyeing every detail of his beautiful face. I didn't want him to catch me staring. Sadly, his features seemed harder now. The cuts on his face from our first encounter that night at the cave were basically healed. He'd tried so hard to keep me safe, virtually facing the nightwalkers on his own, all for me.

I remembered what he'd said to Layla about Daray being right. He wasn't a keeper because he couldn't keep the most important person in his life. Thinking about those words felt like knives cutting through my soul, a horrible sensation I wished I'd never have to face again.

Jayce still had me whether he believed it or not. He'd come around again. Wouldn't he? All I knew is my life wouldn't be the same without him in it. He was the most important part of it. I told myself he needed more time, just a bit more time.

I tried to focus on what the group was saying. There wasn't any point in dwelling over Jayce. He seemed clearly less than interested in me. He never once looked in my direction. Instead, he listened attentively to the ideas the others were pitching. I felt worse by the minute. This had all started because of me.

The group continued making their game plan for taking out the nightwalkers. I didn't bother looking up when someone suggested attacking during the day, even though I knew this would certainly be easier, considering how outnumbered we were. However, fighting like that stooped lower than their level. I hurt tremendously when another suggested I move away, at least for a little while.

"She won't be moving anywhere, so forget about that one!" Garrison's deep voice forbade.

I was pretty sure the comment came from Aiden, but I let it go in one ear and right out the other. His rude remarks couldn't make me feel any worse than I already did. I let my attention drift elsewhere. I still heard everything being said, but the words were more like background noise at that point. The first comment about attacking during the daylight hours brought back a memory I'd nearly forgotten.

I thought it was important and decided to share, so I spoke up. "I don't think we're really that outnumbered."

Everyone stopped talking, all eyes focused on me.

I chose my words carefully and spoke with all the authority I could muster. I needed them to hear what I had to say. "When

I went to the house, Daray took me downstairs. I saw something that didn't seem quite right."

I caught Aiden rolling his eyes.

"The doomahorns and werewolves were being kept as prisoners. They've got them detained in a dungeon downstairs in their house. Maybe there's some way we could convert them? Show them there's a better way to live rather than being held captive. Perhaps we would have the extra power needed to defeat Daray." I felt Jayce lock his stare directly on me. I looked up and met his gaze. I felt my face flush, presumably bright red.

He smiled his perfect smile and announced, "She may be on to something here. If we could somehow make contact or show them they don't have to be prisoners, maybe … they just might want to help us." He gave a wink of approval, and my heart fluttered.

I had to focus back on the group to stop myself from running over, wrapping my arms around him, and never letting go. I listened to everyone discuss tactics. This time, the conversation was directed toward getting us into the dungeon.

In the end, Kaleb's plan seemed to have the most reasonable conclusion, which encompassed all of the necessary time restraints. His plan was extremely tricky to pull off, and only one kind of immortal would be able to do it—the shapeshifter.

The plan sounded really good and doable. However, one part of the concept left a lot to be desired and couldn't be ignored. It came up in the different scenarios more than once. What if the beasts didn't accept or want our help? What if they attacked? The lone shifter would surely perish. There wasn't a plausible way for anyone, shifter or not, to beat those kinds of odds alone. It was a suicide mission.

No way I'd let anyone go, there was absolutely no way! As I glanced around the circle, everyone wore concerned or frustrated expressions on their faces, but Layla caught my attention. She didn't seem to be irritated or disappointed like the others.

She stepped back from our circle and faced the opposite direction. Then without warning, she let out a horrific screech. Everyone immediately stopped talking and turned to see what all the noise was about. She nonchalantly came back and joined the group.

"Umm, Layla?" Jayce said. "Mind telling us what that was all about?"

"Now that I have your attention, I want you to know I've called the other shapeshifters. It's only a matter of time before they arrive."

"The others?" I asked.

"Yes, there are only about twenty known shifters left in the entire world," she said. "Devlin was the shapeshifter who perished trying to save your family. He was my brother, Shanntal."

"Oh, Layla, I'm sorry." I felt like I'd just been kicked in the gut. Why did death and destruction follow me?

She spoke to me in the same way she always had, as my friend. She didn't seem cold or resentful whatsoever. "Shifters have always been around to help protect the other immortals from the wrath of the nightwalkers."

"Oh, Layla. I'm truly sorry. I honestly never knew. The police told me my pet cat died, but I thought they'd been mistaken because we never had a cat. I figured a stray had wandered in or something." A big pit of guilt arose in my stomach, making me feel even worse. I never imagined I could possibly feel any lower. I stood silently and thought about how everyone had been so good to me. What had I done to thank any of them? I hung my head in shame, stepped out of the circle, and walked away.

Garrison and Kaleb followed, and this time I let them. After walking a little ways from the rest of the group, I glanced up at my protectors. I never said anything aloud, but thoughts and questions raced through my mind. What had I cost them? Who had they lost trying to protect me? Why did they bother? No matter how hard I tried, I couldn't spit the words out. The way they both studied me, I knew they understood my pain. I looked deep into their eyes and swore all I saw was my own worthlessness staring me in the face.

Garrison stuck his hand out. "Never leave home without this. Technology makes life so much easier." He handed me my cell.

"Yeah, thanks." I shoved the phone in my pocket.

Kaleb came closer, placed his large hand under my chin, and tilted my head up in a way that forced me to look him in the face. "Don't let me catch you doubting your worth. Shanntal, you are everything to us and mean something to everybody here. You're the change this immortal world needs, and that's the reason we've been waiting for you, why we continue to stand by you, and why we would even die to defend you. Yes, we've all made and will continue to make sacrifices so you can live. Your life is beyond worthwhile, and one day you will understand why. Oh, and just so it's perfectly clear, yes, we do need you here with us."

I felt his sincerity, and smiled at his large mass. "Thank you, Kaleb. It means a lot knowing you think so highly of me. I'm grateful to have someone so loyal and true in my life."

I considered Kaleb the older brother I'd always wanted. Nurturing and caring, everything I imagined an older brother would be. He always looked out for my best interests. Garrison felt more like a younger brother always tagging along. We loved each other, but weren't able to openly speak about our feelings. I loved having him around, though I secretly preferred the conversation and company Kaleb provided.

Garrison grabbed Kaleb by his sleeve, and the two rejoined the others, giving me some time to process everything. I swirled my feet in the sand and drew broken hearts with the tip of my shoe, thinking of all the people who got hurt because of me. What was so special about me? I knew what Kaleb said, but I couldn't believe it. The only thing that seemed real was all the pain I caused. Tears began to swell, but I found myself quite sick of crying all the time, so I choked them back down. Ever since I'd lost my family, it was all I ever seemed to do. I let out a depressed sigh; even they had died because of me. I felt like so much more trouble than I was worth. Maybe everyone would be better off if I just disappeared. As I walked away, someone grabbed ahold of my arm and held me back.

"It's not safe for you to leave. You'll just cause yourself more trouble and grief if you go."

Jayce had stopped me. I felt confused by his gesture. Did it mean he wanted me to stay? Did he forgive me? I looked into his deep brown eyes, expecting they would answer my questions, expecting they'd tell me he'd forgiven me and wanted me back. Instead, he looked away. He couldn't stand to look me in the face. A few days ago we'd meant everything to each other, and now we couldn't even carry on a simple conversation or even look one another in the eye.

"I have to leave, Jayce. Don't you understand? I can't handle any more. It is all too much. How much guilt and pain do I have to suffer through in order to make you understand? I'm so incredibly tired of hurting and don't want to cause any more pain." I pulled my arm away from his reach.

"Shanntal, don't do this. Please."

I couldn't bring myself to listen to him. My stubbornness kicked in and I realized I'd already made up my mind. Leaving would be the best way to fix things. "I'm sorry. I never meant to hurt you or anyone else. I never meant for any of this to happen."

"Stay and sort this out, set things right for everyone. Make our sacrifices worthwhile."

"Jayce, I don't know how to!"

"Don't quit, Shanntal. You can't just walk away. What will you prove by doing that? How will you fix anything? This can't go away by itself, you need to face it."

I screamed. "Don't you understand? I never wanted ... I never asked for any of this. I'm sorry! What more do you want from me?"

I couldn't keep my voice down. I waited for him to say something else, but he didn't. Frustrated, I turned away, and that's when I noticed everyone in the group had stopped talking and was staring at me.

Their silence was more than enough, the final straw. I'd reached my breaking point; the tears and rage I had held back finally consumed me. I let out a blood-curdling scream and took off running down the beach. I had to get away and leave them all behind. I hadn't asked any of them to look after me, and the growing guilt from all their sacrifices and losses was just too much. I couldn't let anyone else get hurt because of me. Come what may, I'd deal with my fate, on my own accord.

I got halfway down the beach, tromping through the debris toward the parking stalls, when I tripped on a log and slammed down hard on the gravel. Cringing in pain, I checked back to see if anyone had noticed. Sure enough, they were all watching. This fueled my anger. I picked myself back up and kept on running. I didn't have a car, but decided running on asphalt would be easier than on sand. I hit the pavement and ran full tilt. My rage gave me unexpected speed and endurance.

About a third of the way up the big hill, I had no choice but to slow down. I could barely breathe. I gasped for air and slowed my pace to a mere walk. Walking would be the only way possible for me to make it to the top of the hill. Now thinking rationally, I was even angrier with myself.

When I made mistakes, I tended to do them big. Go big or don't bother was what my father always said. Stand up for what you believe in, because anything worthwhile always merited a good fight. A good fight? Ha! How ironic. I was far from fighting. I was alone, running away, being nothing but a coward. These weren't the values he'd taught me. I screamed in sheer frustration.

I heard a car coming and moved off to the side. A shiny, black vehicle pulled alongside me.

"Cooled off yet?" Jayce leaned across the passenger seat.

I felt sweaty and defeated. My tantrum had left me quite exhausted. I opened the car door then, took a deep breath before climbing in awkwardly. It was time to face this, even though I felt like disappearing. I knew this needed to be dealt with now. No more running.

Jayce surprised me by not heading back to the beach. Instead, he drove in another direction and turned on a different road. I trusted him enough to find out where we were going once we arrived.

He pulled over by a small boat ramp sitting in between a bunch of greenery. I thought we would keep going, but he managed to park perfectly between two bushes. He shut off the engine, and we sat there, stuck in the car, surrounded by leaves and branches.

I felt so nervous. I couldn't move or speak and wondered what would happen next. We sat for a long while, neither of us saying a word. The quiet made me feel even more uncomfortable. I picked at my fingernails, played with a strand of hair, and looked out the window. Finally, I couldn't take the silence anymore.

"Why did you bring me here, Jayce?" I said, my tone low, hesitant.

He took a minute before looking at me, but when he did, I saw the desperation written across his face. It placed a lump in my throat. I fought the urge to cry. I had no right.

"I'm not sure how to act around you anymore," he said. "Things have become so different."

I didn't know what to say.

He looked out the window and fidgeted with the steering wheel for a minute before letting out a sigh.

"Jayce ..."

"Why did you pick him over me?" He cut me off. "You don't really think you actually love him, do you? Don't you see that he's controlling you? You're just a puppet. Nothing more."

This wouldn't get us anywhere. He was too hurt, and apparently I was still too mad. We'd just end up saying things we'd regret if we had this conversation now. I tried opening my door to take some time to cool off, but couldn't because of how he parked. The bushes outside my door pinned it closed. I had no escape.

"Perfect!" I huffed, sulking back into my seat.

I couldn't leave any time in the near future, so this was coming to blows. Right here, right now. At least one thing made me feel a bit better … I was about to accept responsibility for the pain I'd caused him.

Tingles

~ Chapter Seventeen ~

"Jayce, I've already told you I'm sorry. I'm going to try to explain why I did what I did in the best way possible. I need you to understand I felt obligated because he's the one who saved me. I made a wrong decision. I'm not perfect. I'm sorry it hurt you, but you've got to realize this hurts me too. Do you think I like being away from you? Do you think I enjoy watching you suffer?" I kept my voice calm, but it had a growing sharpness I couldn't avoid.

He looked away, but not before I saw the look upon his face. My comments clearly hurt him more.

Frustrated, I said the first thing that came to mind. "Honestly, how much is one person supposed to endure? I think I've filled the bad luck quota for at least ten lives now." I rolled my eyes and turned my head away so I no longer faced him. I stared out at the greenery filling up the space around my window, and traced my finger along some of the leaves.

We sat quietly for a few minutes before he spoke softly. "I loved you, Shanntal. You had my heart and soul."

I looked directly at him. "Loved?"

"I thought you were my other half, the person to make me whole. Guess we were both mistaken." He sunk his head down.

"Jayce, words aren't going to fix this. We're both saying things we don't really mean. You're hurt because of me, and I am hurt because of everything else. Connect to me. Look inside. See what I see, feel what I feel. Maybe this will help explain better than any words can." I wouldn't back down until he tried. "Connecting might be our last chance to fix things."

I felt him connect. I had a sense of satisfaction knowing he felt everything I did. Connecting would surely help him understand. I thought back to everything that had happened since we'd first parted ways. I ran through every single detail, no matter how big or small, so he knew what I'd been through. I wanted him to understand he was never far from my thoughts.

He witnessed the argument with my uncle and how I found out he'd known all along that I was an immortal. He saw me cry and run out of the house, while trying to escape everyone. I let him feel the confusion and betrayal so he knew how lonesome and alone I felt. I even showed him the moment I called out for Daray.

While he experienced this, his calm face changed to a hard line. I ignored him and kept on going to when we flew through the air. Next, I showed Jayce the horrible run-down house and my unwelcoming reception inside. His hard expression grew angry.

I couldn't stop because of his reactions. I let him view the dungeon and revealed the prisoners. I showed him how Daray pulled out my ring, and he watched as I turned him down. He continued to see Daray storm out of the room and how I became nothing more than another prisoner in the house. He heard my conversation with Ginata, and I showed him how Layla broke through the window to rescue me. Lastly, I brought up all the thoughts I had about him. I needed him to know how many times he crossed my mind while we were apart.

I felt Jayce leave, and I waited anxiously for him to say something, anything. I hoped he understood how much I loved him and how hurt I was by being away.

"I'm sorry for adding to your problems," He spoke, this time looking me in the face.

"You didn't know. Besides, I'm the one to blame here." I looked down.

"I had things all wrong, I'll admit it. I should've connected instead of just imagining what was going on." He lifted my face toward him. "I'm sorry I left you alone. I should have supported you better while you tried to get this figured out."

He said everything I wanted, except … that he still loved me and wanted us to be together.

"I suppose you now understand why I said how much can one person endure."

From the look on his face, I felt confident he understood. I didn't feel or see any of his emotions or memories while we were connected. I was too busy trying to explain my side of the story. I wasn't quite sure how he felt, and it made me uneasy.

Jayce picked up my hand, gently entwining his fingers with mine. I felt his warmth. A warm tingling sensation quickly spread through my body. His penetrating stare remained focused as he looked deeply into my eyes. He moved in closer until he was only a few inches away from my face. Everything began to feel the way it did before all of this happened, but I couldn't let my excitement show. He wasn't finished talking, and I didn't want to be mixing up any signals. I needed him to say the words aloud.

"I'm sorry I wasn't strong enough to keep him away from you. I'm sorry your whole world changed again." With his free hand, he ran his fingers up and down my arm. "One good thing did come out of all this. Since the reunion happened, you've learned who you truly are. Now you get to live the rest of your life with this knowledge."

Tingles shocked me everywhere his fingers touched. He made me melt. All the anger and resentment I'd felt earlier were long gone. I needed Jayce in my life; he was my cure, my light.

He removed his touch from my arm and let go of my hand. Jayce started up the car, and began backing out of the bushes. I was glad we were okay. I smiled at him, when, without warning, he slammed the car into park. My body jerked from the sudden halt. He leaned in, kissing me hard on my lips. He wrapped his fingers in my hair and pulled me closer to him.

The sweet sting of his kiss took me by surprise. I'd nearly forgotten how good it felt. I didn't ever want him to stop. I wanted him to kiss me forever, but he broke away when things began getting pretty heated. His face flushed red. At least one of us had the will to stop.

He wore the biggest smile when he looked at me now. I loved how such a simple thing could brighten up my life. Oh, who was I kidding? I loved every single thing about him. I pulled him back over by the scruff of his shirt and kissed him over and over again. "I love you, Jayce. I always have and I always will."

"I'll always love you too." He gave me a wink and took the car out of park.

We made our way back down to the beach where we found the others exactly as we'd left them. I felt quite embarrassed for how I'd acted before. Garrison and Kaleb both smiled when they saw us approaching. Once we were no more than a few feet away from the group, Jayce suddenly stopped. I crashed into his back because I'd pulled myself behind him, trying to hide until I could figure out what to say to everyone for my earlier behavior. "Jayce?"

He spun around and grabbed onto me as he pulled me into a close embrace. I smiled and felt all my worries disappear. I'd forgotten about the others standing there when he kissed me. As he pulled his lips away from mine, he whispered in my ear, "I love you, Shanntal. Know that I will for eternity."

Smiles from the group greeted us, and I couldn't help but smile back. Standing hand in hand with him, happiness radiated off me. Everyone appeared to be in visibly better moods, and even Aiden smiled at us.

I looked around our circle and noticed there were three faces I didn't recognize. Two females and a massive male had joined since my departure. Layla introduced them.

"Shanntal and Jayce, I would like to introduce you to Allayna, Kynthia, and last, but obviously not least, Kael."

The newcomers all had similar purple eyes. Allayna, the blonde, was slightly on the chubbier side, not fat, just built bigger than an average girl. She was quite pretty, but not exotic looking like Layla.

Kynthia looked the exact opposite of Allayna—quite thin and very tall. Pieces of her jet-black hair hung forward, covering most of her face. She bit her lip nervously, her eyes shifting back and forth as she checked everyone out. The poor girl jumped at every little sound and looked like she wanted to just shy away and go back into the world where she could be alone.

Kael, now there stood a force to be reckoned with. Built similar to a barge, he was absolutely the largest, most muscular being I'd ever met. His muscles bulged off every inch of his well-developed body. He could probably crush a tree between two fingers. He'd be quite frightening if it weren't for the sandy brown hair, accompanied by the biggest, friendliest, toothy smile.

Thanks to them arriving, we now had a better chance. The more help we had on our side, the better. Daray needed to be stopped, and so long as he roamed, the danger of him coming between Jayce and me remained.

The day passed quickly, like they usually did when I was around Jayce. The sun began to set, and Aiden decided it'd be best if we retreated back to their house for the night. Having everyone together meant a better chance for a peaceful evening.

We headed to the car, and I got excited. I'd never been to where Jayce lived and wanted to see where he called home. Did he live in a regular house? Or a run-down shack like the one Daray stayed in?

After a while, we came upon a long, winding driveway located on the edge of town. Trees lined the asphalt, while flowerpots full of bright blossoms were placed sporadically along the road. We followed the drive, which led us up to a beautiful home. The large house had four white pillars, two on either side of the dual front doors.

Jayce and I were the first ones to arrive. He parked just beside the steps leading up to the front door. He walked around to grab my hand as I got out of the car. Together, we walked up the front steps, and he used the opportunity to sneak in another quick kiss.

He unlocked the front door, and we went inside. For a moment, I couldn't breathe as I took in the sights. Was I dreaming? At first glance, the rooms resembled those of a castle, like the one I'd been in a hundred years ago. Suddenly, Daray came to mind, but just for a second. I pushed the thought out of my mind. That castle wasn't up to the challenge of being comparable to this grand home, just like Daray was no comparison to Jayce.

Giant statues of cherubs lined the hallways. The sweet smell of abundant fresh-cut flower bouquets filled the air. Dual staircases covered by lush carpet led the way upstairs, while a sparkling chandelier hung perfectly centered between them. Various paintings of landscapes hung in beautiful, thick frames. I crossed the marble floor, unable to hide my state of awe. Finally, I turned to Jayce. "You actually live here? Just you?"

He laughed. "Yes, I really do live here. No, not by myself. Terran, Aiden, Makan, and Meriel also live here. Layla does too, most of the time. We've lived here for a while now. I know the house is big, but we had to have enough space so we weren't stepping on each other's toes. It's hard to keep peace between the elements all the time."

He started to kiss me just as the front door flung open. A bunch of whistles and cheers greeted us as the others arrived. Yes, everything had gone back to normal.

Meriel suggested the living room would be the best place for everyone to gather so we could continue developing our plan of attack. Everyone sat with his or her kind. The four shapeshifters occupied the soft leather sofa. The element ladies sat on an oversized loveseat, while the element guys sat on a couple of chairs nearby. Garrison and Kaleb sat in some other comfortable looking chairs near Jayce and me. The fairies propped themselves up on edges of bookshelves so they could be the same height as everyone else and wouldn't have to flutter their tiny wings the entire night.

It didn't take long for the conversation to return to the topic of Daray. Everyone knew he'd become one of the most powerful vampires. The only obvious way to destroy him would be to get him alone. Nevertheless, it wouldn't be an easy task to get him away from the others, or to even get close to the others, for that matter. Even with more muscle on our side, the nightwalkers were clearly the more skilled fighters. If this came to face-to-face battle, I wasn't sure we'd stand a chance. We would have to avoid that type of confrontation at all costs.

It started getting pretty late, and the stress of the day had taken a toll on everyone. Jayce suggested we try to sleep while we could. Kael and Garrison offered to take first watch. "Better to be ready and alert in case we have any unexpected company."

Garrison looked at me, and I sensed his worry. If the nightwalkers came tonight, they would undoubtedly have the upper hand. We were in a very dangerous position. Jayce picked up on our increasing apprehension; mind you, Garrison and I weren't hiding our concerns very well. A person with no functioning senses could have picked up on this easily. Makan and Aiden joined our little gathering.

"What's going on?" Aiden asked.

"Shanntal and Garrison are just a bit worried about unexpected company," Jayce said.

"They'd have a lot of nerve coming here," Makan sneered.

"Guys, just calm down. I don't sense anything happening tonight. I've tried to pick up on any hint of them and found nothing. Nothing is a good thing," Jayce reassured.

'That's because they know we'd put up a good fight!" Kael kissed his gigantic, muscular arm.

I couldn't help but laugh and roll my eyes at Kael. His smart mouth couldn't keep anything serious. My reaction fueled the joker, and he continued his flexing and carrying on. Pretty soon, he had everyone laughing.

"What? What's with you people? What's so funny?" he asked, still flexing.

"Oh Kael, thank you. I needed that."

"Anytime." He shot me a big, toothy smile.

Jayce left the room to show everyone where they were sleeping. When he came back I asked, "Where am I going to stay?"

"Beside me. I'm not letting you out of my sight again." He took me by the hand and led me into his bedroom.

We crawled under the blankets, and his arms held me tightly. A moment later, I fell fast asleep.

I never escaped the house. I was still locked away in the room when he'd come back covered in blood, carrying a body. Daray held the corpse close to me, blood pouring out of the wounds. He offered me some. He wanted me to drink blood like they did. When I refused, he chained me downstairs with the others.

In the dungeon the werewolves clawed viciously at me. I put my arms up to protect my face. Every strike the werewolves took sent a jolt of excruciating pain throughout my body. No matter the pain, I couldn't let my guard down. I used my arms to conceal my eyes so I couldn't see what would happen next. I didn't want to see my death come, and felt too weak to fight back. My arms bled heavily from the wounds left by their sharp claws. The scent of the fresh blood taunted the group, making the situation even worse.

A fight broke out between the werewolves and doomahorns. I lowered my arms for a brief second to see what was going on, only to cry out with fright when a doomahorn broke free and headed in my direction. I screamed for help, yanked on my chains while tears streamed down my face. I couldn't break free.

A werewolf slammed into me, knocking me to the ground. My body ached from the blow. The beast snarled out a rumbling growl before coming in for the kill. Then, the doomahorn came back into my sights, standing even closer than before. I didn't know which beast to pay attention to. Which one was going to kill me? I closed my eyes, hoping, wishing someone would rescue me.

I heard the doomahorn's hooves stomp, and the werewolf's growls grew wilder. My eyes opened again when I heard the sound of hooves thundering against the cement floor. The two stood ready for a battle across from one another as if I no longer existed.

When the werewolf smashed into me, my tears were coming down so heavily that the force of the hit sent my tears flying into the air. My tears landed on the doomahorn charging me. Suddenly, the beast transformed into a striking white creature. A single horn rested on top of her beautiful head. The once awful beast turned into a magical unicorn from the touch of my teardrop.

The unicorn pierced her silver horn through the heart of the werewolf. Then she turned around to take on the others. She started killing them in order to help me. Her magic horn opened my shackle, and with a single touch, instantly healed all of my wounds.

She spoke to me through my thoughts and told me her name was Gabriella. She thanked me for saving her from the evil curse the nightwalkers had bestowed upon her. She told me she'd be forever in my debt, and explained she would help me escape to safety. I jumped up on her back, and we ran through the house, both of us escaping unharmed.

I jolted awake and found Jayce's arms were no longer wrapped around me. I reached out for him, but couldn't feel him there. I fumbled around with the nightstand, trying to locate a light of some kind. After knocking over who knows what, I realized there wasn't one there. If Jayce were near, he would have checked on me after the noise I'd just made. This startled me.

The worst thoughts sprang into my mind. What if the nightwalkers had come? What if I was the only one left? I felt safe whenever Jayce was near me, and with him gone, I felt panicky and exposed. "Jayce, where are you?"

A voice answered, but it didn't belong to him. "Everything's all right, Shanntal. Jayce is on watch now. He's okay. Go back to sleep. I'm keeping an eye on you."

I watched the silhouette move to the corner of the room and sit down.

"Garrison?"

"The one and only."

I sighed in relief. "Thanks for staying."

"Glad to be of service. You know, if you ever need to talk, I'm here for you too." His voiced squeaked with the offer.

It was a nice gesture from him, considering I usually ended up talking to Kaleb about stuff. "Thanks, Garrison. I'm glad you're here. Sorry if I snore."

"I've heard you before. Kind of sounds like a freight train." He chuckled.

I laid back down, but no matter how hard I tried, I couldn't go back to sleep. I wanted Jayce beside me. Having only him close by could give me the kind of comfort I needed.

'I'm still with you, just downstairs. Kynthia and I are on watch. Go back to sleep. I'll be back beside you soon enough.'

'Jayce, I really missed being connected to you. I like how we don't need to say things aloud. Hope you know, I am here waiting for you, longing for you, burning for you.'

'Come on, time. Let's get a move on!'

'Honestly, I missed you, and don't ever want to be apart again. I want us to be close, connected, always.'

'Believe me, I understand. We'll just have to keep Daray away. He had his chance. However, I promise you, he'll never get another one, not while I'm around.'

'I love you. I can't bear the thought of being without you. Life doesn't feel worth living if you aren't by my side.'

'Perfect, now I'm satisfied you understand my point. This may mean a fight to the death, but I am prepared to do it just so you know how much you mean to me.'

'Oh, Jayce, please don't let something like that happen. We are getting way ahead of ourselves. I think we are making too much out of this. You're not going to have to fight to the death. Everything will be okay. I've got a feeling.'

'Get some sleep.'

'Good night. I'll be here when your watch is finished. Waiting for you to come back and cuddle.' I closed my eyes, listening to the rhythm of Garrison's breathing. A short while later, I drifted back off to sleep.

I awoke a few hours later with Jayce back in bed beside me. I rolled myself over to admire him. He looked so carefree while he slept. I gently kissed him on the lips without making him stir.

I decided I'd had enough sleep and definitely more than enough nightmares. Why did I keep seeing these kinds of things? How could I think this stuff up? Was there any truth hidden in my dreams? Not wanting to wake Jayce, I stayed where I was and closed my eyes. I remembered back to how Gabriella had saved me from the dungeon. Was there any possibility something like this could actually happen?

Forever

~ Chapter Eighteen ~

I remained snuggled in bed, patiently waiting for Jayce to wake. I felt so safe and secure and would stay here forever if he let me.

He opened his eyes and smiled. "I'd love for you to stay here forever with me." He leaned over and kissed me good morning.

I didn't want to move. I wanted to stay in his big fluffy bed with him by my side. I knew it was wishful thinking, but thought I'd put the suggestion out there anyway.

"Jayce, I've got a perfect plan for today which involves the two of us hiding away in here, away from the rest of the world." I batted my eyelashes, hoping he'd accept my proposal. "What do you say?"

"Tempting ... very tempting." He held me tightly while pondering my offer.

I thought he would agree, but instead he said, "People need to know we are all right. They especially need to know that you are okay. I think you should call your uncle to check in. He's been beside himself thinking he let you and your family down." His tone remained sweet, but it sounded more like an order rather than suggestion.

He was right. It was a definite mood changer as the shock of reality settled in. Surprisingly, I hadn't really thought about Uncle Dane and Auntie Steph since I'd left that night, and I had forgotten they didn't know that I escaped from Daray.

"Oh my, you're absolutely right. They must be worried sick." I hopped out of bed and rummaged through my purse, looking for my cell phone. I dug around before finding it buried deep in the corner. I dialed home.

Auntie Steph answered on the second ring.

"Hi, Auntie Steph." I paused, feeling suddenly nervous. Was she mad at me still? I'd left two nights ago and not on the best of terms.

"Shanntal. Oh, I'm so happy to hear from you!" She surprised me by sounding pleased to hear my voice. "Where are you, honey?"

Her tone took a load of pressure off. What was I thinking? Why did I continue to hurt the people who meant the world to me so easily? How could Daray have such a hold over me?

"I'm fine," I said. "I didn't stay with Daray or the others. I thought it would be better for me to leave." I left out the details of my horrific stay, hoping to avoid panic on her behalf.

"Oh, you didn't?" As predicted, her voice sounded stressed.

"I'm at Jayce's house. Layla, Terran, Aiden, Makan, and Meriel all live here too. I will be staying here for a little while, just until things cool off with Daray and the others. Garrison and Kaleb are here too, and they're staying close to me. Really, we're only staying here because there's more room for everyone."

"Oh, that's where you are. Well, I guess it all sounds acceptable. I'm good, sweetheart, as long as I know you're safe and the others are sticking close by." I heard the relief in her voice after she realized I wasn't alone.

"Is Uncle Dane around?" I asked, feeling apprehensive again. They typically had the opposite reactions to things.

"He sure is, hang on a sec and I'll go get him." She called out for him, and a few seconds later he got on the phone.

"Shanntal, I'm so glad to hear your voice. Are you okay?" he asked, his voice cracked with concern.

"I'm all right. Sorry, I should've listened to you." I paused briefly then explained the situation. "I'm at Jayce's, and all the others are in the next room. I wanted to let you know I'm okay, but we will be staying here for a while. At least until things cool off a little more with Daray and the nightwalkers. There's more room here for everyone, so it seems like the best idea right now."

"You aren't coming home?" He sounded hurt.

"Just for a while, in order to stay safe. Uncle Dane, please understand, I didn't leave the nightwalkers. No, what I mean to say is Daray will be mad when he finds out I'm no longer there. He had stepped out when I kind of made my getaway." I cringed, waiting for his response.

"He doesn't know you left?"

"He'll find out soon enough, or who knows, maybe he already has. It wasn't a pleasant reunion. I discovered Daray keeps prisoners in the house, and he even left me locked in a room after I said I wouldn't marry him." I hadn't wanted to share these details, but needed him to completely understand why I left in the manner I did.

"He did what?" Uncle Dane roared.

"Uncle Dane, please calm down. I'm fine. I've got everyone here, and they're willing to protect me and vow to keep him away. We're prepared should Daray or any other nightwalker try to approach the house. Layla had three more of her kind join us last night. We're ready. You don't have to worry. I'll be fine."

He wasn't hearing a word I said. He started hollering crazy things into the phone. I didn't know what to say to calm him down. I held the phone away from my ear, trying not to go deaf from all his yelling.

Jayce grabbed the phone out of my hand. "Dane … Hello, Dane. Hey, yeah, it's Jayce."

The yelling stopped on the other end of my cell.

Jayce spoke in a calm, rational voice. "I promise you, she's going to be fine. Trust me when I tell you, she's safe."

Maybe it would be better if I went home. Jayce shot me a look and shook his head. I hadn't realized he connected to me. I thought he was too busy, listening attentively and waiting patiently for a chance to speak.

"I understand. Yes … I understand exactly what you mean … trust me, I will … yes, for sure. I promise you … okay … it's settled."

I wanted to know what Uncle Dane said. From the look on Jayce's face, it felt like I was going home. Well, at least he'd tried.

Jayce smile and said, "Oh and Dane, I want you and your wife to know, you're welcome to visit her anytime. Remember, you are always more than welcome here."

Jayce had defused the situation. He was good at calming me down, so I shouldn't have been surprised he was able to do the same to others. "Sure thing … it was nice talking to you also. We'll see you both shortly." He handed the phone back, but not before doing a silly victory dance, showing off his soothing techniques.

"Hi."

"Hello again. I really am sorry, Shanntal." Uncle Dane sounded embarrassed. "I tend to overreact whenever you're involved. I just can't seem to help myself."

"I'm sorry too. Honestly, though, I think flying off the handle tends to be a trait in the family. A rite of passage, so to speak. I guess we should've been born wearing wings to help us fly better."

We both laughed at my poor attempt at humor. Jayce had successfully changed my uncle's state of mind. He was back to his fun loving self, no longer a raging lunatic.

"So, did I hear right? Are you guys coming over?" I was excited by the thought of seeing my family. I missed them. It felt strange, but the time I'd spent away during the past few days seemed longer, more like weeks.

"We'll stop by later this afternoon. I should probably go so we can get ready to leave. I love you, kiddo. I'm glad you're in safe hands." He hung up.

I went near Jayce and wrapped my arms around him. I kissed his left cheek. "Thank you, Jayce." Then I kissed his right cheek. "Thank you, for making my life so wonderful." Lastly, before planting a kiss on his lips, I said, "Thank you for being perfect for me."

He returned kisses in the same manner. "Thank you, Shanntal." He left a kiss on my cheek. "Thank you, for making me so happy." He kissed the other one. "Thank you … for simply being you." Our lips locked in a sweet exchange of passion.

A knock sounded at the bedroom door. The interruption caught us before we got too carried away. I giggled, remembering back to my earlier proposal.

"Guess the plan of hiding out was pretty farfetched." I rolled my eyes mockingly and unwrapped my arms from around his neck.

"More like brilliant!" He gave me another quick kiss, and with a dreadfully sluggish walk, headed toward the door. He pretended the door was too heavy to open. I smiled at his comic attempt to buy us some more alone time. He grinned, straightened himself up, and opened the door. "Yes, how may we assist you?"

"Good morning, you guys." Meriel smirked, giving Jayce a nudge.

"Good morning to you, Meriel." He nudged her back.

Meriel's reaction assured me she was pleased Jayce and I had spent the night in his room, even though nothing really happened between us, only some kisses and snuggling.

"So?" Meriel acted juvenile while standing in the doorway.

We both knew why she was digging. She was snooping to find out news about what had gone on between us.

Jayce shot me a thought. *'Don't let her in on anything. Let her mind wander for a bit. It'll be fun keeping her guessing.'*

Jayce and I never said a word, remaining completely composed.

Finally, she had enough of the game and piped up. "I guess this means you two are back together." She flashed her big beautiful smile at us. "Are you coming downstairs any time soon, or are you staying locked up in here forever?"

I laughed, and she looked at me, confused. I confessed my earlier proposal. "I tried persuading him to stay in here forever, but sadly he turned me down." I bumped Jayce with my hip and pouted.

"Jayce, is that true?"

"Actually, Meriel," I interrupted, before she blasted Jayce for not accepting my offer, "we were just on our way downstairs. I wanted to check in and see how everyone is this morning. I'm quite thrilled because no unwelcomed guests stopped by the entire night."

"Yes, we all made it the *entire* night." She passed Jayce a look I shouldn't have noticed.

I pretended not to see and turned my attention to Jayce, who grinned smugly at her. I shook my head. They were like siblings, poking and prodding at one another just to see who could be more annoying.

"Hello? You guys?" I tried breaking up the unintentional mind war I'd created. "Well, isn't this fun?" I waved my hand in their faces only to get no response. Clearly neither one was paying attention to anything else around them. What were they saying? Finally, I blurted out, "Also, my aunt and uncle should be here pretty soon."

"Really? That's great," Meriel responded. "Can't wait to see them." She gave Jayce a sly eye glance, spun around, and headed downstairs.

I gave him a look of disapproval. A mind war was totally unfair because I had no idea what they were saying. Good things? Bad? Jayce smiled and his brown eyes sparkled as he teased my lips with another kiss. Overcome by his undeniable presence, I quickly forgave him, and we followed Meriel. The three of us joined the others gathered in the living room.

Today seemed different because everyone sat in different places. Species were mixed together. Everybody acted a bit more relaxed and comfortable while they chatted to one another. Laughter was a sure sign things were going well. When the others noticed Jayce and me, the room broke into a round of cheers and whistles. My cheeks heated, and I'm sure my face turned a brilliant shade of red that matched Jayce. I was happy they all approved, but seriously, these rounds of applause needed to stop or we risked the possibility of dying from embarrassment.

I felt magnificent fitting in with everyone. They'd accepted me for me, and I didn't need to pretend I was someone I wasn't. I just had to be myself. I wore the world's biggest smile across my face, feeling incredibly happy being surrounded by my true love and dearest friends. I listened in as everyone resumed their previous discussions. The morning crept onward, and my thoughts of Daray faded, as did the memory of my dream.

The Forest

~ Chapter Nineteen ~

Meriel, Terran, and the three shifter girls wanted to make the most of the daylight and went down to Mystic Beach. Shea and some remaining fairies decided to join the girls, but promised to be back before dusk. So this left Jayce, Garrison, Aiden, Kaleb, Makan, and Kael. The house was quickly clearing out.

My protectors decided to stay close in order to get caught up on some sleep they'd missed out on by keeping watch. They figured by going to bed now, they'd have plenty of energy to keep guard again later tonight.

Kael let out a loud yawn and stretched. Every move made his muscles flex. Smiling his toothy smile, he said, "Yeah, you guys got that right. Sleep now, kick parasite butt tonight." Then he punched his fist into his hand, and let out a bellowing laugh.

So now Aiden, Makan, Jayce, and I remained. Jayce shot Aiden a look, and soon he and Makan headed into the kitchen. We were alone again.

He planted an electrifying kiss on me, which was fine with me. No matter what I couldn't keep my lips off him. I needed him, burned for him. We were lost in our moment of passion, as if no one else in the world existed, until the sound of someone clearing their throat broke things up. Flustered, I looked around to see who had interrupted us.

Aiden seemed a bit red, more so than usual. "Sorry, guys. We've got company."

"Who?" Jayce asked, breathing quite heavily.

"I believe auntie and uncle have arrived."

We jumped up off the couch. "Right. Thanks, Aiden, for not letting them all the way in." I fixed myself quickly. "Do I look okay?"

"You look perfect."

I walked out of the living room first and headed to the front of the house. I saw them standing there, looking around, taken aback by the grandness of the house. They made me smile. I was relieved to see someone else have the same reaction upon first arriving. Their gazes moved throughout the room, scanning the artwork and décor just as I had. Noticing me, they rushed over.

"Shanntal, it's so good to see you." Auntie Steph and Uncle Dane took turns hugging me. Auntie Steph stepped back. "Nice place. I can't believe a bunch of kids live here. This house isn't like anything I've ever seen before, except, well ..."

Uncle Dane and I giggled while we waited for her to continue her statement. We both knew where her train of thought was going.

"A castle. Yeah, that's right, like a fairy tale castle. I swear there was a place like this in the movie I went to the other day." She took another step back to admire the beauty of the house.

Jayce made his entrance. "Nice to see you again, Dane. Oh, this must be your lovely wife Steph who I've heard so much about."

Jayce injected his thoughts. *'I knew she'd be easy to win approval from, even before I met her. Now look ... there's no need to even try.'* He approached her, cupped her hand in his, and leaned down to place a gentle kiss upon it. "It's a pleasure to meet you, Steph."

She giggled and went a shade of pink I'd never seen her wear before. I smiled. Glad I wasn't the only girl that was putty in his hands.

"Come on in. Let's go grab a seat in the living room. It's far more comfortable," Jayce offered.

Auntie Steph nudged me the entire way, acting like a schoolgirl who'd just found out who her friend had a crush on. Jayce clearly loved the attention. Jayce and Auntie Steph chatted, giving Uncle Dane and me some time to talk.

"I'm happy you decided to come. I really wanted to apologize for my behavior earlier. I understand you were only trying to help, but I felt like I owed Daray a chance to show me his side of the story."

"I could never be mad at you for being fair. You are just too trusting. You tend to give people credit even when they don't necessarily deserve it." He spoke low so we didn't disturb Jayce and Auntie Steph. "He's not the same man you once knew, is he?"

"No, not at all. There's nothing left of the person I remembered. The Daray I knew is long gone. I might've seen a glimpse of him, but that was before he locked me in a room." I thought about the fear I felt around him, and especially near the others. I also remembered the frustration and anger that replaced fear when he turned me into a prisoner.

Jayce entered my head. *'Please don't worry. You'll never have to go through that again. I won't ever let you go, not without a fight.'*

Not saying a word, I turned and smiled at Jayce. I knew he was telling me the truth; he needed me as much as I needed him. We were a couple, and splitting us up would be a challenge I didn't think anyone could overcome.

We spent the entire afternoon visit talking and laughing. When the sun began to dip down in the sky that was about the same time Uncle Dane checked his watch. "Oh, Steph, we really should get home. The hour is starting to get quite late."

"We have to leave, *already?*" moaned Auntie Steph. "Really?"

Jayce tried to help relieve the burden of a long farewell. "You can come back anytime you want. You're always welcome. But, Dane's right, it's probably better to go before it gets too dark."

Uncle Dane hurried Auntie Steph along, and they were out the door before the sun had totally set. A few minutes later, everyone else began arriving back at the house.

Kael walked in the living room where everyone was regrouping. "Tonight might be the night." He punched his fists together, looking like a boxer trying to psych out his opponent. "Bring on the beasts."

Garrison and Kaleb followed closely behind Kael. They'd bonded nicely and turned into quite the trio—an enormous, muscular trio. I'd never want to go up against them in a fight; their size alone was intimidating enough.

The sun had completely set so I asked, "Where's Meriel?"

Everyone looked around, but there was no sign of her. I glanced over at Jayce, hoping he'd have some answers. He moved over to the corner of the room, away from everyone else.

"I know where Meriel is," he said. "We've connected. I've found her down by the beach. She knows she should've come home sooner, but she was visiting the mermaids and lost track of time. She's on her way now."

An hour went by, but Meriel still hadn't returned. I looked out the window and found the stars already emerged in the even darker sky.

"Jayce, I'm getting worried. Shouldn't she be home by now?" I leaned in closer so no one could overhear me. "Do you think we need to be concerned?"

"I'll check on her again." He closed his eyes to improve his concentration. This time, he fidgeted and grunted trying to establish a direct line to her.

The whole process seemed different. I'd seen Jayce connect many times before, but it was always done silently and usually unnoticed.

"I can barely see her. What is she still doing in the forest?" he shouted, waving his hands around as if batting branches away.

So much for keeping this under wraps! Everyone overheard him and stopped talking so they could listen carefully as he began describing what he saw.

"Bushes are surrounding Meriel. She's not alone. Someone else is nearby. She's hiding."

People let out fear filled gasps. Night had arrived, and Meriel was alone in the woods. We needed to get to her quickly. Kael transformed into a giant black wolf with purple eyes. He shot out of the living room like a bullet. Garrison looked at Kaleb, who gave a nod, and Garrison ran out after Kael. The others stayed behind, in case the house was ambushed.

The way Jayce connected with Meriel tonight had an entirely different effect on him. At points, he seemed to be in a trance, almost sleepwalking. Then, in the next instant, he'd fidget uncontrollably. The strangest part was how he spoke so loudly. Whenever the two of us had connected, we shared all our communication through internal thoughts. He'd never acted this way while connected to me, nor had I ever seen him behave like this around the elements. He'd always been coherent and could still manage to hold a conversation with those around him. I jumped to the conclusion that something must've been wrong with Meriel, because none of this seemed right to me.

I wanted to know who was near her. Could he see who was there? Before I could ask, he started answering my question on cue. "Lakylee is alone in the forest. She knows Meriel is there, and now she's looking for her."

My heart pounded so hard I thought it would break through my chest. Lakylee came across unstable, her mood fierce and vicious. She was wild. She didn't have the same temperament as the other vampires. What did she want with Meriel?

"Kael's close. So is Garrison, though he's coming into the forest from a different angle. It looks like they're trying to cover as much area as possible." Jayce provided a play-by-play. "They're planning on keeping her contained until they can find out what she wants."

I felt so tense standing there, waiting to see what would happen next. Why was Lakylee alone? Where were the others? Could this be a trap? My mind wouldn't stop racing.

Jayce placed his hand on my shoulder. "Lakylee is getting very close to Meriel. She's only about a hundred yards from her. The guys aren't close enough yet. She's going to beat them to her." He pulled his hand away and clenched his fists together. "Meriel, be still. She's too close," Jayce whispered.

He didn't say or do anything for a few minutes. He stood completely still, resembling a statue. Suddenly, he cried out, "No ... please ... don't!"

We all knew what that meant. Lakylee had reached Meriel first.

"What's happening?" Aiden asked, visibly shaken.

"Lakylee is talking to her." He seemed confused as he described the scene to us. "She isn't aware the others are coming. She's let her guard down and is just talking to Meriel."

"Talking?" Terran asked. "About what?" She held her hands together, trying to stop them from shaking.

"I don't know," Jayce replied.

"Do something! Why don't you do something?" I pleaded to the elements. "Buy her some time. Help her like you did when we needed help."

"We can't," Terran said. "We need to be together for our powers to work. We function as a whole because there's too much of a power struggle working alone, and, sadly, that's the one thing that separates us. Also, the more we use our powers, the weaker we become. It's not safe for us to be vulnerable. It can be devastating for us—well, for everyone, actually."

Jayce continued. "Lakylee is now asking Meriel about Shanntal. She wants to know why she left the house." He paused. "Daray's been causing grief around there. He's accusing them of slaughtering Shanntal's family. The coven denies their involvement, but he won't accept that response. He thinks they're lying. Now, they've split up and gone their own way, but no one wants Lakylee. She doesn't fit properly with the other vampires."

I started feeling sorry for her. It was true; she didn't fit in with the vampires, or the werewolves, for that matter. She was a lone walker. Then I wondered what Daray was up to now. Why would he blame them for my family? Could this be another one of his ploys?

Jayce put up his hands to defend his face and neck. He leaned back until he practically fell over. My heart stopped as I watched helplessly. He appeared to be fighting something off while still connected to Meriel.

Please don't let her get hurt, please don't.

Jayce let out a curdling scream.

Makan punched the wall. Tears poured down his face. "Meriel!" he cried out in an agonizing voice.

Jayce tumbled to the ground. He slowly got onto his knees. A minute passed, then Jayce quickly leaped to his feet and shouted, "Meet your match, beast!"

Hearing those words come from his mouth must've meant Kael and Garrison had arrived. He sounded just like Kael. Jayce remained in his trance as he watched their battle unfold. During this time, he stopped filling us in on any details. We waited, anxiously. About a minute later, Jayce let out an appalling growl, putting everyone even more on edge. He was still in the trance, but looked ready to attack everyone in the room. Unexpectedly, he let out a painful yell, and then fell to the floor.

I waited a few seconds to see what he would do next, but he didn't move. He just stayed on the ground, looking dead.

"Oh my," I gasped. "Jayce, who are you connected to? Jayce, who?" I repeated. "What's going on? Tell me now! Jayce, wake up!" I dropped to my knees and grabbed onto his shirt, shaking him frantically. He slowly awoke, glancing around the room until his eyes focused on me.

I let out a heartbroken whimper. I knew who he meant; he didn't need to say, because I felt the emptiness hit my soul.

He reached his arms out. "I'm so sorry."

Aiden demanded an answer. "Who were you connected to?"

"Garrison." His voice broke. "I'm sorry, Kaleb, Shanntal. He couldn't fight Lakylee off. He tried to help Meriel escape, but she caught him from behind. He never stood a chance. Everything happened too fast, even Kael couldn't help."

Kaleb stood strong and didn't shed a tear. I, on the other hand, was completely hysterical. Garrison was my protector. He wasn't supposed to be gone. I needed him. I managed to walk over to Kaleb, who remained as hard as stone. I wrapped my arms around his broad frame, leaving wet marks on his shirt from my tears. "I'm so sorry. I can't believe this."

Kaleb never made a sound. He simply placed his arms around me and held me close. I felt his pain even though he never said the words aloud. Feeling all eyes on us, I broke out of our embrace and led him into another room where he'd be able to grieve the loss of his brother in peace. We entered the other room, and I closed the door. I sat him down in a chair and looked into his strong eyes. My heart broke seeing all the pain they held.

"Kaleb," I explained softly, "it's okay. He was your brother."

He started to cry. It was distressing watching him. I'd thought of these two as invincible; after all, they were my protectors. Why couldn't I protect them from this? I hugged him tightly while he mourned the loss of his brother.

Jayce came into the room a while later and joined us. "I'm very sorry. I really can't believe this happened. I don't know what to say."

"That's okay," Kaleb said.

I rubbed his broad shoulders to try and comfort him.

Kaleb spoke proudly. "He died protecting, because that's what we do. We know the risks involved, and we still make the choice to face any threat head on." He paused for a minute. "My brother will always be remembered as a protector. He never gave up. A protector, forever." He was done being vulnerable and turned back into stone right before our eyes.

All I could do was support him. "I agree. Protector forever. He'll always be known as my protector."

Jayce relaxed his pose and came a bit closer to us. "Meriel's back now. She's in rough shape and quite weak. It's a miracle Kael got her back here in one piece."

Kaleb and I looked at each other, wiped away our tears, and got up so we could head into the front room with Jayce to check on our friend. Everyone crowded around Meriel. She was conscious and asking for Kaleb. Kaleb and I squeezed our way through the crowd to get near her.

"I'm sorry, Kaleb. Garrison tried protecting me." She gasped sharply, attempting to breathe. "Lakylee attacked when she saw the others come. The guys moved in for an attack because they didn't realize she was only talking. She panicked seeing them closing in around her and just snapped. Kael fought with her first, but she just threw him backward like he was nothing at all. He flew so far, he couldn't get back to us in time."

I looked at Kael, who held her hand while wearing blood stained clothes. Was the blood hers? Maybe Garrison's? I felt sick to my stomach. I couldn't swallow down the lump rising in my throat or stand the sight of him like this, so I made myself focus back on Meriel.

She had tears in her eyes. "Garrison was hunched over. He was trying to lift me up so we could get away faster, but she lunged at him from behind and knocked us both down. She was strong, angry, and ..." Her voice grew quiet. "He couldn't fight her off."

The severity of her weakness became evident as she spoke. Blood stains and dirt covered what was left of her shredded clothes. Lakylee had gone unhinged, clawing a good portion of her. Poor Meriel looked to be in pretty bad shape. I wasn't able to hide my growing concern, and the look upon my face must have said it all.

"Don't worry, Shanntal. I'll heal, I just need time." Meriel smiled weakly then closed her eyes.

Aiden, Makan, and Terran began pushing everyone out of the room to give Meriel some space. "She needs to rest," Terran said.

I nodded and tightly held onto Kaleb's arm as we made our retreat. Jayce was the last one out. I overheard Terran speak to him before he went through the doorway. "Please, Jayce, keep guard tonight. We need to keep her safe. She's far too weak to fight."

Kaleb also heard and looked back nodding. He wanted to show Terran he was ready. He unclenched my arm and went into the group to find Kael. He pulled him aside, and they spoke privately by the big window while staring into the dark, waiting to see what would happen next.

A Glimpse

~ Chapter Twenty ~

The night felt as though it would go on forever. Kael and Kaleb never strayed an inch from the window, not even for a split second. They were on guard, and nothing would be getting past them tonight.

I let out a yawn, quickly followed by another. I felt bad being tired after everything that had happened earlier in the evening, but it was getting quite late. I got up off the couch, walked over to Kaleb, and hugged him tight. "Night, Kaleb. See you in a little while."

He returned the hug along with a nod. He didn't have to say anything. I knew he was still in pain.

I made my way toward the stairs, Jayce following my lead. I retreated up to his bedroom, went over to the bed, and flopped down on the pillows. He crawled in beside me, and pulled the blankets up over us both. Even though I felt so tired, I couldn't fall asleep. So many thoughts raced through my mind. Jayce played with my hair and grazed his fingers along my skin in an effort to soothe me. I rolled over to face him, but all I saw was the outline of his face. I felt along his jawline until I found his lips and ran my fingers across them.

He moved closer, propping himself up while his body pressed gently against mine. His fingertips traced along my shoulders and down my arm. I squeezed in closer, enjoying the shocks from his touch. He continued teasing until I couldn't stand any more.

"Jayce, please."

He obliged, pressing his lips down intensely. I wrapped my arms around his neck, pulling him on top of me. I could get lost in him. This was the life I wanted to live. Kissing him, continually enjoying the sweet sting of our electrifying passion.

A light knock came upon the door, yet another interruption. I moaned in protest when he got up to open the door. Makan stood in the hallway, which was quite dark, but I could still see him clearly.

"Meriel is frail. However, her condition does seem to be improving. Also, I checked in earlier to see how things were going. Kaleb and Kael said they've got tonight covered. So, there's no watch for anyone else this evening."

Jayce nodded in agreement. "Sounds good. Good night." He started closing the door but paused. "Makan, let me know if there's any change with Meriel, okay?"

"Will do. Good night, Shanntal," Makan said, before retreating back downstairs.

Jayce closed the door and came back to bed. He wrapped his arms around me, and we both drifted off swiftly.

I saw Garrison, only to sit back and watch in horror while Lakylee attacked him. It felt like I was there, hiding in the trees, watching the incident unfold. She came up without any warning while he was bent over helping Meriel. He swung around, trying to fight her off, but lost his balance from the unexpected blow. Lakylee seemed so enraged. She was out of control, and in her fit of anger, she clawed savagely at his throat. Then just like that, she disappeared back into the night. With the way she attacked, he never stood a chance of properly defending himself. I continued watching as he lay still on the floor of the forest, bleeding to death. Crying Meriel called out for Kael. He came over, and they both kneeled down to spend the last living moments with Garrison.

The atmosphere of my dream changed. Now, I strolled down the beach, but Garrison was in front of me, unharmed. He looked perfect, just as he always did. He turned and smiled, then thanked me for giving him such a fulfilling life. He finished his thanks by telling me he'd always be in my debt.

I asked him what he meant. What had I done to make it so special? How had his life been so fulfilling? He never got a chance to answer my questions because a bright flash lit up the area where he stood. I looked around but couldn't see him anymore. Garrison was gone, along with the mysterious light.

I was on the beach alone when I heard my name being chanted through the blowing wind. I looked in the same direction the sounds came from just as a dense fog rolled in, covering everything. My blood began to run cold. I knew he was near. I tried to make my escape, but my body didn't cooperate. Instead, I froze.

That's when I saw him clearly. I wanted to get away, but something pulled me in closer. I stood within his reach and he touched my neck, sensually running his icy fingers along my throat. No matter how hard I tried, I was no match against him. Effortlessly, he tilted my head to the side. I fought to straighten my neck, but it wouldn't move. I watched helplessly as he leaned in closer. I felt his cold lips and breath trickling along my neck. A moment later, he bit down, and I cried out from the painful burn as he spilled his venom and drank my blood.

"No, Daray, please don't!" I yelled at the top of my lungs. My voice started off loud, only to become weaker the more I fought. There was no use. My body went cold and limp as he sucked my life away.

Little did I know, Jayce had woken from his sleep when I called out. He connected and saw what was happening. He knew why I'd said those words. He squeezed his eyes shut, placing himself into a trance-like state. A moment later, he gently entered my dream.

I saw Jayce approach out of the corner of my eye, but he started to dim, and everything around me went dark. A new kind of peacefulness took over. Was this what death felt like? It wasn't so bad. The darkness liked me; the darkness wanted me.

Daray had drained most of my blood. My time was just about up, but Jayce hurried over and grabbed my hand. His touch warmed my cold, burning skin. I felt so weak, but couldn't manage to pull myself away. Luckily, Jayce was strong enough to break the hold Daray had over me. I fell into Jayce's arms, and he carried me away. Daray shouted and hissed, but Jayce continued to lead me down the beach away from him. Daray never followed, which surprised me, nor did he put up the fight I'd expected.

Jayce spoke calmly while he continued luring me away to safety. "You're okay, Shanntal. Everything's going to be all right. You are going to wake up." He gave me a gentle nudge, and my eyes opened.

I gasped, choking for air, feeling like I'd woken from the dead. My skin felt cold and my neck hurt badly. There was absolutely no way. Could everything I'd dreamt really have happened? I jumped out of bed and ran into the washroom in Jayce's bedroom. I flicked on the light, only to freak out from my reflection in the mirror. My neck had two red marks, like I'd been bitten.

I raced back into the bedroom. I lifted my hair to show him my neck. "How's this even possible? How did you know? How did you save me?"

"I connected. Daray is getting more powerful, and he wants you. I don't think he's going to stop until he succeeds. Don't worry, this is his method now because he knows he can't get any closer due to all your protection." He grabbed onto my arm and pulled me back into bed. "They're only dreams, he can't actually harm you in them. This is the worst he can do, and trust me, I'll always come for you. I will always save you."

"Promise?"

"I promise." He kissed my neck. His warmth soothed the cool sting of the bite mark.

Jayce fell back asleep, but I couldn't. I really missed Garrison. I wished he would come walking through the door to let me know he's okay, let me know it was all a horrible hoax. I lay there in bed with Jayce's arms wrapped around me, waiting and hoping, but Garrison never came. He really was gone, and once again I felt my heart break.

The night dragged on and I tossed and turned for the remainder of it. I found myself envious of Jayce as he slept peacefully beside me. I was afraid to sleep. What if Daray came back into my dreams again? What if Jayce couldn't get to me in time? I shuddered. Why did I have to lose everyone who mattered to me? How many more lives would mine cost? That was the final straw. I couldn't stay in bed any longer. I got up, looked back at Jayce, who remained motionless, then sighed before heading downstairs.

Kaleb and Kael sat on the couch, keeping watch by the big window. Kaleb was on edge, and I startled him by coming into the room. "Shanntal, wow, didn't expect to see you up so early."

"Couldn't sleep." I looked outside in time to see the sun break along the horizon. The sky was so beautiful, full of pinks, purples, and oranges. One world entered as another left, leaving me caught in the middle of the two. Light made me feel happy but caused me pain. Simultaneously, the dark comforted but also scared me.

Kael stretched and let out a loud yawn. "Well, Kaleb seems like you've got some company. I'm gonna head off, catch some zzz's while I can."

"Sure, man," Kaleb said, watching Kael get to his feet. "Catch you later."

I waved at Kael. I was glad to see him heading to bed. I wasn't in the best of moods and didn't feel much like talking to him. Part of me was mad that he couldn't save Garrison, and part of me knew he would if he could have. I curled up on the couch next to Kaleb and rested my head against his arm. "I really miss him, Kaleb. Do you think he went to the stars?"

"He's in a better place. There's no doubt in my mind." He stared out the window.

We sat there for about an hour, just the two of us. We watched the shadows retreat as the light crawled over everything.

Kaleb broke our silence. "Did he come to you last night?"

Confused by his question, I asked, "Who?"

"Garrison," he said. "I heard when immortals don't go to the stars, they come back for a last visit. A final say, so to speak. He never came to me, so I wondered if perhaps you saw him."

"Oh." Now my dream made a bit more sense. "Yes, he did visit me last night. I dreamt of him."

"What did he show you?" His eyes were intense, searching through my soul to find the answers he longed for.

"He showed me the fight with Lakylee. She was so strong. They'd underestimated her strength. Kael fought her first, but she threw him back as if tossing around a football. Garrison was busy helping Meriel get back on her feet. They were making their getaway when Lakylee came from behind and savagely clawed Garrison's throat. She was so consumed by rage, and he never saw her coming, nor did she realize what she was doing."

Kaleb didn't break his stare. "And?"

"And suddenly we were talking on the beach. He looked good and seemed happy. He thanked me for making his life so fulfilling. He told me he'd be forever in my debt. Kaleb, I don't understand. What did he mean?"

"It's simple, actually. You don't understand how special you truly are. You'll see in time, but he's right, you know, he is in your debt. We all are." He turned his head away and looked back out the window.

I didn't bother to argue or press the issue any further. Garrison's words played on repeat mode in my head, while it felt like everyone spoke to me in riddles. Even Kaleb was doing it to me now. I sat silently pondering the meaning of their words, trying to interpret what they truly meant.

Decisions

~ Chapter Twenty-One ~

Makan came out of the room where Meriel was resting. From the look of him, it was easy to tell he'd been beside her all night. He looked exhausted.

"How's Meriel?" I asked as he passed by.

"She's improving. It's been a rough night. Thankfully, I think she's through the worst of it now. She's up if you want to go in and see her." He motioned his head toward the room.

"Sure." I got up and headed to the doorway. I spun around to see if Kaleb wanted to come, but should've known better, because he stayed right on my tail, shadowing my every move. The bond between Kaleb and I had grown even stronger since the loss of Garrison.

We walked into the room and found Meriel in the same place she'd been the last time we saw her. Her wounds were healing at a rapid rate. They all looked significantly better, but this also made me both happy and mad. I was happy she would be okay, but angry the same fate hadn't come to Garrison.

Meriel looked in our direction and smiled. From her weak smile, we knew she still had lots of pain.

All of my anger left. It was difficult seeing my friend in this state. I held onto Kaleb's hand for support and we both moved closer. "How are you feeling?" I asked, even though the answer was obvious.

"I'm getting better. The healing is coming along." She eyed us both carefully before continuing. "I wanted to tell you both how truly sorry I am for what happened to Garrison. I feel responsible, and I'm honestly sorry." Tears swelled in her eyes.

Kaleb let go of my hand and placed it on Meriel's. "Garrison did exactly what he knew how to do, protect you. He did what needed to be done in order to keep you safe. The world can survive without him, the world can't lose you."

Finally, I understood the real meaning behind his words. Garrison truly was a hero. He'd saved more than Meriel; he'd saved us all. Without the water element, I couldn't imagine what would've happened to any of us. Would she go up to the stars? Would we run out of water? My emotions and mood changed in that instant. All my grief and sorrow was replaced by pure pride. I felt so proud of Garrison for what he'd done. We would be forever in his debt.

Kaleb and I visited for a while. We watched Meriel improve with every passing hour. She grinned, and I turned to see Jayce standing in the doorway smiling at us. The mere sight of him took my breath away. When he smiled at me today, for some reason my heart beat faster and knees weakened. I was glad to be sitting, or I might've fallen down.

He came toward Meriel, stood beside her bed, and examined her closely. "Meriel, looking better I see. Close one, don't you think?" He rubbed her arm softly.

"Yes, I'm beginning to feel much better. I'm very sorry, Jayce. I never meant for any of this to happen." She looked at him, her eyes pleading for forgiveness.

"Rest, Meriel. Just rest."

He turned his attention to Kaleb and me. "Ready for breakfast?"

Kaleb immediately jumped to his feet. "I'm starved," he said, patting his stomach.

I followed the boys into the kitchen, which was rather crowded. Looking at their faces, I felt grateful having such wonderful people in my life. I didn't say much during breakfast. Instead, I enjoyed how everyone moved and interacted with each other. They were similar to a large family; no one was in the way because of how they gracefully maneuvered around one another.

Jayce waited until I had finished eating before he led me outside so we could have a moment alone. I found the fluffy clouds inviting, and I couldn't fight the urge to just lay down and look up at them. We took shelter under a large birch tree in the yard and sat on a patch of grass covered by shadows cast from the leaves above. A light breeze blew, spreading the fragrance of nature all around us. My hand tickled as I brushed it along the blades of grass. I felt Jayce's eyes on me. I looked at him, but sat upright when I noticed something didn't seem right. "Is everything okay?"

"Yes, everything's fine." He didn't sound very convincing.

I tilted my head to the side in disbelief. He was flat out lying. "I know things have been tough, and we had quite the scare with Meriel, but Jayce, she's going to be okay. Also, I'm sorry if I've been acting a bit off. It's because I really miss Garrison. I keep trying to remind myself he died a hero, and I know in time we will get past this, but the look you have in your eyes right now tells me there's something more. What aren't you saying?"

"Nothing." He made himself comfortable in the grass, resting his arms behind his head. "Just drop it."

I decided to leave it alone; he appeared to be in a mood. I'd never seen him this way and assumed he'd probably tell me once he was good and ready. So, I wouldn't push the matter any further.

We spent most of the day outside. Jayce was beside me, though he seemed a million miles away. I tried my best to ignore the building tension and instead focused on the clouds floating above. They reminded me of a time when my sisters and I had stayed in the yard for five hours straight, watching them pass by. We created a game where we'd describe what we saw in the clouds and the others had to point it out. It was our version of hide-and-go-seek and I-spy rolled into one. You had to be quick because the clouds continuously changed in the big sky, and if you didn't spot the object right away, you could waste the entire day waiting for it to reappear.

Another day was coming to an end. I watched the sun dip behind the hills. I rolled onto my stomach to face Jayce. I had done my best to ignore the mood he'd been in practically all day. I couldn't help myself, so I asked the question on my mind. "Do you think Daray's going to come for me soon?"

"I don't know what he's planning," he replied sharply.

"Couldn't you connect? Maybe you could catch a glimpse of what he's planning or even see what he's doing?"

"Is that what you want?" he muttered.

"It might show us what we need to know."

"Fine, I'll try." He closed his eyes to concentrate. Two seconds went by and he opened his eyes back up. "Nothing. I saw nothing."

"Jayce, come on," I said, feeling frustrated by his mood. "You didn't even try. You've been in a mood all day, and I think it's about time you told me what's wrong."

"You want to know what's wrong so badly? Well, it's simple. The elements can't fight for you. It was too close. We almost lost Meriel. This is all crazy!" He threw his arms up in the air, then put his hands on his head, looking like he might pull his hair out. He sighed, shook his head and said, "There's so much more at stake here, yet everyone keeps putting everything on the line for you. This can't happen anymore. Don't you understand? It must stop!"

His words cut through my soul. "I never asked anyone to do this for me." I snapped defensively.

I couldn't believe he'd said such a cruel thing to me. His words came across heartless. I had something else on my mind now ... leave before anything else hurtful gets said and can't be taken back. The house was big enough for us to stay away from each other until things cooled down, or maybe it would be better for me to just go home. He didn't really seem to want me around, so I got up to leave.

He grabbed my arm, holding me in place.

"What?" I snapped sarcastically, trying to yank my arm from his grip. "Haven't you already said everything that's bugging you?" From the look on his face, I could tell he wasn't finished. "Oh lucky me, there's more?"

"I'm not sure I'm built to do this. I love you more than anything in the entire world, but you've got to understand, I can't have you and keep them." He let go of me, pulled his knees up to his chest, and wrapped his arms around them.

Suddenly, I realized how badly this entire situation was tormenting him. Losing my edge, I reached down to hug him, hoping to help ease some of his pain. "Jayce, you don't need to choose."

We embraced, but he held on to me tightly as he shouted, "Yes, yes I do!"

I'd had enough and let go, ending our hug. It seemed pointless to deal with. He was too upset, and I couldn't understand where he was coming from. He wasn't telling me the whole story. How could I help if I didn't know everything going on?

I stood up just as Kaleb came out of the house and began walking toward us. Jayce's anger tore me apart inside. I didn't know how to handle him like this. I kept my eyes straight ahead on Kaleb and never looked back.

Kaleb had his eyes locked on Jayce, but never said a word to him. Instead, he took me by the arm and escorted me back into the house. Everyone crowded in the living room. I looked around but didn't feel like being near anyone. I felt their eyes on me. Were they questioning my worth too? I began feeling like an outsider. Sensing my angst, Kaleb led me up to the room where he was staying. I walked in and sat on the bed while he closed the door.

"What was that all about?" Kaleb asked.

"I'm not entirely sure. I thought maybe you'd know better. Perhaps it's a kind of guy code thing I'm missing?" For some reason, I thought he might have known something I didn't.

"I know at the moment he's feeling torn. He loves you more than anything, but he's the keeper of the elements, which isn't something he can give up easily. It's a big responsibility that was bestowed upon him."

I had to believe Kaleb when he said Jayce loved me. I thought he did too, but the way he'd just acted said something entirely different. It felt more like he hated me. I sighed.

"Look, he feels like he needs to choose, and like right now. The elements aren't safe when you're involved … no offense. Until Daray is destroyed and peace is restored, he will remain torn."

I didn't respond. I just sat there waiting for him to finish his theory.

"The elements want to protect you, and believe me, they will fight. The problem is, every single being on this planet depends on them. So what this boils down to is, they can't risk themselves again for the sake of you. I'm sorry." He tried to break the news gently, but his words still cut.

"I never asked them or anyone else to do this for me," I snarled. I didn't want to cry, but felt the tears coming.

"We know you didn't. That's why we want to help." He patted my shoulder. "You are so stubborn and can't see the whole picture yet. There are bigger things going on in the background here. It will all be revealed in due time." He tried his best to sound wise and supportive.

Blah, blah, blah was all I heard. It was simple. They didn't want me around anymore, and I couldn't blame them one bit. It seemed I'd worn out my welcome, or at least that's how I interpreted these conversations.

Frustrated, I got up, put my hands on my hips, and paced back and forth around the room. What should I do? Where could I go? If I left, would I be safe?

Suddenly, an idea popped in my mind. "Kaleb, I need to go to the beach. Will you come?"

"The beach?" By his expression, it was apparent he didn't agree with my idea.

"Yes, just the two of us. Maybe there's some way to negotiate with Daray and the others. You'll be safe with me. They know we're connected, so they won't harm you."

"Won't harm me? Meh!" He folded his arms in disapproval. "Just like they wouldn't hurt Garrison. You've got a blind spot for that parasite."

"Kaleb! I've got to try something. I can't sit by while everyone else battles for me. I love Jayce. I won't stand by and let him toss me aside, especially due to something like this. He shouldn't have to choose. It isn't right."

He shrugged. "I don't know."

"Whatever, Kaleb. Forget I said anything. I'll go by myself!" I started toward the door. In a flash, Kaleb pressed himself up against the door, blocking me in.

"Did anyone ever tell you that you're far too hotheaded? Geez, man! Settle down."

"Kaleb, I'm warning you. You've got two choices. Either get out of my way, or I'll make you move." I braced myself for impact.

He didn't budge. "Pretty tough talk for a chick."

I rolled my eyes and smirked. He was right. My mouth sure did tend to run off at times. I sulked and went back over to the bed to feel sorry for myself.

"How do you suppose we get past everyone else? It's getting dark, you know, and they're keeping watch," he said a minute later.

"Oh, so you're in, are you?" I grinned.

"Can't let you have all the fun, now, can I? Besides, I'm in the mood to punch a few parasites." He smashed his fists together the same way Kael always did.

"Oh my!" I said, feeling like a clone stood before me. I decided to sneak a peek out the door. We needed to make sure the coast was clear to make our escape. I stuck my head out, but saw Kael walking down the hall toward the room.

"Kael's coming," I said, closing the door quietly. "He can't come, Kaleb, it's too risky."

Right on cue, Kael knocked.

"Got it?" I asked.

He rolled his eyes, shoved me aside, and opened the door.

"What's up?" Kael asked.

"Nothing much. Shanntal and I are just hanging right now." He moved aside so Kael could see me.

I waved.

"Oh, hey, Shanntal. What's going on?" Kael waved back.

"She and Jayce are experiencing some, umm … friction. So we thought we'd hide out in here." Kaleb filled his friend in on some details while I paced around the room.

"Cool, but not cool. Friction isn't cool. Hiding out is cool." Kael muscled his way into the room. He went straight to the bed and sat down, making himself comfy.

Kaleb and I looked at each other, speechless. However, instead of escorting Kael out like I half expected, he abandoned me to go sit down beside his buddy. They both folded their arms and peered up at me, looking innocent.

"Perfect," I said aloud. If I hadn't known any better, I would've sworn they'd planned this.

"What's perfect? Am I missing something? What are you guys up to?"

Kaleb asked, "Why can't we just tell him?"

I shot Kaleb the evil eye. Now we had no choice, so I explained to Kael how Jayce had said the elements weren't safe having me around. I told him how the entire world depended on their survival, and then I filled him in on our plan to make a getaway so everyone would stay safe.

"Wow! That's pretty heavy," Kael said, rubbing his head and trying to process everything.

I briefly studied Kaleb, who seemed quite relieved Kael knew what was going on. Now he wasn't under so much pressure to keep this under wraps. We both looked at Kael, wondering what he would say next.

"I'm in! Where and when are we going?" he asked, punching his fists together.

"Kael," I said, using the most serious tone I had, "I need you to understand, Kaleb will be safe near me because they know we are connected. After what happened to Garrison, Daray owes me this much. I'll try my best to protect you, but there's no guarantee about what might happen. This will be extremely dangerous and we'll be completely outnumbered." I wanted him to be informed of absolutely everything before he committed.

"Don't worry that pretty face of yours. Believe me, I can handle myself." He stood up, flexed his muscles, and flashed his big, toothy smile.

"Well, when you put it that way, who can argue?" I laughed.

He was so big and fierce. His smile, however, made him look like the kindest fellow. He was built like a bear, with the seeming innocence of a child.

We were all in agreement. Kael was coming, and Kaleb seemed pleased.

"We'd better hurry up and get out of here before anyone else comes along or the whole clan decides to join us. Who's on watch?" Kaleb asked.

"Makan and Kynthia. Why?" Kael said.

"Where's Jayce? What if he connects?"

"I saw him just before I came up here. He's not really himself right now. Poor guy's quite depressed. Makan took his shift so he could take some time to pull himself together. He's sitting alone in the back room, sorting through things," Kael explained.

Hearing this made my mission even more important. I needed to get this settled quickly. "Okay, good, everyone's busy. So how do you suppose we get out of here?"

"Let me handle that one." Kael headed over to the window. He wore a mischievous look on his face and nodded once before pushing the window wide open. After providing another toothy smile, followed by a whooshing sound, he transformed. Now a large bird with distinctive, brilliant purple eyes flew directly in front of us.

Kael used his beak to pick up Kaleb by his shirt and lift him out the window. I ran to the window to see what was happening and looked down in time to watch him place Kaleb gently on the lawn near the property line. A few seconds later, he flew back into the room and scooped me up in one swift lift.

Once on my feet, I took a long last look at the big house. I'd miss each and every one of them dearly. They all meant the world to me, and because of this, I would leave. I'd go so they could stay safe. I didn't want any more harm coming to anyone I cared about. This way Jayce wouldn't feel so conflicted, because it simply wasn't right having to choose between the elements and me. I didn't expect him to make the choice, which was far too difficult, and I completely understood.

Even though leaving everyone hurt, it appeared to be the only way I could resolve things once and for all with the nightwalkers.

Perhaps one day this would all be nothing more than a distant memory. Perhaps one day Jayce and I could be together and not have everything go wrong. I knew we were meant to be, and I'd prove it by making things right and keeping everyone safe. With my new sense of determination, I walked out into the night, Kaleb and Kael on either side.

Union

~ Chapter Twenty-Two ~

The three of us made our way through the darkening forest. Being away from the others felt strangely uplifting. I supposed it was because I knew that they would be safer now.

A loud snapping sound came from a branch as it broke into pieces. What caused the break? Was a vampire or werewolf close? Possibly a doomahorn? Or maybe Jayce was coming after us, begging me not to leave. We froze in our places, listening carefully. Another rustling sound came a short distance away, right where we'd just been walking.

We all started feeling far more intense and aware of our surroundings. We quickly realized we weren't the only ones awake and moving around in the thriving forest. A hooting owl flew out of a nearby tree, while a family of raccoons scurried along the ground in the opposite direction. I hadn't really noticed this before; I'd been too wrapped up in myself to see there was more in the world than the three of us.

Moving a little more cautiously, we walked through the thick forest, heading toward the beach. No one really said much now. The guys stayed busy and alert ensuring there were only forest animals nearby. I felt quite nervous when I thought about the unknown ahead of us.

Jayce crossed my mind again. How had everything gotten so mixed up between us? We'd been so happy two days ago, now I was here without him. I couldn't ask him to choose between the elements and me; it wasn't fair. I would've resented him if he'd asked the same of me. It would've been the equivalent of telling me to choose between my family and him. Not a decision made lightly or one likely to go in my favor. So, there I was, leaving with Kaleb and Kael in the middle of the night, heading into the forest. Sacrificing my love to keep Jayce and the elements safe, to keep the world safe. He was right; they couldn't fight for me. My broken heart would mend in time. The losses and sacrifices, well, those would never be forgotten, but at least no more would happen on my behalf.

I was hurting. I didn't want to be away from Jayce. I needed him in my life. I knew it was selfish, but I couldn't help wanting the one person who made me feel happy. Why couldn't it be all about me for once? Suddenly, a sharp pain shot through my stomach. The piercing ache stole my breath and I crouched down, holding myself.

Kaleb placed his hand on my back. "What's wrong?"

Kael stopped walking and came back over to us.

"My stomach really hurts." I sat down gently on an uprooted tree trunk. "I need a minute."

Kael and Kaleb sat on either side of me, constantly scanning the forest to ensure we didn't have any uninvited guests stopping by. A few minutes passed and the pain subsided. I took my time standing, waiting to see if my stomach would act up again. When I felt more like myself, I said to the guys, "We'd better start moving if we plan to reach the beach tonight."

Kael spoke up. "Why don't I shift? I can get you there faster, and Kaleb is quick. He won't take long to catch up to us."

"Absolutely no way! We stick together. No one is running off alone. Think of us as Siamese triplets if you must. We're joined, and there's no way anything will break us apart. Understood?" I folded my arms across my chest to show I meant business. Sure I was a girl, but no way I'd let these big guys push me into anything I didn't think was safe. Our lives depended on it.

Kaleb laughed. "Kael, she won't give. Seriously, we best just do things her way. She's stubborn."

"Stubborn? More like a pain in the—"

"Now, now," Kaleb interrupted. "We've got to stick together. I'm with her no matter what. You can stay too, but only if you listen to what she says. She won't lead us astray."

Kael made a face, admitting defeat. We would take the slower way and stick together, even if it took us all night. Three hours later, we arrived on the road leading to the beach. At least the rest of the way was downhill, making it a much easier walk. We'd have to think up a way for Kael to fly us both up the steep hill. Walking back up would be the killer. We proceeded down the hill, and ten minutes later, we were walking on the sand.

'What do you think you're doing? Are you trying to get yourself killed?'

I gasped, hearing the voice of my love. Tears flooded my eyes, reminding me of what I was giving up.

'I'm sorry, Jayce, but it's the only way. I can't be held responsible for anything else bad that happens, or worse, if anyone gets hurt. This is too much to bear. Please, I don't want you feeling obligated to choose between the others and myself. That's not fair. I already see how much you're hurting just thinking about what to do. So, I'm going to find the vampires and get this all straightened out. I've made my choice, and there's no changing my mind. It's a done deal.'

I hoped he understood what I was trying to do.

'Done deal? How can you even say that?' Jayce shouted in my head.

I couldn't block him out. Perfect, he was miles away and there we were, still fighting.

'Jayce, I'm going to find Daray. I'm sorry, but it's the only way to keep all of you safe. I didn't want the outcome to be like this.'

'Find him for what?' he growled.

'So we can finally finish what we started. Everything's become far too complicated. I want my life back. If fate permits, my life will include you, but if I need to be with him to get simplicity back, so be it.'

'You're nothing like I thought. Do you really think you and that parasite are going to live happily ever after? Ugh, I hope you enjoy your eternity of hell.' Then he left me.

My heart broke into a thousand pieces. This had been my doing, but he'd left not knowing the truth or even putting up much of a fight. He didn't beg or plead, he just said his bit and that was that. Didn't I mean more to him? How could he leave me so easily?

"Oh, Kaleb," I said reaching for a hug. "What have I done?"

"You did what you had to do." He embraced me tightly.

My blood ran cold, a sure sign Daray was close. "Oh no. He's here," I whispered.

Kaleb let go and motioned Kael over with a nod. They took their places on either side of me.

Shea flew frantically in front of my face, her tiny wings fluttering furiously. "Shanntal, what are you doing? This isn't safe. Get out of here!"

I waved my hand, trying to shoo her away. Cleary aggravated, she dove down into Kaleb's pocket and turned on her dimmer. There wasn't time to react to her hastiness; we weren't alone. Lakylee was in sight.

Astonishing! I didn't normally have a reaction from her. This feeling had only happened around Daray. I felt quite surprised to learn I could sense all vampires and even half-breeds. This was great—my own built-in radar for bloodsuckers.

She looked wilder than ever. Kaleb and Kael steadied themselves as she approached. Her strength wouldn't be underestimated or ignored like the last time. Her long, dark hair was a complete mess; pieces stuck straight up. Her clothes were dirty and torn, which I assumed was from her last meeting with Kael.

She snarled when she spotted us.

Kael shifted back into a big black wolf. He returned a vicious growl, showing off his jagged fangs.

"Want some more?" she taunted.

He let out a rage-fueled growl.

"Kael, please. Don't do this," I pleaded.

Kaleb moved in front of the black wolf. He pressed his hand on Kael's chest, reminding him that now wasn't the time or place. Kael toned his growling down. Thankfully, Kaleb had managed to calm him, for the time being.

"Lakylee, I'm surprised to find you down here. Where's Daray?" I asked, taking a step forward.

"How would I know?" she hissed. "Ever since he found you again he's turned his back on us. We've always stood beside him, always been loyal. You ... you were the one who turned your back on him."

"Lakylee, I must see him. Tell me where he is." I took another step forward.

As I made my approach, she hissed and clawed the air. Kael dove forward and stood between us. Kaleb also moved in so he could close the gap if needed.

I took a few more steps until I stood beside Kael. "Lakylee, I'm trying my best to fix this for Daray. I never meant for any of this to happen." I gave her a line I hoped would get to her.

Her feelings for Daray were obvious and explained why she disapproved of me so much. I suspected Daray had feelings for her as well. Why else would he have kept her around so long? They shared a bond, which I disrupted by showing up. I needed to fix the mess I accidently made between them. Then I could have my chance to be with Jayce, and he wouldn't have to choose between the elements or me. It was a perfect plan. All the pieces were there. I just had to put them together again.

"What makes you think you can fix anything?" She eyed me curiously.

"That's between Daray and me," I replied sharply, then awaited her response. I wanted her as fired up as possible so she'd cooperate more when the time came.

Lakylee hissed and snarled. Venom dripped from her fangs, but she quickly licked away the poison, not wanting to waste a single drop. She readied herself, anticipating where to attack first. She shifted her eyes quickly to Kael and then Kaleb, before coming back around where she met my locked stare.

I had her exactly where I wanted. I bravely took another couple steps forward. "Lakylee, it is clear that you care for Daray and want to be together."

She released a defensive growl.

"Look, I'm trying to make sure that happens. We're not the same people from before. I don't belong in the night. We all know this, or at least we both do. I'm in love with Jayce. I understand how much Daray means to you because it's the same way I feel about Jayce."

Lakylee stopped snarling and seemed to be listening. I noticed her relaxed composure gave her the same appealing look the other vampires had. I'd only ever seen her ready to attack.

She brushed her hair off her face and said, "You'd step aside? You think we could be together? Like he was with you?"

Perfect! She was more in love than I'd ever imagined. I could wrap her around my little finger easily, so long as she and Daray ended up together.

"Yes, Lakylee, only this time even better. Things weren't right between us. I knew, by the way, he acted around me. His heart wasn't all in. You have a piece ... the bigger piece."

Her smile started off small and subtle, but continued growing until it stretched across her face. I actually found her attractive when she smiled. She no longer appeared quite so wild or scary.

"I'm really not sure where he is right now. He's either gone into hiding or dropped off the face of the earth. I've been trying to track him, but haven't had any luck."

I winked at Kaleb. It looked like my plan was going to work out perfectly. I would get us close enough to reach the doomahorns and werewolves so we could show them there was a better way to live. We could use this opportunity to teach them they didn't have to stay under the night curse. If they changed their ways, they'd be free and able to live their lives the way they wanted, not as prisoners.

Secretly, I also wanted to get closer to Daray. I knew he was dangerous and evil, but something about him made me think he had another side, a good side. Plus, he seemed to be an essential piece in my life puzzle, and I needed to find out where he fit. Everyone said he'd killed my family, but he'd told me himself that he didn't. Ginata's spirit warned me he was dangerous; however, she'd also said someone else was responsible for their deaths. I needed to get to the bottom of it. Who was behind this, and how could I stop them before they found me or killed anyone else I cared about?

Kael remained in wolf form; he didn't trust Lakylee. I was thankful because I still didn't have much faith in her quite yet either. She seemed calm while she told us everywhere she'd been in her quest to find Daray. She even mentioned how the entire coven had separated when Daray vanished, and that the others took off to the northern tip of the island to find more of their kind.

Driving from one end of the island to the other would've taken about thirteen hours. They had the ability to fly, and they'd split up two days ago. Surely they would've been there by now.

"What happened to the werewolves and doomahorns?" I blurted out, not meaning for my words to sound so direct.

"Ha! They're locked up still. Plus they're getting quite restless. I'll let them loose soon enough." She sounded like her typical evil self, but caught it and hung her head. "Sorry."

You could tell she was trying to refrain from the evil portion of her soul. Some goodness remained trapped beneath the surface; maybe there was still a chance for her.

The daylight hour neared, so Lakylee headed back to Daray's house for shelter, and we followed. Now was our time to get close to the others and see if we could convince them to help us. We arrived at the old, run-down house, and the place made my skin crawl as I thought about everything that went on inside. I readied myself then walked through the door.

The stench of death almost knocked me over. The smell seemed far worse than my last visit. My nostrils stung from the salt of the blood and musky aroma. I pinched my nose closed and held my breath. I looked at Kaleb and Kael for assistance but noticed they too were trying to overcome the stench. I decided to breathe through my mouth. I let go of my nose and motioned for them to do the same. We didn't want to offend her.

Lakylee retreated into the back room, but before leaving us she said, "You can have the run of the house. If the others come back, you're on your own. I never helped. Understood?"

"Got it," I said.

She took one last look at us and closed the door. A minute later, rays of sunlight poked through some of the cracks in the boarded up windows. Another morning arrived.

Changes

~ Chapter Twenty-Three ~

Shea took the opportunity to fly out of Kaleb's pocket. "Are you *crazy*?" she squeaked at us. "We have to leave. This isn't good. What are we even doing here? Come on, guys, let's go!"

I looked to Kaleb for support and then at Kael, who was back in human form. They both shook their heads no, the same as I did.

Shea crossed her tiny arms. She gave us a disapproving shake of her head before diving back into Kaleb's pocket.

We proceeded down the same hallway that Daray had led me through during my previous time in the house. I felt along the wall until I found the panel. I carefully opened the door, took a deep breath, and headed down the dark, squeaky staircase. Kaleb and Kael followed closely behind.

Once we reached the bottom of the stairs, I fumbled around in the darkness, trying to find the light Daray had turned on before. I had to mind what I was doing because I knew what lingered in the shadows. Shea flew out of Kaleb's pocket and began glowing. With her help, I found it easily.

"Ready ... set ... go." I tugged on the string.

The lights flicked on, and the beasts quickly reacted to our presence. Growls and snarls came from the three werewolves locked up in big steel cages. Two doomahorns chained to the wall stomped around, trying to bust free. All of them were clearly starving, and the only thing we seemed to be accomplishing was teasing them as entrees.

"Look at them, they're crazed with hunger." I pointed to the beasts. "We've got to feed them first. They won't listen to us now."

"Oh please! Do you think they've got loads of food just sitting around in a vampire house? Now, what do you suppose we do?" Kaleb snapped, frustrated by the situation.

I got an idea. "Kael, what's the fastest you can go when you're shifted?"

"Fast," he said proudly.

"Good. Fast is good. How are your hunting skills?"

"Hunting? I suppose they're okay. Why? What are you getting at?"

"I need you to hunt right now, and you've got to be quick. Bring the kills back here, but only animals, okay? We aren't feeding them any humans. They need to eat so they'll listen to what we have to say." Deep down I wondered if my crazy plan would even work.

"Yup, I'm on it!" Whoosh! Kael morphed into a large wildcat. He growled and raced up the stairs. Kaleb and I heard the floors squeak above us until he left the house.

"Wow, I have to admit it's pretty handy having him around." I was glad Kaleb talked me into bringing Kael. Now I wasn't sure we could've pulled this off without his help.

Kaleb and I kept our distance from the prisoners. They were so hungry they would've ripped us to shreds had we stood close enough.

Kael returned from his first hunt dragging a deer carcass down the stairs. With a quick flick of his head, he flung the corpse over to the prisoners. The werewolves stuck their claws through the cage bars, tearing pieces off the dead deer. The doomahorns lowered their giant black heads and ate the meat right off the bones.

"Kael, we're going to need more. Lots more!" I said.

The red eyes staring at me suddenly caused me to feel a bit nervous. What if this didn't work? What if they couldn't understand what I was saying? We were running out of alternatives as well as time. No matter what, this plan had to work.

Kael came and went. Every trip he dropped off loads of food for the prisoners. On his last trip, he shifted back into his human form. "Think they've eaten enough yet?" He wiped the sweat from his forehead.

Now I felt really nervous and started to have doubts about the plan. We were trapped underground, and if they decided to attack, I knew we wouldn't stand a chance. These creatures were dark and evil. What if they didn't listen? Was I prepared for this? Were any of us? I took a step back and looked at Kaleb and Kael, who both waited for my directions.

Shea flew out of Kaleb's pocket. Fluttering nearby, she suggested, "Why don't you try a werewolf first? Maybe if we convince them one at a time, we might stand a better chance."

I liked her idea. One would certainly be easier to handle if it decided to attack. I nodded in approval, and Kaleb started walking toward the closest cage.

"No, Kaleb." I pulled him back. "I'm doing this." I didn't want anything to happen to him. He'd done so much already, and I wanted to protect him for once.

"I don't know." He eyed me carefully. "You sure?"

"Kaleb, I must do this myself." I placed my hands on my hips, knowing how much he hated it. "If anything happens, well, you can say I told you so after you rescue me. Okay?"

"Fine, but be careful."

I took my first step nervously as I approached the cage. I gulped down a lump of fear rising up in my throat. I couldn't be afraid; if they sensed fear, everything we were trying to do would be over. Another deep breath followed by another step forward.

The werewolf kept a sharp watch, even though it stayed pressed against the back of the cage. About five feet away, my stomach decided to flip and my palms went sweaty. More doubts ran through my head. All I could think of was how dumb this idea seemed. What was I doing here? The werewolf paced back and forth, letting out low growls.

This is what had to be done, and I was the one who could do it. I took a deep breath and swallowed my fear, then stepped closer. As I calmed myself down, the werewolf mimicked me. We both cooled our adrenaline rushes, looking one another straight in the eye. I placed my hand on the lock.

"Problem, I need a key. I can't open this cage without one." I took my eyes off the beast to look back at Kaleb.

His face changed into a horrible expression. "Shanntal, move!" he yelled.

Instantaneously, I let go of the lock and pulled away from the cage as I felt a breeze against my hair. Shaking, I forced myself to spin around and face the cage. The beast snarled and took another swipe at me. I moved backward until I safely placed myself between Kaleb and Kael. The enraged werewolf continued to aggressively rattle the bars, trying its best to break free.

"Wow! That was way too close," I said, realizing the danger I'd just put myself in. "This won't work. Not like this. We've got to come up with something else."

"Can we talk upstairs for a minute?" Kael asked.

Kaleb nodded.

Disappointed, I followed my friends.

"Listen, maybe if I shift into a werewolf, you can show them the way through your actions with me. Perhaps they won't notice the difference. I am a pretty good actor. Why not let me try?"

"What makes you think you can pull it off?" Kaleb asked.

"Give me a sec." Kael stomped around the hallway before retreating outside. Kaleb and I stared blankly at one another, wondering what he was doing. A few seconds passed, then he returned with a thick chain in his hands.

"This oughta do the trick." He wrapped the chain around his neck and handed me the end.

Whoosh! I now held a werewolf in restraints. My prisoner winked his purple eye and let out a ferocious snarl.

Kaleb took the chain out of my hands. "C'mon. Down you go."

He fought with the chained beast and dragged him down the stairs. I heard Kael snarling and growling the entire way. The overall performance was quite convincing.

I waited a minute before making my way downstairs. The other creatures carried on far worse than before. Werewolves growled and pounded on the on the bars of their cages. The pair of doomahorns scuffed their hooves along the ground, watching with their fire burning eyes.

I walked toward Kaleb and spoke to the beast in his custody. "Do you want to be caged? Do you want to starve?"

Kael let out a snarl and took a swipe at me.

I dodged out of his way. "Or do you want to live another way? Do you want to be free to live your life the way you want?"

Kael calmed himself down. While he did this, the others seemed to settle down too. The plan was working. They were following his lead and treating Kael like an alpha wolf.

I moved closer after his rage changed to calmness. He sat still, watching me as I approached. A mean growl sounded out from behind us. The beast that tricked me earlier started communicating to Kael. I assumed it was telling him to attack while he had the opportunity. Kael responded with a loud, rumbling growl that sounded like a warning to the others. He was in charge now, so they'd better listen up.

The manner in which Kael assumed their identity and mimicked their personality was impressive. If I hadn't seen him shift, I never would have believed he wasn't one of them. I had to take a chance. The window of opportunity was shrinking, and if we didn't act now, it'd be too late.

"I want to show you that I mean you no harm." I took a step and Kael remained still. "I want you to trust me." I stepped even closer. "I want you to know there's a better way to live." I began unraveling the chain from around his neck. "I want you to be free."

He let out a small rumble, taking me by surprise, and I stumbled back a few steps. It took a second to reassure myself that Kael made the noise and he'd never hurt me. I moved back to where I stood before and finished removing the chain.

Kael stood free, acting unsure of what to do next. He let out a fierce growl, and the others responded. Whoosh, he shifted into human form.

I gasped. What was he doing? I looked to Kaleb for assistance.

Kael began speaking. "Thank you for showing me there's a better way to live. Thank you for allowing me to calm my rage." He looked at the others. "I'm free and always will be. I'll never let my rage cage me again."

I followed his lead. "When the moon is full, you will transform. There isn't any way around that part, but you don't have to remain in wolf form all the time. If you learn to tame the rage within, you can have better control over when you transform and when you don't."

The other werewolves pressed up closer to their cage doors.

Kael said, "They'll be all right. They want to know a better way. You can let them out now. They're no longer ruled by rage."

Kaleb grabbed the key off the wall beside him and tossed it over to me. I approached the closest cage. The werewolf was pressed up against the door. I hesitated, afraid of what happened the last time we tried. Was it another trick or real progress? I held my breath and unlocked the lock.

The werewolf pounced forward. The steel cage door knocked me around and smashed against me with a mighty force. I tried to regain my balance, only to be knocked once more. This time, the blow came from the werewolf, and I lost my balance. My arms went up in the air, and the beast sunk its sharp teeth deep into my arm. Blood gushed from my arm, still trapped in the mouth of my attacker. I screamed in pain, pounding my free hand against the powerful jaw, hoping to break the hold. It worked. I yanked my injured arm out when the beast opened its mouth to growl. Hurt and stunned, I tried my best to get away.

Everything felt like a dream, and I wasn't sure which way to go. I heard Kaleb and Kael shouting back and forth to one another, trying to get a handle on the beast before another attack. I stopped stumbling for a minute, in time to receive another smashing blow from the werewolf. The hit shoved me up against the wall. Beside me was the blood-red eye of a doomahorn looking right in my direction.

I thought I'd met my doom. I was about to die, and there wasn't a thing anyone could do to help me. This plan was so stupid; we never should have come. I scrambled to my feet and lifted my wounded arm up to protect my neck and face. I kept my good arm free so I could push the beast off when it came in for the kill. I'd fight as long as I could.

Once again, the werewolf broke free from Kaleb and Kael. I watched in horror as the mass of drool and fur charged straight for me. Excruciating pain radiated through my wounded arm from another bite. I cried out. Blood sputtered out of the new wound and sprayed over everything.

A loud grunt came from the doomahorn beside me. A second later, an agony-filled howl screeched out. The werewolf swayed around before hitting the floor and lying lifeless before me. I stood in a state of disbelief. Thick, murky blood poured out of two gaping puncture holes in its chest.

I tried to move away from the werewolf, but my knees buckled, sending me crashing to the ground. My arm hurt so badly. I couldn't think about anything except the pain. I curled into a fetal position on the floor, feeling ready to faint. Remembering I wasn't safe, I opened my eyes. The red eye of the doomahorn stared back at me.

I clenched my eyes shut, expecting the doomahorn to finish what the werewolf started. A few seconds passed, but nothing else happened. I opened one eye and found the red eye had now become a light shade of blue. The dark fur had changed into a shining white coat. The double horn merged into a longer single horn on top of its beautiful head.

Astounded, I sat up on the floor, cradling my injured arm. I stared in awe at the amazing creature. I glanced around for Kaleb and Kael, wanting to make sure I wasn't the only one seeing this. They both stood with their mouths hung open, while Shea flew beside them wearing a huge smile across her tiny face.

I turned back around just as the newly transformed creature flicked her long, flowing white hair while shaking her head. She shimmered from head to hoof. There was no sign of the evil beast that had been there moments earlier.

Sharp, burning pains shot throughout the bite marks that covered most of my arm. My injuries started getting the better of me. The sight and smell of my blood made me dizzy. I looked to the others for assistance. "Guys, I could really use some help."

From the look on Kaleb's face, I understood the extent of my injuries. I was in pretty rough shape.

The shimmering beauty came over to me first. She placed her shining horn gently down on my arm. I stared at the glorious creature in sheer amazement. She was so beautiful. My eyes drifted down to her horn on my arm because the pain was no longer there. No marks remained; it was as if I'd never been bitten. There was no evidence remaining from my near-death struggle.

This felt so much like a dream. I couldn't comprehend that an honest to goodness unicorn stood before us. How had she fallen under the powers of the nightwalkers to become such an evil beast? I got up from the floor and ran my hands through her silky hair. "Thank you. Thank you so much for saving me." I looked deep into her light blue eyes while I spoke.

'Thank you very much for saving me. I'm forever in your debt. You showed me the way back into the light.'

We all heard the voice of the unicorn, though she hadn't spoken any words aloud.

"What about the other one?" I pointed at the doomahorn still chained up to the wall. Its dark head hung low.

'She will be fine in due time. It may take a while, but when she's ready, she'll come around. Some of us just need a little longer to find the light. Dusk isn't too far off, so we should get out of here.'

I knew she was right, yet still felt terrible about leaving the others behind. We helped her to break free from the spell, so what if we could do the same for the other doomahorn or even the werewolves? Wasn't that worth staying for?

The werewolves paced around frantically in their cages. However, the chained doomahorn didn't seem to be nearly as aggravated. Though her head remained down, the fiery red eyes, which burned so fiercely before, now held a hint of light blue in the center.

"We can't leave. Look!" I pointed at the doomahorn. "Don't you understand? We might not get another chance to help them. So I'm asking, will you help me?"

Not one offered.

I stared at them in disgust. Hadn't they witnessed what happened? Goodness still remained in these creatures. The unicorn proved it. We couldn't just leave them behind.

"Fine," Kaleb said, after a moment.

I felt thankful he'd broken the silence and chose to help me. This sent a rush of happiness throughout me. We were definitely doing a good thing.

Kaleb grabbed onto the chain of the doomahorn and led her upstairs. When they passed by, I noticed her eyes were showing twice as much blue. Definitely a good sign!

The unicorn followed Kaleb and the doomahorn upstairs. Kael decided to stay and help me unlock the werewolf cages, but Kaleb yelled from upstairs. "You've got to get out now. Time's up! Move it!"

Kael and I made a dash for it. We got to the top of the stairs when we heard the door to the back room creak open. Dusk arrived just as Lakylee emerged from her slumber. She took one look at us, then the unicorn, and she let out a ferocious snarl. I paused only long enough to exchange a quick glance with her. Kael grabbed me by the arm, and we ran full speed down the hallway. I heard another snarl followed by a crash that sent wood splinters flying past us. Lakylee must've been quite upset, and the thought of that made me run even faster.

Shea flew between us. "You're just about there, don't slow down!"

We rounded a corner and saw the front door wide open. Kael and I burst through the opening and kept on running right out into the overgrown gardens.

However, I was quickly running out of breath. I didn't have the boys' speed or stamina. I started slowing down just as Kaleb emerged in front of us. Beside him stood two beautiful unicorns. We'd succeeded. It made me feel so proud. We hadn't saved them all, but at least we'd managed to change a couple doomahorns.

"Get on, Shanntal!" Kaleb hollered, leaping onto the bare back of the unicorn.

I forced myself to keep running. When I reached him, he grabbed me by the arm and pulled me up behind him. Kael leapt onto the other one. The unicorns raced away from their prison. I looked back at the house where Lakylee stood alone on the front deck, watching us depart.

The look of betrayal written all over her face weighed heavily on my conscience. For a moment, I even found myself feeling bad for her. She'd shown me a different side, one that wasn't dark or evil like she typically projected. I watched her grow smaller while the distance between us grew larger. Why wasn't she coming after us? Could she also be capable of more? How much goodness remained in her? Then, I had the worst thought, what if I'd just wrecked my chance to find Daray and learn everything he knew about my past life and my family's deaths? Without her help, how would I ever get near him?

United

~ Chapter Twenty-Four ~

Our group traveled farther away from Daray's house, despite the blackening night. I couldn't fight the overwhelming guilt consuming my mind. Lakylee had trustingly opened the house to us, and we betrayed her. Actually, I was the one who had betrayed her, and worst of all, I did it when she'd just started to trust me. It wasn't how she should've been treated, especially after letting her guard down. I knew she had the power and means to track us down, and was fully aware of the fact that she still had two werewolves on her side. The three of them would make a lethal combination.

I deeply regretted the decision to leave Daray's house. We could've made up some kind of story about how the doomahorns transformed into the unicorns. We could have blamed it on the dead werewolf. Oh, who was I kidding? We were fortunate to have made it out alive and in one piece.

The unicorns agreed to stay with us for the night and would go their own way once the sun rose. They were a dream come true for me. Their beauty was even more magnificent than I ever could've imagined. When I read stories to my younger sisters, I'd always been drawn to ones describing the undeniable magic of unicorns. There we were rescuing not only one, but two of them. At that moment, I felt like the girl in those stories.

The forest continued to make sounds and cast shadows around us, putting me more on edge. We weren't in the best position, and I hoped to find some form of shelter soon, mainly before we encountered any wicked vampires or vicious werewolves.

The graceful stride of the unicorns put my worried mind a little more at ease. I found myself calming from the relaxing rhythm of their traveling hooves. Moonlight broke through the treetops, reflecting off their shimmering coats. It helped light up the night and kept the shadows at bay. Their presence reminded me that we had pure goodness on our side. In every book I'd read or movie I'd watched, the good side usually prevailed. I hoped it was true in our case, and that we had enough luck to get us safely through the night.

Regrettably, the further we went, the darker our surroundings got. Even the moonlight couldn't sneak through these thick trees. Shadows flooded around us, casting misleading shapes that played with our minds. After this much time in the forest, the trees and bushes began to look the same. This journey was one of the longest nights I remembered. Whenever I thought day would break, I was shocked to find nothing lighting up the darkened sky. We could've been walking in circles and not known any better.

Perhaps my sense of timing was off due to the fact we were too deep in the forest for me to clearly see the sky. Or maybe because of the simple fact it was the middle of the night, and I was beyond exhausted.

"It feels like we've been going all night," I complained.

"I hear you," Kael said. "My butt is killing me." He hopped off the unicorn and started walking.

"Complain all you want, but we need to keep moving," Kaleb said, pushing us onward.

"Do you think they're going to come after us?" I asked.

"You've seen it for yourself. Lakylee seemed pretty ticked off to me," Kaleb said. "Since she's not with the other vampires, I'm not really sure what she will do. The werewolves are harder for her to control. Either way, we can't afford to leave the chance. Let's keep going."

We sustained our rhythm and kept on moving, this time in silence. So many things raced through my mind. My first thoughts were of Jayce and his warm kisses. Then I wondered how to set things right with Daray. I needed to learn more about my past, and only he knew my secrets. Lastly, I daydreamed about what life would be like after I accomplished this. I needed to be with Jayce, but the situation with Daray still stood in the way.

I remained lost in my thoughts for a while longer, though something began to bother me. No matter how hard I tried, I couldn't make myself believe Daray was as bad as everyone said. Yes, I'd seen the monster in him firsthand, but that same man had also left me alone and unharmed in the vampire house. It made me wonder if the old Daray still lived somewhere inside him too. He'd said kind words about my family, and if he genuinely loved me, what would he gain by killing them? Even the thought of him doing such a thing caused a bit of hatred to grow. If you truly loved someone, you would never want to cause them pain or have them feel a loss, especially the loss of their entire family. That would be an unforgivable act. I had a building suspicion there was more behind this than any of us were aware of. A feeling in my stomach told me Daray would be the key to finding out who was responsible.

I had an unexplainable sense of respect for him that I couldn't deny. Perhaps it was due to the past we'd once shared. After all, our past was one that couldn't be ignored. He'd saved me, searched for me, and then forced himself to let go when he saw I wasn't ready to commit. He'd even somewhat backed off when he realized I loved Jayce with all my heart and soul. Perhaps instead of retaliating, he would just leave me alone so we could end this feud. Then, Jayce and I could be together peacefully, and no one else would get hurt. Lakylee loved Daray, and it was clear he shared feelings for her too. In spite of everything, she managed to fill the void when I was absent from his life.

Another thought surfaced, suddenly bringing me sadness. It would only be a matter of time until the unicorns left us. I felt proud to have helped bring them back from the darkness, and I wanted to share their light with the world. I wanted to show them to all the little girls so they could believe too.

I remembered the moment when the unicorn healed my wounded arm by a single touch of her silver horn. I found myself secretly wanting to ask if she could use her magic once again to heal my breaking heart. I missed Jayce with every ounce of my being. I wondered if he missed me as much. What was he doing? Was he awake and on guard, or sleeping peacefully in his fluffy bed?

I let out a flustered sigh. I had to try very hard to put my mind to rest. If only I could shut these thoughts off completely, just to be numb and think of absolutely nothing for a few minutes. I needed to find some form of peace. Silently, Kaleb reached back and gently slid my arms forward. I rested my head on his back and wrapped my arms around him.

I loved his ability to pick up on my feelings without my having to announce them to the world. He knew when I was in pain or scared, and always knew when I was in serious trouble, sometimes even before I did. He looked back at me when I lifted my head, and I gave him a grateful smile. Kaleb wasn't only my protector; he was my big brother and very best friend.

I knew all these trials were for more than just Jayce and me. They were for literally everyone because I was the one person who risked having the elements destroyed. That wasn't something I could live with. The elements were my friends, and I needed to protect them the best I could. Meriel had been hurt, and Garrison was killed because of me. The truth of the matter was Lakylee never would've been in the forest that night if she weren't searching for me. If I hadn't escaped from Daray, none of this would've happened. I'd figure out a way to track down Daray and sort this out peacefully. Together, we could come up with some kind of agreement that kept him and the other nightwalkers away from the people I cared about. I couldn't bear it if anyone else got hurt. This had to stop.

We came to an opening in the forest, and the unicorns slowed their pace. By this point I felt overwhelmingly tired. I wasn't used to staying up all night. Thirty-nine hours had passed since I'd slept, and the effects had finally caught up.

Kaleb hopped down and lent me his hand for support so I could dismount. Kael followed us further into the field where the grasses and wildflowers were quite tall. The unicorns stayed on the right side of the clearing. Their shimmering heads lowered as they began to feed on the lush greenery.

Kael dropped his large body to the ground. "Guys, I'm beat." He let out a yawn and sprawled across the grassy field. Once settled, he'd completely disappeared from sight.

Kaleb nodded in agreement after watching his sidekick vanish. A second later he flopped down in the wild grass. Once he vanished from view, I heard him say, "Wow, the sky's amazing! Look at them ... they're so ..." and his sentence trailed off with a big yawn.

The tall grass and wildflowers managed to hide their large bodies quickly. Pieces poked up all around to conceal them. It was really good camouflage, and I wished it would be enough to keep us safe. At least we were out of sight from anyone passing by. I wasn't sure this would do anything to protect us from immortals, but hoped it'd be enough for tonight.

The guys made the ground appear so comfortable. I watched the unicorns for a moment while they strolled nearby, still feasting on the greens. They seemed quite peaceful and content. If danger were near, I didn't think they'd remain so relaxed.

Too many doubts raced around, and I couldn't put my mind at ease. This certainly wasn't the safest place to stop. We were completely exposed with little protection, plus, it was the middle of the night. We were the outsiders in this vast forest, which meant anything living there could sneak up from behind, come head on, or even charge us from the sides. Thick trees surrounded the whole area, yet we chose to stop right in the middle. What made the unicorns decide to rest there, of all places? I understood we were in a desperate situation, but seriously, were grass and wildflowers the only protection we could muster?

My body suddenly felt so fatigued. The weight of all the stress and exhaustion pushed me heavily to the ground. I gave in and silently dropped to my knees before lying down. My head rested comfortably near a small patch of clover. I had no strength left to fight with myself over these doubts racing in my mind. Come what may, tonight there was no chance of me going any further. I rolled onto my side and hoped for a four-leaf clover to be somewhere in the patch. Tonight I was betting on some good luck to keep all of us safe.

I enjoyed the magnificent aroma of the lilies, poppies, wildflowers, and daisies. Their heady scent mixed with the sounds of the light breeze—leaves rustling on trees, grasses whistling as they arc with the wind—was a perfect lullaby.

I rolled onto my back and gazed up at the sky. The stars sparkled just as they did every night. They were happy and in love. *Would I ever get to go up to the stars?* I drifted off to sleep.

The morning sun woke me, shining down brightly upon us. Birds chirped happy songs in the distance. Another beautiful day had arrived. There wasn't a cloud to be seen in the bright blue sky.

I sat up to take notice of the tiny clover patch. Sure enough, a lucky four-leaf clover rested right in the center. I'd placed my bet right! We'd managed to make it safely through the entire night. While I sat there contemplating whether or not I should keep the luck with me, one of the unicorns began nibbling. I watched her munch down on the clover.

"Oh, well, there goes my luck," I laughed.

"You? Luck? Now that's a funny one." Kael let out his boisterous laugh.

"Shut up, Kael," I retorted after I heard Kaleb snicker.

It was far too early to deal with the ridiculing. I'd just opened my eyes and needed a few more minutes to find my inner strength, which enabled me to ignore Kael's wisecracks. This early, his comments seemed to penetrate straight through me. I already knew people considered me unlucky. Geez, I probably fit perfectly into the shoes of the unluckiest person on the entire planet. Yet, I didn't need a big oaf telling me things I already knew. I lived this life. I knew the outcome so far, but things were going to change. It was my time to shine.

I'd gathered my bearings and decided I was civil enough to deal with the guys, so I got up and moved closer. I stood above them and shook my head as the two muscle heads wrestled on the ground. They took turns jabbing one another in the stomach and laughed out loud while they pretended to meet the blows.

Kaleb and Kael had bonded so closely. Kael would never replace Garrison, but he was the perfect person to fill the void left behind. Kael was part of our family, and we were both grateful to have him. Besides, all his joking around was good for Kaleb. Personally, I found his jokes quite annoying, especially first thing in the morning, but Kaleb laughed at every single one. Mind you, I was known to be quite cranky when I first woke up.

My stomach interrupted playtime with a loud grumble. They both stopped and looked up. "Wow, totally sorry guys, but I'm starving. We need a plan. Where are we going?"

"Well, you could always go home," Kaleb suggested.

Home? I couldn't think of any other place I'd rather be. "You might be onto something there, Kaleb." I reached into my pocket and pulled out my cell phone. I went to dial, but there was no service. It annoyed me, but really didn't surprise me since we were standing in the middle of a forest. "No service."

A frustrated sigh slipped out of Kaleb's mouth.

"Figures! That's technology for ya," Kael griped.

The boys got up, making it clear we were about to start hiking. One problem—which way was home? I was totally confused as to where we were.

'We'll lead you out safely before we part ways.' The larger unicorn addressed my concerns.

"Thank you," I said graciously.

I took a last glance around. Stunning magenta, violet, peach, yellow, and even some tiny white flowers covered the majority of the landscape. Random patches of clover were scattered all over the place. Small bushes and wild ferns filled the open gaps between the trees, which outlined the clearing.

The tranquility must've appealed to us all. The magnificence of the forest matched the beauty of the unicorns; perhaps it was why they'd stopped here in the first place. I'd always keep this picture fresh in my mind. It would be my tranquility place whenever I needed somewhere peaceful to go. No matter how bad things got, I'd always feel better coming back here, even if it was only in my mind.

The five of us continued on our journey with the unicorns in the lead. In the day, the forest seemed full of bright colors, deep and dark greens that were accompanied with gentle nature sounds. The sun was bright and warm as it cut through the trees, casting away the lurking shadows. Everything seemed better, mostly because we no longer had the threat of running into any nightwalkers.

Jayce lingered in my mind as I daydreamed about the two of us lying in the beautiful ferns, sharing our electrifying kisses among the sweet smelling wildflowers. I missed him more with every passing second.

Loyal Kaleb placed his arm around me. I felt so bad that he was burdened with my pain.

"I'm sorry," I whispered so the others couldn't hear.

He didn't say anything. He just squeezed a little bit harder, and I knew we were bonded together no matter the outcome.

Kael spun around. "What's going on here?" he asked. "Am I missing something?"

"Nope, nothing at all. Kaleb was just keeping me company for a little while." I let go of him so he could catch up to his buddy.

Kael and Kaleb raced ahead, roughhousing their way through the thick bush. From the ruckus they made, I doubted anything would be brave enough to come within two hundred yards.

The unicorns led us steadily in the direction we needed to go. I positioned myself so I could walk between them. I still felt amazed by their presence. Unicorns had always been chalked up to being nothing more than a myth, but these two were the living proof. They blessed me with a new sense of hope because they reminded me there was goodness left in the immortal world—it was just hidden. However, having this kind of goodness on our side made anything possible.

We managed to make our way to a road.

'This is where we must part ways. Shanntal, we'll always be in your debt. Thank you so much for releasing us from the dark spell and showing us the way back into the light where we belong.'

I couldn't help myself. I walked up and wrapped my arms around her neck. "I'm so happy I could help. I hope to see you again soon. Thank you for everything."

'You are most welcome. I'm glad I got the pleasure of meeting you in person.'

Why would she say that? Glad to meet me? I smiled at the glorious animal standing before me, but in the next moment found myself wondering what kind of name would a unicorn have.

'Oh, sweet girl, you know me. We met once before in your dreams. I knew you were coming to save me. We all did.'

"Gabriella?"

'Yes!' She shook her flowing mane. *'I am Gabriella.'*

"Wow!" was all I could say.

Gabriella turned and began to wander away. I quickly proceeded over to the other unicorn, gave her a big hug, and thanked her for everything.

I rejoined the guys, but spun around to take a final look at the unicorns before they departed.

"Thank you again for helping me. I'm so glad I got to believe in you!" I called out. Then, I stepped out of the forest with Kaleb and Kael on either side.

The three of us strolled down the road, enjoying the warmth and freedom of the beautiful, sunny day. A little ways down the road, I pulled my phone out of my pocket.

"Perfect!" I announced to the guys.

They both stopped.

"We've got service!" I waved my phone, accompanied with a silly-happy dance. I was extremely excited to be going home today.

I dialed, and Uncle Dane answered on the second ring.

"Hiya, Uncle Dane. It's Shanntal." I couldn't wipe the smile off my face even if I tried. His voice sounded so nice.

"Heya, kiddo! What's going on?"

"Well, I actually just called to check in and see if you were home. I'm on my way with Kaleb and Kael, but I need to speak with you when I get there. Are you going anywhere today?"

"Nope, should be around all day. Can't wait to see you."

"Great! See you soon then. Love you." I was looking forward to going home. I couldn't contain my excitement. I wanted to run the whole way just to get there quicker.

"So?" Kael teased. "Excited much?"

"So ... he knows we are on our way and he sounds very pleased. I'm sure it won't be a problem for us to stay there. Let's go!"

"Wow! Someone's pretty pumped to get home," Kael said, sounding somewhat hurt.

I knew exactly what he was getting at. "Kael, both you and Kaleb will be staying with me. The three of us are a team now. Wherever one goes, the other two follow." I was glad to have them both on my team.

Kael bestowed a goofy grin as he charged Kaleb, knocking him to the ground. Out popped his renowned laugh. They giggled as they got up, and together we headed home.

Rekindled

~ Chapter Twenty-Five ~

A short time later we arrived on my road. I could see towering evergreens standing proudly in the front yard.

Excitement coursed through me. I couldn't wait to burst through the front door to tell them everything would be okay, and I'd never leave them scared or worried ever again. However, the truth was, I really didn't know how things would turn out. Jayce wasn't speaking to me, and I was trying to keep my distance from the elements and other shifters. Even worse, I still didn't know where Daray was, and I'd just betrayed Lakylee.

Argh! Why did everything always have to be so complicated? I wanted simplicity; I longed for it. How did my life get so turned around again? Would I ever be able to fix things or get it back on the right track?

We arrived on the front lawn, but I stopped prior to reaching the front door. Did I need to knock, or simply walk in? Suddenly, I felt unsure and my excitement was quickly replaced with insecurity. I hadn't been home for a while, and it didn't really feel like my home anymore. After the fight and how I'd left, I felt more like an uninvited houseguest. I lifted my arm to knock, when the front door swung open. Auntie Steph stood in the doorway, wearing a smile that stretched ear to ear.

"What took you so long?" She pulled me in for a long hug.

"Trust me, we came as fast as we could." I hugged her back tightly, forgetting about my previous inhibitions.

"I'm glad to see you guys. I've missed all your faces."

"Hiya, Steph!" Kael said.

"Nice to see you," Kaleb said, a bit more politely.

"Well, come on in. We've been waiting for you all day, it seems like." She stood off to the side, and we walked in. She hugged each of us as we entered.

I felt ridiculous for thinking I didn't belong here. This was my home, and these people were my family. Of course I belonged. Uncle Dane sat on the couch, not bothering to get up. I noticed that there was someone beside him, but couldn't see his or her face because of the way Uncle Dane was sitting. It blocked most of the view. Suddenly, I needed to know who was sitting there, so I walked into the room to greet them properly. My uncle looked at me, wearing the biggest smile, but my heart skipped when I recognized the other person.

"Jayce? What … why are you here?" I froze in my tracks. I felt dumbfounded. Could my mind be playing tricks? I waited to jolt awake from this dream.

"Well, hello to you too," he said.

My heart raced and my stomach filled with butterflies. He looked perfect sitting there in front of me. He was everything I wanted, all that I needed, but it wasn't safe for him to be there. It didn't make any sense. What had happened? What caused him to be here? He knew it wasn't a good idea to be around me.

Jayce got up from the couch and moved closer to me. I noticed the tiny nod he gave my uncle, so I shifted the direction of my stare. Uncle Dane stood up quietly and retreated out of the living room. That's when I looked around and noticed everyone else had also moved into the kitchen. They remained close enough to see and hear what was happening between Jayce and me, but not one spoke a word.

Great, now I felt ambushed. Everyone seemed fine with the fact Jayce was over, but how could they forget about the dangerous situation we were currently in? My emotions were conflicted. I was ecstatic to see him, but at the same time concerned he was there. I realized him being here meant he had chosen me, not the elements. His decision wasn't one I could live with; it didn't sit well. I wouldn't be the one who broke them up. He had to leave.

"Jayce, I'll ask you again. Why are you here?"

"I'm here for you, Shanntal."

"Jayce, you can't be. The elements ..."

He moved a stride closer and cut me off. "I want us more than anything else. Don't you understand? You are my life. I need you."

His words melted me, but reality quickly sank back in. "Jayce, you must think about the elements. You can't leave them because they need you more."

I sat down on the couch, not liking the feeling of being so exposed. I knew everyone was watching and eavesdropping.

Jayce sat beside me. He took my hand and wove his fingers through mine. A familiar warm sensation ran through my entire body.

I pulled my hand out of his grasp. "I can't put you in harm's way." It broke my heart to push him away, but it felt like the right thing to do. I was doing my best to keep him and the others shielded from the wrath of the nightwalkers.

"Everyone knows you mean more to me than anything else ever could. They understand because they feel it too. They've never seen me so connected to another before. You've become a big part of our lives, and in case you wondered, they love you dearly too. The elements also know they cannot fight for you. However, I can, and promise I will." He pulled my hand back over and held it firmly on his lap.

"Jayce." I began tearing up. "Don't get me wrong. I want you more than anything too, but this won't work, not right now. Daray is in hiding. No one knows his whereabouts. Meaning he could show up at any time, and I couldn't live with myself if something happened to you."

"Shanntal, I've never felt the way I do for you, ever in my entire life. I can't bear us being apart. When you're gone, it feels like half of me is missing. Please say you'll have me because I'm not going anywhere until you say you don't want me. Can you do that?" His big brown eyes looked back at me sternly.

Of course you know I won't ever say those words. That's not fair. I want you to stay, Jayce, but it's too dangerous. I can't live with the fear of something happening to you."

"I'll be fine."

"Especially, if it happens because of me. Don't you understand I'm trying to protect you?" I felt frustrated and needed him to understand my reasons. "I have to get things settled with Daray. He's a big piece of this puzzle, and I know he'll be able to set things right for everyone."

"Daray? So, we're back to this again?" Jayce pulled away and got up from the couch.

"Jayce, please try to understand."

"I don't, and I'm not sure I ever will."

I felt completely torn. This was getting us nowhere. Now I was the one that couldn't choose. I needed Jayce so badly, but I wanted him to be safe more. If he stayed, I'd surly be happy having him close, but on the other hand, he'd be in a constant state of danger. If he left, no doubt I'd be miserable, but he'd remain unharmed. So why was this so difficult? The answer was pretty clear. He had to go. I was about to say my conclusion when Kaleb came over and stood between us.

"Sorry to intervene, but, Shanntal, what exactly do you think you're doing?" He asked.

"Kaleb?" I placed a hand on my hip, warning him.

"No offense, but I think you're wrong about this. The nightwalkers automatically win if you continue living your life in fear. Put Daray in the past and leave him there. Doing this will enable you to pursue a future with each other." He pushed Jayce and me closer together.

"Geez, Kaleb! Way to gang up."

He smiled briefly, but then his facial expression hardened. "I feel your pain and how much you hurt when Jayce isn't around. I know how much you love him."

I nodded and looked down. I couldn't handle Jayce staring so intensely at me.

Kaleb continued, "Jayce is a big boy. He's well aware of the dangers. Keep in mind, he's also free to make his own choices, and if I'm not mistaken … I believe he's chosen you."

I slowly lifted my head and looked at Jayce. From the first moment our eyes met, I knew we were meant to be together. I also knew I didn't want him to leave again because I preferred how good I felt when he was close to me. I was at my best when he was by my side. Still confused, I broke eye contact and looked away.

Jayce closed the gap between us. He gently placed his hand under my chin, lifted my head upright, and held it in place. My gaze drifted back to his.

"I was a fool. I shouldn't have let you go. We are meant for each other, I see that." His head tilted slightly when he looked deeper into my eyes. "Don't you?"

I felt the need to look away, even pull away, but couldn't move. If I didn't choose my words carefully, he might give up on me, and I couldn't live with that outcome. I went to speak, but he cut me off by placing a passionate kiss on my lips. I didn't have the strength to fight him off, nor did I want to. I gave my heart back to the man who meant the most to me. I wrapped my arms around him and got lost in our kiss.

Kaleb, who still stood beside us, shouted, "Now that's what I'm talking about! Do you see this love?" He turned to the others. "This is the kind worth fighting for."

"Hear, hear!" Kael cheered.

After Jayce and I had broken out of our embrace, I looked at my aunt and uncle, who stood side by side. They had their arms wrapped around each other, and they both smiled at me. I saw how pleased they were that things were being mended.

Kaleb nudged Jayce. "Great to see ya, man."

"Likewise, Kaleb," Jayce said.

"Uncle Dane, Auntie Steph? I know this isn't the biggest place, but would you mind if we all stayed here for a few nights, just until we can get someplace else arranged?"

"You can stay as long as you like. All of you!" Auntie Steph said. "Don't forget about the basement, it's quite spacious down there. We can easily set up some beds. There's plenty of room for everyone." She looked at my uncle for approval.

"For sure," he agreed.

"See! Everything's all set." She grinned happily. "Oh, and by the way, I already anticipated something like this, so I took the liberty of setting up the basement before you guys arrived."

Uncle Dane laughed. "Of course you did."

Auntie Steph and Uncle Dane were delighted to have me home. I was happy to be back in the place where I could sleep safely in my own bed, take a nice warm shower, and change into clean clothes. I was looking forward to the sweet satisfaction of the small things home provided.

Everyone came out of the kitchen to join us in the living room. Jayce sat by my side and held my hand the entire afternoon. I wasn't sure he'd ever let go again. I felt safe and secure, but most of all, whole.

I sat in a state of awe surrounded by the love of my life, my family, and closest friends. There wasn't any place I'd rather have been.

Dinner came around and with perfect timing because I was starving. Auntie Steph headed into the kitchen and I followed.

"Do you need some help?" I asked.

"Oh, sweetie, I'll always accept your help." She gave me a quick hug.

"I love you, Auntie Steph," I said as we ended our embrace.

"My word! Look at the two of us," she said, quickly wiping her eyes, which had started to tear up. "We're supposed to be preparing dinner, not standing in the kitchen crying. I'm just so glad to have you back home."

"Me too. I sure missed you guys."

"I admit, I'm pretty happy to hear that. We missed you even more. Well, now, before I start crying again, let's get dinner ready for these men." Auntie Steph smoothed her brown, shoulder length hair, straightened out the sweater on her tall, thin frame, and a few seconds later was back to her cheerful self.

"Spaghetti is filling and quite easy to prepare. Think we should make that?"

"Smart girl. Not just a beautiful face. Double threat!" She went to the cupboard, and pulled out noodles and a couple of cans of tomato sauce.

"Can I offer you ladies some help?" Jayce wrapped his arms around my waist before sneaking a quick kiss on my neck.

Oh, how I adored the way his kisses lingered. I felt myself turning into mush in his arms.

"Hey, Jayce, what do you think you're doing, man? Let those girls be girls. They're doing exactly what they're meant to, preparing food for us hungry men. Ha-ha!" Kael joked.

Auntie Steph and I both shot Kael a warning look. He needed to be aware that if he wanted dinner, he'd better quit now, or he'd be the one cooking for everyone else.

"Help? Going once, twice, my final offer." Jayce smiled his devilishly handsome grin.

"Your offer is tempting, but must be declined because it looks like we've got things under control. Thanks, though." I winked, and then he returned to the others.

Auntie Steph and I enjoyed our bonding time as we prepared dinner. It was a great escape from the men, even if it was for only a little while. I'd been growing tired of being the lone female around. Talking to just guys was an all-new experience.

The big pasta feast was ready. Just in time, because everyone seemed good and hungry from the pleasant aroma of basil and oregano coming from the food. There were only four stools along the breakfast bar, so we decided to spread out. Jayce and I let the others sit in the kitchen, and we made ourselves comfortable gathered around the living room table. The candle burning added quite a romantic touch and took my memory back to the time when we lived our lives full of love, not filled with fear.

Uncle Dane held up his glass for a toast. "To true love and dear friends."

"To true love and dear friends," we repeated.

Then it hit me. He was completely right. At that moment, life felt perfect. I was with my best friends, Kaleb, and Kael. I had my family close by and the love of my life beside me.

Jayce and I ate our pasta in our little love cove while the others enjoyed their dinner around the breakfast bar. Once everyone was finished, they made their way back into the living room. I retreated from the group to help Auntie Steph start cleaning up some of the mess.

Uncle Dane and Jayce entered the kitchen.

"Out you ladies go. You've made us a wonderful dinner, but now it's our turn to clean up." Uncle Dane grabbed the cloth out of Auntie Steph's hand and took over washing the larger dishes, which wouldn't fit in the dishwasher.

Jayce took the drying towel out of my hands, but not before giving me another kiss. Auntie Steph and I joined Kaleb and Kael.

"Great dinner, gals!" Kael said. "Sure did hit the spot." He put his hand up toward his mouth, kissed his fingers, and extended his arm as he threw us a kiss. "Fantastico!"

"Thanks, Kael. I'm glad you enjoyed our cooking so much," Auntie Steph said, blushing from the compliment.

After a short while, Jayce and Uncle Dane re-joined the group. Uncle Dane sat down and struck up a conversation. "So what have you guys been up to?"

Kaleb began to explain how we left Jayce and the others behind. Kael got quite excited while he reminisced about our adventure—so excited that he cut Kaleb off in order to tell his version. Kaleb sat quietly while Kael described our meeting with Lakylee down at the beach, and how I convinced her I didn't love Daray, but knew she did. He told them how we went back to the vampire house and freed two of the doomahorns. He got up out of his seat, mimicking my fight with the werewolf. He showed how it attacked me not only once, but a few times, and described how it shredded my arm. As everyone gasped, he quickly mentioned how he and Kaleb had tried to help, but they couldn't get to me.

I gave Kael a stern look, trying to quiet him down, but he paid no attention. We had just lived through an awesome adventure story, and he was all too proud not to share. Thankfully, we'd made it out okay. I looked over at Jayce; his eyes were full of worry, frustration, and fear. I'd never forget that look on his face as long as I lived. It was one I never wanted to see again. I couldn't have said anything to make him understand my reasons, so instead I turned my head away.

Kael continued sharing the gory details of my blood squirting everywhere. I rolled my eyes in protest. He caught my unsubtle hint and skipped over to the part where the doomahorn transformed into a unicorn before our eyes. He kept the mood light by explaining how the unicorn healed my arm. Then he went back into animated detail about how she killed the attacking werewolf.

I shook my head. There was no stopping him.

"Unicorn?" Jayce interrupted.

"I'm serious, look how the horn healed her arm. Shanntal, show them! Show them!" Kael said excitedly.

I shot Kael the dirtiest look I could muster before lifting up my sleeve. I twisted and turned my arm showing them all angles. "It's true, but as you see, I'm totally okay."

"Wow! I never knew they were real." Jayce sat back in the seat. I watched him try to wrap his mind around the fact that unicorns were very much alive. "I've never seen one."

"Maybe you'll have a chance to meet them someday."

Kael picked up his storytelling again, only this time, Kaleb chimed in. They were on a roll traveling back through their lifetimes of various adventures.

Auntie Steph and Uncle Dane sat mesmerized by the different tales being shared. Occasionally, they'd let out an ohhhh or gasp, which made me smile. I imagined all this to be quite mind-boggling for them.

With the stories flowing, I found myself wondering about the conclusion of another one. Would Jayce and I ever get to go up to the heavens? When things went right between us, they were euphoric. Lately, we'd had so many trying and bad times. Yes, we'd worked through them, even when things got really hard and it seemed like we didn't have any hope left. Then there we were, together again. We'd managed to persevere one more time. I hoped this time we'd get it right.

Darkness arrived. The sun had retreated, allowing the moon and stars to make their appearance. Kael and Kaleb offered to split watch, thinking we'd be better safe than sorry. Ten o'clock came around, and as sure as sunrise, Auntie Steph passed along her good nights to us.

"The basement is set up for whoever wants some sleep." Uncle Dane offered. "Jayce, remember you're in with Shanntal, okay?"

This threw me off. Jayce was staying in my room?

"Yes, Dane. She won't be left alone," he assured.

Everything became clear. Uncle Dane didn't want me by myself. I felt safer knowing I wouldn't be alone, but also somewhat excited to be spending the night with Jayce again. I couldn't hide my smile.

Uncle Dane shook his head and gave me a kiss on the head. "You're in safe hands. Good night, Shanntal." He went down the hall and disappeared into his bedroom.

I looked at Jayce. "Wow! You've been busy while I was away. Clearly, you've won over the family."

"Clearly I have." He smiled.

We stayed up for a while longer with Kaleb and Kael. The four of us sat in the living room chatting. It felt nice to be hanging out like normal people. Granted, one of the guys constantly glanced out the window to make sure nothing lurked around outside, but other than that, I considered it normal.

Kaleb let out a yawn followed by a stretch. I felt the same way. Totally beat. The lack of sleep the past few days had finally caught up.

"Kael, are you okay to take the first watch?" I asked.

Kaleb looked at me. "What? I'm fine. I can do first watch."

Kael let out his famous laugh. "Dude, you look like a zombie." Making a creepy face, he stuck his arms up in front of him like a zombie would and mockingly took a few steps.

Kaleb sneered in protest.

"I've got first watch covered. Get some sleep while you can. Before you know it, I'll be the drooling zombie looking for some mushy brains." Kael made a face, causing him to drool all over himself.

It was gross, but we couldn't help but laugh.

Kael returned to his normal pose, with a goofy grin plastered across his face. Always the joker.

"I'll be back in a sec," I said, motioning Kaleb to come with me.

I led the way down the basement stairs. The arrangement was quite welcoming. Uncle Dane and Auntie Steph had set everything up. A couple cots sat beside nightstands topped with bedside lamps. They'd even set up a dresser and placed some photos in fancy frames, creating a more homey feel. This didn't seem like a basement at all, more like a guestroom.

"Wow! I do believe they've been expecting us. This looks fantastic." I could have slept comfortably down there and would have if my own bed weren't waiting for me upstairs.

"Not bad at all," he said, letting out another yawn.

"Kaleb?" I asked while he was lying down on one of the cots.

"Shanntal?" he said, trying to fight off another yawn.

"I wanted to thank you for talking sense into me."

"Anytime."

"I'm also sorry for all the pain you've felt because of me. I never meant for you to carry my burden."

"It's okay." He yawned again.

"I'm really glad you stepped up and made me shut my big mouth before I caused either of us more grief."

"You're welcome. Now, do me a favor?"

"Sure, anything you want."

"Shut up one more time and let me get some sleep." He pulled the blankets up around him.

"Kaleb!" I pushed him in the chest.

He groaned and giggled.

I leaned down and hugged my friend tightly. "Seriously, thank you," I whispered in his ear as I pulled back the blanket. I wished him a good night's sleep and kissed his cheek.

Back upstairs I was greeted by Kael and Jayce.

"You gonna tuck me in too?" Kael asked sarcastically.

"Only if you want me to."

"Perfect, I'll wake you up when I'm ready to get some sleep ... ha-ha!"

"I dare you to try, muscle boy."

"Oh yeah? Look who's talking like she's tough."

"You know I am," I said, flexing.

His awful sense of humor had grown on me. He was boisterous and loud on the surface, but sweet and sensitive on the inside. You just had to look past the layers of muscle to see the caring guy lurking inside. At first, I'd been apprehensive about him joining, but now I couldn't imagine anyone other than him being with us.

"Okay, you two, before this turns into some kind of wrestling match ... I think Shanntal ... that you, umm ... you should say good night. I mean, try to get some sleep while you can. No offense, but you look, well, you look a mess." Jayce waved his hands in the air, outlining me from head to toe.

"Nice!" I snapped with my nastiest tone. "Real nice!"

"Ohhhh!" Kael laughed.

I was mad. After everything I'd just been through, of course I looked a mess. He didn't need to point it out. I headed to my room. "Night, Kael."

"Silent treatment?" Kael giggled as he warned Jayce. "Perhaps you're the one that's in trouble now."

"Jayce," I snapped.

Kael couldn't even pretend to be serious. Using a similar tone to the one I had, he repeated, "Jayce." He proceeded to wave his arms around outlining just like Jayce had done. "Jayce said, 'you look a mess.' She stares at him horrified. I must say, if I had to place money on who would win this round, I'd bet on the mess."

We both looked at him.

Kael blew a kiss at Jayce and flexed all his muscles at me. Then he laughed so hard, he had to lean over, but then lost his balance and landed on the couch.

Jayce shook his head at Kael and turned his focus back to me. "I'm sorry, Shanntal. Honestly, I didn't mean anything bad. I only meant you look like you could use some sleep."

I shot him the dirtiest look. He needed to stop talking, because he was digging himself into a really deep hole.

"I didn't mean it the way you think. My words ... they're coming out wrong." Jayce followed me to bed.

"Ya think?" I snapped.

Kael harassed Jayce the entire way to my room. Even after the door closed, I could still hear Kael laughing from the living room.

"I'm sorry if I offended you. I didn't mean what I said in a bad way. You just look super tired."

Jayce was lucky I actually felt as tired as I looked. "Forgiven this time, but you should never say things like that to a girl. Especially when she is your girlfriend and you're about to share a bed with her!"

"I promise, never again!"

I placed my head on the pillow and pulled the blankets up tight. I hadn't slept in my own bed for quite some time now, and wow, did it ever feel good.

Jayce climbed in beside me. He wrapped his strong arms around my waist and snuggled up close, then whispered in my ear, "You truly are the most beautiful person I've ever known, and I'm so glad you're mine."

Instantly, my mood changed. Not only from his words, but also because of how his body felt close to mine. This was my version of happily ever after. I rolled over so I could look at him. There was just enough light to show me the outline of his face. "I'm so happy you're here. I really did miss you, probably more than you'll ever know."

"I'm here now. I'm not going anywhere."

We were right where we needed to be, right where we should be. I snuggled up closer.

"I love you, Shanntal," he said.

"I love you more," I said back.

"Impossible."

"Then I've done the impossible." I kissed him gently on his lips. "Good night, Jayce." I closed my eyes as we both drifted off to sleep, our bodies still pressed close together.

Named

~ Chapter Twenty-Six ~

A shadowy figure moved seductively through the lingering mist. Struggling against myself, I took a few steps forward, but no matter how hard I tried, I couldn't come up with the inner strength needed to repel him. His undeniable presence made me shiver, and even worse, my legs buckled when he reached over and locked me in an awkward embrace.

He dragged his fingers along my body, which made it difficult for me to warm myself. He gave me a foreign yet excruciating pain I hadn't felt in any of our previous encounters. Eventually, new icy blood coursed throughout my pale body. My reaction to his presence had intensified. I felt changes taking place within and moaned in agony.

He was far too strong and overpowering. Any will to fight recoiled as I surrendered. The changes in my body forced me even closer to him. He had total control of me, with the exception of one thing, and it was by far the most important … my heart. He would never reach that piece of me because it belonged entirely to Jayce. I'd never ask for it back. I would love Jayce, always.

Despite everything happening and the unbearable pain growing inside, I was able to shift my thoughts to Jayce. I pictured his dark hair and deep brown eyes, his perfect smile, muscular body, and Celtic tattoo. I loved his great sense of style. He rocked faded blue jeans and a black t-shirt like no one else. When he paired them up with black and white skater shoes, he stole my breath away.

Thinking of Jayce gave me the power to find some buried strength I needed to force my attacker away. I shoved the vampire off using all of my might. It didn't amount to much, only enough to allow a brief break. Within seconds, the vampire overcame me, and to my dismay, I was once again stuck in his embrace. His icy fingers dragged down my neck, as he leaned in closer and whispered in my ear. I wasn't able to hear him clearly. Hisses and growls took the place of words.

Locked in his deadly grasp, I felt weak and powerless. My life was slipping away. He teased along my mouth before maneuvering down my neck. Agonizing, icy shocks hurt my skin wherever his hands touched. He placed a hard kiss on my mouth, which left a salty taste upon my lips. The flavor lingered, one I didn't know well. Strangely, this unknown flavor managed to ease my pain from the inner radiating chills. He gave me a wicked grin before his lips met my neck, and the pain returned. Once again I was rendered useless. My will, my resentment, my strength, nothing seemed to be enough to keep him away.

I forced my mind back to memories of Jayce so I could remind myself about the time we'd spent together. He had given me the best days of my life so far, and I wasn't ready for our time to be finished. I needed more life, more love, more Jayce. I squirmed until I pulled myself free. My eyes came into focus only to find Daray hadn't been the one holding me. The stranger from the gardens stood before me, flashing his long, sharp fangs. Fresh blood dripped off and trickled down his terrifying pale face. I stumbled backward, but that's when I understood the full extent of my weakness. He'd bitten me, and what I saw was my own blood. My frail body dropped to the ground, craving more of the foreign taste that eased my pain earlier. I was too weak and couldn't find the strength needed to get up. It was too late.

The real Daray arrived and held onto me as I jerked around, losing the last bits of life from my dying body. "Protecting you is all I've ever tried to do. Once I found out you were alive, but lost and cursed by the nightwalkers, I only wanted you to remain safe. I tried everything to keep you in the daylight where you belonged. Shanntal, you're brighter than any sunshine. You're the light leading out of this darkness. You have the ability to heal this immortal world. You can remove the divide that's been placed between us. You weren't supposed to share this fate. It was mine, and I'm sorry you got caught in the middle. This curse was never meant for you." He leaned down, pressed his cool lips on my forehead, and hugged me tightly. "I apologize for not being able to protect you. I promise you, I will make this right."

Unable to speak, I couldn't tell him I forgave him or beg him not to leave my side because I was afraid to die. I didn't want to disappear from this life alone. He would never know the words I wanted to say. He released me from his protective arms to gently lay my dying body on the ground.

A raging growl sounded from his mouth as he revealed his fangs. I saw a look of sheer hatred in his eyes, and his body trembled with rage. He clenched his fists, leapt upward, and smashed into the stranger midair. They hit using brutal force. Every blow sent the other flying. I found it hard to focus on their collisions. They moved so rapidly, back and forth, hit after hit, it wasn't long before I could no longer keep up. My life started to fade, and I hoped with the last of my might that Daray would be strong enough to take out the stranger and finish this once and for all.

My eyes strained when I looked around for the rest of Daray's nightwalkers, but they were nowhere to be seen. He was alone with the stranger and facing his unimaginable strength. I wasn't sure how the stranger had become so strong, or if Daray could beat him. Blackness consumed my eyes and silence filled my ears. I was sure I'd just died because there was nothing left except my mind. I had no senses, no feeling, so I decided to accept the fact I'd met my end. Everything was quiet, and then I heard a voice. A name was spoken and sounded clearer than anything I'd ever heard before. "Donovan."

The stranger had finally been named.

I fought with everything left in me and managed to open my eyes one more time. Disappointment and sadness came into sight. The first clear image I saw was Daray's slain body nearby, dark blood sprawling across the ground.

I heard a growl of protest, only to realize the sound came from somewhere deep inside me. My arms were stretched out, but useless and flailing. Sputtering and sobbing, I cried out, "Why? Why?"

The victorious vampire picked my limp body up from the ground. I had no strength, only a rush of anger and resentment. He placed his face down by my ear and this time spoke clearly. "I'm Donovan. Now you know my name, so make sure you don't forget it!" He bit down with such a powerful force that it jolted me awake.

"Jayce … Jayce …" I fumbled around the bed trying to find him.

"Yes?"

I hesitated. Something about his reply wasn't right. The voice answering me didn't sound anything like Jayce. I shivered from an unexplainable chill. Unable to move out of fear, I squeaked, "Guys?"

But no one came. I felt my heart pounding against my chest, the nightmare still fresh and vivid in my memory. At least I hoped it was only a nightmare. I shook off the panic and screamed. This time, my voice came out nice and loud. Seconds later the bedroom door flung open and the light flicked on. Jayce, Kaleb, and Kael looked ready for battle.

"What's going on?" Jayce asked.

"Can't you feel the chill in the air?" I frantically looked around my room for some sign of him. "I'm sure he was here."

"Daray was here?" Kaleb snarled.

"No, Daray isn't the one we need to worry about. Trust me when I say he means me no harm. Donovan, he's the one who killed my family, and that's who's after me."

"Donovan? Who's he? Where'd he come from?" Kael asked.

"Oh, I know exactly who he is. He's the stranger from that night in the gardens. He's the one that turned Daray." I looked down at my shaking hands, still picturing his pale face and remembering his icy touch.

I was about to explain the details of my dream to the others when I suddenly heard whispers. They were the same kind from earlier, only slightly different, because this time I understood everything perfectly. As the words came to me, I repeated them aloud.

"I don't want you here," he hissed. "Can't you see you don't belong in this world? You've disgraced me by eluding my gift of the night. You weren't meant to receive my offering, yet somehow, here you are." He let out an evil snicker. "Foolish girl, you haven't even figured out how to reap any of the benefits."

I paused; growls and hisses filled my ears.

"You choose to view my gift as a curse, but you … you are the curse. I shall make you pay with your life. That'll be your punishment for continuing to walk among the daywalkers and mortals. Yes, the time has finally come. Soon I will be rid of my curse—once and for all."

"Who does this parasite think he is?" Kael's jaw clenched tightly while he punched his fists together. "He's unreal, truly distorted! Now he's done, 'cause I'm fuming!" Every muscle rippled and veins bulged, intensifying his fury.

Silently, Kaleb shifted his massive body closer to mine. He stood no more than a few inches away, ready for anything.

"Guys, we've got to find Daray. He tried to help, but I think he's dead."

Not one of them budged.

"Guys!" I snapped.

My dreams were becoming more than simple imaginings; they were acting more like premonitions. I had to listen when I was being warned because my dreams kept putting the missing pieces in place. "We've had this all wrong. Daray isn't the threat here, never has been. Believe it or not, he's on our side."

Jayce rolled his eyes.

I wanted to explain what I meant, but couldn't with the weird feeling in the pit of my stomach. Without another word I got off the bed, walked past the guys, and went down the hallway. I knocked once then opened the door to Uncle Dane and Auntie Steph's room. Once their door opened, my blood cooled more severely. Something wasn't right. I flipped on the light in time to catch a glimpse of the speedy shadow fleeing across the room. It raced out the window, leaving the drapes swinging side to side.

Uncle Dane was closest. I rushed to the bed and shook him, making sure he woke up.

"What's going on? I'm up, I'm up!" he said, half asleep.

The guys had followed me into the room, and Jayce bent over to check on Auntie Steph. She too awoke with no trouble. I was relieved they'd remained asleep and we had gotten to their room in time. They were both wide awake now and full of questions, but thankfully neither realized how close they'd just been to death.

Kael's massive body stood in the window, looking past the flowing curtains to see if anything or anyone remained close by. He shut the window and double-checked to make sure it was locked. Kaleb returned from checking out the rest of the house. The whole place was sealed up tightly.

My blood warmed. "He's gone," I said solemnly. I was absolutely furious Donovan had gotten away. He'd come far too close without us even knowing. I couldn't believe he stood in my room, then in the room next door. Now I understood why I'd heard his voice so clearly. Being that close allowed him to simply feed me the lines. He had one thing right. The time was coming, but not my time ... more like his.

"Uncle Dane, why exactly did you ... I mean, why did my family try so hard to keep Daray and the others away? You guys made it your mission to hide me for all these years. Why?"

Reasons

~ Chapter Twenty-Seven ~

The look on his face showed how much he didn't want to answer.

"Uncle Dane, please," I begged. "I need to know the whole story. I can't live on bits and pieces anymore. I need the full truth."

"Oh, kiddo." He paused a moment before saying, "You were, and don't get me wrong, still are a blessing, especially in my books. When everyone throughout the immortal world heard what happened, it made you enemies everywhere. Enemies you couldn't have begun to imagine, and ones you shouldn't have had to face. You were so vulnerable. You were meant to walk with nightwalkers, yet somehow you managed to remain among the daywalkers, and that's what put the entire immortal world on edge. You had the blood of monsters running through your veins, yet basically remained yourself. Your ability and strength was completely unheard of. No one knew what to expect, and therefore, they feared you. Whenever Daray or other nightwalkers were around, you began experiencing subtle changes. Shanntal, you took on their characteristics, and we didn't want that. You're stronger than any curse or gift or whatever they want to call it. You survived, and best of all, you're still you."

"Is that really everything?" I sat down on the edge of the bed while Auntie Steph rubbed my shoulders.

Uncle Dane situated himself beside me, sighed, and then continued. "Unfortunately not."

"Please, I need you to tell me everything."

"The more time you spent around Daray, the harder it became for you to walk in sunlight or act like yourself. With Daray being a newborn vampire, he didn't know how to help you find your way, he was too busy trying to find out himself. With Daray being a full vampire, and your ability to remain among the daywalkers, there wasn't any way to return to the life you shared. You did spend some time together, thinking you could find a way to overcome the differences. We wanted you to be happy, but within a few days of living in the darkness, well, you began turning more into one of them. Your family tried their best to help work things out, but once they realized how much you changed, they decided the only way to save you was to take you away from him. Your parents came in during the daylight hours and walked right out of the house with you. None of the nightwalkers could follow because the sun was high, and that was the last time you ever saw him, until now."

Out slipped a small gasp of disbelief.

"Shanntal, please, you must understand. They were only trying to protect you because they loved you so much and believed in your great potential. So, our family did what was necessary to make sure you didn't slip under the night curse." Uncle Dane's face relaxed, and I saw the love he held for me in his eyes.

"Did Daray understand why I couldn't be near him?"

"I cannot answer that." Uncle Dane shrugged. "I don't know how his reasoning skills work."

I looked at Jayce, whose features remained neutral. He connected, and without so much as a word I knew he got where I was coming from. I felt him all through me and understood his sympathy and recognized his support. More importantly, I felt reassured knowing he was on my side and it was okay for me wanting to know about my past. Finding out what happened all those years ago would be the only way I'd ever be able to move my life forward. Perhaps it would also help us understand what exactly we were up against.

"I want you to know something else. Before your parents did what they did, they tried their best to explain to Daray why being around him wasn't good for you. They told him it would only cause you more pain and suffering. He agreed that night because he saw how the changes were taking their toll on you, but he still didn't let you go. So Daray left them no choice, and that's when the decision was made to take you away. They had to go to these extremes in order to keep you the way you're meant to be. Over the years, your family moved from place to place trying to keep you hidden from nightwalkers. They even called upon the protectors for assistance, and that's how Garrison and Kaleb entered your life. Any time a nightwalker was present, the protectors would keep guard and help the family stow you away. After a while, well it just got easier to hide you."

"I guess poor Daray never really saw the situation in the same light as my family. It explains a lot about his behavior toward me, though. I understand things far better now."

I was especially thankful for my family and the extremes they went to. They didn't have to look after me in the manner they did. They'd chosen to help me, and I appreciated their support. Their love and sacrifices gave me the strength and courage I needed so I could remain myself. I never would have made it this far without them.

I'd never forget the faces of my biological parents. They'd brought me into this world and loved me during my eighteen human years. I would continue to love them for many more lifetimes. But my immortal family, well, they'd taken me in as one of their own, and stood by me throughout my immortal years. They'd even given their lives in order to protect me, and for that, I'd be eternally grateful. I owed them so much. For loving me when they didn't have to, and protecting me when they didn't need to. They helped me live my life to the fullest and never asked for a single thing in return. They were a wonderful family, and I felt honored to be considered a part of it for so many years. My emotions took over. I felt so loved, and all the love I received fueled my power. Love gave me the strength to survive.

I finally understood why Daray had searched for me all those years. He missed having a proper chance to gain some closure. He'd held onto our love, but as more time passed, the more his resentment grew toward my family for hiding me. I couldn't blame him or them. I was glad my family took the measures they did; I just wished Daray could've had a chance to deal with my departure on his own terms. Things might've been different between daywalkers and nightwalkers if he'd gotten that chance. Perhaps he never would've grown into a monster or become quite so hostile if his pain were dealt with sooner.

Undying ageless love—only to find out in the end, it wasn't the kind of love meant to last. Daray and I weren't soul mates. I knew this because of how love felt with Jayce. Jayce was unquestionably my soul mate, just as Lakylee was Daray's.

"We've got to find Daray. I think he could be in some serious trouble. Donovan's here for me and won't stop until he gets what he came for. All this mayhem started the night Daray turned, and when he accidently saved me. That's the point where Donovan became the threat. When I lost my memory, I'd forgotten all about him. The fact is, Daray managed to save me. He tried his best to help me. Think about it ... with all the changes going on during his transition, for a newborn vampire to even bother trying, well that means a lot. The monster owns him now, but not his soul. I know that's still intact."

The guys rolled their eyes. They remained reluctant to help a nightwalker, especially Daray. After all, he'd been responsible for many of our problems. Even though we'd had it all wrong before, they didn't quite see it that way.

"You guys, please. We've got to find him. He needs our help."

"Fine, all right," Jayce agreed.

Kaleb and Kael both nodded.

Time sure was a funny beast. One minute you could have everything figured out, and a second later, find yourself completely lost. I was getting myself back on track. Another track, but at least this time it was the right one. We were going vampire hunting. We would save Daray and destroy Donovan.

My blood chilled. "We've got company," I announced as the guys readied themselves in my aunt and uncle's bedroom.

A few moments passed with no sign of anyone. My anticipation grew until it erupted. I pushed Kael out of the way so I could see for myself who was there. I pressed my face up against the glass, and a glowing streak of blue-green eyes flashed by. I jumped back, but the eyes came up closer.

From the light in the bedroom, we saw Lakylee standing outside the window. Her pale skin glistened in the night, casting a sense of innocence across her face. She nodded in the direction of the front door, and then disappeared.

"Stay here and be ready," I said to the guys. "You'll need to protect Auntie Steph and Uncle Dane. Please don't let anything happen to them. I'll be fine. Lakylee and I have an understanding."

Kaleb began to protest, but Uncle Dane and Auntie Steph stood speechless. Kael looked ready to kill. Jayce somehow managed to calm the group down by explaining he'd stay connected. If he sensed any danger, we'd know right away. Then they could take out Lakylee or any other nightwalker before they even knew what hit them.

I walked out of the bedroom, closing the door tightly behind me. I heard their low chatter as I made my way down the hall. I felt nervous. Lakylee and I had an understanding, but that was before I decided to betray her. What would she be like now? Was this a trap or still a truce? Only one way to tell, and before Jayce or anyone else could intervene, I opened the front door.

Lakylee stood alone. The light cast from the full moon lit up the night perfectly. As she stood on my front porch, I saw how flawless her pale skin looked under the moonlight, while her long, wild hair flowed gently in the night breeze. She looked beautiful, but two sets of red eyes quickly caught my attention as they moved behind her. She'd brought the werewolves along. They raced back and forth around the neighborhood, their noses stuck straight up in the air. I froze in terror when one ran toward an unsuspecting neighbor. Why was he outside? Didn't he know what lurked after dark? I fought the urge to yell out to warn him. The neighbor bent down by a bush in the middle of his yard and picked up a cat. The cat set its sight on the closest wolf and clawed the man in a frantic attempt to get down. I heard 'ouch' as he let go. The cat ran full speed to the front door, with the man hurrying closely behind. He glanced around the street, saw us, and waved. However, his face changed after Lakylee turned to him. His eyes grew large, mouth hung wide open, and he slammed the door shut.

A giggle accidently slipped out at the situation. He had risked his own life to get a cat back inside. Silly man! Nightwalkers had no interest feeding off a cat. However, under different circumstances, he would've been another story. No doubt about it.

Lakylee seemed less than impressed by his reaction, but really, what did she expect? Nightwalkers had created their own reputation, and everyone had heard the horror stories. Thankfully, the wolves weren't there to hurt anyone. They were actually helping keep our neighborhood safe by pacing around the premises, scouting for unwanted guests.

I slowly let out my breath so my voice didn't reveal how scared I'd truly been. "Lakylee, what brings you here tonight?"

Truce

~ Chapter Twenty-Eight ~

She eyed me up and down before speaking. "You know what happens. You've seen Daray's death in your dreams, and I will not live without him. I'm here to help you. Actually, we're here to help." She motioned at the roaming werewolves. "Donovan mustn't get anywhere near you, and we both know he came much too close tonight. He needs to be stopped, and you need our help. If Donovan reaches you, I'll surely lose Daray when he tries to avenge your death. I won't allow that to happen. Daray's not strong enough to take Donovan on alone." She swayed anxiously in front of me.

Her movements were hypnotic. I stared, wanting to respond, but all I could think about were all the ways she could've taken me out, then and there. She stopped swaying, which enabled me to gather my thoughts. Once my head cleared, I moved out of the doorway and invited her in.

This was an event I never thought would occur. Lakylee invited into my house as a friend—an ally. She was fierce and strong, a definite asset to have on our side. The two immortal worlds had been separated by battles for so long, yet there we were, coming together as one.

Lakylee and I spoke alone in the living room. In those moments, I realized that when hostilities weren't present, the nightwalkers could be quite likeable.

Kaleb and Kael slowly made their way into the living room. There was a definite sore spot I hadn't taken into account before they entered. I felt Kaleb's pain once he and Kael focused in on Lakylee. I wasn't sure they would ever overcome the loss of Garrison. I knew how much they missed him, because I felt the same sadness and hatred. Garrison had been a big part of our lives, and Lakylee was the one who had taken him away from us.

The living room seemed smaller with Lakylee and the guys so close. The usually spacious room felt no bigger than a broom closet. I wanted to keep some distance between her and the others because, in truth, I didn't completely trust her yet and wasn't entirely sure how well Kaleb or Kael would handle seeing her. I couldn't bring myself to ask them to let it go and forget about everything. I'd never forget Garrison, so what gave me the nerve to ask something like that of them? Instead, I kept my words and thoughts to myself and stood in the middle. I'd try my best to break up anything, should something start. I was the neutral one with both parties on my side.

"This room isn't big enough to hold this meeting," Lakylee said, obviously feeling the tension rising.

I nearly broke down when I saw Kaleb's expression. Garrison had been his brother. This was terrible of me to place his murderer in the same room. Yes, she'd offered us help, but at what price?

Uncle Dane and Auntie Steph were on either side of Jayce as they entered the room, and he said, "We could always move this gathering to my house."

"Jayce? What about the elements? We can't put them at risk. There's too much at stake, and this isn't their battle. The entire world would be in jeopardy if something happened to them."

"This is their fight, just the same as it is for each and every one of us. Getting rid of Donovan will enable our worlds to live peacefully. We should respect each other for the qualities and differences we have. After all, aside from the food we consume or the hour in which we wake, there really isn't that much difference. We all shoot to the stars with our soul mates, live for eternity, and share the same basic needs. Our worlds are related in many ways."

I looked around, gathering everyone's responses. Did others feel the same way? They all nodded, giving Jayce their approval. Even through the window the werewolves nodded in agreement.

"I understand there were sacrifices on both sides, but let's not let the lives of our lost brothers and sisters be in vain," Jayce went on. "Help them be a part of this change and set things right. Their deaths will have new meaning, and in the end, they will have died for a better purpose."

Jayce was absolutely right. There were losses on both sides, and by coming together, we could mend old wounds and come up with the strength to destroy Donovan. Donovan had separated our two worlds with his way of thinking and put us at odds with each other. Without him, there could be peace.

"Okay, gang, so do we have a truce?" Jayce asked.

"For Garrison!" Kaleb said.

"Truce," Kael agreed.

"For sure. Count me in!" Lakylee said.

Scratches sounded at the window. Lakylee nodded and said, "They're in. They think it'll be fun kicking Donovan's butt."

"Okay, it seems things are settled. Remember, from this point on we are all on the same team. This must be a group effort, us against him. Let's go to my place. There's more room, and we could use the space to bring in others and get them up to speed. We need everyone on the same page," Jayce said.

Lakylee and the werewolves agreed to meet us there. Uncle Dane offered to drive us in his trusty, four-door red car. Auntie

Steph and Uncle Dane sat up front, while Jayce, Kaleb, and I sat in the backseat. I looked out the window and every once in a while caught a glimpse of fur. Kael followed in his wolf form, since there hadn't been enough room in the car for everyone. Kael and Kaleb hadn't felt right leaving us, because no one could really believe what was taking place.

I leaned over and whispered to Kaleb. "I'm sorry. I never thought about how hard this would be on you. She offered to help us, and honestly, the only thing I thought about was beating Donovan. I'm sorry for the toll my selfishness has taken on your emotions. I didn't mean to be so heartless."

He looked surprised. "Uh … thank you, but just so you know, what you're doing isn't selfish. As a matter of fact, it's exactly the opposite. You're the key. You're helping peace overcome years of fighting by taking a stand, and I'm beside you one hundred percent. I understand the reasons we were summoned to protect you. The measure of your worth is beyond words." He smiled whole-heartedly. "I miss Garrison, but remember he died protecting Meriel. His actions saved her, you, and the rest of world. He died with his honor intact."

"The fact remains, Garrison should be here with us. I was only thinking about what I wanted when I brought the one responsible for his death into our lives. Now she's up close and personal, and I wanted you to know I understand how hard this must be for you. That's all I'm trying to get across. I understand, Kaleb, and I'm sorry."

He nudged me. "You worry too much. I'm fine. This is going to be a good thing. I can feel it. Besides, we could really use all the help we can get against this Donovan guy, and she's definitely a strong fighter. Honestly, she's a great asset to have on our side."

"Yes, she truly is," I said, thinking about how fierce Lakylee was.

"Only if we can trust her …" His voice trailed off and he stared out the window.

"We can, Kaleb. I'm sure of it."

He turned back toward me and looked me straight in the eye. "I'll trust your judgment. I'm with you always, and so is Kael. We go wherever you do. I promise we will destroy anything with the intention of causing you harm."

"Thanks, Kaleb. I'm counting on that. Remember, I'm nothing more than a big wimp."

"Oh, I remember, all right." He rolled his eyes. "Mouthy as anything, but a complete wimp. Too bad you can't fight with words or they'd be in *big* trouble. Ha-ha!"

"Funny, real funny," I sneered.

Kaleb seemed okay after all. I was relieved this wasn't too hard for him. I couldn't bear seeing him hurt like that again. I knew the loss of Garrison would never subside, but the sting wouldn't be as immense as more time passed.

'You just did a really good thing there.' Jayce smiled.

'Thanks. I just didn't want him to have to deal with anything uncomfortable.'

'Losing you would be the one thing he couldn't handle. Remember, he's here because of you, and only you.'

I didn't respond. I needed a moment to myself. I thought about how thankful I felt having such amazing people in my life. They were all very special to me. I'd do anything for each and every one of them and knew I could expect the same in return. For once in my life, I felt lucky.

Jayce placed our entwined hands on his lap and squeezed them together tightly. If he hadn't been able to connect to understand everything I felt, I wasn't sure he'd ever comprehend how much I truly loved him. It was more than I could describe with words and greater than I could possibly ever show him.

'You are my life.' Jayce squeezed my hand tightly. *'I love you.'*

'I love you more.'

'Impossible.'

'Then I've done the impossible.' I smiled.

'Yes, yes you have.' He squeezed my hand even tighter.

He broke our connection and joined in on the conversation in the car around us. Everyone spoke about how strange it felt to have this kind of outcome, and how no one ever expected it. A new immortal world was about to be born. It would be a better place for us all and a safer place for the mortals living among us. New rules would have to be made after the death of Donovan because this type of change would be like nothing known before.

I drifted into my own little place and daydreamed about a life with our two worlds combined. I imagined tranquility, where immortals gathered peacefully instead of on battlefields. I was sure there'd be some resistance, possibly from both sides, but overall I figured it would be pretty easy to come up with a plan that would work for everyone. We'd need to appoint leaders who were familiar with both sides. If they already had existing alliances, perhaps that would be enough to reassure any of the doubters. My mind raced with possibilities. This had to be the right thing; it felt right from my head down to my toes.

I pulled myself back into reality and returned with a different feeling as we traveled during the night; nightwalkers on our side. I felt stronger. We didn't have to run in fear or worry if a vampire or werewolf lurked around the next corner. We only had to worry about Donovan, but at least I could sense him. His presence felt like nothing I've ever come across. My senses would give us ample time to prepare or defend.

A short while later we arrived at the grand house, which felt absolutely incredible. I really missed my friends and couldn't wait to see everyone. I found it difficult being away from them—we'd all been so close before—and I hoped with any luck that we could pick up right where we'd left off. Picking sides was a very hard thing to do and not much fun. When I left my friends, I'd picked a side. I'd done so with good intentions, because I was trying to keep them safe, but lesson learned. I'd never make that mistake again. I would stand my ground. My true friends would support me while standing by my side.

Lakylee stood partially hidden alongside the house while two werewolves paced eagerly around the edge of the property scouting for intruders. When she realized we were approaching, she revealed herself completely. Our group gathered and headed up to the front doors. Once inside, I was shocked to find no one came to greet us. Where were the others? Had something gone wrong? I immediately shook the intrusive thoughts from my head. No, it wouldn't happen like that. This was the beginning of a great change. Have faith, I told myself. It will all work out.

Our group bunched together as we moved through the lower level of the house. Lakylee walked alongside Kaleb, but neither of them seemed bothered by the fact. Kael stayed near Uncle Dane and Auntie Steph, while the two wolves walked on either side of me. Jayce was up front, leading the way. We must've been quite the sight. Never in all eternity had our worlds walked together like this. It was a sure sign this change was real, and we were taking our first steps together.

We neared the living room when I heard voices. I recognized some, while others not so much. All the voices sounded quite happy as they chatted back and forth. One by one, we entered the crowded living room, and to my surprise, everyone was waiting for us. When I said everyone, I meant everyone. The elements, fairies, shapeshifters, four vampires from the coven, and three werewolves filled the living room. Even the two unicorns rescued from the vampire house stood outside the open window looking in.

Previously sworn enemies sat amongst one other, talking like lifelong friends. Aiden and Terran conversed casually with a couple werewolves, while the unicorns exchanged deep conversation with a vampire trio. I was left in a state of awe taking in the scene. The best part for me was how everyone appeared to be enjoying one another's company. You couldn't fake the smiles filling the room.

"Hey, gang!" Jayce announced loudly.

Everyone quieted down. I glanced over at Kaleb as I quickly wiped a stray tear from my cheek. Thankfully, he hadn't noticed. I didn't want him to see me all emotional. Yes, this was big, and yes, it was fantastic, but other than talking, nothing had really happened yet. My eyes met Kael, who faced the opposite direction. If he would've caught me being mushy, I'm sure I never would've heard the end of it.

My sense of worry became lighter when I scanned the room and located Layla and Meriel. Meriel gave me a tiny wave, while Layla flashed her gorgeous smile. Meriel looked great. She had still been in rough shape the last time I'd seen her. It was quite the relief to see she'd made a complete recovery. I beamed back at my two friends. My smile reached ear to ear.

"Thank you all for coming tonight," Jayce began. "I'm really glad to see so many of you here. We'll have to continue spreading the word to the others unable to attend. I don't want to start off on the wrong note, but please be warned … some may need a little more convincing. Just be patient with them. Not everyone can adapt easily to change. We'll need to give them more time to process this. We also need to decide on a designated person, perhaps one for each side so they can be available to address any grievances." Jayce paused to ensure he had everyone's full attention.

It was such a sight, seeing all the different immortals in one room. I found myself wishing Daray were around to witness the birth of our new world. I needed to stop worrying. We'd find him soon enough so he'd be part of this too.

"First things first." Jayce turned to face me. "Shanntal, you're the reason we've come together. You alone have managed to heal some wounds we've bestowed upon one another."

I felt my face blush from being put on the spot. I wished someone would do something to take the spotlight off me. I really didn't feel much different from anyone else. He spoke like I had super powers or something.

"We swear to you here and now to protect you with our lives. To each and every one of us, you are the most significant being in this room because you're Donovan's threat. When you harness the power of light and strength of the dark, he won't stand a chance. As long as you walk in both worlds, you'll have access to their powers. What we promise now is to do whatever you ask. Every being in this room will look out for you, no matter the cost. Consider this ... we will follow our leader and be ready wherever you need us. This truce was made possible because of you."

"Oh, Jayce," I sputtered, quite embarrassed by his speech. "I don't have powers. Well, maybe the power to find trouble from miles away." I laughed, but it was a sad and true fact. Trouble seemed to follow me. "Besides, there's absolutely no way *anyone* should be put at risk, especially for me. Am I right, or what?" I looked out to the crowd for support but found none. They all took his side. He was building me up, but too much. I was a wimp. How could I possibly go up against the likes of Donovan? Most significant person—ha! More like the person to get us in the deepest amount of trouble.

I made eye contact with a vampire who said, "If you really think these barriers can be removed, then I'd fight with you."

"I truly believe there's a better way for us all to live," I said.

"I will fight too!" shouted another vampire, raising her arms high.

"Me too!" Pledged a unicorn and werewolf in unison.

Pretty soon all the people and creatures had announced they would not only fight beside me, but also for me. I felt overwhelmed by their devotion. Simply knowing I had them on my side made me feel even stronger. Suddenly, I felt invincible, like nothing and no one could stop me.

"I promise to fight for all of you!" I shouted to the group. Cheers broke out across the room, and I felt like a queen who just found her victory.

Our gathering broke as dawn neared. The nightwalkers needed to get back to their shelters, and some had to feed before returning. Yawns came out of the daywalkers because we weren't used to being up all night. It was clear we were losing steam.

Now that we had everyone on the same page, things would be easier to deal with. Priority number one: find Daray. Priority two: destroy Donovan. Their order of arrangement was not set in stone, but I really hoped it was the order in which they happened. I didn't want my dream coming true. I wanted Daray and Lakylee to have their chance to be happy together, and I wanted a chance to make amends with Daray. I'd gotten the privilege of seeing both of them differently—sides I never thought were possible, but thanks to the opportunity, I now considered both friends. I wanted Daray and Lakylee to share the same kind of happiness I'd found with Jayce.

Our final nightwalker guests said their thanks and goodbyes, while the elements began showing everyone else to their rooms. Jayce and I put Auntie Steph and Uncle Dane in the guest room beside his.

"I never thought this day would come, kiddo. You're truly a gift, Shanntal, and we're so happy to be a part of your family. You make us proud," Uncle Dane said.

Auntie Steph nodded in agreement.

He gave me a hug before entering the bedroom. Auntie Steph hugged me, and we exchanged our good nights.

I had a good feeling the tables were about to turn. If this plan worked out, it would allow everyone to live as equals. Prisoners and enemies were from a past time; from this point forward we were friends. Equals above all else!

Sauda

~ Chapter Twenty-Nine ~

Jayce and I managed to get a few hours of rest, as did some of the others in the house. The majority of the daywalkers had remained at the grand home. Some found sleeping during the day an easy adjustment, while others struggled a bit more. We decided it'd be best to stay in groups, which would allow people to take sleep breaks without everyone going at once. It would be tough to hunt and track vampires, because in order to fight like nightwalkers, we needed to act like them. Staying awake all night would provide the only chance to find Donovan and destroy him.

I had to be extra careful too. If what Uncle Dane had told me earlier held any truth, I didn't want to be walking the night too long. No way would I ever willingly live that lifestyle. The thought of scrounging around in the darkness for blood made my skin crawl and stomach turn. I wasn't sure if that's exactly how life went for them, but it was the picture I had in my head. My imagination showed me more than enough to ensure I never wanted to find out the real deal.

Thankfully, the day went by rather quickly. Before long, the sun began to set. It was time. We needed to get a lot done tonight. Finding Daray was at the top of the list. Someone, somewhere, must've seen him. He couldn't have just disappeared. Could he?

I grew anxious as I waited by the window, watching the warm sun make her way out of the sky. The oranges, reds, pinks, and purples were breathtaking as they always were, but tonight I was looking forward to seeing the stars.

The sky darkened, and then Sitara and her love came out first, making their nightly appearance. Her sparkle showed how happy and completely in love she was with her partner, and since he was up there, it left no doubt he felt the same way about her. While I was busy admiring the happy couple, a thought came to mind. If Jayce really was my soul mate, why weren't we up in the stars celebrating our love? Would we ever get that chance?

'One day, Shanntal, don't rush it. Let's enjoy what we have between us now. Enjoy our time down here knowing we will be together forever, and one day, when destiny decides, we will be sent up to the stars.' Silently, Jayce wrapped his arms around my mid-section and pulled me in tightly. He placed his warm kisses down the back of my neck, which sent little shocks zapping everywhere he touched. I was lost in the moment, but red eyes caught my attention as they raced by the window. I jumped backward, knocking into Jayce.

"Something's out there," I said, a bit more excited than necessary. Those freaky red eyes had really startled me. I still wasn't quite used to our new union. I supposed the whole idea would take a bit of time to seem normal. After all, we were trying to let the past become the past.

"We have some guests," Jayce announced, much calmer.

Aiden entered the room with a crowd following closely behind. There were at least six new nightwalkers alongside him.

One of the female vampires stood out to me. She moved gracefully, but the sight of her had me defensive. I singled in on her as the group came closer. Had we known each other before? All I clearly understood at this point was that everything in me told me to pay special attention to her. What I didn't understand was why I had that feeling.

She looked ferocious, yet completely seductive. She flicked her long, black hair as her deep green eyes glanced around the room, taking in the sights. Then she finally met my gaze.

She raised an eyebrow, parted her lips into a partial sneer, and daringly walked right over, pushing people out of the way with her every step. She wasn't messing around or waiting for a proper introduction.

She seemed very familiar, but I couldn't place her. This set off another internal warning flag, and automatically my defenses were up. Who was she?

Kaleb and Kael sensed my tension and assumed their traditional stance on either side of me. No one wanted an uproar in the house, but our new guest had a certain way about her that put me on edge.

"So, you're the one who walks both worlds. Hmm … different than I pictured," she huffed, still eyeing me closely. "I don't foresee you playing the role of a fool, so you must understand Donovan won't be easy to go up against." She took another step forward. "No offense, but you don't look like much for him to be worried about."

Kaleb and Kael puffed their chests up to show her I wasn't alone in this fight.

"Those who are at odds with him … well, let me put it this way, they don't usually last too long." She let out an evil giggle and moved out of my space, but continued to eye me.

"Listen up, vampire!" I shouted, my body ramrod straight with rage. "This immortal world has been ripped in two because of Donovan. So let's get one thing clear—I'm not going anywhere. I will rid the world of Donovan in order to let these changes live. I believe they will grow into something great. Everyone else here sees, understands, and agrees with what I'm trying to do."

She took notice of the eyes focused on us.

"Everyone here has vowed to ensure these changes are made. Don't you see? It's too late to turn back. We've already started, and nothing will stop us!" I folded my arms across my chest and stood my ground.

"Oh ... I see, all right." This time, she came right close. I caught the stench of death and allure on her breath. The sight of her fangs didn't intimidate me, so I stayed my ground and never moved a muscle.

I thought this was when the fight would break out, but she surprised me. She let out a playful giggle and retreated back into her own space. "The fact you have the nerve to stand in front of me and state your case showing no sign of fear, well, that's impressive!"

"Thank you," I replied, slightly shocked.

"I will stand by you because I can see you're true to your word. I've got a feeling about you, Shanntal ... I've got a feeling!" She waved her finger at me during her statement.

She backed off the intensity level, which made me feel much better. I was so caught up in our interaction, I'd forgotten about everyone else. The entire room had stopped to watch the outcome of our introduction. She laughed, noticing a few people letting out sighs of relief.

"Relax, everyone. Everything is just fine. It was a test to see if she's all that they say she is. I am impressed. By the way, my name is Sauda, which means dark beauty." Again, she giggled and took the opportunity to flip her long, black hair.

My mouth dropped open. Seriously? Dark beauty? Who did this vampire think she was? Before I could pipe up and say something, she carried on with her introduction.

"I've come from afar. News traveled to my land about what you're doing here, and, well ... let's just say, I'm intrigued." Sauda looked back in my direction. "I had to come to see for myself if the chatter held any truth. I also wanted to find out if you were everything they said. I must admit, I understand why Donovan's going through so much trouble. You're like no one I've ever crossed paths with before."

Crossed paths? Why where her words triggering questions in my mind? I couldn't shake the feeling of déjà vu, but now wasn't the time for me to be filled with wonder. She had come to help us. I needed to accept that and bury these suspicious thoughts.

I shot out my hand. "Good to meet you, Sauda. We're happy to have you on board."

She shook my hand. After we separated, Sauda turned around to chat to the nightwalkers that had come with her. Kaleb and Kael stuck close by me. I gave them a quick nod to thank them without having to say the words aloud. We remained near the new group of nightwalkers, which enabled me to overhear Sauda speaking to the others. Despite my change of heart, I still couldn't let it go. There was something about her that made me want to know more. Something that kept me on guard.

Sauda's group shared their opinions about what we were doing and predicted how it would all play out. I was about to lose interest, but then Sauda said something to snag my attention. "Daray is going to go crazy when he hears about this."

I spun her around. "Daray? You know him?" I snapped impatiently. "Tell me where he is!" My gut instinct was right. I knew she was important. I just knew it!

"Easy, now." She pulled herself out of my reach.

Embarrassed, I took a couple steps back.

"Of course I know him. Everyone knows of Daray, but I had the pleasure of spending time with him not so long ago. He's been all over the map, going from coven to coven in search of Donovan. He's trying to track him, but I know he won't find him, because Donovan, well, he's something else altogether."

"He just might find him," I said, remembering my dream, then hoped with everything in me that Daray never found Donovan. I didn't want that one coming true.

"One thing I find amusing is he's doing it to try and get Donovan to leave you alone. It's such a romantic gesture! He searched for you, found you, and now he's fearlessly confronting your foe. I wish someone like Daray tracked me down or stood up for me like that. He's so striking, so powerful, and did I mention extremely good-looking?"

Clearly, Daray had another admirer. I saw the fire in Sauda's eyes as she spoke of him. She seemed a bit confused as to why Daray would bother to go to these extremes for me, but remained helpful as she informed me of the details from their meeting. Perhaps a bit too helpful, especially in the way she gushed over Daray and me. She spoke like we were still a couple.

Lakylee was listening in and decided she'd heard enough. She pushed her way through the crowd to partake in our conversation. "Where do you come from, Sauda? When did you see Daray last?"

Sauda's guard instantly went up when Lakylee entered the picture. "What does it matter to you?"

"Oh, it matters. Look, save yourself some time, I couldn't care less about where you come from. The only part of the conversation that matters to me is the part concerning Daray, and that's because I'm looking for him. Now, spit it out. Where is he?" Lakylee snapped. She was rough around the edges, which sometimes made it difficult seeing the friendlier side of her.

From Sauda's lack of response I assumed Lakylee had intimidated her, being a half-breed and all. Lakylee had strength unlike any of the others. I would've stopped talking too. Clearly, Sauda had hit a sore spot, by the way, she spoke of Daray, and Lakylee made that fact known. You needed to look deep, past all the layers, in order to find the true Lakylee. The wildness was her defense mechanism, her protection from being different. I understood how she worked because I'd done the same thing from time to time. Wearing a shield, allowing only a select few to ever see the real you because it was too hard trying to blend in. Being one of a kind ... sometimes had its drawbacks.

Watching the elements trying to scramble out of the room snapped me out of my thoughts and back into the moment. Lakylee was angry, and Sauda didn't seem to be backing down. The elements were on the right track, better to be safe than sorry. It was time for them to move to safety. Layla, Kynthia, and Allayna moved up front, placing themselves as barriers between the elements and everyone else. The elements were top priority; if any of us wanted to survive, they had to remain safe.

Frantically, I looked around before spotting Uncle Dane and Auntie Steph huddled together in the corner of the room. They seemed to be in good spirits, despite the escalating friction between nightwalkers. Kaleb nodded at Kael, and I saw him grab Jayce, and then the two of them moved closer. As the guys approached, I saw relief in Auntie Steph's eyes. Kaleb never left my side. We were one.

When the tensions rose, our worlds separated once again. It truly was a shame, but seemed necessary. Lakylee had a short temper, especially where Daray was concerned. Now this self-proclaimed dark beauty stood here, claiming interest in Daray, and was ironically the last to see him. I wasn't sure if this scenario would push Lakylee over the edge. We needed to stay prepared, at least until everyone could learn to get along.

After the initial assessment of one another, or the fact Sauda lost their staredown, she began to calmly explain everything. "Lakylee, I come from a place called Forest Falls. It's located on the south side of the mainland. Just before dawn, Daray came to our coven seeking shelter. I didn't have the heart to turn him away, so I let him in. That's when he first spoke of his search for

Donovan. He holds such anger toward him for stealing his love and his life."

Lakylee shot me a look that gave me goose bumps. I needed Sauda to shut her mouth before she said something that would hurt our newly formed alliance.

"How did you know where to find us?" I interrupted.

"It wasn't until after Daray left that the chatter from other covens came, telling us what you were doing here."

"How long ago did you see him, Sauda?" I prodded.

"He left our place about three nights ago. However, the chatter started two days before that. Word is spreading quickly, and I've heard from others, Donovan is close by. He's probably here already. Bad thing for Daray because it means he went in the wrong direction. He headed east after parting from us."

"No, actually that's really good news! The further Daray goes, the less of a chance he'll have of running into Donovan. It'll keep him safe. Right?" I looked at Lakylee, hoping she agreed.

She gave a quick nod and retreated to the group of werewolves. I hoped we found Daray soon because I wanted them to be happy. The love they shared was a darker kind, but true nonetheless. If I hadn't come here, or Ginata and I hadn't used the Ouija board that night, maybe their love would still be growing strong. I needed to fix things between them, because if Daray could love Lakylee, I'd be free to love Jayce forever with no interference.

The night crept along. Nothing much had happened, except an increase in tension between some of the allies and newcomers. With so many newcomers arriving during the night, the cycle kept repeating, just as it had between Lakylee and Sauda. However, the biggest problem with so many gathered was we'd inadvertently put up a wall that Donovan would never be able to cross. We needed to split up in order to find him or allow him to find me.

Destiny

~ Chapter Thirty ~

Aiden was on the same page as I was. He announced to the group, "We'll be breaking off into groups and keeping them fairly small. They will remain large enough to ensure no one gets taken off guard. Groups of four should be okay, so long as every group is accompanied by a number of fairies. We are doing this because it will help lessen the risk for all involved."

Some mumbled, but overall, everyone seemed to be in agreement.

Aiden continued. "One new rule must come into play, so fairies, please listen up. Your glow power must only be used as a defense mechanism against Donovan or his followers. Please be careful not to use your light around any ally nightwalkers."

There were many fairies available, and having the power of their glows on our side was extremely helpful. It was instant sunlight.

The first group consisted of Lakylee the half-breed, Sauda the vampire, Kynthia the shapeshifter, Gabriella the unicorn, and a number of fairies. They were going to Uncle Dane's house. Donovan had been there last, so our home seemed like the best starting point to try and pick up a trail.

Before departing, Lakylee shot me a less than thrilled look because of the fact Sauda had ended up in her group. I shrugged. There wasn't much I could do; Aiden was the one who paired them up.

The next group consisted of Layla, Taini the werewolf, Jayce, and a very nice looking vampire guy, who I'd never been properly introduced to. They were going to be on lookout down at the beach.

Jayce gave me a quick kiss, then nonchalantly turned away to head out.

Funny, he thought I'd let him go as easily as that. "Why you? Why do you need to go? You're supposed to be here with me!" I grabbed his arm, trying to keep him from moving further away.

He turned to face me, and at first I saw fear in his eyes, but then I saw the fight. "Shanntal, I have to do this. We need as many daywalkers as possible in the groups. We're clearly outnumbered here. It's the only way to even things out and make sure everyone sticks to the plan."

"But—"

He cut me off with a passionate kiss. "I love you, Shanntal, and I must do this because of how much I love you. I'll be fine, so try not to worry. We are going down to the beach, only because it's where we've had run-ins before."

"Jayce ... that's exactly what I'm afraid of."

"I'll be back before you even have time to miss me." He wouldn't change his mind. "Kaleb and Kael will stay close to you. I know you'll be safe with them around." He gestured, and they came closer.

"I love you, Jayce. Please tell me you understand how much because I refuse to live without you."

"I know how much," he said. "But, Shanntal, you need to know I love you even more." He kissed my forehead and pulled away. "I'll be back soon. I promise."

I let go, but held my breath while his group disappeared into the darkness. Something made me want to go give Aiden a piece of my mind. How dare he send Jayce out to search for Donovan? Jayce also needed to be safe. He should've been protecting me, protecting them. I kept my mouth closed because I knew deep down inside he had to go. We all had our part to play in this.

I listened to Aiden assemble the next group consisting of the other unicorn, Allayna the shapeshifter, and Fadan and Keita, who were both werewolves. He instructed them to take first watch at the vampire house.

Allayna expressed some concern. "Aiden, I'm not sure about this. Don't you think a better idea would be to have at least one vampire in our group? After all, we are going to a vampire house."

"My decision is final. This is for your safety."

"My safety?"

"We already agreed it would be better for non-vampires to watch the house. Remember that is their home, after all."

"*We?*" she challenged.

"Yes, we, the elements. We as a whole are making the groups up in a way that protects and benefits everyone."

Allayna nodded, seeming satisfied by his response. Their group assembled and a moment later headed to their stakeout point. A few fairies followed closely behind.

The once crowded house had cleared out. There were only a few of us remaining, and the time had come for us to find out what our roles were going to be in all this.

"The rest should be ready in case he comes to the house. Everyone here will be guarding Shanntal, understood?" Aiden went on to say, "We elements must be kept safe, and so we will be locking ourselves together in a room. While we are locked away, we ask that you only call upon us if absolutely necessary. Every time our powers are called upon, our physical being becomes weaker. I would like to keep my human form, as do the others, so we will only use our powers under dire circumstances."

"We will try our best to not bother you guys," Kaleb said.

It didn't seem fair they were involved in all this again. I understood they wanted to help keep balance, but there was too much at stake, especially when the entire world needed them. The situation had become too dangerous.

A few straggling nightwalkers who weren't placed into earlier groups were directed by Aiden to patrol the area surrounding the house. Uncle Dane, Auntie Steph, Kaleb, and Kael were instructed to stay by my side inside the house. Then Aiden led the elements upstairs to safety. We were as ready as we could be.

Donovan, tonight is the night. Tonight your evil way ends.

'Well said!' Jayce entered my mind.

'Are you at the beach now?'

'Just about, but I wanted to say, I love you very much. Don't worry, there won't be any heroic moves, just whatever's necessary.'

'Jayce, please be careful. I love you.'

I didn't feel our connection break, and it made me feel better. He left me feeling like he was still standing beside me.

The moon was full, and the breeze was strong, blowing winds of change throughout the night air. We were ready to put these changes into action.

The uneventful night dragged on and on, and I started getting annoyed. Where was Donovan? Why hadn't he shown himself? I tried to ask Jayce if their group had any luck, but couldn't reach him. We weren't connected any longer. Aggravated, I stepped outside for some air and walked along the terrace on the front of the house. Everyone had come together, which was a step in the right direction. So why wasn't this part of the plan working out how we thought?

We were willing to fight for these changes because they would make life better for everyone. I grew impatient with the waiting game. I wanted ... better yet, I needed things sorted out. This plan had to be implemented before anyone else I cared about got hurt. Frustrated, I paced back and forth, trying to blow off steam before I erupted. After a few minutes, I began to calm down and thought about the bigger picture. No news was good news. Right?

It was in my moment of clarity when I noticed how awfully quiet the night sounded. Nothing moved. Even the wild winds had died down to a silent breeze. No sounds came from anywhere, leaving the illusion that the eerie night had swallowed up the rest of the world. There were at least four nightwalkers nearby, yet I didn't see or hear any of them. I stood still and looked out into the darkness. The moon lit up the tops of the trees and reflected off the dew-covered ground, making it easier for me to see, but more moments passed and still nothing stirred. Had they left?

I was about to go warn the others when the silhouette of a person coming up the driveway caught my eye. I paused. Knee-high mist lingered on top of the driveway, giving the approaching individual quite the floating effect. Shivers rippled down my spine, my heart pounded, and my palms began to sweat. Was I about to face Donovan, on my own, right then and there? I swallowed hard and braced myself.

The figure came closer, and I bravely took a step off the terrace. It kept approaching, but no matter how hard I tried I couldn't make out who it was. Taking another few steps further away from the terrace, I proceeded onto the driveway. Only a small distance remained between the advancing individual and myself. The mist cleared, and I instantly recognized him.

"Daray," I shouted excitedly as I ran over to hug him.

He didn't take to my embrace; instead, he remained hard and cold. "Shanntal."

I let go of him and quickly stepped back. I'd forgotten how we'd left things. The last time we saw one another, a lot of hurtful things had been said and done. Even though I was relieved to see him, I never thought about how much my rejection had hurt him. "Daray, may we talk for a minute?"

"I suppose so." He stood with his arms folded, resembling a statue.

"I never wanted things to be like this. Look at us now. We don't even know one another. I want you in my life, but as a friend."

He huffed.

"Daray, please."

"Fine, say what you will, but just so we're clear, I'm only here to figure out what's going on. And, by the looks of things, you're the only one around that I can talk to. Now start explaining." His eyes shifted toward the door.

I followed his stare. Kaleb and Kael stood in the doorway, their gigantic chests pushed out even further than normal. Even though we had a truce with the nightwalkers, they still had their guard up when it came to me.

"Guys, look, Daray found us!" I said, trying to assure them everything was okay without having to say the words aloud.

Kaleb nodded. "I see that."

His eyes never moved off Daray for a second. I looked at Kael, who wore a similar unwelcoming expression.

"Guys, could we get a few minutes alone? We have some things to talk about." I didn't want them to scare Daray off. I knew they meant well, but their pose was one ready for battle. We'd never be able to work things out with them breathing down our necks.

Kael pulled a reluctant Kaleb into the house by his arm. I let out a sigh. This was all so weird, yet somehow seemed right. Nightwalkers were once the enemy, and now we were friends, even allies. Sure, there might've been some wounds that needed more time to heal, but I hoped when these changes occurred, those old wounds would mend completely.

I sat down on the steps, and Daray sat alongside me. He was so handsome. I couldn't deny the fact. Any girl would've been happy knowing someone like him had searched for her for a century, happy someone like him could hold onto a love considering all the changes he'd been through. If I'd never found Jayce, I would've run away with Daray in a heartbeat. However, Jayce was my life now, just as Lakylee was his.

"I'd like to start off with I'm sorry. I feel awful that things turned out this way for us. Our lives are destined to be entwined for all of eternity, but not in the way we thought. Our engagement brought us into the gardens, and that's the reason you became immortal. It's the same reason I did. Don't you see? We exist because of each other. Our very existence, the position we are in today, that was the purpose of our meeting all those years ago. Destiny had a plan for us. Love was just the beginning of the time we'd share together. This destiny right here, right now, will bring two worlds together. Life will change for everyone when it becomes one world. It must be the reason we escaped the night death came for us."

"Destiny? That's what you consider this? I say it's more like a cruel case of irony!" he spoke harshly. "It's ironic to think I spent an eternity looking for my true love, only to track her down and find out she doesn't love me anymore. Destiny. Ha! I'm cursed to walk the night, cursed to feed off the blood of the mortals, and cursed to walk alone."

"Daray, I don't want you to be alone."

"What are you saying?"

"I'm saying, you're not alone. You never have been. Lakylee loves you more than I ever could. Your obsession with finding me held you stuck in a place where you never had a chance to recognize what blossomed between the two of you. Lakylee loves you, and she can't live without you."

The hardened face he wore moments before relaxed. "She loves me?"

"Yes, she does, Daray."

"What about you?" he asked.

"Daray, we have too many challenges to face. Too many odds stacked up against us."

"It wasn't always that way."

"No, you're right, it wasn't. Please understand I'll always be thankful for the time we spent together. I owe you my very existence. I do love you, but now, as a friend. Jayce is my true love. We want to spend our eternity together, just as Lakylee wants to spend hers beside you. Think about it, she's been there the whole time. You must see she'd do anything for you."

"Well, she did manage to fill the void left by your disappearance." I nodded.

"Just between us, I actually stopped looking for you. It's been about two decades since I bothered trying. I figured you were dead, in the stars, or on the other side of the world. It wasn't until I located you through the Ouija board that my hope came back. When I found you down at the beach, I instantly knew our chance was gone and I'd wasted my immortality on a prize that couldn't be mine. I saw the love between you and Jayce. The sparks are visible to everyone. Your love is so strong."

"Yes, I agree, but, Daray, you had a prize the entire time. Your sights were just set on the wrong trophy. Don't you see?"

"I suppose I do. Lakylee always comes into my thoughts, and she's always been very loyal. I feel quite lonely when she's not around." He looked at me, showing a sensitivity I'd never known before. "I must find her and tell her how I feel." He jumped up off the steps.

I pulled on the sleeve of his coat. "Now's not the time, Daray. Donovan's very close, and everyone has split up into groups to try and find him. You'll be safe, but please, just stay here. I know they'll be back before dawn. Be patient, you'll have your chance to tell her soon enough."

"I know you mean well, but you of all people should understand. I must tell her before it's too late. I won't live in that same manner, wasting my eternity. I refuse to let it happen again." He looked at me for understanding.

He found it. I understood exactly what he meant.

I gave my old love and new friend a hug before wishing him well on his journey. It was so romantic; he was off to tell the girl who loved him exactly how much he loved her back. The thought of their reunion brought butterflies to my stomach the same way Jayce did. Daray and I had both found our soul mates, and above all else, remained friends while doing so. I watched him retreat down the darkened driveway.

When Daray left my sight, I felt a strange chill in the night air. I tried to once again spot the nightwalkers that were supposed to be keeping watch. Still no sign of them … where were they? A dark, uneasy feeling grew in the pit of my stomach. Something didn't feel right. I walked further down the driveway, contemplating if I should head out in search of them myself.

The sound of howls came from the direction opposite where Daray headed. Even though I heard them, I couldn't shake my suspicion something wasn't quite right. Although I couldn't see anything wrong, the hairs on my arms stood on end, and chills ravaged down my back. Better to be safe than sorry. I decided to head back to the comfort and security waiting back inside. I would grab the others so we could go out and search around the premises as a group.

I spun around to face the house, and to my astonishment, I'd gone quite a way further than I'd realized. The way the windows were all lit up made the giant home look very welcoming. I felt at ease again and laughed at myself for being so paranoid.

A branch snapped nearby.

Yikes! I dashed toward the house. I ran as fast as I could, but the house appeared to be moving further away from me. Every passing second caused my panic to grow stronger. I had to stop myself for a minute. This felt crazy! My mind must've been playing tricks on me. The house couldn't move away. My senses were on overdrive.

Time to calm down. I needed to listen. If someone were close, I'd hear footsteps or more breaking branches. My ears strained for some kind of noise. Nothing but sheer silence, not even the wind. The night was as quiet as death, and it confirmed the fact something wasn't right. I took another look around, but still nothing moved. I decided to get off the driveway while making my way back to the house. I'd feel safer being somewhat hidden among the trees and shrubs that lined the driveway.

I pushed myself along as branches and twigs scratched me and tugged on my clothes. I kept my hands up to try and protect my face from the incoming branches. This was a much slower route, but I did feel better being hidden. I was only about fifty yards away from the front door, and for a brief moment, I debated going the rest of the way on the driveway. However, the bad feeling kept getting worse. Nope, I'd stay hidden. This path was working well for me so far.

Thud! I tripped. Branches jabbed and poked at me as I fell. I smashed my head into the base of the tree trunk. I cried out in pain as the throbbing began. I touched along my hairline and felt the warmth of blood. Oh no, this really wasn't good. I tried getting up, but the dizziness won and forced me back to the ground. I lay bleeding in the shrubs, hoping and wishing someone would find me soon. Someone who was on my side.

I tried connecting to Jayce. Maybe if he sensed my pain, he'd lead the others out of the house to help. I concentrated the best I could, despite my oozing and throbbing pain. However, it was no use. He didn't connect back.

Every minute my pain grew more and more unbearable. I found it difficult to keep my eyes open. "Help me … anyone? Help!" I shouted feebly. The sound of my voice pounded like nails through my throbbing skull.

I heard no response, nothing but unwelcoming silence. My eyes closed and I drifted into unconsciousness.

Healing

~ Chapter Thirty-One ~

I awoke safe and sound, tucked into Jayce's bed. Had this been just another one of my dreams? I balanced on my elbows before attempting to sit up. The shocking pain in my head felt all too real. I lay back down, reached up, and found bandages wrapped around my head.

"Jayce?" I called out. "Anyone?"

A moment later the door opened. I stared in disbelief; Jayce looked more beat up than I felt.

"Oh no … what happened?" I placed my hands over my mouth to stop my gasp, or at least hide it a bit better.

He moved slowly, but came and sat down beside me on the bed. From the look on his face, I already knew it was bad news. "I guess you can see we ran into some trouble."

"What happened?" I repeated.

"We met nightwalkers down at the beach that were opposed to what we're doing. They tried to stop us because they foolishly believe Donovan's created the proper way of life. They feel those gifted from the night belong in the night, and daywalkers should stay in the light where they *let us survive*." He paused for a moment. "They're unbelievably ignorant. He's brainwashed them. We fought, and sadly there were significant casualties on both sides."

"Who?" I sobbed. None of this was supposed to happen. Donovan should've been the casualty, the only one. My imagination ran wild. From the sight of Jayce, I knew there'd been brutal fighting.

"Many more nightwalkers and daywalkers joined us while you slept. Unfortunately, the fighting grew too intense. Most of the newcomers backed out, and those who didn't ..." He let out a defeated sigh. "Well, there's no way to soften it, they didn't survive."

"No!" This was exactly the opposite of what I wanted to hear.

"The group sent to the vampire house never came back. Allayna, Fadan, and Keita were all killed. Donavon showed up there and didn't take to their company. The unicorn traveling with them managed to get away. She arrived here in time to warn us, but unfortunately died a few hours ago from her injuries."

I sat upright; sadness turned to pure anger. Despite the pain I was in, I clenched my fists and pounded them against the bed.

Jayce continued, "My group lost the vampire. Taina, the werewolf is injured, but she'll be okay in the long run. Layla got injured too, but her injuries are minor compared to everyone else."

I'd reached my breaking point. A rage boiled inside I'd never known or felt before. I would've fought until death, ripping Donovan into pieces, had he been close enough. Donovan needed to die, and I was set on doing it myself. After all the lives stolen, the loved ones he'd taken from me, I was sure I'd feel no remorse. I was out for revenge. He'd created me; now he was about to regret everything about me.

"I've got to see Gabriella." I tried to stand, but my head injury had other plans. I spun out and lost my balance.

"You must rest." Jayce tried to put me back into bed.

I fought him off and managed to stumble a few steps toward the door.

"You're too stubborn, Shanntal. Do you even remember what happened? Do you know where they found you?"

I stopped. It took a minute before the events came back into my mind. "Yes, I know where I was, Jayce," I snapped. "I walked there myself."

"And?"

"Well, I remember feeling uneasy because I couldn't find the four nightwalkers keeping watch. Daray arrived, and we chatted. When he left, I followed him a little ways, trying to spot the others. Something didn't feel right to me, so I got off the driveway and took cover in the bushes. I couldn't find any of them, so I decided to go back to the house, but I tripped."

"Oh, you found them all right. You tripped on their corpses!"

"What?"

"Donovan was here, but must've retreated when Daray arrived. I never thought the day would come when I'd be thankful to know Daray was around. But I am. If he hadn't come when he did, who knows what would have happened. Kaleb told me you wandered off by yourself. What were you thinking?"

"Really?" I asked, quite surprised. "Donovan was here?"

"Yeah, and from where you and the nightwalkers' remains were found, he was really close."

I began to panic. "Jayce, we have a huge problem."

"What?"

"I couldn't tell he was here. Having all these nightwalkers around is causing my body to adapt. I can't sense him."

Donovan was too strong, and we needed a way to know whenever he was near. The extra edge we had on our side had just disappeared.

Jayce stared with a blank expression.

"Are you able to connect?" I asked.

"No. I've already tried. I wanted to get a feel for him, see how he thinks and figure out his plan, but I can't reach him." Frustrated, he ran his hands through his hair, trying to stimulate a connection.

Things weren't going as planned. We were banged up and bruised, and it wouldn't lead us to a victory. "Jayce, please help me. I need to get to Gabriella. She's got the ability to heal our wounds, and we have to be ready before nightfall."

"Fine, all right! Only because I really hurt, and if she can take this pain away, I'm all for it." He placed his arms around me for support, and we made our way downstairs.

I didn't see a body in the house that wasn't battered. Things were starting to look pretty bad. What if we were in over our heads? What if Donovan's strength made him invincible? What if this became a battle with no end? Could I handle being the one responsible for more lives lost?

We found Gabriella just outside the house, feeding under the tree where Jayce and I had argued days before. Despite everything, I was glad that day was behind us.

"Gabriella, I'd like to ask you for a favor." I approached her slowly.

She stopped eating and looked in my direction. My breath was momentarily caught when the sun shimmered on her silky white hair, making her horn sparkle like a thousand diamonds. *'Yes, Shanntal, my dear friend, what may I do for you?'*

Jayce remained behind while I advanced toward the enchanting beauty. As I got closer, I saw her sadness. Her blue eyes now held a darker tinge of gray in the center of them. Then I remembered Jayce had told me the other unicorn died from her injuries. I wrapped my arms around her neck. "I'm so very sorry for your loss. I never thought things would turn out this way. Please forgive me."

'Forgive you?'

"Yes, this is all because of me. It's my fault things are going wrong."

'That's quite a heavy load to carry and one you shouldn't lug around. Fate and destiny decide what happens and the time it will

come about. Child, there's nothing you could've done differently to have changed the outcome of all that's been done. It's what is meant to be.' She nuzzled her nose against me.

"But, if I hadn't fallen down. If I'd only …" Her touch made my negativity disappear, and I felt a sense of peace wash over me. We stood silently for a few minutes, enjoying each other's company.

Jayce sat down as he watched the healing process begin. He was absolutely mesmerized by Gabriella and her magical ways.

'Shanntal, if I remember correctly, you came to ask me for a favor. What can I do to help you?'

I felt better than I had in days. During our visit, Gabriella managed to heal more than my head wounds. She healed my guilty conscience too. I was ready for action and prepared to do whatever necessary to rid the world of Donovan.

"Could I bother you to use your magic to heal some of the wounded? I don't want them suffering on my behalf. It was my fight, and they've risked everything to protect me. I'd like to return the honor, with your help, of course."

'I would be more than happy to help you. However, please remember, this is the only time I'm able to step in. Destiny has already mapped everything out for each ad every one of us.'

"Thank you, Gabriella. I promise, I won't ask again." I hugged my friend.

Everything about her amazed me. Especially since I'd seen her in my dreams before we met, but mostly because she was the one creature that lived in every little girl's imagination. I still couldn't wrap my head around the fact I had her here with me. Undoubtedly, she was the single most magnificent creature that ever lived, and to call her my friend was the greatest gift I could've ever received.

I assisted Jayce up from the ground. Gabriella remained still while I delicately brought him to her. He was in pretty rough shape and appeared to be getting worse. Jayce leaned his arm on her for balance, and Gabriella carefully shook her long flowing white mane. Within a few seconds, the healing treatment began to take effect, and he stood upright. His hand remained on her for healing and no longer for support. After another minute had passed, most of his visible wounds disappeared.

"Thank you, Gabriella," he said gratefully.

'Consider it my pleasure, Jayce.'

"We'll gather the others and bring them out. Thank you again for doing this!"

Jayce and I rounded up the least injured so they could help carry out the ones in worse condition. We managed to get the wounded daywalkers to form a line in front of Gabriella. Graciously, she took the time to heal each and every one.

A steady flow of thanks came from the mended. The healing from a unicorn left you feeling better than imaginable. It left a sensation like you could jump up to the stars and dance among the clouds. Our momentum was back and much better than before. We were all in good spirits, full of life, and filled with love.

Another evening quickly arrived. I strolled closer to Gabriella. "Thank you so much for helping everyone today."

'You're more than welcome, Shanntal.'

"I ... umm ... I mean *we* really can't thank you enough. When the nightwalkers arrive, I'll help gather up their wounded so you can heal them too."

'I'm sorry, but I won't be able to help them, Shanntal. My magic only helps those with pure hearts. I'm afraid the nightwalkers aren't pure anymore. They roam the night, meaning they live another way.'

"Oh," I said, feeling discouraged again. Our worlds were still torn. What she said made sense, but I wished there was a way to overcome the divide remaining between us.

'Please try not to worry. They've got the means available to mend themselves. I just can't assist them with the process.'

"Thanks for everything you've done for us. I sure do appreciate your help, and so do the others. I understand you can't do anything for the nightwalkers. It's unfortunate, but I really do understand."

This setback made me wonder if the plan to join our two worlds could even happen. No matter what steps we took forward, everything boiled back down to good versus evil, and we couldn't find a way around it.

The nightwalkers had a reputation and for just cause. They were killers, simple as that. They chose to feed on mortals rather than animals. Once mortal blood was spilled, it signified the end of their pure heart. They were all given a choice, but the thirst was powerful, and often too much to handle. Their lack of willpower became the decision maker on how they'd spend the rest of their lives. Animal blood just didn't quite quench the thirst, which eventually drove them to feed off the mortals. Once they tasted human blood, that's when the power trip took over. Some killed for the thrill, while others only killed when absolutely necessary as a means of survival. Either way, there was no forgiving the taking of innocent lives. It wasn't their fault, just part of the curse. They received a gift of beautiful, ageless immortality, but attached to it was a hefty price—death. Death surrounded and consumed them. It left them no escape because they were dead themselves. The venom killed once it made contact, but blood fed the immortality, allowing them to rise once again.

A puzzling question came into my mind. If I was immortal because of a vampire, how could she heal me? I turned to ask, but she was no longer there.

The sky had become dark much earlier than usual. A thick cloud cover arrived from the incoming storm. The earlier cool breeze started blowing fiercely. I pulled my sweater tightly around me and hurried toward the house.

Contact

~ Chapter Thirty-Two ~

I was only about thirty feet from the house when lightning lit up the darkened sky. A couple of seconds passed by before I heard the thunder rumble. The wind quickly picked up, blowing in a chill that wasn't there moments earlier. Another roar came from the threatening sky, causing me to jump. The rhythmic storm moved in rapidly and was showing no mercy as it prepared to unleash its wrath upon us. I looked around for Gabriella, but she still wasn't anywhere to be seen. Come to speak of it, no one was. They'd all been healed and gone inside.

I watched three streaks of lightning split off into all directions. I used that as my cue to head indoors. The storm was going to be nasty once it hit. I looked around one more time for Gabriella, only to end up with the same luck as before. There was no sign of her. I needed to stop worrying. She was a unicorn and had probably already found shelter from the storm.

I was about to plant my foot on the steps of the house, but something seemed off. My hair stood on end, but I wasn't quite sure why. Whatever was going on, it had me ready and alert. I glanced over to my right just as the lightning lit up the sky. Nothing seemed out of the ordinary, so I looked to my left, awaiting the next strike. The rain erupted, drenching everything in seconds. I shivered from the cool downpour soaking my clothes, but remained in place because I needed to know if someone was there. It was a feeling that I couldn't ignore. The next lightning strike came, and I scanned the tree line. On the far left side, in the spot where the trees thinned out, I caught a glimpse of a dark silhouette just as it stepped back into the trees, and the thunder rolled again.

Had I actually seen someone, or was I just being paranoid? I used my best efforts to blink the rain away. I even raised my hands to make a visor for my eyes. It was pointless. No matter how hard I tried, the night was so dark and the rain too heavy for me to see anything clearly. Yet, the more I thought about what had caught my eye, the more likely it seemed. Shiver tremors rolled across my body, confirming my doubts. Deep down, I knew I had seen someone. Sure, the rain was cold, but not enough to cause this kind of reaction. Every hair stood on end, and the harsh shivers continued. Maybe it was what we'd been waiting for? Was this the time we would fight to make our big changes happen?

I wanted … actually, I needed to be sure of what I saw before warning everyone. I waited rather impatiently for more lightning to strike. I tapped my foot as if that would make it happen faster. I needed light to see who lurked within the trees. I felt fired up and ready. Come on, bring on the fireworks!

BOOM! The thunder crashed, and I jumped about two feet off the ground. I wanted lightning, not thunder. Sheesh! Yeah, I was ready, for anything except a loud sound. I shook it off. I had to be as ready as I could be.

A few seconds later, lightning illuminated the darkened sky. I squinted, trying to reduce the rain in my eyes while I looked at the place I thought I'd spotted someone. Sure enough, movement, just down from where I looked the first time. I quickly wiped the rain out of my eyes. I couldn't believe it. The individual no longer hid among the trees; he used this opportunity to reveal himself. Our eyes connected, and without a doubt, I knew who he was … Donovan.

My heart pounded harder than ever before. I waited for him to lunge at me like he had that night in the gardens. Disappointment. He made no attempt to come forward.

His pale, sunken face, dark eyes, and bloody mouth looked the same as they had in my dream. He squared himself off and locked his icy stare with mine. Donovan opened his mouth wide and revealed his fangs, accompanied by an eerie smile. Instead of coming forward, he remained lurking through the trees, pacing back and forth. The lightning passed, and once again the sky went dark.

I spun around, wanting to warn everyone that he was here. My mouth opened to shout for help, but something made me stop. All I thought about was how I didn't want anyone else hurt because of me. This fight was between the two of us, and we had an opportunity to settle this here and now. The last one standing would have the world the way they wanted.

Instead of moving closer to the house, I went against my better judgment and decided to trust my instincts. I started toward the trees. My shoes splashed with every step in the slippery grass. I felt my socks getting soaked while the heavy rain chilled me right to the bone.

As I approached, I thought the wet ground might actually help me out. It might benefit me should I need to escape. I could slip and fall down easily, then camouflage myself in mud and disappear. It could enable me a chance to crawl away unseen.

Nonsense! I fought the cowardly thoughts from my head. I would stand and fight. The time had come for someone to fight back; I wouldn't run or hide anymore.

Sopping wet and fired up, I finally reached the tree line. I wiped the rain from my face and glanced around but couldn't see him anywhere. He was toying with me, always playing these ridiculous games, and I'd grown very tired of the antics. "Donovan, you big coward. I'm here! I'm the one you want. Show yourself!" I held my arms out as I shouted at the trees. I spun around trying to catch a glimpse of him, but he never appeared, and this fueled my anger even more. My rage hit a boiling point, sending adrenaline pumping rapidly through my veins. I was ready to fight. I'd never been more ready for anything in my entire life. I clenched my fists. "Where are you? You wanted this, now you hide? Are you scared? Not used to someone who'll fight back?" I ranted while I spun myself around one more time, and then it happened ... our eyes locked.

He crept out from behind the large tree only a few feet away from where I stood. The sight of him made me grind my teeth and ball up my fists, as I hardened my stance. He came over and stood in front of me, so I did the first thing that came to mind. I lunged. I knocked him to the ground, punching and kicking as hard as I possibly could. Every blow connected, but he just laughed. He remained ruthless, provoking me to do worse than I already was. I needed to act fast. I rolled over, got myself up off the ground, and kicked him in the ribs. He coiled from the blow, but never stopped laughing.

His laughing made me livid. Donovan remained on the ground looking up at me. From that stance, it seemed I had the upper hand, but the awful laughter escaping from between his fangs left me with an overwhelming urge to lose it. I had to do worse to shut him up. I moved in closer to kick him again, hoping it would be the time that silenced his laughter.

I lifted my leg back to gather momentum, swung forward, but with a swift movement of his arm, he hit the back of my planted knee, sending me spilling down on top of him.

"Now, isn't this much better? Let's get a bit more up close and personal." He licked his bloody tongue down the side of my face.

Disgusted, I dug my elbows into him and scurried away in an attempt to get back on my feet. The games were done. He wasn't playing around anymore. I'd gotten his attention. I had regained most of my balance and was just about all the way up when he took hold, and in an effortless motion, flung me backward through the air. I landed hard on my back, knocking the wind out of me. I choked for air as I rolled around in pain.

Donovan strolled over casually. He sat on top of me, pinning me to the ground while I lay helpless and injured. I kicked and squirmed using every ounce of strength I could find, but I wasn't strong enough to move him. He had complete control now.

"You've surprised me." He cocked his head slightly to the side. "I didn't think you had it in you. Quite the fight you've started here." His cold fingers dragged down my cheek. "I must admit … I rather enjoy this side of your demeanor."

I squirmed. My skin burned from his icy touch. I had to get up and find help. Why had I been so reckless and stupid? How did I think I could take him on alone? Why hadn't Kaleb or Jayce sensed I was in trouble? I needed them now, more than ever before.

I opened my mouth, about to call for help, when Donovan interrupted me.

"Thinking about calling for help?" His tone was razor sharp. "Do it! I want them to watch you perish."

"Why are you doing this to me?" I cried.

"You got in the way. That's all. You were never supposed to become immortal. This gift wasn't meant for you, it was for Daray. However, once you are gone, things can finally happen the way they were meant to all those years ago."

"I didn't ask for this." I looked for understanding deep in his cold eyes.

"I know you didn't. Yet, everyone seems to treat you as some kind of superior being, but we both know you aren't. You are nothing more than a mistake. I promise you this right here and now, I will kill anyone who tries to protect you. I've waited far too long for this to end."

"No!" I cried. The faces of Jayce, Kaleb, Kael, and the others flashed through my mind. "Please, leave them alone."

"Oh yes!" he taunted. "They will all disappear, the same way your family did. Now, call them! I want them around to witness your ending."

I didn't respond.

"Call them!" he snapped.

I stayed silent.

"Why won't you call them?" His voice grew impatient.

I wasn't about to play his game the way he wanted. I wouldn't grant him the satisfaction he craved. So I remained silent.

In retaliation, his fist smashed down hard on my face. I cried out and turned my head to the side, trying to protect myself. His vulgar act split my lip open. The taste of salty blood filled my mouth as it spilled out of the fresh wound.

He dragged my face back toward him, his fingers playing with my blood. "Answer me!" he ordered.

Something seemed different; his touch no longer hurt as it had before. An urge instructed me to suck on my bottom lip. I started drinking my own blood, and shockingly, doing so made me feel strong again. A growing power surged, starting in the pit of my stomach. Soon, the new power overshadowed any pain I felt. I deliberately chose to ignore Donovan, knowing how much my silence would anger him. He was used to having all the control, and I enjoyed not giving him the satisfaction.

"Answer me, stupid girl."

I smirked instead of responding, and he hit me again. More blood flowed, this time from the other side of my mouth. I welcomed the discomfort for another minute until … the unspeakable happened.

Fangs

~ Chapter Thirty-Three ~

Fangs ripped through my gums, leaving a euphoric sensation. I felt powerful, superior even. Letting out a horrific snarl, I pushed Donovan off me like nothing more than a feather. He smashed through the trees, sending debris flying everywhere.

I got up from the ground and stood for a minute, taking the time to feel my fangs and admire my newly acquired strength. The vampire in me had finally come out. He'd pushed too far and made me too angry. He let the beast loose, and now he was about to meet his match.

I started toward him, and to my pleasure he appeared shaken by the fact I was coming after him. "Scared?" I teased, quickening my stride. I uprooted a nearby tree and threw it at him.

The tree hit, and he fell to the ground. When he stood up, I latched onto another so I could take joy in knocking him down once again. I felt invincible. I threw blow after blow and didn't allow him much of a chance to fight back.

The best part of my new powers was I had no regrets doing any of it. My remorse and compassion were buried deep within. Rage, resentment, and bitterness were the feelings coming out of me now. The memories of my family, Ginata and her parents, Garrison, and the many other friends who died because of this beast flashed fresh in my mind. The monster would pay for their deaths, and would do so by losing his own life.

I became consumed by my increasing rage. I felt strong, wild, and fierce, with only one thing on my mind—destroy Donovan. I became so lost in my dark thoughts that I didn't notice when he took hold of a tree. *Smash!* I flew back from the delivered hit. Branches scratched me while leaves flew off in every direction. I sailed through the air, landing on a bunch of broken branches, which helped break my fall. I picked myself up, and to my surprise, no pain. Not a thing. Brushing myself off, I did what needed to be done, and charged again.

Whack! Whack! My newly arrived vampire stone hands pounded against Donovan. The thought of everything he'd done to my family fueled my fury, allowing me to punch him over and over again.

Our battle continued on fairly even ground, mimicking the sounds of the storm. Unfortunately, a problem arose, and we both noticed about the same time as the pace of our fight slowed. We were both immortal, so there wasn't any easy way to kill each other. In truth, I didn't even know if I could stake Donovan, and thankfully he never took advantage of the fact. Fighting just used up all our energy, and we weren't even doing damage to one another. The surrounding forest felt the brunt of our run-in.

In a final attempt to battle, we lunged at one another, colliding in mid-air. The encounter sent us flying backward in opposite directions. I landed hard on a rocky part of the ground, but the fall didn't hurt me whatsoever. My skin grew harder and thicker with every passing minute. I was changing, and quite rapidly; the vampire I had locked inside was practically free.

I found my new experience of fighting absolutely exhausting and welcomed the much needed break. I'd never done hand-to-hand combat before, and it wasn't anything like I expected. I thought I could hurt him, make him feel pain like he caused so many others, but I was wrong. He was made of stone; no heart lived in him.

"It's not so bad being a vampire, right?" he asked smugly. "Why couldn't you have just accepted the fact you shared my gift in the beginning? Everything could have been different for you, but no, that's not the choice you made. Instead, you tried so hard to fight it, but look at how much you're enjoying yourself now. Life only gets better from here."

"Gift? You call this a gift? You've ruined my life! Yes, your *curse* has consumed me, I'll admit to that, but all you've really done is brought out the worst in me. I don't thank you for any of this. I hate you more than ever. *I will never walk the night!*"

"My young opponent, the change is already done. You'll never walk during the day again." His taunting laugh echoed through the forest.

"Liar! You lie!" I cried. This couldn't be the end. It just couldn't.

The rain eased, or at least I no longer sensed the wetness any more. My blood grew colder as more minutes went by, then the moment arrived when my skin fully hardened. It felt like I wore a protective suit made of thick ice or heavy metal. So many changes occurred in me that I no longer felt like myself. He'd brought out the beast, and I didn't know how or if I could turn myself back. Tears should have flowed, but I was so angry I couldn't make them come. My heart broke on the inside, but thanks to my new demeanor I couldn't show any of my pain on the outside. I stomped my feet and screamed in utter frustration.

Donovan grinned wickedly as he watched my unraveling.

I looked down at the hardened skin covering my body. It didn't even resemble mine; I looked so pale, so dead. I felt my fangs, but this time I cringed. They were so sharp, completely lethal.

Donovan appeared undeniably amused.

My senses continued to heighten. Soon everything looked and sounded different. I could see as clearly at night as I'd once viewed the world during the daylight hours. I turned my head when I heard noises coming from the distance. Jayce and the others poured out of the house, racing toward the trees. More sounds rustled, this time from the opposite side. I spotted Daray, Lakylee, and the other nightwalkers approaching.

We'd made a truce that remained strong. Daywalkers and nightwalkers still came together regardless of what just happened or what I was experiencing. As a group, we could continue to change the way things had once been done. We were immortals, plain and simple, with no need for the day or night dividing us. Immortals needed to feel free during both times. Coming together now, showing no signs of animosity toward one another, was proof this would work. We were all on the same team. We believed in the same purpose ... there was a way to live among each other in peace.

The only thing that wouldn't work anymore was me. I had changed and needed to figure out exactly how to live with myself this way. I couldn't pretend everything would be okay between Jayce and me because these circumstances led back to the same problem, which had separated me from Daray all those years ago. How could we survive if one was a monster and the other wasn't? Despite everyone coming together, I couldn't get past the obvious problems. The lifestyles were vastly different, and no matter how much I loved him, I didn't know how to overcome the obstacles ahead.

Uncle Dane and Auntie Steph quickly made their way over to me. Seeing the disappointment evident on their faces broke what was left of my heart. Uncle Dane froze in his steps; tears swelled in his eyes, but he remained strong. He never shed a single tear, but instead clenched his fists tightly. Auntie Steph took one good look and started crying uncontrollably.

I'd turned into the one thing we worked so hard to avoid. They'd protected me for years, as did my family, and I failed them all. I'd been defeated and changed into a monster. The worst part was I'd done this all on my own. If only I'd called for help or connected to Jayce, maybe things would've ended differently for me, or maybe Donovan would've gotten his chance to kill more of the people I loved. Despite what I had become, I knew I'd done the right thing. They were all safe now.

My eyes shifted between Kaleb and Kael, who now made their approach. Kael appeared somewhat repulsed by my new demeanor, but Kaleb looked at me in the same caring way he always had. He would remain beside me no matter what, through the light and deep into the darkness—we were one.

Jayce, on the other hand, was another story altogether. I knew this would destroy him and wasn't quite sure I could handle watching him go through any more pain. I sighed, trying to avoid eye contact the best I could.

Time froze momentarily as I stood and thought about how we may never get to be together like we once were. Jayce had shown me what love felt like, and what it meant to live again. Even when our problems had stemmed from impossible scenarios, we managed to work things out. However, this seemed so much worse. No matter my changes, it still couldn't numb my heartbreak.

Multiple scenarios ran through my head as I pondered the possible outcomes, hoping at least one would show me how we could have a future together. It was no use. Not after I'd already come up with my own conclusion. After all, the same scenario happened a hundred years ago with this exact type of relationship. Sure, we were different people, but it would probably end the same way. It would be too difficult to carry on with the life we'd created. He had to walk during the day hours, whereas I'd be confined to roaming the night. We already had too many odds stacked up against us, and although we'd managed to pull through every other time, I wasn't sure we stood a chance. Once again, we'd become the couple in an impossible relationship.

Jayce moved closer. So close, my nose practically touched his chin. He tilted my head up, forcing me to meet his gaze. Just when I thought things couldn't possibly get worse, I realized I was totally wrong. While looking deep into his eyes, something happened. I saw our hopes and dreams fade, along with the layers of pain he'd been trying to downplay. He didn't need to say words aloud. I knew him too well; he couldn't fool me. I understood everything from just a look in his eyes.

When Jayce realized I understood, tears swelled in his eyes. He let go of my face and walked away. I knew by the way he paced back and forth that he was trying to come up with some kind of elaborate plan to change me back. I wanted to tell him not to waste his time, tell him not to even bother. I wanted to tell him I had already accepted the fact it wasn't possible, but I remained silent.

Lakylee emerged from the gathering crowd. She smiled sympathetically at first, but her facial expression hardened as she took notice of my changes. She hissed and spun around wildly. "What have you done to her?"

"What have I done?" Donovan laughed. "It's already done! It always has been. I've just helped her along with the evolving bit, that's all. She likes herself better this way. Don't you, Shanntal?" He stood proud of his victory.

I hung my head in shame. I didn't want to be a vampire. I liked my life and wanted it back. I didn't want to be stuck walking the night or having to kill in order to survive. I wanted to see the sun rise and bask in her glorious rays.

From the corner of my eye, I saw Lakylee step out of view. Curiosity got the better of me, so I looked up to see where she went. That's when I detected the level of crazed she was. The vicious warrior we all knew had come out to play. She snarled and hissed as she closed in on Donovan. He scrambled, looking to the other nightwalkers for assistance. Not one moved to help him.

My transformation might've ruined who I was, but certainly not what I was about. My friends, family, and even my allies were angry, hurt, and disappointed in the same ways I was. No one wanted this fate for me, no one except Donovan.

Realizing he was on his own, Donovan did his best to escape. It was quite a pathetic sight. He managed to scramble about ten feet away before Lakylee attacked. She ripped and tore, showing no mercy as he cried out, begging for her to stop. I turned my head away, finding it too difficult to watch their fight unfold. I imagined she'd used these same kinds of moves on Garrison. Bitterness grew inside. Why was my life so hard? Why did everything turn out in the worst possible way whenever I was involved? Didn't I deserve any sort of happiness? That was it! I vented my frustration with a blood-curdling scream.

Lakylee paused when I screamed, allowing Donovan the opportunity to push her off of him. Looking injured, he stumbled around before spotting an opening in the crowd. It appeared he would get to make his great escape after all. Lakylee noticed it unfold about the same time as I did. She hollered at Sauda, who stood the closest to Donovan, to stop him. However, Sauda didn't react. Instead, she remained in a somewhat dazed state checking out the nail polish on her manicured fingernails. Donovan bolted past her.

Everyone groaned, unable to believe what happened. Sauda just let the person who had single-handily destroyed my life get away. I was furious. I wanted him to be held accountable for everything he'd done. Unfortunately, all I could do was stare in disbelief.

Thankfully, Daray acted fast. Using super speed, he raced past Sauda, knocking Donovan to the ground. Daray destroyed the chance for him to escape.

Even more enraged, Lakylee got up in Sauda's face. She hissed, "What's wrong with you, Sauda? Were you just going to let him get away? Is your loyalty with him or us?"

"Of course it's with you guys." She huffed nonchalantly.

"Really?" sneered Lakylee. "It sure doesn't seem like that, since *you* were the one who almost let him escape!"

"Look, there's no need to get yourself all worked up. I knew he wouldn't get too far. Haven't you noticed how many others are around here?"

Lakylee released a grisly growl and clenched her jaw.

I decided to step in before things got out of control. "Listen, Sauda, the level of frustration here is insane, but surely you can appreciate the sensitivity of the situation. This man ..." I paused for a moment as her eyes shifted over to Donovan. "Allow me to rephrase. This monster has hurt so many people."

Someone interrupted me with a sarcastic laugh.

"Okay, okay, who am I kidding? Yeah, we all know that's quite an understatement. Seriously, though, he's *killed* so many people, and I'm pretty sure they weren't only the ones I cared about. His way of living isn't right. If they can live peacefully above us, then why can't we down here? Do you understand what I am saying?"

"Yes, I get it," she replied, using a softer tone.

Just when I thought the conversation was over, Sauda piped up. "But ... I know if Daray hadn't gotten a chance to shine, someone else surely would have. Besides, I really didn't want to break a nail. See, they were just done." She flashed her fancy nails at the group.

A few laughs sounded, but Lakylee grumbled at her response. Sauda certainly was different. I couldn't say I'd ever met a diva nightwalker before.

Meanwhile, Daray and the others delivered a few extra blows to the monster while he was on the ground.

Donovan looked defeated. He foolishly thought by changing me, things would go back to the way they were. He expected me to sit back, accept my fate, and act like nothing would be done about it. Well, it might've been true for me, but was he ever wrong about my friends. They were standing up for me, and he wouldn't get away with this.

Four werewolves intervened and picked Donovan up off the ground. They held onto him tightly as he thrashed around, trying to break loose.

"What are you going to do with him?" I asked.

In order to try and comfort me, Daray placed his arm protectively around me. "Don't worry, Shanntal. You're too pure to share this fate. This was my fate. It was never meant for you, but somehow you ended up caught in the middle. I promise you, all the wrongs will be made right."

His words didn't help me feel better, so I pulled myself out of his half-embrace. "Although this fate wasn't meant to be mine, destiny seemed to think otherwise. Look at me, Daray. There's no going back!"

Donovan let out a wicked laugh, but quickly stopped when the werewolves roughed him up some more.

Uncle Dane and Auntie Steph moved closer to me. I stared blankly, unsure of what to do or say. They positioned themselves on either side of me and tightly held my hands.

"We love you no matter what time of day you walk," Uncle Dane said.

"You'll always be our sweet Shanntal," Auntie Steph assured.

I squeezed their hands appreciatively, but it caused them both to squirm.

"Oh, you guys, I'm awfully sorry," I apologized while relaxing my grip. I'd forgotten about my new strength attached to these powers.

Too bad I wasn't strong enough to defeat Donovan or keep myself from changing. If only I'd called out for help when I first saw him. I went in bravely to face the beast, only to end up losing the battle. What made me think I could handle it on my own? I knew I was in over my head, yet something still made me charge over there. What the heck was wrong with me? I didn't feel right in my new body. I shouldn't have fangs. I didn't want to live this way. I wanted to scream, but instead hung my head shamefully.

I overheard Jayce talking to someone, but didn't recognize the voice. Curiosity won, so I lifted my head. At first glance, I saw Sauda flip her hair, but just past her was a glimpse of Jayce talking to one of the vampire guys who had arrived with Sauda. The sight of Jayce stole my breath, and for a brief moment our eyes locked, but I felt nothing. We were no longer connected.

I had to face the truth. The same thing happened before with Daray and me. The only difference was the fact that I was the one who had been turned into the vampire. History seemed to be repeating itself, which meant I was the one about to lose my true love. I made myself look into his eyes, but the amount of pain I saw forced us both to look away.

My emotions were being contradictory. I felt love, yet couldn't have it. I felt strong, yet I was weak. My only true emotion was bitterness. My life had been stolen, along with the lives of my family and friends, and I resented every single second of it.

It was in the next moment when I made up my mind. I was going to die. As soon as the sun rose, I would put myself out of my misery. There was no way I would ever kill an innocent or end up confined to an eternity of endless roaming nights. That was not the life I was born to live.

Jayce stormed over and looked me square in the eyes. "I'll love you forever. Remember? You said that! Those are your words. This isn't forever, so get that stupid idea out of your head. I won't let you die, especially like that. I mean it, Shanntal. Lose that idea right now!"

I was shocked. "You knew what I was thinking?"

"Of course I did. We are always connected. You can't feel me because of your changes, but maybe you'll feel this." His warm lips pressed against mine.

His kiss stung my mouth. Sharp shocks zapped my lips. The warmth of him, his kiss, it all hurt my skin, so I pulled away. "I can't do this."

"I understand." He placed his hand gently under my chin, tilted my head up to make me look him in the face again. "Please don't give up on us. There's got to be a way. I promise, we'll figure this out."

Everything had changed, and I wasn't handling my new reality very well. Sure, I admit at one point in time I actually envied the vampires. I loved their seductiveness and appeal. I admired their methods of sucking in their lovers, and how they seduced their prey until the moment the hunger arrived. No one saw them coming until it was too late. Their strength was undeniably impressive, and the night really wasn't that bad. I'd often found something about the darkness comforting.

The problem for me was I couldn't be with Jayce the way we were before. I needed that because he had become the best part of my life. Another thing I had a hard time with was acknowledging the fact I'd have to kill innocents to survive. The sheer thought of taking the life of another placed a pit in my stomach. Man, I couldn't even kill Donovan, even after everything he'd done to me and the people I cared about most. How would I ever survive as a vampire? I wasn't a killer and never could be.

I felt defeated, ashamed, and all because I had been too stupid to call for help when I had the chance. Now, I'd managed to lose everything that mattered and didn't see how I could ever get it back.

As I stood lost in my thoughts, everyone continued to come together in my defense. Aiden and Makan assisted the werewolves in holding Donovan captive. Kael and Kaleb chatted to Daray and Lakylee, trying to decide what they should do with him. Uncle Dane and Auntie Steph and Layla never strayed too far from me. Layla had stayed a very loyal friend through everything, and even though I had changed, our bond remained intact.

The nightwalkers seemed disappointed that Donovan managed to change me, but still treated me the same way as they did before. I hadn't killed anyone, so I guessed I wasn't totally like them—at least not yet.

"Tie him up and let the sun turn him to ash," someone shouted.

"Cut off his head!" yelled a wolf.

"Cut out his black heart!" screamed Meriel.

"Don't! You guys, please. No one deserves that. There's got to be another way. Show some mercy," I begged.

Here I was pleading for the man who had not only killed my family, but also turned me into another one of his nightwalkers. I wasn't sure why, but the thought of him being killed made me miserable. I didn't want anyone else to die … not even him.

I walked toward Donovan, who was still being held. I moved closer so I could look him square in the eye. "Don't you see there's a better way? Look around you. This is the proof." I pointed at all the different beings gathered. Vampires, werewolves, daywalkers, elements, a unicorn, fairies, and shapeshifters, all stood mixed with each other, showing no animosity because they stood united.

Donovan eyed the group closely. I remained hopeful, waiting to see if he understood and could accept what we'd done. Considering his predicament, it was clearly in his best interest to agree. Being united was far better than being at odds with one another.

"I do see what you mean," he replied.

"Guys, please let him go. This isn't right. No one deserves to have their life taken from them." I looked Donovan straight in the eye as I emphasized my point. "No one!"

Reluctantly, they let go of their grip on him one by one. From their expressions, it was easy to tell how crazy they thought I was. However, out of respect they did as I asked. Donovan was free to roam around and do whatever he wished. I gave him the chance he never offered anyone else—he was free to go live his life in peace.

Donovan stood free, although somewhat uneasily. He glanced around the group nervously. After all, these were the same beings who held him captive moments before. I really couldn't blame him as he turned and cautiously eyed me up and down.

I truly hoped he could blend in easily, allowing us to leave the past behind. I felt obligated, so I reassured him. "It's really okay. No tricks. You're free to go and live your life."

Donovan continued to look at me, but that's when I saw his uncertainty begin to unravel.

Right then I decided to forgive Donovan for all of the dreadful things he had done. No, I wasn't being rash or searching for an easy road in hopes he'd somehow wind up lost along the way. Perhaps the higher ups, destiny, karma, or whatever you wanted to call them, would take notice of my gesture and decide to reward me by taking it easier on the people I cared about. Or maybe forgiving him would simply allow for my own peace of mind. In any event, this sudden wave of forgiveness was a way for us to end the hostilities we'd carried around for so long, especially on Donovan's behalf. He had hated me for over a hundred years, and it was high time to let go of the grudge. This was a chance at a clean slate ... a fresh start for all.

"Donovan ..." I said sincerely, "I forgive you."

His mouth dropped open, and stunned gasps sounded from the others.

I hoped my act of forgiveness would be accepted, but he didn't offer a response; instead, he looked away. I decided to follow his gaze, which now rested on Sauda. Confused and somewhat disappointed, I left my attention on both of them, hoping for some sort of explanation, while everyone else took to gossiping about what I had just said.

The smugness he'd worn earlier had left his face. It was replaced with a softer look, making his monstrous ways fade. However, I knew this had nothing to do with my gesture. What was the reasoning behind his newly found demeanor?

I found myself curious. What exactly was going on? Then, it hit me. We had never suspected something was going on between them, even though Sauda had been the one who didn't bother to stop him during his escape attempt.

The closer I watched, the more subtle hints I began to pick up on. Donovan appeared to plead to Sauda without saying any words aloud. However, he didn't need to because his actions were evident in the way he looked at her. He may as well been screaming at the top of his lungs. Why was he pleading with her? I even saw him mouth the words, 'I'm sorry.' She acknowledged with a small shrug that would've gone unnoticed had my keen eye not been watching. Had anyone else noticed their secretive connection?

Suddenly, things didn't feel right anymore. I was no longer full of forgiveness; I was overflowing with suspicion. We had clearly missed something, but before I could say a word, Donovan's gaze shot back at me. They were full of fury, and his rage caused me to swallow my words. Once more, his eyes shifted to Sauda, who had turned her back on him. His fists clenched as he shed a single tear.

I waved frantically to get the guys' attention, but there wasn't enough time for them to act. Donovan shot out of his spot, aiming directly for me.

Lights

~ Chapter Thirty-Four ~

I prepared to defend myself, but Meriel smiled sweetly as she stepped in front to shield me. All I thought about was how irresponsible it was for her to pull such a stunt. The world could live without me; no one could live without her.

"No!" I screamed. I tried to shove her out of the way, but her feet were glued to the spot.

Uncle Dane, who stood closest, heard my scream and saw what was about to happen. In the last second, he jumped in front of us. Donovan slammed hard into our trio. Meriel and I both stumbled from the blow, but Donovan held on as he ripped apart Uncle Dane's throat. Blood spilled, while Uncle Dane let out an agonized gurgle, and cast a helpless glance toward his wife. After Donovan let go, my uncle fell limply to the ground.

The next sounds I heard were Auntie Steph's distraught screams mingled with my own.

Auntie Steph raced over to Uncle Dane's side. She tried to stop the bleeding as he moaned weakly.

He had saved Meriel and me. He sacrificed himself to save us from the monster I'd just shown pity to. Uncle Dane had been so brave, so selfless, but he wasn't supposed to die. This wasn't right … it just wasn't right.

Devastated, I faced Donovan. "How could you? How could you do something so awful after I just spared your life?"

An evil smile spread across Donovan's face. "Now you've lost what I have. We are even."

"What does that mean?" I heard Jayce ask. "What did you lose?"

"I lost her … Oh, nevermind. What does it matter? We are even now."

I had never felt such hatred before. I screamed at the top of my lungs. No words came, just a sound to release the pain and anger I felt.

"Oh, I'll show you what even looks like," growled Lakylee.

The nightwalkers took to dealing with Donovan. The mercy I'd shown him had been a huge mistake, and there was no way I'd do it again. I turned my back on him, ignoring his pleas for help. The last sound I heard from him was a pained scream. The nightwalkers had rid the world of the monster named Donovan; he'd never hurt anyone ever again.

My focus was on Uncle Dane, who lay weak on the ground, blood spilling out of his horrific wounds. I knelt down and held his hand. "Please don't go. Please … I need you. I can't do this alone."

I choked on my sobs, unable to see him through my blurred eyes. I was thankful my tears had returned in order to smudge the sight of him because I didn't want to see how bad the wounds actually were. I already knew things weren't looking good, but I couldn't lose him too. More and more tears flowed.

Auntie Steph calmly placed a caring hand on my shoulder. "Shanntal, honey, it is our time. You're fine now, and you always will be. Your friends love you, so remember you'll never be alone. Friends are the family we choose for ourselves."

This was no time for advice. Uncle Dane gasped, holding onto his last bit of life. Auntie Steph should've been a complete mess too. He was her husband, her soul mate. I didn't understand. The only thing clear was how wrong this all felt.

Gabriella came toward the group surrounding Uncle Dane. I spotted her, got up, and pushed my way through the crowd, pleading for help. "You've got to help him. Please heal him. He can't die. He just can't! Save him!"

'Shanntal, I'm sorry. You already know I cannot help him. I warned you of this the last time. I'm not able to step in again. Destiny has its own plans, and I shall not interfere.'

"Your magic is the only way to save his life!" I shouted.

'I truly am sorry, my dear Shanntal, but there's nothing I can do for him.'

Grief-stricken, I spun around in time to witness my beloved uncle take his last breath. My friends came nearer to comfort me as I reeled from my pain. Condolences poured in, and as much as I appreciated their support, it wasn't enough. My uncle was gone. He was dead.

I looked at Auntie Steph, whose beloved husband had just died, but strangely she wore the biggest smile across her face. It was official; she'd snapped. She absolutely beamed happiness from head to toe. I was mystified. Was she delirious? Had his death pushed her over the edge?

"Shanntal, we have loved you since the first moment you came into our lives, and I hope you know we will for all time. Please don't be sad. This is how it was supposed to be. Keep your faith and hopes alive, knowing we'll always be with you." She winked before turning her head toward the sky as if waiting for something.

Everything I'd ever known had changed, and the one person who I could always count on was gone. Always with me, nonsense! She uttered impossible words. Uncle Dane was dead.

Something astonishing happened. A brilliant pink light reached down to embrace my uncle's corpse, and it lifted him easily into the night sky. In the light, Uncle Dane appeared alive and well. He smiled and waved before blowing me a kiss. Then the light brought him closer to Auntie Steph, and a moment later, the light consumed her too. The pair stood locked in a romantic embrace—rays of light sprouting out all around them.

I quickly checked around to see if the lights were too bright for any nightwalkers. I didn't want anyone else hurt. To my surprise, everyone appeared fine and wore smiles on their lit up faces. This light was different and seemed harmless. I giggled at my moment of stupidity. In the midst of the confusion, I momentarily forgot I'd become a nightwalker. If the light did hurt, surely I would've felt it too.

Relieved no one was hurt, I turned back around in time to see my aunt and uncle kiss passionately. They were beautiful, and it brought me a sense of joy knowing they were so happy together.

My uncle spoke, while Auntie Steph held his hand tightly. "Shanntal, you're going to be okay. Please trust everything will work out the way it should. I hope you always remember how much we love you. We are extremely proud to have had the chance to call you family. Keep making us proud, kiddo!"

"Thank you for always being there. I love you both more than you'll ever know."

Auntie Steph's eyes twinkled. "No sweetheart, we completely get it because we love you just as much."

The surrounding light carried them gently into the night sky, and the glow around them seemed to brighten the higher they went. Finally, I understood the magnificence of what we were witnessing. Instantly my sadness changed into sheer delight. Auntie Steph and Uncle Dane were in love, alive, happy, and would be together forever ... united with the other stars.

A set of dazzling lights shot streaks across the sky. They looked like fireworks exploding, welcoming them to their new life. We'd just witnessed the biggest honor one could receive in the immortal world. The sight was heartbreaking, but indescribably beautiful.

Jayce spoke in a low voice so only I could hear. "Now do you understand why I didn't want to rush our trip to the stars?"

I nodded, realizing the only way to go up there meant the end of a lifetime down here.

He kissed me gently on the cheek, while squeezing my hand tightly.

I felt the fire of our passion ignite, so I leaned in and gave him a real kiss. Sadly, it didn't last long because of how the kiss burned, so I flinched away, trying to avoid the shock.

He backed off in order to give me space, which allowed my new reality to sink back in. I was a nightwalker, and no matter how hard we tried, this would be the hardest thing we ever had to work through. I loved his warm kisses, but with my blood running cold, they were far too painful for me to stand.

Jayce wore a calm expression as he looked toward Gabriella and nodded.

The nightwalkers formed a tight circle around me, just as a harsh hunger hit me. Suddenly, I was starving, craving the taste of blood like I'd never wanted anything else before. I eyed everyone, trying to locate my prey. I heard the sound of blood pulsating through a nearby heart, causing a bit of excitement as I imagined how good it would taste. I growled in agony from the hunger pains, and my eyes locked on Meriel. She'd seemed eager to put herself in danger before, so why not now?

I took a step forward, licking my lips. Thoughts rummaged my mind, teasing me about what she would taste like. Her blood, my hunger, it made my mouth water uncontrollably. I couldn't take it any longer and lunged at her. Instead of sinking my fangs into her neck, I smashed up against a wall of vampires and werewolves. They covered every inch of my sight and closed the circle in tighter around me. Meriel disappeared from my sights.

In a panic, I looked around for Jayce, but never saw him in my view. Gabriella, Kaleb, and Kael were also nowhere to be seen. The daywalkers had left me behind.

"Help me!" I shouted. "Someone, please!"

The space around me grew darker and smaller. I tried to push through the fangs surrounding me, but they were too strong. I crouched down, wrapped my arms tight around my knees, and rocked back and forth. Where was Jayce, Kaleb, or even Kael? How could they leave me behind? What could I do to get myself out of this mess? My stomach wrenched from the hunger pains. I had to feed and needed to do it soon. There was no time left; I needed to act, it was now or never. I did the first thing that came to mind and sprang up trying to make an escape. I'd just about cleared the height of their shoulders, but two angry werewolves yanked on my pant legs, which slammed me down to the ground. I got up quickly, eager to leap again. However, the gruesome growls coming from the nightwalkers immediately made me shrink back. The circle clenched tighter around me. Is this what the end of my life looked like? How would they finish me off? I waited ...

Many moments passed before a break happened in the circle. I watched Gabriella move gracefully toward me. Her mane and coat were shining brighter than the stars, which allowed her to cast off the darkness left from the nightwalkers. When our eyes met, I wondered if she saw me begging for help or if she saw me as one of them. I couldn't bring myself to say the words aloud; instead, I buried my pleas for help down deep inside. I had to accept my fate. I was a vampire now, and that meant walking alongside my fellow nightwalkers.

'My child, please come forward.' Gabriella stood before me, shaking her mane. Little rays of light flew off her and covered me like specks of dust.

The circle the nightwalkers formed began to recede when the specks of light clung to me. I found myself wrapped up in their beauty. They resembled the star that took Uncle Dane and Auntie Steph. These tiny lights were beautiful, but I soon noticed they weren't the same because these lights hurt my eyes. I closed them tightly, hoping the burning would stop.

"We'll take things from here, guys," Jayce said.

I opened my eyes, but squinted from the brightness. I saw Jayce shake Daray's hand and heard him say, "Seriously, I can't thank you enough. We couldn't have done this without your help."

"What's going to happen to her?" Daray asked.

Lakylee held onto Daray's hand, wearing a worried look. She bobbed up and down, trying to see what was going on with me. Now able to see past the circle, I found no one had left. Everyone stayed to make sure I was okay. These were my friends who truly loved and cared about me. I felt a rush of warmth that caused the tiny flicks of light clinging to me become brighter. The more I thought about how loved I was, the bigger and brighter the lights grew.

"It looks like she'll be just fine," Jayce said, his perfect smile beaming at me.

"We'll be back at nightfall to check in on her. Good luck!" Lakylee said.

The group of nightwalkers headed off to find shelter before another day dawned.

My dearest friends resumed the circle and surrounded me. Jayce, Kaleb, Kael, Layla, the elements, even shy Kynthia had stuck around. Other daywalkers who came to fight stood mixed in among my friends. When I took in each and every one of their faces, the lights on me grew. My eyes locked with Jayce, and suddenly I was consumed in a white light so bright and pure it mimicked the sun.

I felt strange, weak, and even somewhat faint. I stumbled, briefly losing my balance, but managed to catch myself and plant my feet firmly back on the ground. I needed to hold it together and stay in one place, but as my world spun, it made me more disoriented. The bright lights covered everything until I couldn't see. I couldn't stand the brightness anymore. I closed my eyes, trying to avoid the light, but behind my eyelids seemed to be just as bright. I couldn't escape it. I growled, feeling cranky and irritated, but an idea crept into my mind and gave me a bit of hope. Maybe the light meant Jayce and I would get our turn to visit the stars? After all, my human life was over. No matter how hard I tried to accept the change, I still considered being a vampire the end of my life.

I took comfort in the thought of heading up to the stars with my love. The idea made the pain from the light seem not quite so unbearable. The brilliant glow continued to shine around me for what felt like hours. It hadn't taken that long for Uncle Dane and Auntie Steph, so why was it taking so long for me? I reached out, but couldn't feel Jayce. It wasn't possible to shoot up to the stars alone, was it? I tried opening my eyes, but the light was still too bright. I shut them and took a deep breath.

Suddenly, a perfect peacefulness took over, like nothing I'd ever felt before. The only comparable moment I had was when I knew I was in love with my soul mate, and Jayce expressed his harmonizing love in return. I knew without a doubt that I was safe, loved, and no matter what happened next, the rest of my life would be an amazing adventure.

The lights ruptured and a gentle voice spoke. 'My child, you're pure of heart and always will be. For this reason, I can set you free. You don't need to be confined to the night, just be as you once were. Consider it my time to be your savior. Now open your eyes and accept my gift. It's my way to thank you for saving me from the darkness.'

Gabriella placed her horn gently against my chest, close to my heart. A fierce rage burned deep inside me, so I pulled away, but she stepped forward, closing the gap between us. Again her horn touched, only this time the contact radiated a rush of warmth, consuming my body. My mouth tingled; reaching up, I felt the fangs retreat into my gum line. Her powers were really working. She was healing me.

It wasn't long before the light around us faded and I felt more like myself. Well, almost … minus the little bit of fear lingering over what would happen when the sun rose. What if the night curse wasn't completely gone from my body? Would I turn to ash when sunlight touched me?

Sunlight

~ Chapter Thirty-Five ~

I held my breath as the sunlight breached the horizon. Another day arrived, filling the sky with beautiful shades of pinks and oranges while chasing away the shadows. Quite nervous, I stood in place as the sunlight covered my entire body. The sun felt warm on my skin, but, thankfully, I never burst into flames, so I began to relax. The worst was behind me. I had managed to return to the state where I truly belonged.

"Thank you so much, Gabriella." I was so grateful for my friend. "I don't know how to possibly repay you for doing this for me."

'Consider us even. Remember, you were the one who risked everything to save me from the pits of darkness. I will never forget your bravery. The higher ups won't either, so they decided it was only right to allow me the ability to rescue you during your time of despair.'

"But, I thought you couldn't heal nightwalkers?"

'My dear, you're too pure to ever be one of those. You changed into a vampire because of what was already buried deep inside. Donovan brought out the worst in you, yet you still showed him mercy even when you thought your world would never be the same. You have compassion running through your veins and a true heart to match. That's why I was able to do this for you.'

"But ... what about the blood?" I asked, disgusted with myself for consuming as much as I did. I felt appalled when I thought about the things I wanted to do to my dear friend Meriel.

'The blood was yours and spilled because of Donovan. You never drew blood nor took it from someone else. You did what was necessary for your survival. You had to evolve. This was all part of the path destiny mapped out for you, for all of us. It's what was meant to be.'

The nightmarish days and nights of fighting, running, and hiding were all over. Better yet, he'd never get a chance to ruin our new alliance or hurt anyone else. With Donovan gone, my past could finally stay safely behind me. I had the love of my life by my side and the best friends anyone could ask for. Everything would be all right.

'This is the right way, your way.'

"My way," I said the words aloud, pondering their meaning. Then I had a better idea. "Everything happened because of how we all came together. The worlds are no longer separated. Immortals are allies from this point forward. So it's our way!"

Gabriella nodded her head in approval.

"I truly do appreciate all the help." I hugged my dear friend. Our embrace took the warm sting out of the morning sun and returned my skin to normal. "Thank you from the bottom of my heart."

Everyone stood not too far off in the distance. They'd given us room so Gabriella could have the space needed in order to heal me. It was time for us to rejoin the crowd.

Meriel noticed our return first. She ran over and hugged me. "I'm so glad to see you, as you. Does everything feel okay now?"

"Yes, I'm just as I was." I smiled wryly, thinking of all the changes I'd undergone in the past twenty-four hours.

Everyone welcomed me back with open arms and well wishes. A big hug came from behind, lifting my feet right up off the ground. Only one person I knew could or would do something like that. "Kael ... can't breathe!" I choked out.

The moment my feet touched the ground, he spun me around to face him. "Man oh man! Am I *ever* glad to have you back!" He smothered me with another hug. "No offense, but those fangs ... ugh ... gross. They didn't suit you at all!" Kael poked his teeth out pretending they were fangs. Drool poured out of his mouth.

Everyone laughed.

I imagined I must've been quite the sight. This left me feeling slightly disgusted, but I decided to ignore it. I never hurt Meriel, so there wasn't any reason to beat up myself over what hadn't happened.

"Kael, all I can say is I'm really glad to be myself. Life just wouldn't work out with me being a nightwalker. Blood, darkness, no heartbeat, as appealing as those may sound, it just wasn't meant for me. I mean no offense to the nightwalkers. All the power to them, it's just that lifestyle wasn't my thing. The fangs kept making me bite my lip."

"They were too big for your face," Kaleb smirked.

Kael bellowed his infamous laugh.

"Besides, that laugh of yours called me back to the light. I love it! I missed it. I couldn't imagine life without you as part of it." Kael beamed and I smiled, realizing I'd just inadvertently fed his ego.

Kael puffed out his chest. He was in a state of awe over himself, another girl who couldn't live without him.

I decided to let him relish it a while longer.

Kaleb never said a word when I embraced his large mass. He'd always remained loyal. Even when I was at my worst, he somehow still saw the real me. He was the best friend I could've ever asked for, and I felt like the absolute luckiest girl to have him in my life. He smiled as we broke out of our embrace, and let his eyes lead the way to Jayce.

Jayce was the most remarkable sight in my eyes. The glorious morning sky accentuated his dark silhouette perfectly. He resembled an angel who'd fallen from the sky just for me.

'You truly are my angel. Now bring that beautiful face of yours over here!'

I ran to him. Jayce locked me in his arms and swung me around, lifting my feet off the ground. When he placed me back down, he used the opportunity to plant a hot kiss on me.

My lips stung, but in the best way imaginable, because it was the stuff I lived for. Now that all the craziness was behind us, we could enjoy our chance to simply be together, forever. I leaned forward to capture another pleasant sting from his soft, warm lips.

Hoots and hollers sounded from the group. Jayce and I had a way about us that somehow involved everyone. When we were happy, they were too. Happy was how things would be from here on out.

The morning went by quickly. Our visitors began to head on their way. Jayce and I thanked everyone for their support and for coming together when we needed them most. The days of daywalkers versus nightwalkers were over. No matter how we came to be, we were all immortals. Everyone had found a place in the new world so we could now function as a whole.

As our usual group headed into the house, the elements smiled, along with my dear friend Layla. However, one face in the group really stood out. The face belonged to Meriel. She wore the world's biggest smile, but I saw through it instantly. I wondered if an apology would be part of the message she was about to bestow.

"Meriel?" I inquired.

"I know … I know. You must be beyond upset with me. I was so stupid and reckless, and for that I am truly sorry. I never meant for anything to happen to your aunt and uncle."

"If they hadn't gone to where they went, I admit we would have a serious problem. Meriel, I can't hold a grudge, because they are happy and together. That's what matters to me most. Just knowing they are safe takes a big load off my shoulders. Plus, I am beyond proud, and I'll never forget what Uncle Dane did for you."

Meriel's smile faded, revealing the pain and guilt hidden in her eyes. Her voice cracked as she said, "Honestly, I only tried to help. I thought you'd been through enough, and believed when he saw me in his path it would make him stop." Her head hung low. "I admit ... I got caught up in all the action and adventure."

I couldn't allow myself to stay mad or leave any chance for this to fester and ruin our friendship. I knew she meant well, especially because her actions were meant to save me. We had to deal with this right now, and considering where my family went, I'd already forgiven her. She needed to know we were okay, so I decided to make light of the situation. "Caught up in the adventure. Ha! What are we ever going to do with you? Listen, my friend, you need to find another way to produce those adrenaline rushes. Know what I mean, crazy girl?" I winked, trying to show I wasn't upset. "Ever think of trying things like skydiving or riding motorcycles? Maybe boxing a big, brutal chick?"

We both laughed, picturing tiny Meriel boxing some ogre.

"Just find some kind of *normal* release to get you revved up. Don't force me to make you spar with Jayce, or even scarier yet, Kael."

Kael perked up. "What about me?"

"Sparring Kael. How about we take you on?" I said.

"Bring it on!" Meriel bellowed.

He rolled his eyes then returned his attention to Kaleb as they walked through the front door.

We laughed.

"No matter what it is, I know you'll be great with whatever you decide to take on."

"Thanks." She giggled softly. We embraced to re-seal our friendship.

"You're welcome, but please promise me one thing. Stay out of trouble! I can't keep having people save you." I poked her in the stomach before breaking free from our hug. I made the comment in a joking manner, but at the same time I was quite serious. I'd lost two very dear people protecting her. Meriel was an element, and therefore I felt she needed to stop acting so reckless.

After we had gone inside, it was finally time for some food and a bit of sleep. The night had been quite long for everyone; sleep was on top of the to-do list for many.

Jayce and I bypassed the food and made our way straight upstairs to his room. I walked in first with him following closely behind. I wasn't sure he'd ever let me out of his sight again, but was thankful he cared enough to stick around through the tough times. He never gave up on me, not even when it seemed like all was lost.

Jayce closed the bedroom door, and my heart fluttered. It was so good to see him like this, wearing a sweet smile meant for me. For a short while I thought I'd lost him, lost us, but we were lucky because destiny decided we were meant to be.

I was about to tell him how happy I was, but he suddenly looked uncomfortable and got a strange glint in his eye. I wondered what was going on. Prior to me asking, he rushed over to the bed and pushed me flat out on my back. He gripped my hands tightly in his.

"Don't ever scare me like that again. I love you too much." He left me pinned down, looking into my eyes. "Promise me, no matter what happens in the future, you'll never give up on us again. Ever!"

"Jayce …" I tried to speak, but he kissed me in a way he'd never done before.

We were completely connected; hearts and souls entwined. We'd been made for each other.

"I love you, Jayce," I said, after our kiss.

"I love you more."

"Impossible."

"Then I've done the impossible." He placed another steamy kiss on me.

Then he rolled over me and sprawled himself out on the bed. I took the opportunity to snuggle up. He wrapped his arms around me, and he held me so close I felt his heartbeat as his breath caressed my neck and shoulders. Safe and sound, I fell asleep locked in his arms.

I awoke with a smile because neither of us had broken our loving embrace. I rolled over, which woke Jayce up, so I kissed him good afternoon.

"Good morning, beautiful. Or should I say afternoon?"

Laughter rang out from downstairs, and one laugh stood out. Kael—his laughter was so distinct and loud. Jayce and I both giggled as we climbed out of bed and went downstairs to join the others.

Aiden, Makan, Meriel, Terran, Layla, Kaleb, and Kael all sat talking in the living room.

"Whoa!"

I heard a female voice behind us, so I moved out of the way to let her pass.

"Quite the night, if you know what I mean. Like, right?" Kynthia breezed by enthusiastically.

"Yup!" Kael nodded, his toothy grin spreading.

"All I can say is wow!" she continued. "Like, total wow!"

"Wow, yup, you've said the right word," Kael agreed. "Not much else can describe it."

Kynthia paced around the room. "Geez, and I mean serious geez. Did last night really happen?"

Her outgoing, chatty demeanor took me by surprise. The timid girl we'd met at Mystic Beach seemed completely confident, far from the shy girl she portrayed earlier.

"I watched it unfold with my own two eyes. Total craziness! Shanntal ... those fangs ... man oh man!" Kael snickered.

"Totally unreal!" Kynthia giggled as she sat down beside him. "No one will believe this, it's far too bizarre."

"Sure they will," said Kael. He exchanged a look with Kynthia, causing his cheeks to blush just as hers did.

At that moment, everything became clear. A love spark was growing between them, and the thought made me incredibly happy for them. I squeezed Jayce's hand tightly because I was lucky enough to have found my love spark.

I counted down the hours until dusk, because I wanted to thank the nightwalkers, I mean, friends, for coming to my rescue. Finally, nightfall arrived as Jayce led me in the direction of the trees. This time, everyone followed closely behind. I shivered as the memory of my previous encounter replayed, fresh in my mind. Things had turned out so differently from what I'd thought. A positive outcome arrived in the end, just not what I expected.

A rush of sadness consumed me when I looked at the spot where Uncle Dane took his last breath. He'd died protecting us, but his life should never have ended like that. Yes, I was happy they had gone up to the stars, but I truly missed them both and would have rather known that they were cuddled up safe and sound in the comfort of their own home. I felt the tears form, but before any could escape, Jayce took hold of my hand.

"Get ready," Jayce said. Using his free hand, he pointed up to the sky.

My eyes followed the direction in which he pointed, and a beautiful pink smudge danced its way across the sky before settling right above us. The pink streak gathered into a star and sparkled brighter than any diamond I'd ever seen. A few seconds later, Sitara and her love arrived, followed by the other happy couples.

I knew who the pink star was, but I needed to hear the words just to be sure. Looking at Jayce, tears in my eyes, I asked, "Is that really them?"

"Yes, that star is Uncle Dane and Auntie Steph," he said, wiping some tears off my cheeks.

Their star twinkled and I knew it was a wink from Uncle Dane. Even though they were miles above me, I knew they'd always be close, and I would never be alone.

"Wow!" A realization hit me, so I said, "That's pretty cool. I never knew they were older than Sitara."

"They're not," Jayce replied.

"Then how come they get to come out first?"

"Your uncle received the greatest honor because he sacrificed himself to save you and Meriel. He lost his life without fear and did so with pure love in his heart. You're a very important person, Shanntal, as is Meriel, and because he saved you both, they will get to shine first from this night forward. Everyone will know how he saved Meriel, but most of all, how he saved the one who brought our immortal worlds together."

I felt a lump grow in my throat, but quickly swallowed it down before the tears started again.

"All of this has happened because of you. We're proud to call you our friend," spoke a male voice from behind us.

I turned around, and Daray and Lakylee emerged.

"Hiya, guys!" I said, excited to finally see them.

Lakylee let go of Daray's hand in order to give me a big hug. "I'm so glad to see you're back to yourself."

"Thanks to you." I noticed the others beginning to gather. "Thanks to all of you!"

Daray winked, and I winked back.

It was unbelievable. Together as one, no longer labeled daywalkers or nightwalkers, we were immortals. Best of all, we were friends. I admired our group as I looked around at the people surrounding me. We'd done it. We had found the better way of life and did so by working together.

Five new faces emerged out of the woods. A female with long, fire red hair and dark eyes led the group. Something about them seemed familiar, though I wasn't entirely sure I'd seen any of them before.

"Glad to see you're lacking fangs," she teased. "They didn't look quite right on you."

"Umm ... thanks," I said, uncertain.

"I knew it!" Sauda huffed knowingly as she appeared from behind their group. "Don't recognize her, do you?"

Surprised to see Sauda still around, I shook my head.

"I'm Taini," said the red-head. "I suppose I must look pretty different when I'm not wearing my fur coat."

"Oh my," I said, taken back. "You're the ... you guys are the werewolves, aren't you?"

"We sure are!" said the tall blond fellow, pulling proudly on his beard.

He was quite nice looking, but I never would've suspected he'd once been a werewolf.

"Holy! What? No way, how is this even possible?" I didn't mean to sound like a skeptic, but this was incredible. "Wait ... really, you're the wolves?"

They laughed. Sure, I was kind of embarrassed by my reaction, but the news was absolutely huge! I couldn't help but ask the questions racing around in my mind. I needed to know what happened.

Taini spent the next few minutes explaining how the wolves had achieved the ability to change whenever they needed to. If they were in some sort of danger or their anger got the better of them, they would revert back into the wolf form. Therefore, they'd always have to be mindful not to let the rage overcome them. Another part of taming the wolf meant they would undoubtedly change whenever the moon was full. The wolf needed at least one night to run free so it wouldn't become restless and consume them again.

While Taini shared the story, I smiled while staring at her in disbelief. The breakthrough was truly amazing, but somewhat unbelievable. If they weren't standing before me, I never would've believed it.

"You still don't have a grasp on how truly special you really are, but believe me when I say, we sure do. This was all possible because of you," Lakylee added.

Daray agreed. "I'm pleased to say, she's totally right. You've shown each and every one of us that there's a better way. You have taught us how to live together peacefully, and you've even managed to remind the blackest of hearts it could still do the most important thing. It could still love."

Lakylee wrapped her arms around Daray, and then kissed his neck. "Even this is because of you. You're truly a gift and make life better for everyone, all the way around."

"Thank you, guys." I smiled.

Daray looked different now. The darkness that haunted him was gone. I felt pleased, knowing he'd found happiness. I knew love had led him and Lakylee to each other, and nothing would interfere with their happiness.

Sauda still tagged around, hanging off Daray's every word, but Lakylee seemed to be somewhat more tolerant of her. I wondered what made Sauda stick around, but I noticed how her eyes focused on Lakylee. Perhaps there was a friendship in the making, or was something else going on? I shook the suspicion away. I was just happy to see Lakylee was no longer alone. She'd become a part of something where she belonged and was loved.

We were similar in so many ways, which was quite uncanny at times. We were both one of a kind, had walked alone for some time, managed to overcome the odds, and in the end came together with those who surrounded us. We'd found our place in the world, true love, and friendship in each other.

****

Some immortals are born, while others are made. Some have the ability to move and bend the constraints of time, giving the gift of everlasting life. Immortals will always be part of everyday life. Some may hide from you, while others choose to make their presence known during the first encounter. We are everywhere. We could be your neighbor down the street, a person on the bus in the seat next to you, or maybe even the shadow stalking in the distance. The easiest way to spot us is to look up into the night skies where our most honored will be happy to greet you. Always remember that thanks to these sacrifices and changes we've made together, today we are able to walk as *'one.'*

****

Escaped the Night is my debut novel.

Thank you for deciding to pick it up with all the ample choices out there.

You're a gem in my books!

XOXO Jenn XOXO

****

Did you like the story? Leave a review. If you loved it, please share this story with a friend. Even if you didn't enjoy it, please leave your feedback so I can improve the craft on my next novels.

www.escapedthenight.com

For our younger generation (6 –10 years), I have written

Sammie Street Adventures – Stormy Saturday

<u>Warning!</u> Read this book at your own risk. It may cause:

- Increased imagination
- Sibling bonding
- Messy bedrooms
- Instant relief from boredom on rainy days

Grab a copy of this story for our younger generation.

An adventure starts with the turn of a page.

www.sammiestreet.com

Reader Reviews:

Sabrina Ford from Sabrina's Paranormal Palace
http://sabrinasparanormalpalace.blogspot.ca/

Have you ever read a book where it stays with you days after you're done? Escaped the Night is that book for me. I fell in love with the characters and world Jennifer has written.

Shanntal is a girl who is lost after the death of her family. She goes to live with her aunt and uncle but soon finds out things are not what they seem. She has always felt different from her family, but it's not until she meets Jayce that things start to come clear. Her memories start to some back and Shanntal finds out that she is a unique Immortal that can walk both in the light and dark. She can bring both worlds together but only if she can fight the darkness inside herself. With the love of Jayce and all her new friends, Shanntal stands up to the darkness ... but she needs to be careful as it has plans of its own for her.

Jennifer puts a new spin on the supernatural beings we all have come to love. If you want a book filled with Immortals of all kinds and a love that will take your breath, then Escaped the Night is the book for you. Jennifer is an author to watch. 5/5 stars

Reader Reviews:

Kristina Haecker from Kristina's Books & More rated it 5 of 5 stars
http://kristinasbooksandmore.blogspot.ca/

This is Jennifer Blyth's fantastic debut novel!

Escaped the Night is a breathtaking paranormal romance that has the most amazing line up of paranormal creatures I've ever seen in one novel! It has vampires, werewolves, faeries, shapeshifters, unicorns, immortals, and more! The characters are all great as well! There are ones you hate, ones you love, and ones that make you laugh. Shanntal is the main character and despite having been through and sacrificed a lot, she stays strong through the entire novel! She is very brave, stubborn, protective of those she loves, and has a good heart! All the qualities that make up a great character! Jayce is every girl's fantasy. Handsome, tattooed, charming, romantic, and protective. He introduces Shanntal to the incredible world of the daywalkers VS the nightwalkers, along with all of the other creatures. All of the minor characters are just as entertaining, and really get you rooting for them throughout the novel.

The story is unique! It has many different factors that come together and make a really great book! It has the perfect mix of action and romance. The story had me smiling, laughing, and crying. At the end I had a huge smile on my face and was left feeling completely satisfied. Everything was wrapped up nicely with a big bow on top! (Or a pretty cover!) I really liked that the cover had some hidden significance that was hidden in the story!

The writing is fresh, gruesome at times, beautiful in others. The descriptions were a big part of the story and they do not disappoint! I love how Jennifer captures all the different scenes perfectly. The pacing was perfect for the story, starting off slow and ending with a bang! Just when you think you've figured out what has happened, it changes. A hint of suspense was always present.

Escaped the Night is a wonderful paranormal romance that I definitely recommend to anyone that likes the genre! It is a tale of true love and good overcoming evil, as well as a coming of age story. It's an addictive read that will have you connecting to the characters and will make you not want to put it down!

I will definitely be reading more from Jennifer Blyth! I really hope she chooses to do a sequel!

Thank you to Jennifer for providing the review copy!

About the Author

Jennifer Blyth, author of the easy-to-read book Sammie Street Adventures – Stormy Saturday www.sammiestreet.com has tried her writing hand with her debut novel Escaped the Night. Jennifer manages to take her readers on an adventure with the turn of the page. www.escapedthenight.com

Jennifer currently lives in Calgary, Alberta, Canada with her daughter and urban zoo. Jennifer is an animal lover with her dogs, cats, fish, and even pet frogs. This lady keeps herself busy. She reads, writes, and makes sure to use her imagination any chance she gets.

Jennifer is a huge fan of the arts and is an avid music lover. She has just about every genre on her playlist. She is always listening to her music while writing, editing, and even brainstorming. Perhaps one day she'll disclose some of her favorite tunes to us. Jennifer also loves the paranormal world. If there are books, movies, TV shows, there's a pretty good chance she's enjoying it, just as you are.

Keep this author in mind. Jennifer has loads of new ideas that will be reaching the pages soon.

CPSIA information can be obtained at www.ICGtesting.com
Printed in the USA
BVOW02s0624260216

438023BV00001BA/2/P